W9-BQM-759

HOME TRUTHS

BOOKS BY MAVIS GALLANT

The Other Paris
Green Water, Green Sky
My Heart Is Broken
A Fairly Good Time
The Pegnitz Junction
From the Fifteenth District
Home Truths

Sixteen Stories

HOME TRUTHS

MAVIS GALLANT

Random House
New York

To Nelly McMillan

Published in the United States by Random House, Inc., New York.

Home Truths was originally published in hardcover by Macmillan of Canada, A Division of Gage Publishing Limited, in 1981.

"With a Capital T" was first published in *Canadian Fiction Magazine*. All other stories originally appeared in *The New Yorker*.

Library of Congress Cataloging in Publication Data

Gallant, Mavis.
Home truths.

Reprint. Originally published: Toronto, Canada: Macmillan of Canada, © 1981.
I. Title.
PR9199.3.G26H6 1985 813'.54 84-45757
ISBN 0-394-53198-1

Manufactured in the United States of America
2 4 6 8 9 7 5 3

CONTENTS

AT HOME

THANK YOU FOR THE LOVELY TEA

That year, it began to rain on the twenty-fourth of May – a holiday still called, some thirty years after her death, Queen Victoria's Birthday. It rained – this was Canada – until the middle of June. The girls, kept indoors, exercising listlessly in the gym, quarrelled over nothing, and complained of headache. Between showers they walked along spongy gravel paths, knocking against spiraea bushes that suddenly spattered them with water and white. It was the last lap of term, the dead period between the end of exams and the start of freedom. Handicrafts and extra art classes were improvised to keep them busy, but it was hopeless; glooming over their desks, they quarrelled, dreamed of summer, wrote plaintive letters home. Their raincoats were suddenly hot and heavy, their long black stockings scratchy and damp.

"Life is Hell," Ruth Cook wrote on the lid of a desk, hoping that someone would see it and that there would be a row. It was the slow time of day – four o'clock. Yawning over a drawing of flowerpots during art class, she looked despairingly out the streaked window and saw Mrs. Holland coming up the walk. Mrs. Holland looked smart, from that distance. Her umbrella was furled. On her head was a small hat, tilted to one side, circled with a feather. She looked smart but smudged, as if paint had spilled over the outline of a drawing. Ruth took her in coldly, leaning on a plump, grubby hand. Mrs. Holland was untidy – she had heard people say so. She was emotional. This, too, Ruth had overheard, always said with disapproval. Emotion meant "being American"; it meant placing yourself unarmed in the hands of the enemy. Emotion meant not getting one's lipstick on straight, a marcel wave coming apart in wild strands. It accounted for Mrs. Holland's anxious blue eyes, for the button missing on a blouse, the odds and ends forever falling out of purse or pocket. Emotion was worse than bad taste; it was calamitous. Ruth had only to look at Mrs. Holland to see what it led to. Mrs. Holland passed up the front steps and out of sight. Ruth went back to her bold lettering: "Life is Hell." Any other girl in the room, she thought with satisfaction, would have gone importantly up to the desk and whispered that a lady had come to take her to tea, and could she please go and get ready now? But Ruth knew that things happened in their own good time. She looked at her drawing, admired it, and added more flowerpots, diminishing to a fixed point at the center of the page.

"Well done," said Miss Fischer, the art teacher, falsely, strolling between the ranks of desks. If she saw "Life is Hell," she failed to comment. They were all cowards; there was no one to fight. "Your horizon line is too low," said Miss Fischer. "Look at the blackboard; see how I have shown Proportion."

Indicating patience and self-control, Ruth looked at the blackboard, over it, around it. The blackboard was filled with receding lines, the lesson having dealt with Perspective as well as Proportion. Over it hung a photograph of the King – the late King, that is. He had died that year, and so had Kipling (although far less fuss was made about him), and the girls had to get used to calling Kipling "our late beloved poet" and the Prince of Wales "King Edward." It was hopeless where the

Prince was concerned, for there hung the real King still, with his stiff, elegant Queen by his side. He had died on a cold January day. They had prayed for him in chapel. His picture was in their prayer books because he was head of the Church – something like that. "It is a year of change," the headmistress had said, announcing his death.

"It's a year of change, all right," Ruth said softly, imitating the headmistress's English accent. Even the term "headmistress" was new; the old girl, who had retired to a cottage and a faithful spinster friend, had been content with "principal." But the new one, blond, breathless, pink-cheeked, was fresh from England, full of notions, and felt that the place wanted stirring up. "I'm afraid I am progress-minded," she told the stone-faced, wary girls. "We must learn never to fear change, provided it is for the best." But they did fear it; they were shocked when the tinted image of George V was taken down from the dining-room wall and the famous picture of the Prince of Wales inspecting the front during the Great War put in its place. The Prince in the photo was a handsome boy, blond, fresh, pink-cheeked – much like the new headmistress, in fact. "A year of change," the headmistress repeated, as if to impress it forever on their minds.

Scrubbing at her flowerpots with artgum, Ruth thought it over and decided there had been no real change. She had never met the King and didn't care for poetry. She was still in school. Her mother had gone to live abroad, but then she had never been around much. The only difference was that her father had met unfortunate Mrs. Holland.

Coming into the flagged entrance hall, Mrs. Holland was daunted by the chilly gloom. She stared at the row of raincoats hanging from pegs, the sombre portraits of businessmen and clergymen on the walls. Governess-trained, she considered herself hopelessly untutored, and attached to the smell of drying coats an atmosphere of learning. Someone came, and went off to fetch the headmistress. Mrs. Holland sat down on a carved bench that looked like a pew. Irreligious but fond of saying she would believe in something if only she could, she gazed with respectful interest at the oil portrait of the school's chief financial rock, a fruit importer who had abandoned Presbyterianism for the Church of England when a sudden rise in wealth and status demanded the change. Although he wore a gay checked suit and looked every inch himself, a small-town Presbyterian go-getter, Mrs. Holland felt he must, surely, be some sort of Anglican dignitary; his portrait was so much larger than the rest; besides, the hall was so hushed and damp that religion had to come into it somewhere. She recalled a story she had been told – that the school had been a Bernardine abbey, transported from England to Canada stone by stone. The lightless corridors, the smell of damp rot emanating from the linen cupboards, the drafts, the cunning Gothic windows with Tudor panes, the dark classrooms and sweating walls, the chill, the cold, the damp, the discomfort, wistfully British, staunchly religious, all suggested this might indeed have been the case. How nice for the girls, Mrs. Holland thought, vaguely but sincerely.

In point of fact, the school had never been an abbey. Each of its clammy stones had been quarried in North America, and the architectural ragout was deliberate; it was intended to provide the pupils with character and background otherwise lacking in a new continent. As for the fruit importer, the size of his portrait had to do only with the size of his endowment. The endowment had been enormous; the school was so superlatively uncomfortable that it cost a fortune to run. The fruit importer's family had been – still were – exceedingly annoyed. They wished he would take up golf and quit meddling in church affairs. He could not help meddling. Presbyterianism had left its scar. Still, he felt uneasy, he was bound to admit, if there were nuns about, or too much incense. Hence his only injunction, most difficult to follow: The school should be neither too High nor too Low. Every regime had interpreted this differently. The retiring principal, to avoid the vulgarity of being Low, had brought in candles and Evensong. The new headmistress, for her part, found things disturbingly High, almost Romish. The white veils the girls wore to chapel distressed her. They were so long that they made the girls look like Carmelite nuns, at least from the waist up. From the waist down, they looked like circus riders, with their black-stockinged legs exposed to garter level. The pleated serge tunics were worn so short, in fact, that the older girls, plump with adolescence, could not sit down without baring a pink inch between tunic and stocking top. The modernism she had threatened took form. She issued an order: lengthen the tunics, shorten the veils. Modernism met with a mulish and unaccountable resistance. Who would have believed that young girls, children of a New World, would so obstinately defend tradition? Modernism, broadmindedness foundered. The headmistress gave up the fight, though not her claim to the qualities in which she took greatest pride.

It was broadmindedness now that compelled her to welcome Mrs. Holland briskly and cordially, ignoring Mrs. Holland's slightly clouded glance and the cigarette stain on the hand she extended. Ruth's father had rung up about tea, so it was quite in order to let Ruth go; still, Mrs. Holland was a family friend, not a parent – a distinction that carried its own procedure. It meant that she need not be received in the private sitting room and given cake but must wait in the office. It meant that Ruth was not to go alone but must be accompanied by a classmate. Waved into the office, Mrs. Holland sat down once more. She propped her umbrella against her chair, offered the headmistress a cigarette. The umbrella slid and fell with a clatter. The cigarette was refused. Reaching for her umbrella, Mrs. Holland tipped her case upside down, and cigarettes rolled everywhere. The headmistress, smiling, helped collect them, marvelling at the variety of experience inherent in teaching, at the personal tolerance that permitted her contact with a woman of Mrs. Holland's sort.

"My hair's all undone, too," said Mrs. Holland, wretchedly, clutching her properties. And, really, watching her, one felt she had too much for any one woman to handle – purse, umbrella, and gloves.

The headmistress retrieved the last cigarette and furtively dropped it in the wastebasket. "With all this rain, one can hardly cope with one's hair," she said, almost as cordially as if Mrs. Holland were a parent. Resolved to be lenient, she remembered that Ruth's father's money did, after all, lend the situation a certain amount of social decency. The headmistress had heard, soon after her arrival, this wayward story of divorce and confusion – Ruth's parents divorced; Ruth's mother, who had behaved badly, gone abroad; the sudden emergence of Mrs. Holland – and she had decided that Ruth ought to be watched. There might be tendencies – what someone less broadminded might have called bad blood. But Ruth was a placid girl, to all appearances – plump, lazy, rather Latin in looks, with glossy blue-black hair, which she brushed into drooping ringlets. In spite of the laziness, one could detect a nascent sense of leadership; she was quite bossy, in fact. The headmistress was satisfied; like the school, the imitation abbey, Ruth was almost the real thing.

Summoned, Ruth came in her own good time. Conversation between the two women had frozen, and they turned to the door with relief. Ruth was trailing not one friend but two, May Watson and Helen McDonnell. The three girls stood, berets on their heads, carrying raincoats. Their long black legs looked more absurd than ever. They shook hands with Mrs. Holland, mumbling courteously. For some reason, they gave the appearance of glowering, rather like the portraits in the hall.

"What time do we have to be back, please?" said Ruth.

"I expect Mrs. Holland will want to bring you back soon after tea," said the headmistress. She made a nervous movement toward Mrs. Holland, who, however, was collecting her belongings without difficulty. The girls were being taken to the tearoom of a department store, Mrs. Holland said. "I *am* pleased," said the headmistress, too enthusiastically. The girls glanced at her with suspicion. But her pleasure was authentic; she had feared that they might be going to Ruth's house, where Mrs. Holland, the family friend, might seem too much at home. Mrs. Holland pressed on the headmistress a warm, frantic farewell and followed the girls out. It had begun to rain again, the slow warm rain of June. Mrs. Holland, distracted, stopped to admire the Tudor-Gothic façade of the school, feeling that this was expected, and was recalled by the fidgeting of her charges. There was more fumbling, this time for car keys, and, at last, they were settled – Ruth in front, as a matter of course (the car was her father's), and Helen and May in back.

"Out of jail," said Ruth, pulling off her beret and shaking out her hair.

"Is it jail, dear? Do you hate it?" said Mrs. Holland. She drove carefully away from the curb, mindful of her responsibilities. "Would you rather – "

"Oh, Ruth," Helen protested, from the back. "You don't mean it."

"Jail," said Ruth, but without much interest. She groped in the side pocket on the door and said, "I left a chocolate bar here last time I was out. Who ate it?"

"Perhaps your father," said Mrs. Holland, wishing Helen had not interrupted that most promising lead about hating school.

"He hates chocolate. You know that. He'd be the last person to eat it. But honestly," she said, placid again, "just listen to me. As if it even mattered."

Situations like this were Mrs. Holland's undoing. The absence of the chocolate bar, Ruth's young, averted profile, made her feel anxious and guilty. The young, to her, were exigent, full of mystery, to be wooed and placated. "Shall we stop somewhere and get another chocolate bar?" she said. "Would you like that?"

It was terrible to see a grown woman so on the defensive, made uneasy by someone like Ruth. Helen McDonnell, taller than the others, blond, ill at ease, repeated her eternal prayer that she might never grow up and be made unhappy. As far as she knew, there were no happy adults, other than teachers. She looked at May, to see if she had noticed and if she minded, but May had turned away and was staring at her pale, freckled reflection in the window, thrown back from the dark of the rainy streets. She knew that May was grieving for an identical face, that of her twin, who this year had been sent to another school, across the continent. Driving through thicket suburbs and into town now, they passed May's house, a white house set back on a lawn.

"There's your house, May," Ruth said, twisting around on the front seat. "How come you're a boarder when you are right near?"

"How about you?" said May, angrily.

Ruth twisted a curl and said, "Haven't got a mother at home, that's why."

"Would you like to live at home?" said Mrs. Holland eagerly, and Ruth stiffened. Oh, if only she could teach herself not to be so spontaneous! Instead of drawing the child toward her, she drove her away.

"It's much better to board," said Helen, before Ruth could reply. "I mean, you learn more, and they make you a lady."

"Don't be so stupid," said Ruth, and May said, "Who cares about that?"

Helen, reminded that these two would grow up ladies in any case, colored. But then, she thought, seeing the three of us together, no one could tell. They wore the same uniform, and who was to guess that Ruth's father was rich and May's clever? As long as she had the uniform, everything was all right. Pious, Helen repeated another prayer – that God might miraculously give her different parents.

Furious with Helen for having again interrupted, Mrs. Holland clamped and relaxed her gloved hands on the wheel. Traffic lights came at her through a blur of rain. If only she and Ruth were alone. If only Ruth, with the candor Ruth's father was so proud of, would turn to her and say, "Are you and Daddy getting married?" Then Mrs. Holland might say, "That depends on you, dear. You see, your father feels, and I quite agree ..." Or if Ruth were hostile, openly hating her, if it were a question of winning her confidence, of replacing the mother, of being a sister, a companion, a friend ... But the girl was closed, indifferent. She seemed unable to grasp the importance of Mrs. Holland in her father's life. There was an innocence, a lack of prudence, in her references to the situation; she said things that made shame and caution fill Mrs. Holland's heart. She was able to remark, casually, to Helen and May, "My father and Mrs. Holland drove all the way to California in this car," reducing the trip (undertaken with many doubts, with fear, with a feeling that hotel clerks were looking through and through her) to a simple, unimportant outing involving two elderly people, long past love.

They crawled into the center of town, in the wake of streetcars. Mrs. Holland, afraid for her charges, drove so slowly that she was a traffic hazard. An irritated policeman waved them by.

"Is the store all right?" Mrs. Holland said to Ruth. "Would you rather go somewhere else?" She had circled the block twice, looking for a parking space.

Ruth, annoyed by all this caution, said, "Don't ask me. It's up to the girls. They're the guests."

But neither of the girls could choose. Helen was shy, May

absorbed. Mrs. Holland found a parking place at last, and they filed into the store.

"I used to come here all the time with my sister," May said, suddenly coming to as they stood, jammed, in the elevator. "We came for birthdays and for treats. We had our birthdays two days in a row, because we're twins and otherwise it wouldn't be fair. We wore the same clothes and hardly anybody could tell us apart. But now," she said, echoing a parental phrase, "we have different clothes and we go to different schools, because we have to develop separate personalities."

"Well," said Mrs. Holland, unable to take this in. "Have you a sister?" she said to Helen.

There was a silence; then Helen blurted out, "We're seven at home."

"How nice," said Mrs. Holland. But Helen knew that people said this just to be polite, and that being seven at home was just about the most shameful thing imaginable.

"Are your sisters at school with you?" Mrs. Holland asked.

Everyone in the elevator was listening. Helen hung her head. She had been sent to school by an uncle who was also her godfather and who had taken his duties seriously. Having promised to renounce Satan and all his works in Helen's name, he uprooted her, aged six, from her warm, rowdy, half-literate family and packed her off to school. In school, Helen had been told, she would learn to renounce Satan for herself and, more important, learn to be a lady. Some of the teachers still remembered her arriving, mute and frightened, quite as frightened as if the advantages of superior schooling had never been pointed out. There were only three boarders Helen's age. They were put in the care of an elderly housekeeper, who filled a middle role, neither staff nor servant. After lessons they were sent to sit with her, in her red-papered, motto-spangled room. She taught them hymns; the caterwauling got on her nerves, but at least they sat still while singing.

She supervised their rushed baths and murderously washed their hair. Sometimes some of the staff wondered if more should not be done for the little creatures, for although they were clean and good and no trouble, the hand that dressed them was thorough but unaffectionate, and they never lost the wild-eyed hopelessly untidy look of unloved children. Helen now remembered very little of this, nor could she imagine life away from school. Her uncle-godfather conscientiously sent her home each summer, to what seemed to her a common, clamorous, poverty-stricken family. "They're so loud," she would confide to the now quite elderly person who had once taught her hymns. "Their voices are so loud. And they drink, and everything." She had grown up to be a tall, quiet girl, much taller than most girls her own age. In spite of her height she wore her short, ridiculous tunic unselfconsciously. Her dearest wish was to wear this uniform as long as she could, to stay on at the school forever, to melt, with no intervening gap, from the students' dining hall to the staff sitting room. Change disturbed her; she was hostile to new girls, could scarcely bear it when old girls came back to be married from the school chapel. Hanging over the stairs with the rest of the girls, watching the exit of the wedding party from chapel to street, she would wonder how the bride could bear to go off this way, with a man no one knew, having seen school again, having glimpsed the girls on the stairs. When the headmistress said, in chapel, confusing two esteemed poets, "The old order changeth, girls. The Captains and Kings depart. Our King has gone, and now our beloved Kipling has left us," Helen burst into tears. She did not wish the picture of George V to leave the walls; she did not want Kipling to be "the late." For a few days afterward, the girls amused themselves by saying, "Helen, listen. The Captains and Kings depart," so that they could be rewarded, and slightly horrified, by her astonishing grief. But then they stopped, for her shame and silence after such outbursts were disconcerting. It never became a joke, and so had to be abandoned.

Mrs. Holland and her guests settled into an oval tearoom newly done up with chrome and onyx, stuffed with shoppers, smelling of tea, wet coats, and steam heating. Helen looked covertly at Mrs. Holland, fearing another question. None came. The waitress had handed them each a giant, tasselled menu. "I'll have whatever the rest of them have," Helen said, not looking at hers.

"Well," said Ruth, "*I'll* have chocolate ice cream with marshmallow. No, wait. Strawberry with pineapple."

May forgot her sister. The choice before her was insupportable. "The same as Ruth," she said, at last, agonized and uncertain.

Mrs. Holland, who loathed sweets, ordered a sundae, as a friendly gesture, unaware that in the eyes of the girls she had erred. Mothers and their substitutes were expected to drink tea and nibble at flabby pâté sandwiches.

As soon as their ice cream was before them, Ruth began again about the chocolate bar. "My father never eats chocolate," she said, quite suddenly. "And he knew it was mine. He'd never touch anything that wasn't his. It would be stealing."

"Maybe it got thrown away," said May.

"That'd be the same as stealing," said Ruth.

Mrs. Holland said, "Ruth, I do not know what became of your bit of chocolate."

Ruth turned to Mrs. Holland her calm brown eyes. "Goodness!" she said. "I never meant to say you took it. Anyway, even if you did make a mistake and eat it up sometime when you were driving around – Well, I mean, who cares? It was only a little piece, half a Cadbury bar in blue paper."

"I seldom eat chocolate," said Mrs. Holland. "If I had seen it, let alone eaten it, I should certainly have remembered."

"Then he must have had somebody else with him," said Ruth. The matter appeared to be settled. She went on eating, savoring every mouthful.

Mrs. Holland put down her spoon. The trend of this outing, she realized now, could lead only to tears. It was one of the situations in her life – and they were frequent – climaxed by a breakdown. The breakdown would certainly be her own: she wept easily. Ruth, whose character so belied her stormy Latin looks, had rarely wept since babyhood. May, the thin, freckled one, appeared quite strung up about something, but held in by training, by discipline. I lack both, Mrs. Holland thought. As for the big girl, Helen, Mrs. Holland had already dismissed her as cold and stupid. Mrs. Holland said softly, "*Les larmes d'un adolescent*." But it doesn't apply to cold little Canadians, she thought.

"I know what that means," said Ruth. She licked her spoon on both sides.

Mrs. Holland's phrase, the image it evoked, came from the outer circle of experience. Disturbed, the girls moved uneasily in their chairs, feeling that nothing more should be said.

"Don't you girls *ever* cry?" said Mrs. Holland, almost with hostility.

"Never," said Ruth, settling that.

"My sister cried," said May. She turned her light-lashed gaze to Helen and said, "And Helen cries."

"I don't," said Helen. She drew in, physically, with the first apprehension of being baited. "I do not."

"Oh, Helen, you do," said May. She turned to Ruth for confirmation, but Ruth, indifferent, having spoken for herself, was scooping up the liquid dregs of her ice cream. "Do you want to see Helen cry?" said May. Like Mrs. Holland, she seemed to have accepted the idea that one of them was going to break down and disgrace them; it might as well be Helen.

Or perhaps the remark went deeper than that. Mrs. Holland, who could barely follow Ruth's mental and emotional spirals, felt unable, and disinclined, to cope with this one. May leaned forward, facing Helen. Mrs. Holland suddenly answered "No," too late, for May was saying, in a pretty, piping voice, "Hey, Helen, listen. The King has left us, and Kipling is dead."

Helen failed to reward her. She stared, stolid, as if the words had been in a foreign language. But there remained about the table the knowledge that an attempt had been made, and Mrs. Holland and Helen, both natural victims, could not look away from May, or at each other. Ruth had finished eating. She sighed, stretched, began to tug on her coat. She said to Mrs. Holland, "Thankyouverymuchforalovelytea. I mean, if our darling new headmistress asks did we thank you, well, we did. I was afraid I might forget to say it later on."

"Thanks for a lovely tea," said May. She had been afraid to speak, in case the effort of forming words should release the tight little knot of tears she felt in her throat. It was so much more difficult to be cruel than to be hurt.

"Thank you," said Helen, as if asleep.

I can only hope they thanked you," the headmistress said when Mrs. Holland delivered them, safe, half an hour later. "Girls are apt to forget."

"They thanked me," said Mrs. Holland. The three girls had curtsied, muttering some final ritual phrase, and vanished into an area of dim, shrill sound.

"Study hall," said the headmistress. "Their studies are over for the term, but they respect the discipline."

"Yes, I suppose they do."

"It was kind of you to take them out," said the headmistress. She laid her cold pink hand on Mrs. Holland's for a moment, then withdrew it, perplexed by the wince, the recoil. "One forgets how much it can mean at that age, a treat on a rainy day."

"Perhaps that's the answer," Mrs. Holland said.

The headmistress sensed that things were out of hand, but she had no desire to be involved; perhaps the three had been noisy, had overeaten. She smiled with such vague good manners that Mrs. Holland was released and could go.

From an upstairs window, Ruth watched Mrs. Holland make her way to the car. May and Helen were not speaking. Helen was ready to forgive, but to May, who had been unkind, the victim was odious, and she avoided her with a kind of prudishness impossible to explain to anyone, let alone herself. They had all made mistakes, Ruth thought. She wondered if she would ever care enough about anyone to make all the mistakes those around her had made during the rainy-day tea with Mrs. Holland. She breathed on the window, idly drew a heart, smiled placidly, let it fade.

JORINDA AND JORINDEL

A summer night: all night someone has been learning the Charleston.

"I've got it!" the dancer cries. "I've got it, everybody. Watch me, now!" But no one is watching. The dancer is alone in the dining room, clinging to the handle of the door; the rest of the party is in the living room, across the hall. "Watch me!" travels unheard over the quiet lawn and the silent lake, and then dissolves.

The walls of the summer house are thin. The doors have been thrown back and the windows pushed as high as they will go. Young Irmgard wakes up with her braids undone and her thumb in her mouth. She has been dreaming about her cousin Bradley; about an old sidewalk with ribbon grass growing in the cracks. "I've got it," cried the witch who had captured Jorinda, and she reached out so as to catch Jorindel and change him into a bird.

Poor Mrs. Bloodworth is learning to dance. She holds the handle of the dining-room door and swivels her feet in satin shoes, but when she lets go the handle, she falls down flat on her behind and stays that way, sitting, her hair all over her face, her feet pointing upward in her new shoes. Earlier, Mrs. Bloodworth was sitting that way, alone, when, squinting through her hair, she saw Irmgard sitting in her nightgown on the stairs. "Are you watching the fun?" she said in a tragic voice. "Is it really you, my sweet pet?" And she got to her feet and crawled up the stairs on her hands and knees to kiss Irmgard with ginny breath.

There is prohibition where Mrs. Bloodworth comes from. She has come up to Canada for a party; she came up for just one weekend and never went away. The party began as a wedding in Montreal, but it has been days since anyone mentioned the bride and groom. The party began in Montreal, came down to the lake, and now has dwindled to five: Irmgard's mother and father, Mrs. Bloodworth, Mrs. Bloodworth's friend Bill, and the best man, who came up for the wedding from Buffalo. "Darling pet, may I always stay?" said Mrs. Bloodworth, sobbing, her arms around Irmgard's mother's neck. Why she was sobbing this way nobody knows; she is always crying, dancing, embracing her friends.

In the morning Mrs. Bloodworth will be found in the hammock outside. The hammock smells of fish, the pillow is stuffed with straw; but Mrs. Bloodworth can never be made to go to bed. Irmgard inspects her up and down, from left to right. It isn't every morning of the year that you find a large person helplessly asleep. She is still wearing her satin shoes. Her eyeballs are covered with red nets. When she wakes up she seems still asleep, until she says stickily, "I'm having a rotten time, I don't care what anybody says." Irmgard backs off and then turns and runs along the gallery – the veranda, Mrs. Bloodworth would say – and up the side of the house and into the big kitchen, where behind screen doors Mrs. Queen and Germaine are drinking tea. They are drinking it in silence, for Germaine does not understand one word of English and Mrs. Queen is certainly not going to learn any French.

Germaine is Irmgard's *bonne d'enfant*. They have been

together about a century, and have a history stuffed with pageants, dangers, near escapes. Germaine has been saving Irmgard for years and years; but now Irmgard is nearly eight, and there isn't much Germaine can do except iron her summer dresses and braid her hair. They know a separation is near; and Irmgard is cheeky now, as she never was in the past; and Germaine pretends there have been other children she has liked just as well. She sips her tea. Irmgard drops heavily on her lap, joggling the cup. She will never be given anything even approaching Germaine's unmeasured love again. She leans heavily on her and makes her spill her tea. Germaine is mild and simple, a little dull. You can be rude and impertinent if necessary, but she must never be teased.

Germaine remembers the day Irmgard was kidnapped. When she sees a warm August morning like this one, she remembers that thrilling day. There was a man in a motorcar who wanted to buy Irmgard ice cream. She got in the car and it started moving, and suddenly there came Germaine running behind, with her mouth open and her arms wide, and Molly, the collie they had in those days, running with her ears back and her eyes slits. "Stop for Molly!" Irmgard suddenly screamed, and she turned and threw up all over the man's coat. "*Le matin du kidnap*," Germaine begins softly. It is a good thing she is here to recall the event, because the truth is that Irmgard remembers nothing about that morning at all.

Mrs. Queen is standing up beside the stove. She never sits down to eat, because she wants them to see how she hasn't a minute to waste; she is on the alert every second. Mrs. Queen is not happy down at the lake. It is not what she expected by "a country place." When she worked for Lady Partridge things were otherwise; you knew what to expect by "a country place." Mrs. Queen came out to Canada with Lady Partridge. The wages were low, and she had no stomach for travel, but she was devoted to Lady P. and to Ty-Ty and Buffy, the two cairns. The cairns died, because of the change of air, and after Lady P. had buried them, she went out to her daughter in California, leaving Mrs. Queen to look after the graves. But Mrs. Queen has never taken to Canada. She can't get used to it. She cannot get used to a place where the railway engines are that size and make that kind of noise, and where the working people are as tall as anyone else. When Mrs. Queen was interviewing Irmgard's mother, to see if Irmgard's mother would do, she said she had never taken to the place and couldn't promise a thing. The fancy might take her any minute to turn straight around and go back to England. She had told Lady Partridge the same thing. "When was that, Mrs. Queen?" "In nineteen ten, in the spring." She has never felt at home, and never wants to, and never will. If you ask her why she is unhappy, she says it is because of Ty-Ty and Buffy, the cairns; and because this is a paltry rented house and a paltry kitchen; and she is glad that Ty-Ty and Buffy are peacefully in their graves.

The party last night kept Mrs. Queen awake. She had to get up out of her uncomfortable bed and let the collies out of the garage. They knew there was a party somewhere, and were barking like fools. She let them out, she says, and then spent some time on the gallery, looking in the living-room window. It was a hot, airless night. (She happens to have the only stuffy room in the house.) The party was singing "Little Joe." Apparently, she did not see Mrs. Bloodworth dancing and falling down; at least she doesn't mention it.

Mrs. Queen is not going to clean up the mess in the living room. It is not her line of country. She is sick, sore, and weary. Germaine will, if asked, but just now she is braiding Irmgard's hair. Eating toast, Irmgard leans comfortably against Germaine. They are perfectly comfortable with each other, but Mrs. Queen is crying over by the stove.

Irmgard's cousin Bradley went back to Boston yesterday. She should be missing him, but he has vanished, fallen out of summer like a stone. He got on the train covered with bits of tape and lotion, and with a patch on one eye. Bradley had a terrible summer. He got poison ivy, in July, before coming here. In August, he grew a sty, which became infected, and then he strained his right arm. "I don't know what your mother will say," Irmgard's mother said. At this, after a whole summer of being without them, Bradley suddenly remembered he had a father and mother, and started to cry. Bradley is ten, but tall as eleven. He and Irmgard have the same look – healthy and stubborn, like well-fed, intelligent mice. They often stare in the mirror, side by side, positively blown up with admiration. But Bradley is superior to Irmgard in every way. When you ask him what he wants to be, he says straight off, "A mechanical and electrical engineer," whereas Irmgard is still hesitating between a veterinary and a nun.

"Have you dropped Freddy now that Bradley is here?" It seems that she was asked that a number of times.

"Oh, I still like Freddy, but Bradley's my cousin and everything." This is a good answer. She has others, such as, "I'm English-Canadian only I can talk French and I'm German descent on one side." (Bradley is not required to think of answers; he is American, and that does. But in Canada you have to keep saying what you are.) Irmgard's answer – about Freddy – lies on the lawn like an old skipping rope, waiting to catch her up. "Watch me," poor Mrs. Bloodworth said, but nobody cared, and the cry dissolved. "I like Freddy," Irmgard said, and was heard, and the statement is there, underfoot. For if she still likes Freddy, why isn't he here?

Freddy's real name is Alfred Marcel Dufresne. He has nine sisters and brothers, but doesn't know where they are. In winter he lives in an orphanage in Montreal. He used to live there all the year round, but now that he is over seven, old enough to work, he spends the summer with his uncle, who has a farm about two miles back from the lake. Freddy is nearly Irmgard's age, but smaller, lighter on his feet. He looks a tiny six. When he comes to lunch with Irmgard, which they have out in the kitchen with Germaine, everything has to be cut on his plate. He has never eaten with anything but a spoon. His chin rests on the edge of the table. When he is eating, you see nothing except his blue eyes, his curly dirty hair, and his hand around the bowl of the spoon. Once, Germaine said calmly, uncritically, "You eat just like a pig," and Freddy repeated in the tone she had used, "*comme un cochon*," as if it were astonishing that someone had, at last, discovered the right words.

Freddy cannot eat, or read, or write, or sing, or swim. He has never seen paints and books, except Irmgard's; he has never been an imaginary person, never played. It was Irmgard who taught him how to swim. He crosses himself before he goes in the water, and looks down at his wet feet, frowning – a worried mosquito – but he does everything she says. The point of their friendship is that she doesn't have to say much. They can read each other's thoughts. When Freddy wants to speak, Irmgard tells him what he wants to say, and Freddy stands there, mute as an animal, grave, nodding, at ease. He does not know the names of flowers, and does not distinguish between the colors green and blue. The apparitions of the Virgin, which are commonplace, take place against a heaven he says is "*vert*."

Now, Bradley has never had a vision, and if he did he wouldn't know what it was. He has no trouble explaining anything. He says, "Well, this is the way it is," and then says. He counts eight beats when he swims, and once saved Irmgard's life – at least he says he did. He says he held on to her braids until someone came by in a boat. No one remembers it but Bradley; it is a myth now, like the *matin du kidnap*. This year, Bradley arrived at the beginning of August. He had spent July in Vermont, where he took tennis lessons and got poison ivy. He was even taller than the year before, and he got down from the train with pink lotion all over his sores and, under his arm, a tennis racket in a press. "What a little stockbroker Bradley is," Irmgard heard her mother say later on; but Mrs. Queen declared that his manners left nothing wanting.

Bradley put all his own things away and set out his toothbrush in a Mickey Mouse glass he travelled with. Then he came down, ready to swim, with his hair water-combed. Irmgard was there, on the gallery, and so was Freddy, hanging on the outside of the railings, his face poked into the morning-glory vines. He thrusts his face between the leaves, and grins, and shows the gaps in his teeth. "How small he is! Do you play with him?" says Bradley, neutrally. Bradley is after information. He needs to know the rules. But if he had been sure about Freddy, if he had seen right away that they could play with Freddy, he would never have asked. And Irmgard replies, "No, I don't," and turns her back. Just so, on her bicycle, coasting downhill, she has lost control and closed her eyes to avoid seeing her own disaster. Dizzily, she says, "No, I don't," and hopes Freddy will disappear. But Freddy continues to hang on, his face thrust among the leaves, until Bradley, quite puzzled now, says, "Well, is he a friend of yours, or what?" and Irmgard again says, "No."

Eventually, that day or the next day, or one day of August, she notices Freddy has gone. Freddy has vanished; but Bradley gives her a poor return. He has the tennis racket, and does nothing except practice against the house. Irmgard has to chase the balls. He practices until his arm is sore, and then he is pleased and says he has tennis arm. Everybody bothers him. The dogs go after the balls and have to be shut up in the garage. "Call the dogs!" he implores. This is Bradley's voice, over the lake, across the shrinking afternoons. "Please, somebody, call the dogs!"

Freddy is forgotten, but Irmgard thinks she has left something in Montreal. She goes over the things in her personal suitcase. Once, she got up in the night to see if her paintbox was there – if that hadn't been left in Montreal. But the paintbox was there. Something else must be missing. She goes over the list again.

"The fact is," Bradley said, a few days ago, dabbing pink lotion on his poison ivy, "I don't really play with any girls now. So unless you get a brother or something, I probably won't come again." Even with lotion all over his legs he looks splendid. He and Irmgard stand side by side in front of the bathroom looking glass, and admire. She sucks in her cheeks. He peers at his sty. "My mother said you were a stockbroker," Irmgard confides. But Bradley is raised in a different political climate down there in Boston and does not recognize "stockbroker" as a term of abuse. He smiles fatly, and moves his sore tennis arm in a new movement he has now.

During August Freddy no longer existed; she had got in the habit of not seeing him there. But after Bradley's train pulled out, as she sat alone on the dock, kicking the lake, she thought, What'll I do now?, and remembered Freddy. She knows what took place the day she said "No" and, even more, what it meant when she said "Oh, I still like Freddy." But she has forgotten. All she knows now is that when she finds Freddy – in his uncle's muddy farmyard – she understands she hadn't left a paintbox or anything else in Montreal; Freddy was missing, that was all. But Freddy looks old and serious. He hangs his head. He has been forbidden to play with her now, he says. His uncle never wanted him to go there in the first place; it was a waste of time. He only allowed it because they were summer people from Montreal. Wondering where to look, both look at their shoes. Their meeting is made up of Freddy's feet in torn shoes, her sandals, the trampled mud of the yard. Irmgard sees blackberries, not quite ripe. Dumb as Freddy, having lost the power to read his thoughts, she picks blackberries, hard and greenish, and puts them in her mouth.

Freddy's uncle comes out of the foul stable and says something so obscene that the two stand frozen, ashamed – Irmgard, who does not know what the words mean, and Freddy, who does. Then Freddy says he will come with her for just one swim, and not to Irmgard's dock but to a public beach below the village, where Irmgard is forbidden to go; the water is said to be polluted there.

Germaine has her own way of doing braids. She holds the middle strand of hair in her teeth until she has a good grip on the other two. Then she pulls until Irmgard can feel her scalp lifted from her head. Germaine crosses hands, lets go the middle strand, and is away, breathing heavily. The plaits she makes are glossy and fat, and stay woven in water. She works steadily, breathing on Irmgard's neck.

Mrs. Queen says, "I'll wager you went to see poor Freddy the instant that Bradley was out of sight."

"Mmm."

"Don't 'Mmm' me. I hope he sent you packing."

"We went for a swim."

"I never saw a thing like it. That wretched boy was nothing but a slave to you all summer until Bradley came. It was Freddy do this, come here, go there. That charming English Mrs. Bustard who was here in July remarked the same thing. 'Irmgard is her mother all over again,' Mrs. Bustard said. 'All over again, Mrs. Queen.'"

"*Mrs. Bustard est une espèce de vache*," says Germaine gently, who cannot understand a word of English.

"Irmgard requires someone with an iron hand. 'A hand of iron,' Mrs. Bustard said."

Irmgard was afraid to tell Freddy, "But we haven't got our bathing suits or any towels." He was silent, and she could no longer read his mind. The sun had gone in. She was uneasy, because she was swimming in a forbidden place, and frightened by the water spiders. There had been other bathers; they had left their candy wrappers behind and a single canvas shoe. The lake was ruffled, brown. She suggested, "It's awfully cold," but Freddy began undressing, and Irmgard, not sure of her ground, began to unbuckle her sandals. They turned their backs, in the usual manner. Irmgard had never seen anybody undressed, and no one had ever seen her, except Germaine. Her back to Freddy, she pulled off her cotton dress, but kept on her bloomers. When she turned again, Freddy was naked. It was not a mistake; she had not turned around too soon. He stood composedly, with one hand on his skinny ribs. She said only, "The water's dirty here," and again, "It's cold." There were tin cans in the lake, half sunk in mud, and the water spiders. When they came out, Irmgard stood goosefleshed, blue-lipped. Freddy had not said a word. Trembling, wet, they put on their clothes. Irmgard felt water running into her shoes. She said miserably, "I think my mother wants me now," and edged one foot behind the other, and turned, and went away. There was nothing they could say, and nothing they could play any longer. He had discovered that he could live without her. None of the old games would do.

Germaine knows. This is what Germaine said yesterday afternoon; she was simple and calm, and said, "*Oui, c'est comme ça. C'est bien malheureux. Tu sais, ma p'tite fille, je crois qu'un homme, c'est une déformation.*"

Irmgard leans against Germaine. They seem to be consoling each other, because of what they both know. Mrs. Queen says, "Freddy goes back to an orphan asylum. I knew from the beginning the way it would end. It was not a kindness, allowing him to come here. It was no kindness at all." She would say more, but they have come down and want their breakfast. After keeping her up all night with noise, they want their breakfast now.

Mrs. Bloodworth looks distressed and unwashed. Her friend has asked for beer instead of coffee. Pleasure followed by gloom is a regular pattern here. But no matter how they feel,

Irmgard's parents get up and come down for breakfast, and they judge their guests by the way they behave not in pleasure but in remorse. The man who has asked for beer as medicine and not for enjoyment, and who described the condition of his stomach and the roots of his hair, will never be invited again. Irmgard stands by her mother's chair; for the mother is the mirror, and everything is reflected or darkened, given life or dismissed, in the picture her mother returns. The lake, the house, the summer, the reason for doing one thing instead of another are reflected here, explained, clarified. If the mirror breaks, everything will break, too.

They are talking quietly at the breakfast table. The day began in fine shape, but now it is going to be cloudy again. They think they will all go to Montreal. It is nearly Labor Day. The pity of parties is that they end.

"Are you sad, too, now that your little boy friend has left you?" says Mrs. Bloodworth, fixing Irmgard with her still-sleeping eyes. She means Bradley; she thought he and Irmgard were perfectly sweet.

Now, this is just the way they don't like Irmgard spoken to, and Irmgard knows they will not invite Mrs. Bloodworth again, either. They weigh and measure and sift everything people say, and Irmgard's father looks cold and bored, and her mother gives a waking tiger's look his way, smiles. They act together, and read each other's thoughts – just as Freddy and Irmgard did. But, large, and old, and powerful, they have greater powers: they see through walls, and hear whispered conversations miles away. Irmgard's father looks cold, and Irmgard, without knowing it, imitates his look.

"Bradley is Irmgard's cousin," her mother says.

Now Irmgard, who cannot remember anything, who looked for a paintbox when Freddy had gone, who doesn't remember that she was kidnapped and that Bradley once saved her life – now Irmgard remembers something. It seems that Freddy was sent on an errand. He went off down the sidewalk, which was heaving, cracked, edged with ribbon grass; and when he came to a certain place he was no longer there. Something was waiting for him there, and when they came looking for him, only Irmgard knew that whatever had been waiting for Freddy was the disaster, the worst thing. Irmgard's mother said, "Imagine sending a child near the woods at this time of day!" Sure enough, there were trees nearby. And only Irmgard knew that whatever had been waiting for Freddy had come out of the woods. It was the worst thing; and it could not be helped. But she does not know exactly what it was. And then, was it Freddy? It might have been Bradley, or even herself.

Naturally, no child should go near a strange forest. There are chances of getting lost. There is the witch who changes children into birds.

Irmgard grows red in the face and says loudly, "I remember my dream. Freddy went on a message and got lost."

"Oh, no dreams at breakfast, please," her father says.

"Nothing is as dreary as a dream," her mother says, agreeing. "I think we might make a rule on that: no dreams at breakfast. Otherwise it gets to be a habit."

Her father cheers up. Nothing cheers them up so fast as a new rule, for when it comes to making rules, they are as bad as children. You should see them at croquet.

SATURDAY

I

After the girl across the aisle had glanced at Gérard a few times (though he was not talking to her, not even trying to), she went down to sit at the front of the bus, near the driver. She left behind a bunch of dark, wet, purple lilac wrapped in wet newspaper. When Gérard followed to tell her, she did not even turn her head. Feeling foolish, he suddenly got down anywhere, in a part of Montreal he had never seen before, and in no time at all he was lost. He stood on the curb of a gloomy little street recently swept by a spring tempest of snow. A few people, bundled as Russians, scuffled by. A winter haze like a winter evening sifted down through a lattice of iron and steel. The sudden lowering of day, he saw, was caused by an overhead railway. This railway was smart and new, as if it had been unpacked out of sawdust quite recently and snapped into place.

What was it for? "Of all the unnecessary … " Gérard muttered, just as his father might. Talking aloud to oneself was a family habit. You could grumble away for minutes at home without anyone's taking the least notice. "Yes, they have to spend our money somehow," he went on, just as if he were old enough to vote and pay taxes. Luckily no one heard him. Everyone's attention had been fixed by a funeral procession of limousines grinding along in inches of slush. The Russian bundles crossed themselves, but Gérard kept his hands in his pockets. "Clogging up the streets," he offered, as an opinion about dying and being taken somewhere for burial. At that moment the last cars broke away, climbed the curb, and continued along the sidewalk. Gérard pressed back to the wall behind him, as he saw the others doing. No one appeared astonished, and he supposed that down here, in the east end, where there was a funeral a minute, this was the custom. "Otherwise you'd never have any normal traffic," he said. "Only all these hearses."

He thought, all at once, Why is everybody looking at me?

He was smiling. That was why. He could not help smiling. It was like a cinématèque comedy – the black cars in the whitish fog, the solemn bystanders wiping their noses on their gloves and crossing themselves, and everyone in winter cocoon clothes, with a white bubble of breath. But it was not black and gray, like an old film: it was the color of winter and cities, brown and brick and sand. What was more, the friends and relations of the dead were now descending from their stopped cars, and he feared that his smile might have offended them, or made him seem gross and unfeeling; and so, in a propitiatory gesture he at once regretted, he touched his forehead, his chest, and a point on each shoulder.

He had never done this for himself. Until now, he had never craved approval. From the look of the mourners, they were all Protestants anyway. He wanted to tell them he had crossed himself by mistake; that he was an atheist, from a singular and perhaps a unique family of anti-clerics. But the mourners were too grieved to pay attention. Even the men were sobbing. They held their hands against their mouths, they blinked and choked, they all but doubled over with pain – they were laughing at something. Perhaps at Gérard? Well, they were terrible people. He had always known. He was relieved to see one well-behaved person among them. She had been carried from her car and placed, with gentle care, in a collapsible aluminum wheelchair. Loving friends attended her, one to hold her purse, another to tie her scarf, a third to tuck a fur robe around her knees. Gérard had often been ill, and he recognized on her face the look of someone who knows about separateness and nightmares and all the vile tricks that the body can play. Her hair was careless, soft, and long, but the face seemed thirty, which was, to him, rather old. She turned her dark head and he heard her say gravely, "Not since the liberation of Elizabeth Barrett ... "

The coffin lay in the road. It had been let down from a truck, parked there as if workmen were about to jump out and begin shovelling snow or mending the pavement. The dead man must have left eccentric instructions, Gérard thought, for his coffin was nothing more than pieces of brown carton stapled together in a rough shape. The staples were slipping out: that was how carelessly and above all how cheaply the thing had been done. Gérard had a glimpse of a dark suit and a watch chain before he looked away. The hands, he saw, rested upon a long white envelope. He was to be buried with a packet of securities, as all Protestants probably were. The crippled woman touched Gérard on the arm and said, "Just reach over and get it, will you? " – that way, casually, used to service. No one stopped Gérard or asked him what he thought he was doing. As he slipped the envelope away he knew that this impertinence, this violation, would turn the dead man into a fury where he was concerned. By his desire to be agreeable, Gérard had deliberately and foolishly given himself some bad nights.

Jazz from an all-night program invaded the house until Gérard's mother, discovering its source in the kitchen, turned the radio off. She supposed Gérard had walked in his sleep. What else could she think when she found him kneeling, in the dark, with his head against the refrigerator door? Beside him was a smashed plate and the leftover ham that had been on it, and an overturned stool. She knelt too, and drew his head on her shoulder. His father stood in the doorway. The long underwear he wore at all times and in every season showed at his wrists and ankles, where the pajamas stopped. Without his teeth and without his glasses he seemed younger and clearer about the eyes, but frighteningly helpless and almost female. His head and his hands were splashed with large, soft-looking freckles.

"He looks so peaceful," the old man said. "This is how he always looks when we aren't around."

She did not answer, for once, "Oh, nobody cares," but her expression cried for her, "What useless, pointless remark will you think of next?" She clasped her son and tried to rock him. As Gérard resisted, she held still. Of all her children, he was the one with whom she blundered most. His uneven health, his moods, his temper, his choked breathing, were signs of starvation, she had been told, but not of the body. The mother was to blame. How to blame? How? Why not the father? They hadn't said. Her daughters were married; Léopold was still small; in between came this strange boy. One of Queen Victoria's children had been flogged for having asthma. Why should she think of this now? She had never punished her children. The very word had been banned.

Gérard heard his father open the refrigerator and then heard him pouring beer in a glass.

"He's been out with his girl," his father said. "She's no Cleopatra, but it's better than having him queer."

All Gérard felt then was how her grip slackened. She said softly, "Get rid of that girl. Just until you've passed your exams. Look at what she's doing to you. One day you'll meet her in the street and you'll wonder why you fought with your mother over her. Get rid of her and I'll believe everything you ever say. You've never walked in your sleep. You came in late. You were hungry … "

"What about the funeral?" the old man said. "Whose funeral?"

"Leave him," said his mother. "He's been dreaming."

Gérard, no longer refusing, let his mother rock him. If it had been a dream, then why in English? Dreaming in English made him feel powerless, as if his mind were dying, ill-fed from the soil. They spoke English at home, but he, Gérard, tried to dream in French. He read French; he went to French movies; he tried to speak it with his little brother; and yet his mind made fun of him and sent up to the surface "Elizabeth Barrett." The family had not deserted French for social betterment, or for business reasons, but on the matter of belief that set them apart. His mother wanted English to be freedom, at least from the Church. There were no public secular schools, but that was only part of it. Church and language were inextricably enmeshed, and you had to leave the language if you wanted your children brought up some other way. That was how it was. It was as simple, and as complex, as that. But (still pressed to his mother) he thought that here in the house there had never been freedom, only tension and conversation (oh, such a lot of conversation!) and a few corrupted qualities disguised as "speaking your mind," "taking a stand," and "drawing the line somewhere." Caressed by his mother, he seemed privileged. Being privileged, he weakened, and that meant even his rage was fouled. He had so much to hate that he seemed to carry in his brain a miniature Gérard, sneering and dark.

"If you would just do something about your children instead of all the time thinking about yourself," he heard his mother say. "Oh, anything. Do anything. Who cares what you do now? Nobody cares."

There had been a shortage of bedrooms until Gérard's five sisters married. His mother kept for her private use a sitting room with periwinkle paper on the walls. It could have done as a bedroom for the two boys, but her need for this extra space was never questioned. She had talks with her daughters there, and she kept the household accounts. Believing it her duty, she read her children's personal letters and their diaries as long as they lived under her roof. She carried the letters to the bright room and sat, leaning her head on her hand, reading. If someone came in she never tried to hide what she read, or slip it under a book, but let her hand fall, indifferently. In this room Gérard had lived the most hideous adventure of his life. Sometimes he thought it was a dream and he willed it to be a dream, even if it meant reversing sleeping and waking forever and accepting as friends and neighbors the strangers he saw in his sleep. He would remember it sometimes and say, "I must have dreamed it." His collection of pornography was heaped in plain sight on his mother's desk. There were the pictures, the books carefully dissimulated under fake covers, and the postcards from France and India turned face down. His mother sat with these at her elbow, and, of course, he could see them, and she said, "Gérard, I won't always be here. I'm not immortal. Your father is thirty years older than I am but he didn't have to bear his own children and he's as sound as this house. He might very well outlive me. I want you to see that he is always looked after and that he always uses saccharine to sweeten his tea. There is a little box I slip in his pajama pocket and another in the kitchen. Promise me. Now, the sweater you had on yesterday. I want to throw it out. It's past mending. I don't want you to sulk for a week, and that's why I'm asking you first." He wanted to say, "Those things aren't mine, I've got to give them back." He saw through her eyes and all at once understood that the cards from India were the worst of all, for they were all about people scarcely older than Léopold, and the reason they looked so funny was that they were starving to death. All Gérard had seen until now was what they were doing, not who they were, or could be. Meanwhile the room rocked around him, and his mother stood up to show that was all she had to say.

She did not sleep in the pretty room, but in a Spartan cell where there were closets full of linen and soap, and a shelf of preserves behind a curtain, and two painters' stepladders, and two large speckled mirrors in gilt frames. One wall was covered with photographs of a country house the children had never seen, and of her old convent school. The maid, when there was one, went freely in without knocking if she needed a jar of fruit or clean bedsheets. Even when her daughters married and liberated their rooms one by one, she stayed where she was. The bed was hard and narrow and the old man could not comfortably spend the night. For years Gérard had slept in a basement room that contained a Ping-Pong table, and from which he could hear, at odd hours, the furnace coming to life with a growl. A lighted tank of tropical fish separated two divans, one of which was used now by his father, now by his little brother. He had never understood why his father would suddenly appear in the middle of the night, and why the little brother, aged three and four and five, was led, stumbling and protesting, to finish the night in his mother's bed. Gérard was used to someone's presence at night, the warm light of the tank had comforted him. Now that he had a room of his own and slept alone in it, he discovered he was afraid of the dark.

His mother sat by his bed, holding his hand, until he pretended to be asleep. His door was open and a ray from the passage bent over the bed and along the wall. "I'm sure I must be pale," she said, though her cheeks and brow were rosy. She believed her children had taken her blood to make their own and that hers was diminished. Having had seven babies, she could not have left much over a pint. Bitterly anti-clerical, she sometimes hinted that nuns had the best of it after all. Gérard had been wrong to wake her; he had no business walking in his sleep. Tomorrow was what she called "a hell day." It was Léopold's ninth birthday, she was without help, and twenty-two people were going to sit down to lunch. Directly after the meal, she was to take all the uneaten cake to an aged religious who had once been a teacher of hers and was now ending her life bedridden in a convent for the old. The home was seventy miles north of the city, but might have been seven hundred. One son-in-law had undertaken to drive her. Instead of coming back with him, she proposed to spend the night. This meant that another son-in-law would have to fetch her the next day. The interlocked planning this required surpassed tunnelling under the Alps. "Hell day," she said, but she said it so often that Gérard supposed most days were some kind of hell.

The first thing he did when he wakened was light a cigarette, the second turn on his radio. He felt oddly drunk, as if he might miss his footing stumbling down to breakfast. She was already prepared for the last errand of the day. She wore a tweed suit and her overnight case stood in the hall. She moved back and forth between the kitchen and the dining room. His father, still in underwear and pajamas, sat breakfasting at the counter in the kitchen. She paused and watched him stir too much sugar into his coffee, but did not, this time, remark on it. The old man, excited, tapped his spoon on his saucer.

"It was a movie," he said. "Your dream. I saw it, I think, in a movie about an old man. You've dreamed an old man's dream. I've looked through the paper," he said, pushing it toward his son. "There's nothing about that funeral. It couldn't have been a funeral. Anyway, not anyone important."

"Leave him," said the mother, patiently. "He dreamed it. There is something you can do today. Take over the dog. *Completely*. Léopold has him now." Gérard knew it was his father thus addressed. He held his cup in both hands. "As for you, Gérard, I want a word with you."

"Another thing I thought," continued the old man. "Maybe they were making a movie around there and you got mixed up with the crowd. What you took for a railway was some kind of scaffolding, cameras. Eh?"

"Gérard, I want you to ... " She turned to her husband: "Back me up! He's your son, too! Gérard, I want you to tell that girl you're too young to be tied to one person." Her face was blazing, her eyes brilliant and clear. "What will you do when she starts a baby? Marry her? I want you to tell that girl there's no money to inherit in this family, and that after Léopold's education is finished there won't be a cent for anybody. Not even us."

"She's not really a dancer," said the old man, forestalling the next bit. "She gives dancing *lessons*. It's not the same thing."

"I don't care what she gives. What about your son?"

Gérard was about to say, "I did tell her," but he remembered,"I never got there. I only started out."

He stopped hearing them. He had set his cup down as his mother spoke his name, and pushed it to the back of the counter. As his father handed him the paper, he remembered, he had taken it with his left hand, and opened it wide instead of carefully folding it, as he usually did. This was so important that he did not hear what was said after a minute or two. He had always given importance to his gestures, noticing whether he put his watch or his glasses to the left or the right of a bedlamp. He always left his coffee cup about four inches from the edge of the counter. When he studied, he piled his books on the right, and whatever text he was immediately using was at his left hand. His radio had to be dead center. He saw, and had been noticing for some time, that his mind was not keeping quiet order for him anymore and that his gestures were not automatic. He felt that if he did not pay close attention to everything now, something literally fantastic could happen. Gestures had kept things controlled, as they ought to be. Whatever could happen now was in the domain of magic.

II

The conviction that she was married against her will never leaves her. If she had been born royal it could not have been worse. She has led the life of a crown princess, sapped by boredom and pregnancies. She told each of her five daughters as they grew up that they were conceived in horror; that she could have left them in their hospital cots and not looked back, so sickened was she by their limp spines and the autumn smell of their hair, by their froglike movements and their animal wails. She liked them when they could reason, and talk, and answer back – when they became what she calls "people."

She makes the girls laugh. She is French-Canadian, whether she likes it or not. They see at the heart of her a sacrificial mother; her education has removed her in degree only from the ignorant, tiresome, moralizing mother, given to mysterious female surgery, subjugated by miracles, a source of infinite love. They have heard her saying, "Why did I get married? Why did I have all these large dull children?" They have heard, "If any of my children had been brilliant or unusual, it would have justified my decision. Yes, they might have been narrow and warped in French, but oh how commonplace they became in English!" "We are considered traitors and renegades," she says. "And I can't point to even one of my children and say, 'Yes but it was worth it – look at Pauline – or Lucia – or Gérard.' " The girls ought to be wounded at this, but in fact they are impermeable. They laugh and call it "Mother putting on an act." Her passionate ambition for them is her own affair. They have chosen exactly the life she tried to renounce for them: they married young, they are frequently pregnant, and sometimes bored.

This Saturday she has reunited them, the entire family and one guest, for Léopold's ninth birthday. There are fourteen adults at the dining-room table and eight at the children's, which is in the living room, through the arch. Léopold, so small he seems two years younger than nine, so clever and quick that other children are slightly afraid of him, keeps an eye on his presents. He has inherited his brother's electric train. It is altogether old-fashioned; Gérard has had it nine years. Still, Léopold will not let anyone near it. It is his now, and therefore charmed. If any of these other children, these round-eyed brats with English names, lays a hand on the train, he disconnects it; if the outrage is repeated, he goes in the kitchen and stands on a stool and turns off the electricity for the whole house. No one reprimands him. He is not like other children. He is more intelligent, for one thing, and so much uglier. Unlike Gérard, who speaks French as if through a muslin curtain, or as if translating from another language, who wears himself out struggling for one complete dream, Léopold can, if he likes, say anything in a French more limpid and accurate than anything they are used to hearing. He goes to a private, secular school, the only French one in the province; he has had a summer in Montreux. Either his parents have more money than when the others were small, or they have chosen to invest in their last chance. French is Léopold's private language; he keeps it as he does his toys, to himself, polished, personal, a lump of crystalline rock he takes out, examines, looks through, and conceals for another day.

Léopold's five sisters think his intelligence is a disease, and one they hope their own children will not contract. Their mother is *bright*, their father is *thoughtful* (*deep* is another explanation for him), but Léopold's intelligence will always show him the limit of a situation and the last point of possibility where people are concerned; and so, of course, he is bound to be unhappy forever. How will he be able to love? To his elder brother, he seems like a small illegitimate creature raised in secret, in the wrong house. One day Léopold will show them extraordinary credentials. But this is a fancy, for Léopold is where he belongs, in the right family; he has simply been planted – little stunted, ugly thing – in the wrong generation. The children at his table are his nieces and nephews, and the old gentleman at the head of the adult table, the old man bowed over a dish of sieved, cooked fruit, is his father. Léopold is evidence of an old man's foolishness. His existence is an embarrassment. The girls wish he had never been born, and so they are especially kind, and they load him with presents. Even Gérard, who would have found the family quite complete, quite satisfactory, without any Léopold, ever, has given the train (which he was keeping for his own future children) and his camera.

When Léopold is given something, he walks round it and decides what the gift is worth in terms of the giver. If it seems cheap, he mutters without raising his eyes. If it seems important, he flashes a brief, shrewd look that any adult, but no child, mistakes for a glance of complicity. The camera, though second-hand, has been well received. It is round his neck; he puts down his fork and holds the camera and makes all the children uneasy by staring at each in turn and deciding none of them worth an inch of film.

"Poor little lad," says his mother, who flings out whatever she feels, no matter who is in the way. "He has never had a father – only a grandfather."

The old man may not have heard. He is playing his private game of trying to tell his five English-Canadian sons-in-law apart. The two Bobs, the Don, the Ian, and the Ken are interchangeable, like postage stamps of the Queen's profile. Two are Anglicans, two United Church, and the most lackluster is a Lutheran, but which is he? The old man lifts his head and smiles a great slow smile. His smile acquits his daughters; he forgives them for having ever thought him a shameless old person; but the five sons-in-law are made uneasy. They wonder if they are meant to smile back, or something *weird* like that. Well, they may not have much in common with each other, but here they are five together, not isolated, not alone. Their children, with round little noses, and round little blue eyes, are at the next table, and two or three babies are sleeping in portable cots upstairs.

It is a windy spring day, with a high clean sky, and black branches hitting on the windows. The family's guest that day is Father Zinkin, who is dressed just like anyone, without even a clerical collar to make him seem holy. This, to the five men, is another reason for discomposure; for they might be respectful of a robe, but *what* is this man, with his polo-necked sweater and his nose in the wine and his rough little jokes? Is he really the Lord's eunuch? I mean, they silently ask each other, would you trust him? You know what I mean ... Father Zinkin has just come back from Rome. He says that the trees are in leaf, and he got his pale jaundiced sunburn sitting at a sidewalk café. This is Montreal, it is still cold, and the daughters' five fur coats are piled upstairs on their mother's bed. They accept the news about Rome without grace. If he thinks it is so sunny in Rome, why didn't he stay there? Who asked him to come back? That is how every person at that table feels about news from abroad, and it is the only sentiment that can ever unite them. When you say it is sunny elsewhere, you are suggesting it is never sunny here. When you describe the trees of Rome, what you are *really* saying is there are no trees in Montreal.

Why is he at the table, then, since he brings them nothing but unwelcome news? The passionately anti-clerical family cannot keep away from priests. They will make an excuse: they will say they admire his mind, or his gifts with language – he speaks seven. He eats and drinks just like anyone, he has travelled, and been psychoanalyzed, and is not frightened by women. At least, he does not seem to be. Look at the way he pours wine for Lucia, and then for Pauline, and how his tone is just right, not a scrap superior. And then, he is not Canadian. He does not remind them of anything. None of the children, from Lucia, who is twenty-nine, to Léopold, nine today, has been baptized. Father Zinkin sits down and eats with them as if they were. Until the girls grew up and married they never went to church. Now that they are Protestants they go because their husbands want to; so, their mother thinks, this is what all the fighting and the courage came to, finally; all the struggling and being condemned and cut off from one's own kind: the five girls simply joined another kind, just as stupid.

No, thinks the old father at the head of the table: more stupid. At any rate, less interesting. Less interesting because too abstract. You would have to be a genius to be a true Protestant, and those he has met ... At night, when he is trying to get to sleep, he thinks of his sons-in-law. He remembers their names without trouble: the two Bobs, the Don, the Ian, and the last one – Keith, or Ken? Ken. Monique married Ken. Alone, in the dark, he tries to match names and faces. Are both Bobs thin? Pink in the face? Yes, and around the neck. They lose their hair young – something to do with English hairbrushes, he invents. The old man droops now, for the sight of his sons-in-law can send him off to sleep. His five daughters – he knows their names, and he knows his own sons. His grandchildren seem to belong to a new national type, with round heads, and quite large front teeth. You would think some Swede or other had been around Montreal on a bicycle so as to create this new national type. Sharon, and Marilyn and Cary and Gary and Gail. Cary and *Gary*.

"Nobody cares," his wife says, very sharply.

He has been mumbling, talking to himself, saying the names of children aloud. She minds because of Father Zinkin. When she and her husband are alone, and he talks too much, repeats the same thing over and over, she squeezes her eyes until only a pinpoint of amber glows between the lids, and she squeezes out through a tight throat, "All right, all *right*," and even, "Shut UP" in a rising crescendo of three. Not even her children know she says "Shut up" to the old man; "nobody cares" is just a family phrase. When it is used on Don Carlos, the basset, now under the children's table, it makes him look as if he might cry real tears.

She speaks lightly, quickly now, in English. She sits, very straight, powdered and pretty, and says, in a musical English all her own, not the speech of the city at all, "They say Jews look after their own people, but it's not true. I was told about some people who had a very old sick father. They had to tie him to a chair sometimes, because he would go downtown and steal things or start to cry in the street. As they couldn't afford a home for him, and he wouldn't have gone anyway, they decided to leave him. They moved half the furniture away and the old man sat crying on a chair and saw his family go. He sat weeping, not protesting, and his children slouched out without saying goodbye. Yes, he sat weeping, a respectable old man. Now, this man's wife gave Russian lessons to earn her living, and one day, when she was giving a lesson to a woman I know, she said, 'Come to the window.' My friend looked out and saw an old-fashioned Jew going by. The woman said, 'That was my husband.' She seemed pleased with herself, as though she had done what was right for her children."

"Was he dead?" asks Gérard. He is always waiting for some simple, casual confirmation about the existence of ghosts.

"No, of course not. He was just an old man, and someone had taken him in. Some Russian. So," she concedes, "he was looked after." But, as she likes her stories cruel, so that her children will know more about life than she once did, unhappy endings are her habit. She feels obliged to add, "Someone took him in, but probably gave him a miserable time. He must be dead now. This was long ago, during the last war, when people were learning Russian. It was the thing to do then."

Her children are worried by this story, but perhaps the father has not heard it. He is still eating his fruit, taking a mouthful and then forgetting to swallow. Suddenly something he has been thinking silently must have excited him, for he taps his spoon on the edge of the glass dish.

"As you get old you lose everything," he says. "You lose your God, if you ever had one. When you know they want you to die, you want to live. You want to be loved. Even that."

His children are so embarrassed, so humiliated, they feel as if ashes and sand were being ground in their skins. The sons-in-law are revolted. They look at their plates. Honestly, they can never come to this house without something being said about religion or something personal.

"You lose your parents," the old man continues. "You have to outlive them. Everything is loss." Before they can say "nobody cares" he is off once more: "No need for priests," he mutters. "If there is no sin, then no need for redemption. Dead words. Tell me, Father whoever you are," (he asks the glass dish of fruit) "will you explain why these words should be used?" Muttering – he has been muttering all his life.

"Oh, shut *up*," they are thinking. A chorus of silent English: "Shut *up*!" If only the old man could hear the words, he would see a great black wall; he would hear a sigh, a rattle, like the black trees outside the windows, hitting the panes.

The old man shakes his head over his plate: No, no, he never wanted to marry. He wanted to become a priest. Either God is, or He is not. If He is, I shall live for Him. If He is not, I shall fight His ghost. At forty-nine he was married off by a Jesuit, who was an old school friend. He and the shy, soft, orphaned girl who had been placed in a convent at six, and had left it, now, at eighteen, exchanged letters about comparative religion. She seemed intelligent – he has forgotten now what he imagined their life could ever be like. Presently what they had in common was her physical horror of him and his knowledge of it, and then they had in common all their children.

III

When the old man had finished his long thoughts, everyone except Gérard and Father Zinkin had disappeared. The small children were made to kiss him – moist reluctant mouths on his cheek – "before Granpa takes his nap." Léopold, who never touched anyone, looked at him briefly through his new camera and said softly to him, and only to him, "*Il n'y a pas assez de lumière*." Their dark identical eyes reflected each other. Then everyone vanished, the women to rattle plates in the kitchen, Léopold to his room, the five fathers to play some game with the children at the back of the house. He sat in his leather armchair, sometimes he slept, and he heard Gérard protesting, "I know the difference between seeing and dreaming."

"Well, it was a waking dream," said the priest. "There is no snow on the streets, but you say there had been a storm."

The old man looked. The white light in the room surely was the reflection of a snowy day? The room seemed filled with white furniture, white flowers. The priest, because he was dressed like Gérard, tried to sound like a young man and an old friend. Only when the priest turned his head, seeking an ashtray, did the old man see what Father Zinkin knew. His interest in Gérard was intellectual. His mind was occupied with its own power. The old man imagined him, narrow, suspicious, in a small parish, lording it over a flock of old maids. They were thin, their eyebrows met over their noses.

Gérard said, "All right, what if I was analyzed? What difference would it make?"

"You would be yourself. You would be yourself *without effort*."

The old man had been waiting for him to say, "it would break the mirror;" for what is the good of being yourself, if you are Gérard?

"What I mean is, you can't understand about this girl. So there's no use talking about her."

"I know about girls," said the other. "I went out. I even danced."

It struck the old man how often he had been told by priests they knew about life because they had, once, danced with girls. He was willing to let them keep that as a memory of life, but what about Gérard, as entangled with a woman as a man of thirty? But then Gérard lost interest and said, "I'd want to be analyzed in French," so it didn't matter.

"It wouldn't work. Your French isn't spontaneous enough. Now, begin again. You were on the street, it was daylight, then you were in the kitchen in the dark."

How the old man despised this self-indulgence! He felt it was not his business to put a stop to it. His wife stopped it simply by coming in and beginning to talk about herself. When she talked about her children she seemed to be talking about herself, and when the priest said, to console some complaint she was making, "The little one will be brilliant," meaning Léopold, he seemed to be prophesying a future in which she would shine. Outside, the others were breaking up into groups, carrying cots, ushering children into cars. It would take a good ten minutes, and so she sat perched on the arm of a sofa with her hat on her head and her coat on her arm, and said, "Léopold will be brilliant, but I never wanted him. I'd had six children, five close together. French Canadians of our background, for I daren't say class, it sounds so ... Well, we, people like ourselves, do *not* usually have these monstrous families, regardless of what you may have been told, Father. My mother had no one but me, and when she tried having a second child, it killed her. When I knew I was having Léopold I took ergot. I lay here, on this very sofa, in the middle of the afternoon. Nothing happened, and nothing showed. He was born without even a strawberry mark to condemn me."

She likes to shock, the old man remembered. How much you can take is measure of your intelligence. So she thinks. Oddly enough, she can be shocked.

She stopped speaking and sighed and smoothed the collar of her coat. When she thought, "My son Gérard is sleeping with a common girl," it shocked her. She thought, now, seeing him slouch past the doorway, scarcely able to wait for the house to empty so that he could go off and find that girl and spend a disgusting Saturday night with her, "Gérard knows. He looks at his father, and me, and now he knows. Before, he only thought he knew. He knows now why the old man follows me up the stairs."

She said very lightly, "My son has sex on the brain. It's all he thinks about now. I suppose all boys are the same. You must have been that way once, Father." Really, that was farther than she had ever gone. The priest looked like a statue resembling the person he had been a moment before.

Once she had departed the house seemed to relax, like an animal that feels safe and can sleep. The old man was to walk the dog and do something about his children. Those had been his instructions for the day. Oh, yes, and he was to stop thinking about himself. He put on his hat and coat and walked down the street with Don Carlos. Don Carlos dug the wet spring lawns with tortoiseshell nails. Let off the leash, he at once rolled in something horrible. The old man wanted to scold, but the wind made all conversation between himself and the dog impossible. The wind suddenly dropped; it was to the old man like a sudden absence of fear. He could dream as well as Gérard. He invented: he and Don Carlos went through the gap of a fence and were in a large sloping pasture. He trod on wildflowers. From the spongy spring soil grew crab apple trees and choke cherries, and a hedge of something he no longer remembered, that was sweet and white. Presently they – he and the dog – looked down on a village and the two silvery spires of a church. He saw the date over the door: 1885. The hills on the other side of the water were green and black with shadows. He had never seen such a blue and green day. But he was still here, on the street, and had not forgotten it for a second. Imagination was as good as sleepwalking any day.

Léopold stood on the porch, watching him through his camera. He seemed to be walking straight into Léopold's camera, magically reduced in size.

"Why, Léo," he said. "You're not supposed to be here," not caring to show how happy it made him that Léopold was here. They were bound so soon to lose each other – why start?

"Wouldn't."

"Wouldn't what?"

"Wouldn't go to Pauline's. She's coming back to get us for supper."

"I don't want anything more to eat today."

"Neither do I. And I'm not going."

Who would dare argue with Léopold? He put his camera down. One day he would have the assurance of a real street, a real father, a real afternoon.

"Well, well," his father said. "So they're all gone." He felt shy. He would never have enough of Léo – he would never know what became of him. He edged past and held the door open for the dog.

"All gone. *Il n'y a que moi*." Léopold, who never touched anyone, pressed his lips to his father's hand.

UP NORTH

When they woke up in the train, their bed was black with soot and there was soot in his Mum's blondie hair. They were miles north of Montreal, which had, already, sunk beneath his remembrance. "D'you know what I sor in the night?" said Dennis. He had to keep his back turned while she dressed. They were both in the same berth, to save money. He was small, and didn't take up much room, but when he woke up in that sooty autumn dawn, he found he was squashed flat against the side of the train. His Mum was afraid of falling out and into the aisle; they had a lower berth, but she didn't trust the strength of the curtain. Now she was dressing, and sobbing; really sobbing. For this was worse than anything she had ever been through, she told him. She had been right through the worst of the air raids, yet this was the worst, this waking in the cold, this dark, dirty dawn, everything dirty she touched, her clothes – oh, her clothes! – and now having to dress as she lay flat on her back. She daren't sit up. She might knock her head.

"You know what I sor?" said the child patiently. "Well, the train must of stopped, see, and some little men with bundles on their backs got on. Other men was holding lanterns. They were all little. They were all talking French."

"Shut up," said Mum. "Do you hear me?"

"Sor them," said the boy.

"You and your bloody elves."

"They was people."

"Little men with bundles," said Mum, trying to dress again. "You start your fairy tales with your Dad and I don't know what *he'll* give you."

It was this mythical, towering, half-remembered figure they were now travelling to join up north.

Roy McLaughlin, travelling on the same train, saw the pair, presently, out of his small red-lidded eyes. Den and his Mum were dressed and as clean as they could make themselves, and sitting at the end of the car. McLaughlin was the last person to get up, and he climbed down from his solitary green-curtained cubicle conspicuous and alone. He had to pad the length of the car in a trench coat and city shoes – he had never owned slippers, bathrobe, or pajamas – past the passengers, who were drawn with fatigue, pale under the lights. They were men, mostly; some soldiers. The Second World War had been finished, in Europe, a year and five months. It was a dirty, rickety train going up to Abitibi. McLaughlin was returning to a construction camp after three weeks in Montreal. He saw the girl, riding with her back to the engine, doing her nails, and his faculties absently registered "Limey bride" as he went by. The kid, looking out the window, turned and stared. McLaughlin thought "Pest," but only because children and other men's wives made him nervous and sour when they were brought around camp on a job.

After McLaughlin had dressed and had swallowed a drink in the washroom – for he was sick and trembling after his holiday – he came and sat down opposite the blond girl. He did not bother to explain that he had to sit somewhere while his berth was being dismantled. His arms were covered with coarse red hair; he had rolled up the sleeves of his khaki shirt. He spread his pale, heavy hands on his knees. The child stood between them, fingertips on the sooty window sill, looking out at the breaking day. Once, the train stopped for a long time; the engine was being changed, McLaughlin said. They had been rolling north but were now turning west. At six o'clock, in about an hour, Dennis and his mother would have to get down, and onto another train, and go north once more. Dennis could not see any station where they were now. There was a swamp with bristling black rushes, red as ink. It was the autumn sunrise; cold, red. It was so strange to him, so singular, that he could not have said an hour later which feature of the scene was in the foreground or to the left or right. Two women wearing army battle jackets over their dresses, with their hair piled up in front, like his mother's, called and giggled to someone they had put on the train. They were fat and dark – grinny. His mother looked at them with detestation, recognizing what they were; for she hated whores. She had always acted on the desire of the moment, without thought of gain, and she had taken the consequences (Dennis) without complaint. Dennis saw that she was hating the women, and so he looked elsewhere. On a wooden fence sat four or five men in open shirts and patched trousers. They had dull, dark hair, and let their mouths sag as though they were too tired or too sleepy to keep them closed. Something about them was displeasing to the child, and he thought that this was an ugly place with ugly people. It was also a dirty place; every time Dennis put his hands on the window sill they came off black.

"Come down any time to see a train go by," said McLaughlin, meaning those men. "Get up in the *night* to see a train."

The train moved. It was still dark enough outside for Dennis to see his face in the window and for the light from the windows to fall in pale squares on the upturned vanishing faces and on the little trees. Dennis heard his mother's new friend say, "Well, there's different possibilities." They passed into an unchanging landscape of swamp and bracken and stunted trees. Then the lights inside the train were put out and he saw that the sky was blue and bright. His mother and McLaughlin, seen in the window, had been remote and bodiless; through their transparent profiles he had seen the yellowed trees going by. Now he could not see their faces at all.

"He's been back in Canada since the end of the war. He was wounded. Den hardly knows him," he heard his mother say. "I couldn't come. I had to wait my turn. We were over a thousand war brides on that ship. He was with Aluminium when he first came back." She pronounced the five vowels in the word.

"You'll be all right there," said McLaughlin. "It's a big place. Schools. All company."

"Pardon me?"

"I mean it all belongs to Aluminum. Only if that's where you're going you happen to be on the wrong train."

"He isn't there now. He hates towns. He seems to move about a great deal. He drives a bulldozer, you see."

"Owns it?" said McLaughlin.

"Why, I shouldn't *think* so. Drives for another man, I think he said."

The boy's father fell into the vast pool of casual labor, drifters; there was a social hierarchy in the north, just as in Heaven. McLaughlin was an engineer. He took another look at the boy: black hair, blue eyes. The hair was coarse, straight, rather dull; Indian hair. The mother was a blonde; touched up a bit, but still blond.

"What name?" said McLaughlin on the upward note of someone who has asked the same question twice.

"Cameron. Donald Cameron."

That meant nothing, still; McLaughlin had worked in a place on James Bay where the Indians were named MacDonald and Ogilvie and had an unconquered genetic strain of blue eyes.

"D'you know about any ghosts?" said the boy, turning to McLaughlin. McLaughlin's eyes were paler than his own, which were a deep slate blue, like the eyes of a newly born child. McLaughlin saw the way he held his footing on the rocking train, putting out a few fingers to the window sill only for the form of the thing. He looked all at once ridiculous and dishonored in his cheap English clothes – the little jacket, the Tweedledum cap on his head. He outdistanced his clothes; he was better than they were. But he was rushing on this train into an existence where his clothes would be too good for him.

"D'you know about any ghosts?" said the boy again.

"Oh, sure," said McLaughlin, and shivered, for he still felt sick, even though he was sharing a bottle with the Limey bride. He said, "Indians see them," which was as close as he could come to being crafty. But there was no reaction out of the mother; she was not English for nothing.

"You seen any?"

"*I'm* not an Indian," McLaughlin started to say; instead he said, "Well, yes. I saw the ghost, or something like the ghost, of a dog I had."

They looked at each other, and the boy's mother said, "Stop that, you two. Stop that this minute."

"I'll tell you a strange thing about Dennis," said his mother. "It's this. There's times he gives me the creeps."

Dennis was lying on the seat beside her with his head on her lap.

She said, "If I don't like it I can clear out. I was a waitress. There's always work."

"Or find another man," McLaughlin said. "Only it won't be me, girlie. I'll be far away."

"Den says that when the train stopped he saw a lot of elves," she said, complaining.

"Not elves – men," said Dennis. "Some of them had mattresses rolled up on their backs. They were little and bent over. They were talking French. They were going up north."

McLaughlin coughed and said, "He means settlers. They were sent up on this same train during the depression. But that's nine, ten years ago. It was supposed to clear the unemployed out of the towns, get them off relief. But there wasn't anything up here then. The winters were terrible. A lot of them died."

"He couldn't know that," said Mum edgily. "For that matter, how can he tell what is French? He's never heard any."

"No, he couldn't know. It was around ten years ago, when times were bad."

"Are they good now?"

"Jeez, after a *war*?" He shoved his hand in the pocket of his shirt, where he kept a roll, and he let her see the edge of it.

She made no comment, but put her hand on Den's head and said to him, "You didn't see anyone. Now shut up."

"Sor 'em," the boy said in a voice as low as he could descend without falling into a whisper.

"You'll see what your Dad'll give you when you tell lies." But she was halfhearted about the threat and did not quite believe in it. She had been attracted to the scenery, whose persistent sameness she could no longer ignore. "It's not proper country," she said. "It's bare."

"Not enough for me," said McLaughlin. "Too many people. I keep on moving north."

"I want to see some Indians," said Dennis, sitting up.

"There aren't any," his mother said. "Only in films."

"I don't like Canada." He held her arm. "Let's go home now."

"It's the train whistle. It's so sad. It gets him down."

The train slowed, jerked, flung them against each other, and came to a stop. It was quite day now; their faces were plain and clear, as if drawn without shading on white paper. McLaughlin felt responsible for them, even compassionate; the change in him made the boy afraid.

"We're getting down, Den," said his Mum, with great, wide

eyes. "We take another train. See? It'll be grand. Do you hear what Mum's telling you?"

He was determined not to leave the train, and clung to the window sill, which was too smooth and narrow to provide a grip; McLaughlin had no difficulty getting him away. "I'll give you a present," he said hurriedly. But he slapped all his pockets and found nothing to give. He did not think of the money, and his watch had been stolen in Montreal. The woman and the boy struggled out with their baggage, and McLaughlin, who had descended first so as to help them down, reached up and swung the boy in his arms.

"The Indians!" the boy cried, clinging to the train, to air; to anything. His face was momentarily muffled by McLaughlin's shirt. His cap fell to the ground. He screamed, "Where's Mum? I never saw *any*thing!"

"You saw Indians," said McLaughlin. "On the rail fence, at that long stop. Look, don't worry your mother. Don't keep telling her what you haven't seen. You'll be seeing plenty of everything now."

ORPHANS' PROGRESS

When the Collier girls were six and ten they were taken away from their mother, whom they loved without knowing what the word implied, or even that it existed, and sent to their father's mother. Their grandmother was scrupulous about food, particularly for these underfed children, and made them drink goat's milk. Two goats bought specially to supply the orphans were taken by station wagon to a buck fifty miles away, the girls accompanying them for reasons of enlightenment. A man in a filling station was frightened by the goats, because of their oblong eyes. The girls were not reflected in the goats' eyes, as they were in each other's. What they remembered afterwards of their grandmother was goat's milk, goat eyes, and the frightened man.

They went to school in Ontario now, with children who did not have the same accent as children in Montreal. When their new friends liked something they said it was smart. A basketball game was smart, so was a movie: it did not mean elegant, it just meant all right. Ice cream made out of goat's milk was not smart: it tasted of hair.

Their grandmother died when the girls were seven and

eleven and beginning to speak in the Ontario way. Their mother had been French-Canadian – they were now told – but had spoken French and English to them. They had called her Mummy, a habit started when their father was still alive, for he had not learned French. They understood, from their grandmother, and their grandmother's maid, and the social worker who came to see their grandmother but had little to say to them, that French was an inferior kind of speech. At first, when they were taken away from their mother, Cathie, the elder girl, would wake up at night holding her head, her elbows on her knees, saying in French, "My head hurts," but a few minutes later, the grandmother having applied cold wrung-out towels, she would say in English, "It's better."

Mildred had pushed out two front teeth by sucking her thumb. She had been doing that forever, even before they were taken away from their mother. Ontario could not be blamed. Nevertheless, their grandmother told the social worker about it, who wrote it down.

They did not know, and never once asked, why they had been taken away. When the new social worker said to Cathie, "Were you disturbed because your mother was unhappy?" Cathie said, "She wasn't." When the girls were living with their mother, they knew that sometimes she listened and sometimes could not hear; nevertheless, she was there. They slept in the same bed, all three. Even when she sat on the side of the bed with her head hanging and her undone jagged-cut hair hiding her eyes, mumbling complaints that were not their concern, the children were close to her and did not know they were living under what would be called later "unsheltered conditions." They never knew, until told, that they were uneducated and dirty and in danger. Now they learned that their mother never washed her own neck and that she dressed in layers of woollen stuff, covered with grease, and wore men's shoes because some man had left them behind and she liked the shape or the comfort of them. They did not know, until they were told, that they had never been properly fed.

"We ate chicken," said Cathie Collier, the elder girl.

"They say she served it up half raw," said their grandmother's maid. "Survet" said the maid for "served," and that was not the way their mother had spoken. "The sheets was so dirty, the dirt was like clay. All of yez slept in the one bed," said the maid.

"Yes, we slept together." The apartment – a loft, they were told, over a garage; not an apartment at all – must still exist, it must be somewhere, with the piano that Mildred, the little one, had banged on with her palms flat. What about the two cats who were always fighting or playing, depending on their disposition? There were pictures on the wall, their mother's, and the children's own drawings.

"When one of the pictures was moved there was a square mass of bugs," said the grandmother's maid. "The same shape as the pitcher."

"To the day I die," said the social worker from Montreal to her colleague in Ontario, "I won't forget the screams of Mildred when she was dragged out of that pigsty." This was said in the grandmother's parlor, where the three women – the two social workers, and the grandmother – sat with their feet freezing on the linoleum floor. The maid heard, and told. She had been in and out, serving coffee, coconut biscuits, and damson preserves in custard made of goat's milk. The room was heated once or twice a year: even the maid said her feet were cold. But "To the day I die" was a phrase worth hearing. She liked the sound of that, and said it to the children. The maid was from a place called Waterloo, where, to hear her tell it, no one behaved strangely and all the rooms were warm.

Thumb-sucker Mildred did not remember having screamed, or anything at all except the trip from Montreal by train. "Boy, is your grandmother ever a rich old lady!" said the maid from Waterloo. "If she wasn't, where'd you be? In an orphung asylum. She's a Christian, I can tell you." But another day, when she was angry with the grandmother over something, she said, "She's a damned old sow. It's in the mattress and she's lying on it. You can hear the bills crackle when you turn the mattress Saturdays. I hope they find it when she dies, is all I can say."

The girls saw their grandmother dead, in the bed, on that mattress. The person crying hardest in the room was the maid. She had suddenly dyed her hair dark red, and the girls did not know her, because of her tears, and her new clothes, and because of the way she fondled and kissed them. "We'll never see each other again," said the maid.

Now that their grandmother had died, the girls went to live with their mother's brother and his wife and their many children. It was a suburb of Montreal called Ahuntsic. They did not see anything that reminded them of Montreal, and did not recall their mother. There was a parlor here full of cut glass, which was daily rubbed and polished, and two television sets, one for the use of the children. The girls slept on a pull-out divan and wrangled about bedclothes. Cathie wanted them pushed down between them in a sort of trough, because she felt a draft, but Mildred complained that the blankets thus arranged were tugged away from her side. She was not properly covered and afraid of falling on the floor. One of their relations (they had any number here on their mother's side) made them a present of a box of chocolate almonds, but the cousins they lived with bought exactly the same box, so as to tease them. When Cathie and Mildred rushed to see if their own box was still where they had hidden it, they were bitterly mocked. Their Ontario grandmother's will was not probated and every scrap of food they put in their mouths was taken from the mouths of cousins: so they were told. Their cousins made them afraid of ghosts. They put out the lights and said, "Look out, she is coming to get you, all in black," and when Mildred began to whimper, Cathie said, "Our mother wouldn't try to frighten us." She had not spoken of her until now. One of the cousins said, "I'm talking about your old grandmother. Your mother isn't dead." They were shown their father's grave, and made to kneel and pray. Their lives were in the dark now, in the dark of ghosts, whose transparent shadows stood round their bed; soon they lived in the black of nuns. Language was black, until they forgot their English. Until they spoke French, nothing but French, the family pretended not to understand them, and stared as if they were peering in the dark. They very soon forgot their English.

They could not stay here with these cousins forever, for the flat was too small. When they were eight and twelve, their grandmother's will was probated and they were sent to school. For the first time in their lives, now, the girls did not sleep in the same bed. Mildred slept in a dormitory with the little girls, where a green light burned overhead, and a nun rustled and prayed or read beside a green lamp all night long. Mildred was bathed once every fortnight, wearing a rubber apron so that she would not see her own body. Like the other little girls, she dressed, in the morning, sitting on the floor, so that they would not see one another. Her thumb, sucked white, was taped to the palm of her hand. She caught glimpses of Cathie sometimes during recreation periods, but Cathie was one of the big girls, and important. She did not play, as the little ones still did, but walked up and down with the supervisor, walking backwards as the nun walked forward.

One day, looking out of a dormitory window, Mildred saw a rooftop and an open skylight. She said to a girl standing nearby, "That's our house." "What house?" "Where Mummy lives." She said that sentence, three words, in English. She had not thought or spoken "Mummy" since she was six and a half. It turned out that she was lying about the house. Lying was serious; she was made to promenade through the classrooms carrying a large pair of shears and the sign "I am a liar." She did not know the significance of the shears, nor, it seemed, did the nun who organized the punishment. It had always been associated with lying, and (the nun suddenly remembered) had to do with cutting out the liar's tongue. The tattling girl, who had told about "Where Mummy lives," was punished too, and made to carry a wastebasket from room to room with "I am a basket-carrier" hung round her neck. This meant a tale-bearer. Everyone was in the wrong.

Cathie was not obliged to wear a rubber apron in her bath, but a muslin shift. She learned the big girls' trick, which was to take it off and dip it in water, and then bathe properly. When Mildred came round carrying her scissors and her sign Cathie had had her twice-monthly bath and felt damp and new. She said to someone, "That's my sister," but "sister" was a dark scowling little thing. "Sister" got into still more trouble: a nun, a stray from Belgium, perhaps as one refugee to another, said to Mildred, swiftly drawing her into a broom-cupboard, "Call me Maman." "Maman" said the child, to whom "Mummy" had meaning until the day of the scissors. Who was there to hear what was said in the broom-cupboard? What basket-carrier repeated that? It was forbidden for nuns to have favorites, forbidden to have pet names for nuns, and the Belgian stray was sent to the damp wet room behind the chapel and given flower-arranging to attend to. There Mildred found her, by chance, and the nun said, "Get away, haven't you made enough trouble for me?"

Cathie was told to pray for Mildred, the trouble-maker, but forgot. The omission weighed on her. She prayed for her mother, grandmother, father, herself (with a glimpse in the prayer of her own future coffin, white) and the uncles and aunts and cousins she knew and those she had never met. Her worry about forgetting Mildred in her prayers caused her to invent a formula: "Everyone I have ever known who is dead or alive, anyone I know now who is alive but might die, and anyone I shall ever know in the future." She prayed for her best friend, who wanted like Cathie to become a teacher, and for a nun with a mustache who was jolly, and for her confessor, who liked to hear her playing the Radetzky March on the piano. Her hair grew lighter and was brushed and combed by her best friend.

Mildred was suddenly taken out of school and adopted. Their mother's sister, one of the aunts they had seldom seen, had lost a daughter by drowning. She said she would treat Mildred as she did her own small son, and Mildred, who wished to leave the convent school, but did not know if she cared to go and live in a place called Chicoutimi, did not decide. She made them decide, and made them take her away. When the girls were fifteen and nineteen, and Mildred was called Desaulniers and not Collier, the sisters were made to meet. Cathie had left school and was studying nursing, but she came back to the convent when she had time off, not because she did not have anywhere else to go, but because she did not want to go to any other place. The nuns had said of Cathie, laughing, "She doesn't want to leave – we shall have to push her out." When Cathie's sister, Mildred Desaulniers, came to call on her, the girls did not know what to say. Mildred wore a round straw hat with a clump of plastic cherries hanging over the brim; her adoptive brother, in long trousers and bow tie, did not get out of the car. He was seven, and had slick wet-looking hair, as if he had been swimming. "Kiss your sister," said Mildred's mother, to Cathie, admonishingly. Cathie did as she was told, and Mildred immediately got back in the car with her brother and snatched a comic book out of his hands. "Look, Mildred," said her father, and let the car slow down on a particular street. The parents craned at a garage, and at dirty-legged children with torn sneakers on their feet. Mildred glanced up and then back at her book. She had no reason to believe she had seen it before, or would ever again.

THE PRODIGAL PARENT

We sat on the screened porch of Rhoda's new house, which was close to the beach on the ocean side of Vancouver Island. I had come here in a straight line, from the East, and now that I could not go any farther without running my car into the sea, any consideration of wreckage and loss, or elegance of behavior, or debts owed (not of money, of my person) came to a halt. A conqueror in a worn blazer and a regimental tie, I sat facing my daughter, listening to her voice – now describing, now complaining – as if I had all the time in the world. Her glance drifted round the porch, which still contained packing cases. She could not do, or take in, a great deal at once. I have light eyes, like Rhoda's, but mine have been used for summing up.

Rhoda had bought this house and the cabins round it and a strip of maimed landscape with her divorce settlement. She hoped to make something out of the cabins, renting them weekends to respectable people who wanted a quiet place to drink. "Dune Vista" said a sign, waiting for someone to nail it to a tree. I wondered how I would fit in here – what she expected me to do. She still hadn't said. After the first formal Martinis she had made to mark my arrival, she began drinking rye, which she preferred. It was sweeter, less biting than the whiskey I remembered in my youth, and I wondered if my palate or its composition had changed. I started to say so, and my daughter said, "Oh, God, your accent again! You know what I thought you said now? 'Oxbow was a Cheswick charmer.'"

"No, no. Nothing like that."

"Try not sounding so British," she said.

"I don't, you know."

"Well, you don't sound Canadian."

The day ended suddenly, as if there had been a partial eclipse. In the new light I could see my daughter's face and hands.

"I guess I'm different from all my female relatives," she said. She had been comparing herself with her mother, and with half sisters she hardly knew. "I don't despise men, like Joanne does. There's always somebody. There's one now, in fact. I'll tell you about him. I'll tell you the whole thing, and you say what you think. It's a real mess. He's Irish, he's married, and he's got no money. Four children. He doesn't sleep with his wife."

"Surely there's an age limit for this?" I said. "By my count, you must be twenty-eight or -nine now."

"Don't I know it." She looked into the dark trees, darkened still more by the screens, and said without rancor, "It's not my fault. I wouldn't keep on falling for lushes and phonies if you hadn't been that way."

I put my glass down on the packing case she had pushed before me, and said, "I am not, I never was, and I never could be an alcoholic."

Rhoda seemed genuinely shocked. "I never said *that*. I never heard you had to be put in a hospital or anything, like my stepdaddy. But you used to stand me on a table when you had parties, Mother told me, and I used to dance to 'Piccolo Pete.' What happened to that record, I wonder? One of your wives most likely got it in lieu of alimony. But may God strike us both dead here and now if I ever said you were alcoholic." It must have been to her a harsh, clinical word, associated with straitjackets. "I'd like you to meet him," she said. "But I never know when he'll turn up. He's Harry Pay. The writer," she said, rather primly. "Somebody said he was a new-type Renaissance Man – I mean, he doesn't just sit around, he's a judo expert. He could throw *you* down in a second."

"Is he Japanese?"

"God, no. What makes you say that? I already told you what he is. He's white. Quite white, *entirely* white I mean."

"Well – I could hardly have guessed."

"You shouldn't have to guess," she said. "The name should be enough. He's famous. Round here, anyway."

"I'm sorry," I said. "I've been away so many years. Would you write the name down for me? So I can see how it's spelled?"

"I'll do better than that." It touched me to see the large girl she was suddenly moving so lightly. I heard her slamming doors in the living room behind me. She had been clumsy as a child, in every gesture like a wild creature caught. She came back to me with a dun folder out of which spilled loose pages, yellow and smudged. She thrust it at me and, as I groped for my spectacles, turned on an overhead light. "You read this," she said, "and I'll go make us some sandwiches, while I still can. Otherwise we'll break into another bottle and never eat anything. This is something he never shows *anyone*."

"It is my own life exactly," I said when she returned with the sandwiches, which she set awkwardly down. "At least, so far as school in England is concerned. Cold beds, cold food, cold lavatories. Odd that anyone still finds it interesting. There must be twenty written like it every year. The revolting school, the homosexual master, then a girl – saved!"

"Homo *what*?" said Rhoda, clawing the pages. "It's possible. He has a dirty mind, actually."

"Really? Has he ever asked you to do anything unpleasant, such as type his manuscripts?"

"Certainly not. He's got a perfectly good wife for that."

When I laughed, she looked indignant. She had given a serious answer to what she thought was a serious question. Our conversations were always like this – collisions.

"Well?" she said.

"Get rid of him."

She looked at me and sank down on the arm of my chair. I felt her breath on my face, light as a child's. She said, "I was waiting for something. I was waiting all day for you to say something personal, but I didn't think it would be that. Get rid of him? He's all I've got."

"All the more reason. You can do better."

"Who, for instance?" she said. "You? You're no use to me."

She had sent for me. I had come to Rhoda from her half sister Joanne, in Montreal. Joanne had repatriated me from Europe, with an air passage to back the claim. In a new bare apartment, she played severe sad music that was like herself. We ate at a scrubbed table the sort of food that can be picked up in the hand. She was the richest of my children, through her mother, but I recognized in her guarded, slanting looks the sort of avarice and fear I think of as a specific of women. One look seemed meant to tell me, "You waltzed off, old boy, but look at me now," though I could not believe she had wanted me only for that. "I'll never get married" was a remark that might have given me a lead. "I won't have anyone to lie to me, or make a fool of me, or spend my money for me." She waited to see what I would say. She had just come into this money.

"Feeling as you do, you probably shouldn't marry," I said. She looked at me as Rhoda was looking now. "Don't expect too much from men," I said.

"Oh, I don't!" she cried, so eagerly I knew she always would. The cheap sweet Ontario wine she favored and the smell of paint in her new rooms and the raw meals and incessant music combined to give me a violent attack of claustrophobia. It was probably the most important conversation we had.

"We can't have any more conversation now," said Rhoda. "Not after that. It's the end. You've queered it. I should have known. Well, eat your sandwiches now that I've made them."

"Would it seem petulant if, at this point, I did not eat a tomato sandwich?" I said.

"Don't be funny. I can't understand what you're saying anyway."

"If you don't mind, my dear," I said, "I'd rather be on my way."

"What do you mean, on your way? For one thing, you're in no condition to drive. Where d'you think you're going?"

"I can't very well go that way," I said, indicating the ocean I could not see. "I can't go back as I've come."

"It was a nutty thing, to come by car," she said. "It's not even all that cheap."

"As I can't go any farther," I said, "I shall stay. Not here, but perhaps not far."

"Doing what? What *can* you do? We've never been sure."

"I can get a white cane and walk the streets of towns. I can ask people to help me over busy intersections and then beg for money."

"You're kidding."

"I'm not. I shall say – let me think – I shall say I've had a mishap, lost my wallet, pension check not due for another week, postal strike delaying it even more – "

"That won't work. They'll send you to the welfare. You should see how we hand out welfare around here."

"I'm counting on seeing it," I said.

"You can't. It would look – " She narrowed her eyes and said, "If you're trying to shame me, forget it. Someone comes and says, 'That poor old blind bum says he's your father,' I'll just answer, 'Yes, what about it?' "

"My sight *is* failing, actually."

"There's welfare for that, too."

"We're at cross-purposes," I said. "I'm not looking for money."

"Then waja come here for?"

"Because Regan sent me on to Goneril, I suppose."

"That's a lie. Don't try to make yourself big. Nothing's ever happened to you."

"Well, in my uneventful life," I began, but my mind answered for me, "No, nothing." There are substitutes for incest but none whatever for love. What I needed now was someone who knew nothing about me and would never measure me against a promise or a past. I blamed myself, not for anything I had said but for having remembered too late what Rhoda was like. She was positively savage as an infant, though her school tamed her later on. I remember sitting opposite her when she was nine – she in an unbecoming tartan coat – while she slowly and seriously ate a large plate of ice cream. She was in London on a holiday with her mother, and as I happened to be there with my new family I gave her a day.

"Every Monday we have Thinking Day," she had said, of her school. "We think about the Brownies and the Baden-Powells and sometimes Jesus and all."

"Do you, really?"

"I can't *really*," Rhoda had said. "I never met any of them."

"Are you happy, at least?" I said, to justify my belief that no one was ever needed. But the savage little girl had become an extremely careful one.

That afternoon, at a matinée performance of *Peter Pan*, I went to sleep. The slaughter of the pirates woke me, and as I turned, confident, expecting her to be rapt, I encountered a face of refusal. She tucked her lips in, folded her hands, and shrugged away when I helped her into a taxi.

"I'm sorry, I should not have slept in your company," I said. "It was impolite."

"It wasn't that," she burst out. "It was *Peter Pan*. I hated it. It wasn't what I expected. You could see the wires. Mrs. Darling didn't look right. She didn't have a lovely dress on – only an old pink thing like a nightgown. Nana wasn't a real dog, it was a lady. I couldn't understand anything they said. Peter Pan wasn't a boy, he had bosoms."

"I noticed that, too," I said. "There must be a sound traditional reason for it. Perhaps Peter is really a mother figure."

"No, he's a *boy*."

I intercepted, again, a glance of stony denial – of me? We had scarcely met.

"I couldn't understand. They all had English accents," she complained.

For some reason that irritated me. "What the hell did you expect them to have?" I said.

"When I was little," said the nine-year-old, close to tears now, "I thought they were all Canadian."

The old car Joanne had given me was down on the beach, on the hard sand, with ribbons of tire tracks behind it as a sign of life, and my luggage locked inside. It had been there a few hours and already it looked abandoned – an old heap someone had left to rust among the lava rock. The sky was lighter than it had seemed from the porch. I picked up a sand dollar, chalky and white, with the tree of life on its underside, and as I slid it in my pocket, for luck, I felt between my fingers a rush of sand. I had spoken the truth, in part; the landscape through which I had recently travelled still shuddered before my eyes and I would not go back. I heard, then saw, Rhoda running down to where I stood. Her hair, which she wore gathered up in a bun, was half down, and she breathed, running, with her lips apart. For the first time I remembered something of the way she had seemed as a child, something more than an anecdote. She clutched my arm and said, "Why did you say I should ditch him? *Why?*"

I disengaged my arm, because she was hurting me, and said, "He can only give you bad habits."

"At my age?"

"Any age. Dissimulation. Voluntary barrenness – someone else has had his children. Playing house, a Peter-and-Wendy game, a life he would never dare try at home. There's the real meaning of Peter, by the way." But she had forgotten.

She clutched me again, to steady herself, and said, "I'm old enough to know everything. I'll soon be in my thirties. That's all I care to say."

It seemed to me I had only recently begun making grave mistakes. I had until now accepted all my children, regardless of who their mothers were. The immortality I had imagined had not been in them but on the faces of women in love. I saw, on the dark beach, Rhoda's mother, the soft hysterical girl whose fatal "I am pregnant" might have enmeshed me for life.

I said, "I wish they would find a substitute for immortality."

"I'm working on it," said Rhoda, grimly, seeming herself again. She let go my arm and watched me unlock the car door. "You'd have hated it here," she said, then, pleading, "You wouldn't want to live here like some charity case – have me support you?"

"I'd be enchanted," I said.

"No, no, you'd hate it," she said. "I couldn't look after you. I haven't got time. And you'd keep thinking I should do better than *him*, and the truth is I can't. You wouldn't want to end up like some old relation, fed in the kitchen and all."

"I don't know," I said. "It would be new."

"Oh," she cried, with what seemed unnecessary despair, "what did you come for? All right," she said. "I give up. You asked for it. You can stay. I mean, I'm inviting you. You can sit around and say, 'Oxbow was a Cheswick charmer,' all day and when someone says to me, 'Where jer father get his accent?' I'll say, 'It was a whole way of life.' But remember, you're not a prisoner or anything, around here. You can go whenever you don't like the food. I mean, if you don't like it, don't come to me and say, 'I don't like the food.' You're not my prisoner," she yelled, though her face was only a few inches from mine. "You're only my father. That's all you are."

CANADIANS ABROAD

IN THE TUNNEL

Sarah's father was a born widower. As she had no memory of a mother, it was as though Mr. Holmes had none of a wife and had been created perpetually bereaved and knowing best. His conviction that he must act for two gave him a jocular heaviness that made the girl react for a dozen, but his jokes rode a limitless tide of concern. He thought Sarah was subjective and passionate, as small children are. She knew she was detached and could prove it. A certain kind of conversation between them was bound to run down, wind up, run down again: you are, I'm not, yes, no, you should, I won't, you'll be sorry. Between eighteen and twenty, Sarah kept meaning to become a psychosociologist. Life would then be a tribal village through which she would stalk soft-footed and disguised: that would show him who was subjective. But she was also a natural *amoureuse*, as some girls were natural actresses, and she soon discovered that love refused all forms of fancy dress. In love she had to show her own face, and speak in a true voice, and she was visible from all directions.

One summer, after a particularly stormy spring, her father sent her to Grenoble to learn about French civilization – actually, to get her away from a man he always pretended to think was called Professor Downcast. Sarah raged mostly over the harm her father had brought to Professor Downcast's career, for she had been helping with his "Urban and Regional Studies of the Less Privileged in British Columbia," and she knew he could not manage without her. She did not stay long in Grenoble; she had never intended to. She had decided beforehand that the Alps were shabby, the cultural atmosphere in France was morbid and stifling, and that every girl she met would be taking the civilization course for the wrong reason. She packed and caught a bus down the Napoleon Route to the Mediterranean.

Professor Downcast had been forced to promise he would not write, and so, of course, Sarah would not write her father. She wanted to have new friends and a life that was none of his business. The word "Riviera" had predicted yellow mornings and snowy boats, and crowds filling the streets in the way dancers fill a stage. Her mind's eye had kept them at a distance so that they shimmered and might have been plumed, like peacocks. Up close, her moralist's eye selected whatever was bound to disappoint: a stone beach skirted with sewage, a promenade that was really a through speedway, an eerie bar. For the first time she recognized prostitutes; they clustered outside her hotel, gossiping, with faces like dead letters. For friends she had a pair of middle-aged tourists who took her sightseeing and warned her not to go out at night by herself. Grenoble had been better after all. Who was to blame? She sent her father a letter of reproach, of abuse, of cold reason, and also of apology – the postmark was bound to be a shock. She then began waiting round American Express for an answer. She was hoping it would be a cable saying "Come on home."

His feelings, when he got round to describing them, filled no more than one flimsy typewritten page. She thought she was worth more than that. What now? She walked out of American Express, still reading her letter. A shadow fell over the page. At the same time a man's soft voice said, "Don't be frightened."

She looked up, not frightened – appraising. The man was about twice her age, and not very tall. He was dressed in clean, not too new summer whites, perhaps the remains of a naval officer's uniform. His accent was English. His eyes were light brown. Once he had Sarah's attention, and had given her time to decide what her attention would be, he said his name was Roy Cooper and asked if she wouldn't like to have lunch with him somewhere along the port.

Of course, she answered: it was broad daylight and there were policemen everywhere – polite, old-fashioned, and wearing white, just like Roy Cooper. She was always hungry, and out of laziness had been living on pizzas and ice cream. Her father had never told her to keep experience at bay. For mystery and horror he had tried to substitute common sense, which may have been why Sarah did not always understand him. She and Roy Cooper crossed the promenade together. He held her arm to guide her through traffic, but let go the minute they reached the curb. "I've been trying to talk to you for days now," he said. "I was hoping you might know someone I knew, who could introduce us."

"Oh, I don't know anyone *here*," said Sarah. "I met a couple of Americans in my hotel. We went to see this sort of abandoned chapel. It has frescoes of Jesus and Judas and …" He was silent. "Their name was Hayes?"

He answered that his car was parked over near the port in the shade. It was faster to walk than drive, down here. He was staying outside Nice; otherwise he wouldn't bother driving at all.

They moved slowly along to the port, dragging this shapeless conversation between them, and Sarah was just beginning to wonder if he wasn't a friend of her father's, and if this might be one of her father's large concrete jokes, when he took her bare arm in a way no family friend would have dared and said look here, what about this restaurant? Again he quickly dropped her arm before she could tug away. They sat down under an awning with a blue tablecloth between them. Sarah frowned, lowered her eyes, and muttered something. It might have been a grace before eating had she not seemed so determined; but her words were completely muffled by the traffic grinding by. She leaned forward and repeated, "I'd like to know what your motives are, exactly." She did not mean anything like "What do you want?" but "What is it? Why Roy Cooper? Why me?" At the back of her mind was the idea that he deserved a lesson: she would eat her lunch, get up, coolly stroll away.

His answer, again miles away from Sarah's question, was that he knew where Sarah was staying and had twice followed her to the door of the hotel. He hadn't dared to speak up.

"Well, it's a good thing you finally did," she said. "I was only waiting for a letter, and now I'm going back to Grenoble. I don't like it here."

"Don't do that, don't leave." He had a quiet voice for a man, and he knew how to slide it under another level of sound and make himself plain. He broke off to order their meal. He seemed so at ease, so certain of other people and their reactions – at any moment he would say he was the ambassador of a place where nothing mattered but charm and freedom. Sarah was not used to cold wine at noon. She touched the misty decanter with her fingertips and wet her forehead with the drops. She wanted to ask his motives again but found he was questioning hers – laughing at Sarah, in fact. Who was she to frown and cross-examine, she who wandered around eating pizzas alone? She told him about Professor Downcast and her father – she had to, to explain what she was doing here – and even let him look at her father's letter. Part of it said, "My poor Sarah, no one ever seems to interest you unless he is

no good at his job
small in stature, I wonder why?

'Marxist-Leninist' (since you sneer at 'Communist' and will not allow its use around the house)
married or just about to be
in debt to God and humanity.

I am not saying you should look for the opposite in every case, only for some person who doesn't combine all these qualities at one time."

"I'm your father's man," said Roy Cooper, and he might well have been, except for the problem of height. He was a bachelor, and certainly the opposite of a Marxist-Leninist: he was a former prison inspector whose career had been spent in an Asian colony. He had been retired early when the Empire faded out and the New Democracy that followed no longer required inspection. As for "debt to God and humanity," he said he had his own religion, which made Sarah stare sharply at him, wondering if his idea of being funny was the same as her father's. Their conversation suddenly became locked; an effort would be needed to pull it in two, almost a tug-of-war. I could stay a couple of days or so, she said to herself. She saw the south that day as she would see it finally, as if she had picked up an old dress and first wondered, then knew, how it could be changed to suit her.

They spent that night talking on a stony beach. Sarah half lay, propped on an elbow. He sat with his arms around his knees. Behind him, a party of boys had made a bonfire. By its light Sarah told him all her life, every season of it, and he listened with the silent attention that honored her newness. She had scarcely reached the end when a fresh day opened, streaky and white. She could see him clearly: even unshaven and dying for sleep he was the ambassador from that easy place. She tossed a stone, a puppy asking for a game. He smiled, but still kept space between them, about the distance of the blue tablecloth.

They began meeting every day. They seemed to Sarah to be moving toward each other without ever quite touching; then she thought they were travelling in the same direction, but still apart. They could not turn back, for there was nothing to go back to. She felt a pause, a hesitation. The conversation began to unlock; once Sarah had told all her life she could not think of anything to say. One afternoon he came to the beach nearly two hours late. She sensed he had something to tell her, and waited to hear that he had a wife, or was engaged, or on drugs, or had no money. In the most casual voice imaginable he asked Sarah if she would spend the rest of her holiday with him. He had rented a place up behind Nice. She would know all his friends, quite openly; he did not want to let her in for anything squalid or mean. She could come for a weekend. If she hated it, no hard feelings. It was up to her.

This was new, for of course she had never *lived* with anyone. Well, why not? In her mind she told her father, After all, it was a bachelor you wanted for me. She abandoned her textbooks and packed instead four wooden bowls she had bought for her father's sister and an out-of-print Matisse poster intended for Professor Downcast. Now it would be Roy's. He came to fetch her that day in the car that was always parked somewhere in shade – it was a small open thing, a bachelor's car. They rolled out of Nice with an escort of trucks and buses. She thought there should have been carnival floats spilling yellow roses. Until now, this was her most important decision, for it supposed a way of living, a style. She reflected on how no girl she knew had ever done quite this, and on what her father would say. He might not hear of it; at least not right away. Meanwhile, they made a triumphant passage through blank white suburbs. Their witnesses were souvenir shops, a village or two, a bright solitary supermarket, the walls and hedges of villas. Along one of these flowering barriers they came to a stop and got out of the car. The fence wire looked tense and new; the plumbago it supported leaned every way, as if its life had been spared but only barely. It was late evening. She heard the squeaky barking of small dogs, and glimpsed, through an iron gate, one of those stucco bungalows that seem to beget their own palm trees. They went straight past it, down four shallow garden steps, and came upon a low building that Sarah thought looked like an Indian lodge. It was half under a plane tree. Perhaps it was the tree, whose leaves were like plates, that made the house and its terrace seem microscopic. One table and four thin chairs was all the terrace would hold. A lavender hedge surrounded it.

"They call this place The Tunnel," Roy said. She wondered if he was already regretting their adventure; if so, all he had to do was drive her back at once, or even let her down at a bus stop. But then he lit a candle on the table, which at once made everything dark, and she could see he was smiling as if in wonder at himself. The Tunnel was a long windowless room with an arched whitewashed ceiling. In daytime the light must have come in from the door, which was protected by a soft white curtain of mosquito netting. He groped for a switch on the wall, and she saw there was next to no furniture. "It used to be a storage place for wine and olives," he said. "The Reeves fixed it up. They let it to friends."

"What are Reeves?"

"People – nice people. They live in the bungalow."

She was now in this man's house. She wondered about procedure: whether to unpack or wait until she was asked, and whether she had any domestic duties and was expected to cook. Concealed by a screen was a shower bath; the stove was in a cupboard. The lavatory, he told her, was behind the house in a garden shed. She would find it full of pictures of Labour leaders. The only Socialist the Reeves could bear was Hugh Dalton (Sarah had never heard of him, or most of the others, either), because Dalton had paid for the Queen's wedding out of his own pocket when she was a slip of a girl without a bean of her own. Sarah said, "What did he want to do that for?" She saw, too late, that he meant to be funny.

He sat down on the bed and looked at her. "The Reeves

versus Labour," he said. "Why should you care? You weren't even born." She was used to hearing that every interesting thing had taken place before her birth. She had a deadly serious question waiting: "What shall I do if you feel remorseful?"

"If I am," he said, "you'll never know. That's a promise."

It was not remorse that overcame him but respectability: first thing next day, Sarah was taken to meet his friends, landlords, and neighbors, Tim and Meg Reeve. "I want them to like you," he said. Wishing to be liked by total strangers was outside anything that mattered to Sarah; all the same, quickened by the new situation and its demands, she dressed and brushed her hair and took the path between the two cottages. The garden seemed a dry, cracked sort of place. The remains of daffodils lay in brown ribbons on the soil. She looked all round her, at an olive tree, and yesterday's iron gate, and at the sky, which was fiercely azure. She was not as innocent as her father still hoped she might turn out to be, but not as experienced as Roy thought, either. There was a world of knowledge between last night and what had gone before. She wondered, already, if violent feelings were going to define the rest of her life, or simply limit it. Roy gathered her long hair in his hand and turned her head around. They'd had other nights, or attempts at nights, but this was their first morning. Whatever he read on her face made him say, "You know, it won't always be as lovely as this." She nodded. Professor Downcast had a wife and children, and she was used to fair warnings. Roy could not guess how sturdy her emotions were. Her only antagonist had been her father, who had not touched her self-confidence. She accepted Roy's caution as a tribute: *he*, at least, could see that Sarah was objective.

Roy rang the doorbell, which set off a gunburst of barking. The Reeves' hall smelled of toast, carpets, and insect spray. She wanted southern houses to smell of jasmine. "Here, Roy," someone called, and Roy led her by the hand into a small sitting room where two people, an old man and an old woman, sat in armchairs eating breakfast. The man removed a tray from his knees and stood up. He was gaunt and tall, and looked oddly starched, like a nurse coming on duty. "Jack Sprat could eat no fat" came to Sarah's mind. Mrs. Reeve was – she supposed – obese. Sarah stared at her; she did not know how to be furtive. Was the poor woman ill? *No*, answered the judge who was part of Sarah too. *Mrs. Reeve is just greedy. Look at the jam she's shovelled on her plate.*

"Well, this is Sarah Holmes," said Roy, stroking her hair, as if he was proving at the outset there was to be no hypocrisy. "We'd adore coffee."

"You'd better do something about it, then," said the fat woman. "We've got tea here. You know where the kitchen is, Roy." She had a deep voice, like a moo. "You, Sarah Holmes, sit down. Find a pew with no dog hair, if you can. Of course, if you're going to be fussy, you won't last long around *here* – eh, boys? You can make toast if you like. No, never mind. I'll make it for you."

It seemed to Sarah a pretty casual way for people their age to behave. Roy was older by a long start, but the Reeves were *old*. They seemed to find it natural to have Roy and Sarah drift over for breakfast after a night in the guesthouse. Mr. Reeve even asked quite kindly, "Did you sleep well? The plane tree draws mosquitoes, I'm afraid."

"I'll have that tree down yet," said Mrs. Reeve. "Oh, I'll have it down one of these days. I can promise you that." She was dressed in a bathrobe that looked like a dark parachute. "We decided not to have eggs," she said, as though Sarah had asked. "Have 'em later. You and Roy must come back for lunch. We'll have a good old fry-up." Here she attended to toast, which meant shaking and tapping an antique wire toaster set on the table before her. "When Tim's gone – bless him – I shall never cook a meal again," she said. "Just bits and pieces on a tray for the boys and me." The boys were dogs, Sarah guessed – two little yappers up on the sofa, the color of Teddy-bear stuffing.

"I make a lot of work for Meg," Mr. Reeve said to Sarah. "The breakfasts – breakfast every day, you know – and she is the one who looks after the Christmas cards. Marriage has been a bind for her. She did a marvellous job with evacuees in the war. And poor old Meg loathed kids, still does. You'll never hear her say so. I've never known Meg to complain."

Mrs. Reeve had not waited for her husband to die before starting her widow's diet of tea and toast and jam and gin (the bottle was there, by the toaster, along with a can of orange juice). Sarah knew about this, for not only was her father a widower but they had often spent summers with a widowed aunt. The Reeves seemed like her father and her aunt grown elderly and distorted. Mrs. Reeve now unwrapped a chocolate bar, which caused a fit of snorting and jostling on the sofa. "No chockie bits for boys with bad manners," she said, feeding them just the same. Yes, there she sat, a widow with two dogs for company. Mr. Reeve, delicately buttering and eating the toast meant for Sarah, murmured that when he *did* go he did not want poor Meg to have any fuss. He seemed to be planning his own modest gravestone; in a heightened moment of telepathy Sarah was sure she could see it too. To Sarah, the tall old man had already ceased to be. He was not Mr. Reeve, Roy's friend and landlord, but an ectoplasmic impression of somebody like him, leaning forward, lips slightly parted, lifting a piece of toast that was caving in like a hammock with a weight of strawberry jam. Panic was in the room, but only Sarah felt it. She had been better off, safer, perhaps happier even, up in Grenoble, trying not to yawn over "*Tout m'afflige, et me nuit, et conspire à me nuire.*" What was she doing here, indoors, on this glowing day, with these two snivelly dogs and these gluttonous old persons? She turned swiftly, hearing Roy, and in her heart she said, in a quavering spoiled child's voice, "I want to go home." (How many outings had she ruined for her father. How many picnics, circuses, puppet shows, boat rides. From how many attempted holidays had he been fetched back with a telegram from whichever relation had been trying to hold Sarah down for a week. The strong brass chords of "I want my own life" had always been followed by this dismal piping.)

Roy poured their coffee into pottery mugs and his eyes met Sarah's. His said, Yes, these are the Reeves. They don't matter. I only want one thing, and that's to get back to where we were a few hours ago.

So they were to be conspirators: she liked that.

The Reeves had now done with chewing, feeding, swallowing, and brushing crumbs, and began placing Sarah. Who was she? Sarah Holmes, a little transatlantic pickup, a student slumming round for a summer? What had she studied? Sociology, psychology, and some economics, she told them.

"Sounds Labour" was Mr. Reeve's comment.

She simplified her story and mentioned the thesis. "Urban and Regional Studies of the Less Privileged in British Columbia," as far as Mr. Reeve was concerned, contained only one reassuring word, and that was "British." Being the youngest in the room, Sarah felt like the daughter of the house. She piled cups and plates on one of the trays and took them out to the kitchen. The Reeves were not the sort of people who would ever bother to whisper: she heard that she was "a little on the tall side" and that her proportions made Roy seem slight and small, "like a bloody dago." Her hair was too long; the fringe on her forehead looked sparse and pasted down with soap. She also heard that she had a cast in one eye, which she did not believe.

"One can't accuse her of oversmartness," said Mrs. Reeve.

Roy, whose low voice had carrying qualities, said, "No, Meg. Sarah's jeans are as faded, as baggy, as those brown corduroys of yours. However, owing to Sarah's splendid and enviable shape, hers are not nearly so large across the beam end." This provoked two laughs – a cackle from Jack Sprat and a long three-note moo from his wife.

"Well, Roy," said Tim Reeve, "all I can say is, you amaze me. How do you bring it off?"

"What about me?" said Sarah to herself. "How do *I* bring it off?"

"At least she's had sense enough not to come tramping around in high-heeled shoes, like some of our visitors," said Mrs. Reeve – her last word for the moment.

Roy warned Sarah what lunch – the good old fry-up – would be. A large black pan the Reeves had brought to France from England when they emigrated because of taxes and Labour would be dragged out of the oven; its partner, a jam jar of bacon fat, stratified in a wide extent of suety whites, had its permanent place on top of the stove. The lowest, or Ur, line of fat marked the very first fry-up in France. A few spoonfuls of this grease, releasing blue smoke, received tomatoes, more bacon, eggs, sausages, cold boiled potatoes. To get the proper sausages they had to go to a shop that imported them, in Monte Carlo. This was no distance, but the Reeves' car had been paid for by Tim, and he was mean about it. He belonged to a generation that had been in awe of batteries: each time the ignition was turned on, he thought the car's lifeblood was seeping away. When he became too stingy with the car, then Meg would not let him look at television: the set was hers. She would push it on its wheeled table over bumpy rugs into their bedroom and put a chair against the door.

Roy was a sharp mimic and he took a slightly feminine pleasure in mocking his closest friends. Sarah lay on her elbow on the bed as she had lain on the beach and thought that if he was disloyal to the Reeves then he was all the more loyal to her. They had been told to come back for lunch around three;

this long day was in itself like a whole summer. She said, "It sounds like a movie. Are they happy?"

"Oh, blissful," he answered, surprised, and perhaps with a trace of reproval. It was as if he were very young and she had asked an intimate question about his father and mother.

The lunch Roy had described was exactly the meal they were given. She watched him stolidly eating eggs fried to a kind of plastic lace, and covering everything with mustard to damp out the taste of grease. When Meg opened the door to the kitchen she was followed by a blue haze. Tim noticed Sarah's look – she had wondered if something was burning – and said, "Next time you're here that's where we'll eat. It's what we like. We like our kitchen."

"Today we are honoring Sarah," said Meg Reeve, as though baiting Roy.

"So you should," he said. It was the only attempt at sparring; they were all much too fed and comfortable. Tim, who had been to Monte Carlo, had brought back another symbol of their roots, the Hovis loaf. They talked about his shopping, and the things they liked doing – gambling a little, smuggling from Italy for sport. One thing they never did was look at the Mediterranean. It was not an interesting sea. It had no tides. "I do hope you aren't going to bother with it," said Tim to Sarah. It seemed to be their private measure for a guest – that and coming round in the wrong clothes.

The temperature in full sun outside the sitting-room window was thirty-three degrees centigrade. "What does it mean?" said Sarah. Nobody knew. Tim said that 16°C. was the same thing as 61°F. but that nothing else corresponded. For instance, 33°C. could not possibly be 33°F. – No, it felt like a lot more.

After the trial weekend Sarah wrote to her father, "I am in this interesting old one-room guesthouse that belongs to an elderly couple here. It is in their garden. They only let reliable people stay in it." She added, "Don't worry, I'm working." If she concealed information she did not exactly lie: she thought she *was* working. Instead of French civilization taught in airless classrooms she would study expatriates at first hand. She decided to record the trivia first – how visitors of any sort were a catastrophe, how a message from old friends staying at Nice brought Tim back from the telephone wearing the look of someone whose deepest feelings have been raked over.

"Come on, Tim, what was it?" his wife would call. "The who? What did they want? An invitation to their hotel? Damned cheek. More likely a lot of free drinks here, that's what they want." They lived next to gas fires with all the windows shut, yelling from room to room. Their kitchen was comfortable providing one imagined it was the depth of January in England and that sleet was battering at the garden. She wanted to record that Mr. Reeve said "heith" and "strenth" and that they used a baby language with each other – walkies, tummy, spend-a-penny. When Sarah said "cookie" it made them laugh: a minute later, feeding the dogs a chocolate cookie, Meg said, "Here, have a chockie bicky." If Tim tried to explain anything, his wife interrupted with "Come on, get to Friday." Nobody could remember the origin of the phrase; it served merely to rattle him.

Sarah meant to record this, but Professor Downcast's useful language had left her. The only words in her head were so homespun and plain she was ashamed to set them down. The heat must have flattened her brain, she thought. The Reeves, who never lowered their voices for anyone, bawled one night that "old Roy was doting and indulgent" and "the wretched girl is in love." That was the answer. She had already discovered that she could live twenty-four hours on end just with the idea that she was in love; she also knew that a man could think about love for a while but then he would start to think about something else. What if Roy never did? Sarah Cooper didn't sound bad; Mrs. R. Cooper was better. But Sarah was not that foolish. She was looking ahead only because she and Roy had no past. She did say to him, "What do you do when you aren't having a vacation?"

"You mean in winter? I go to Marbella. Sometimes Kenya. Where my friends are."

"Don't you work?"

"I did work. They retired me."

"You're too young to be retired. My father isn't even retired. You should write your memoirs – all that colonial stuff."

He laughed at her. She was never more endearing to him than when she was most serious; that was not her fault. She abandoned the future and rearranged their short history to suit herself. Every word was recollected later in primrose light. Did it rain every Sunday? Was there an invasion of red ants? She refused the memory. The Reeves' garden incinerator, which was never cleaned out, set oily smoke to sit at their table like a third person. She drank her coffee unaware of this guest, seeing nothing but butterflies dancing over the lavender hedge. Sarah, who would not make her own bed at home, insisted now on washing everything by hand, though there was a laundry in the village. Love compelled her to buy enough food for a family of seven. The refrigerator was a wheezy old thing, and sometimes Roy got up and turned it off in the night because he could not sleep for its sighing. In the morning Sarah piled the incinerator with spoiled meat, cheese, and peaches, and went out at six o'clock to buy more and more. She was never so bathed in love as when she stood among a little crowd of villagers at a bus stop – the point of creation, it seemed – with her empty baskets; she desperately hoped to be taken for what the Reeves called "part of the local populace." The market she liked was two villages over; the buses were tumbrils. She could easily have driven Roy's car or had everything sent from shops, but she was inventing fidelities. Once, she saw Meg Reeve, wearing a floral cotton that compressed her figure and gave her a stylized dolphin shape, like an ornament on a fountain. On her head was a straw hat with a polka-dot ribbon. She found a place one down and across the aisle from Sarah, who shrank from her notice for fear of that deep voice letting the world know Sarah was not a peasant. Meg unfolded a paper that looked like a prescription; slid her glasses along her nose; held them with one finger. She always sat with her knees spread largely. In order not to have Meg's thigh crushing his, her neighbor, a priest in a dirty cassock, had to squeeze against the window.

"She doesn't care," Sarah said to herself. "She hasn't even looked to see who is there." When she got down at the next village Meg was still rereading the scrap of paper, and the bus rattled on to Nice.

Sarah never mentioned having seen her; Meg was such a cranky, unpredictable old lady. One night she remarked, "Sarah's going to have trouble landing Roy," there, in front of him, on his own terrace. "He'll never marry." Roy was a bachelor owing to the fact he had too many rich friends, and because men were selfish.... Here Meg paused, conceding that this might sound wrong. No, it sounded right; Roy was a bachelor because of the selfishness of men, and the looseness and availabilty of young women.

"True enough, they'll do it for a ham sandwich," said Tim, as if a supply of sandwiches had given him the pick of a beach any day.

His wife stared at him but changed her mind. She plucked at her fork and said, "When Tim's gone – bless him – I shall have all my meals out. Why bother cooking?" She then looked at her plate as if she had seen a mouse on it.

"It's all right, Meg," said Roy. "Sarah favors the cooking of the underdeveloped countries. All our meals are raw and drowned in yogurt." He said it so kindly Sarah had to laugh. For a time she had tried to make them all eat out of her aunt's bowls, but the untreated wood became stained and Roy found it disgusting. The sight of Sarah scouring them out with ashes did not make him less squeamish. He was, in fact, surprisingly finicky for someone who had spent a lifetime around colonial prisons. A dead mosquito made him sick – even the mention of one.

It is true that Roy has never lacked for pretty girls," said Tim. "We should know, eh, Roy?" Roy and the Reeves talked quite a lot about his personal affairs, as if a barrier of discretion had long ago been breached. They were uncomfortable stories, a little harsh sometimes for Sarah's taste. Roy now suddenly chose to tell about how he had met his own future brother-in-law in a brothel in Hong Kong – by accident, of course. They became the best of friends and remained so, even after Roy's engagement was broken off.

"Why'd she dump you?" Sarah said. "She found out?"

Her way of asking plain questions froze the others. They looked as if winter had swept over the little terrace and caught them. Then Roy took Sarah's hand and said, "I'm ashamed to say I wasn't gallant – I dumped the lady."

"Old Roy probably thought, um, matrimony," said Tim. "Eh, Meg?" This was because marriage was supposed to be splendid for Tim but somehow confining for his wife.

"She said I was venomous," said Roy, looking at Sarah, who knew he was not.

"She surely didn't mean venomous," said Tim. "She meant something more like, moody." Here he lapsed into a mood of his own, staring at the candles on the table, and Sarah remembered her shared vision of his unassuming gravestone; she said to Roy in an undertone, "Is anything wrong with him?"

"Wrong with him? Wrong with old Tim? Tim!" Roy called,

as if he were out of sight instead of across the table. "When was the last time you ever had a day's illness?"

"I was sick on a Channel crossing – I might have been ten," said Tim.

"Nothing's the matter with Tim, I can promise you that," said his wife. "Never a headache, never a cold, no flu, no rheumatism, no gout, nothing."

"Doesn't feel the amount he drinks," said Roy.

"Are you ever sick, Mrs. Reeve?" Sarah asked.

"Oh, poor Meg," said Tim immediately. "You won't get a word out of her. Never speaks of herself."

"The ailments of old parties can't possibly interest Sarah," said Meg. "Here, Roy, give Sarah something to drink," meaning that her own glass was empty. "My niece Lisbet will be here for a weekend. Now, *that's* an interesting girl. She interviews people for jobs. She can see straight through them, mentally speaking. She had stiff training – had to see a trick cyclist for a year."

"I abhor that subject," said Roy. "No sensible prison governor ever allowed a trick cyclist anywhere near. The good were good and the bad were bad and everyone knew it."

"Psycho-whatnot does not harm if the person is sound," said Meg. "Lisbet just went week after week and had a jolly old giggle with the chap. The firm was paying."

"A didactic analysis is a waste of time," said Sarah, chilling them all once more.

"I didn't say that or anything like it," said Meg. "I said the firm was paying. But you're a bit out of it, Roy," turning to him and heaving her vast garments so Sarah was cut out. "Lisbet said it did help her. You wouldn't believe the number of people she turns away, whatever their education. She can tell if they are likely to have asthma. She saves the firm thousands of pounds every year."

"Lisbet can see when they're queer," said Tim.

"What the hell do you mean?" said Roy.

"What did she tell you?" said Meg, now extremely annoyed. "Come on, Tim, get to Friday."

But Tim had gone back to contemplating his life on the Other Side, and they could obtain nothing further.

Sarah forgot all about Mrs. Reeve's niece until Lisbet turned up, wearing a poncho, black pants, and bracelets. She was about Roy's age. All over her head was a froth of kinky yellow hair – a sort of Little Orphan Annie wig. She stared with small blue eyes and gave Sarah a boy's handshake. She said, "So you're the famous one!"

Sarah had come back from the market to find them all drinking beer in The Tunnel. Her shirt stuck to her back. She pulled it away and said, "Famous one what?" From the way Lisbet laughed she guessed she had been described as a famous comic turn. Roy handed Sarah a glass without looking at her. Roy and Tim were talking about how to keep Lisbet amused for the weekend. Everything was displayed – the night racing at Cagnes, the gambling, the smuggling from Italy, which bored Sarah but which even Roy did for amusement. "A picnic," Sarah said, getting in something she liked. Also, it sounded cool. The Hayeses, those anxious tourists at her hotel in Nice, suddenly rose up in her mind offering advice. "There's this chapel," she said, feeling a spiky nostalgia, as if she were describing something from home. "Remember, Roy, I mentioned it? Nobody goes there ... you have to get the keys from a café in the village. You can picnic in the churchyard; it has a gate and a wall. There's a river where we washed our hands. The book said it used to be a pagan place. It has these paintings now, of the Last Judgment, and Jesus, naturally, and one of Judas after he hung himself."

"Hanged," said Roy and Lisbet together.

"Hanged. Well, somebody had really seen a hanging – the one who painted it, I mean."

"Have you?" said Roy, smiling.

"No, but I can imagine."

"No," he said, still smiling. "You can't. All right, I'm for the picnic. Sunday, then. We'll do Italy tomorrow."

His guests got up to leave. Tim suddenly said, for no reason Sarah could see, "I'm glad I'm not young."

As soon as the others were out of earshot Roy said, "God, what a cow! Planeloads of Lisbets used to come out to Asia looking for Civil Service husbands. Now they fly to Majorca and sleep with the waiters."

"Why do we have to be nice to her, if you feel like that?" said Sarah.

"Why don't you know about these things without asking?" said Roy.

My father didn't bring me up well, Sarah thought, and resolved to write and tell him so. Mr. Holmes would not have been nice to Lisbet and then called her a cow. He might have done one or the other, or neither. His dilemma as a widower was insoluble; he could never be too nice for fear of someone's taking it into her head that Sarah wanted a mother. Also, he was not violent about people, even those he had to eliminate. That was why he gave them comic names. "Perhaps you are right," she said to Roy, without being any more specific. He cared for praise, however ambiguous; and so they had a perfect day, and a perfect night, but those were the last: in the morning, as Sarah stood on the table to tie one end of a clothesline to the plane tree, she slipped, had to jump, landed badly, and sprained her ankle. By noon the skin was purple and she had to cut off her canvas shoe. The foot needed to be bandaged, but not by Roy: the very sight of it made him sick. He could not bear a speck of dust anywhere, or a chipped cup. She remembered the wooden bowls, and how he'd had to leave the table once because they looked a little doubtful, not too clean. Lisbet was summoned. Kneeling, she wrapped Sarah's foot and ankle in strips of a torn towel and fixed the strips with safety pins.

"It'll do till I see a doctor," Sarah said.

Lisbet looked up. How small her eyes were! "You don't want a doctor for that, surely?"

"Yes, I do. I think it should be X-rayed," Sarah said. "It hurts like anything."

"Of course she doesn't," said Roy.

Getting well with the greatest possible amount of suffering, and with your bones left crooked, was part of their code. It seemed to Sarah an unreasonable code, but she did not want to seem like someone making a fuss. All the same, she said, "I feel sick."

"Drink some brandy," said Lisbet.

"Lie down," said Roy. "We shan't be long." It would have been rude not to have taken Lisbet on the smuggling expedition just because Sarah couldn't go.

In the late afternoon Meg Reeve strolled down to see how Sarah was managing. She found her standing on one foot hanging washing on a line. The sight of Sarah's plaid slacks, bought on sale at Nice, caused Meg to remark, "My dear, are you a Scot? I've often wondered, seeing you wearing those." Sarah let a beach towel of Roy's fall to the ground.

"Damn, it'll have to be washed again," she said.

Meg had brought Roy's mail. She put the letters on the table, face down, as if Sarah were likely to go over the postmarks with a magnifying glass. The dogs snuffled and snapped at the ghosts of animal-haters. "What clan?" said Meg.

"Clan? Oh, you're still talking about my slacks. Clan *salade niçoise*, I guess."

"Well, you must not wear tartan," said Meg. "It is an insult to the family, d'you see? I'm surprised Roy hasn't ... Ticky! Blue! Naughty boys!"

"Oh, the dogs come down here and pee all over the terrace every day," said Sarah.

"Roy used to give them chockie bits. They miss being spoiled. But now he hasn't time for them, has he?"

"I don't know. I can't answer for him. He has time for what interests him."

"Why do you hang your washing where you can see it?" said Meg. "Are you Italian?" Sarah made new plans; next time the Reeves were invited she would boil Ticky and Blue with a little sugar and suet and serve them up as pudding. I must look angelic at this moment, she thought.

She said, "No, I'm not Italian. I don't think so."

"There are things I could never bring myself to do," said Meg. "Not in my walk of life."

The sociologist snapped to attention. Easing her sore ankle, Sarah said, "Please, what is your walk of life, exactly?"

It was so dazzling, so magical, that Meg could not name it, but merely mouthed a word or two that Sarah was unable to lip-read. A gust of incinerator smoke stole between them and made them choke. "As for Tim," said Meg, getting her breath again, "you, with all your transatlantic money, couldn't buy what Tim has in his veins."

Sarah limped indoors and somehow found the forgotten language. "Necessity for imparting status information," she recorded, and added "erroneous" between "imparting" and "status." She was still, in a way, half in love with Professor Downcast.

She discovered this was a conversation neither Roy nor Lisbet could credit. They unpacked their loot from Italy on the wobbly terrace table – plastic table mats, plastic roses, a mermaid paperweight, a bottle of apéritif that smelled like medicine, a Florentine stamp box ... "Rubbish, garbage," Sarah said in her mind. "But Roy is happy." Also, he was drunk. So was Lisbet.

"Meg could not have said those things," said Roy, large-eyed.

"Meg doesn't always understand Sarah," said Lisbet. "The accent."

"Mrs. Reeve was doing the talking," said Sarah.

"She wouldn't have talked that way to an Englishwoman," said Roy, swinging round to Sarah's side.

"Wouldn't have dared," said Lisbet. She shouted, "Wouldn't have dared to me!"

"As for Tim, well, Tim really is the real thing," said Roy. "I mean to say that Tim really *is*."

"So is my aunt," said Lisbet, but Roy had disappeared behind the white net curtain, and they heard him fall on the bed. "He's had rather a lot," said Lisbet. Sarah felt anxiety for Roy, who had obviously had a lot of everything – perhaps of Lisbet too. And there was still the picnic next day, and no one had bought any food for it. Lisbet looked glowing and superb, as if she had been tramping in a clean wind instead of sitting crouched in a twilit bar somewhere on the Italian side. She should have been haggard and gray.

"Who was driving?" Sarah asked her.

"Took turns."

"What did you talk about?" She was remembering his "God, what a cow!"

"Capital punishment, apartheid, miscegenation, and my personal problems with men. That I seem cold, but I'm not really."

"Boys, boys, boys!" That was Meg Reeve calling her dogs. They rolled out of the lavender hedge like a pair of chewed tennis balls. They might well have been eavesdropping. Sarah gave a shiver, and Lisbet laughed and said, "Someone's walking on your grave."

The sunlight on the terrace next morning hurt Roy's eyes; he made little flapping gestures, meaning Sarah was not to speak. "What were you drinking in Italy?" she said. He shook his head. Mutely, he took the dried laundry down and folded it. Probably, like Meg, he did not much care for the look of it. "I've made the picnic," Sarah next offered. "No reason why I can't come – we won't be doing much walking." She stood on one leg, like a stork. The picnic consisted of anything Sarah happened to find in the refrigerator. She included plums in brandy because she noticed a jar of them, and iced white wine in a thermos. At the last minute she packed olives, salted peanuts, and several pots of yogurt.

"Put those back," said Roy.

"Why? Do you think they'll melt?"

"Just do as I say, for once. Put them back."

"Do you know what I think?" said Sarah after a moment. "I think we're starting out on something my father would call The Ill-Fated Excursion."

For the first time ever, she saw Roy looking angry. The vitality of the look made him younger, but not in a nice way. He became a young man, an ugly one. "Liz will have to drive," he said. "I've got a blinding headache, and you can't, not with *that*." He could not bring himself to name her affliction. "How do you know about this place?" he said. "Who took you there?"

"I told you. Some Americans in my hotel. Haynes – no, Hayes."

"Yes, I can imagine." He looked at her sidelong and said, "Just who were you sleeping with when I collected you?"

She felt what it was like to blush – like a rash of needles and pins. He knew every second of her life, because she had told it to him that night on the beach. What made her blush was that she sensed he was only pretending to be jealous. It offended her. She said, "Let's call the picnic off."

"I don't want to."

She was not used to quarrels, only to tidal waves. She did not understand that they were quarrelling now. She wondered again what he had been drinking over in Italy. Her ankle felt in a vise, but that was the least of it. They set off, all three together, and Lisbet drove straight up into the hills as if pursuing escaped prisoners. They shot past towns Sarah had visited with the Americans, who had been conscientious about churches; she saw, open-and-shut, views they had stopped to photograph. When she said "Look," nobody heard. She sat crumpled in the narrow back seat, with the picnic sliding all over as they rounded the mountain curves, quite often on the wrong side.

"That was the café, back there, where you get the key," Sarah had to say twice – once very loudly. Lisbet braked so they were thrown forward and then reversed like a bullet ricocheting. "Sarah knows about this," said Roy, as if it were a good thing to know about. That was encouraging. She gripped her ankle between her hands and set her foot down. She tested her weight and managed to walk and hop to the cool café, past the beaded curtain. She leaned on the marble counter; she had lost something. Was it her confidence? She wanted someone to come and take her home, but was too old to want that; she knew too many things. She said to the man standing behind the counter, "*J'ai mal*," to explain why she did not take the keys from him and at once go out. His reaction was to a confession of sorrow and grief; he poured out something to drink. It was clear as water, terribly strong, and smelled of warm fruit. When she gestured to show him she had no money, he said, "*Ça va*." He was kind; the Hayeses, such an inadequate substitute for peacocks, had been kind too. She said to herself, "How awful if I should cry."

The slight inclination of Roy's head when she handed the keys to him meant he might be interested. She felt emboldened: "One's for the chapel, the other's the gate. There isn't a watchman or anything. It's too bad, because people write on the walls."

"Which way?" Lisbet interrupted. She chased her prisoners another mile or so.

Sarah had told them no one ever came here, but they were forced to park behind a car with Swiss license plates. Next to the gate sat a large party of picnickers squeezed round a card table. There was only one man among them, and Sarah thought it must be a harem and the man had been allowed several wives for having been reasonable and Swiss until he was fifty. She started to tell this to Roy, but he had gone blank as a monument; she felt overtaken by her father's humor, not her own. Roy gave the harem an empty look that reminded her of the prostitutes down in Nice, and now she knew what their faces had been saying. It was "I despise you." The chapel was an icebox; and she saw Roy and Lisbet glance with some consternation at the life of Jesus spread around for anyone to see. They would certainly have described themselves as Christians, but they were embarrassed by Christ. They went straight to Judas, who was more reassuring. Hanged, disembowelled, his stomach and liver exposed to ravens, Judas gave up his soul. His soul was a small naked creature. Perceiving Satan, the creature held out its arms.

"Now, *that* man must have eaten Sarah's cooking," said Roy, and such were their difficulties that she was grateful to hear him say anything. But he added, "A risk many have taken, I imagine." This was to Lisbet. Only Sarah knew what he meant. She fell back and pretended to be interested in a rack of postcards. The same person who trusted visitors not to write their names on paintings had left a coin box. Sarah had no money and did not want to ask Roy for any. She stole a reproduction of the Judas fresco and put it inside her shirt.

Roy and Lisbet ate some of the picnic. They sat where Sarah had sat with the Americans, but it was in no way the same. Of course, the season was later, the river lower, the grass drooping and dry. The shadows of clouds made them stare and comment, as if looking for something to say. Sarah was relieved when the two decided to climb up in the maquis, leaving her "to rest a bit" – this was Lisbet. "Watch out for snakes," Sarah said, and got from Roy one blurred, anxious, puzzled look, the last straight look he ever gave her. She sat down and drank all the brandy out of the jar of plums. Roy had an attitude to people she had never heard of: nothing must ever go wrong.

An accident is degrading for the victim. She undid the towelling strips and looked at her bloated ankle and foot. Of course, it was ugly; but it was part of a living body, not a corpse, and it hurt Sarah, not Roy. She tipped out the plums so the ants could have a party, drank some of the white wine, and, falling asleep, thought she was engaged in an endless and heated discussion with some person who was in the wrong.

She woke up cramped and thirsty on the back seat of the car. They were stopped in front of the café and must have been parked for some time, for they were in an oblique shadow of late afternoon. Roy was telling Lisbet a lie: he said he had been a magistrate and was writing his memoirs. Next he told her of hangings he'd seen. He said in his soft voice, "Don't you think some people are better out of the way?" Sarah knew by heart the amber eyes and the pupils so small they seemed a mistake sometimes. She was not Sarah now but a prisoner impaled on a foreign language, seeing bright, light, foreign eyes offering something nobody wanted – death. "Flawed people, born rotten," Roy went on.

"Oh, everyone thinks that now," said Lisbet.

They were alike, with fortunes established in piracy. He liked executions; she broke people before they had a chance to break themselves. Lisbet stroked the back of her own neck. Sarah had noticed before that when Lisbet was feeling sure of herself she made certain her neck was in place. *Neurotic habit*, Sarah's memory asked her to believe; but no, it was only the gesture of someone at ease in a situation she recognized. Tranquil as to her neck, Lisbet now made sure of her hair. She patted the bright steel wool that must have been a comfort to her mother some thirty-five – no, forty – years before.

I am jealous, Sarah said to herself. How unwelcome. Jealousy is only ... the jealous person is the one keeping something back and so ...

"Oh, keys, always keys," said Roy, shaking them. He slammed out in a way that was surely rude to Lisbet. She rested her arm over the back of the seat and looked at Sarah. "You drank enough to stun a rhinoceros, little girl," she said. "We had to take you out behind the chapel and make you be sick before we could let you in the car." Sarah began to remember. She saw Roy's face, a gray flash in a cracked old film about a catastrophe. Lisbet said, "Look, Sarah, how old are you? Aren't you a bit out of your depth with Roy?" She might have said more, but a native spitefulness, or a native prudence, prevented her. She flew to Majorca the next day, as Roy had predicted, leaving everyone out of step.

Now Roy began hating; he hated the sea, the Reeves, the dogs, the blue of plumbago, the mention of Lisbet, and most of all he hated Sarah. The Reeves laughed and called it "old Roy being bloody-minded again," but Sarah was frightened. She had never known anyone who would simply refuse to speak, who would take no notice of a question. Meg said to her, "He misses that job of his. It came to nothing. He tried to give a lot of natives a sense of right and wrong, and then some Socialist let them vote."

"Yes, he liked that job," Sarah said slowly. "One day he'd watch a hanging, and the next he'd measure the exercise yard to see if it was up to standard." She said suddenly and for no reason she knew, "I've disappointed him."

Their meals were so silent that they could hear the swelling love songs from the Reeves' television, and the Reeves' voices bawling away at each other. Sarah's throat would go tight. In daytime the terrace was like an oven now, and her ankle kept her from sleeping at night. Then Roy gave up eating and lay on the bed looking up at the ceiling. She still went on shopping, but now it took hours. Mornings, before leaving, she would place a bowl of coffee for him, like an offering; it was still there, at the bedside, cold and oily-looking now, when she came back. She covered a tray with leaves from the plane tree – enormous powdery leaves, the size of her two hands – and she put cheese on the leaves, and white cheese covered with pepper, a Camembert, a salty goat cheese he had liked. He did not touch any. Out of a sort of desperate sentiment, she kept the tray for days, picking chalky pieces off as the goat cheese grew harder and harder and became a fossil. He must have eaten sometimes; she thought of him gobbling scraps straight from the refrigerator when her back was turned. She wrote a letter to her father that of course she did not send. It said, "I've been having headaches lately. I wind a thread around a finger until the blood can't get past and that starts a new pain. The headache is all down the back of my neck. I'm not sure what to do next. It will be terrible for you if I turn out to have a brain tumor. It will cost you a lot of money and you may lose your only child."

One dawn she knew by Roy's breathing that he was awake. Every muscle was taut as he pulled away, as if to touch her was defilement. No use saying what they had been like not long before, because he could not remember. She was a disgusting object because of a cracked ankle, because she had drunk too much and been sick behind a chapel, and because she had led an expedition to look at Jesus. She lay thinking it over until the dawn birds stopped and then she sat up on the edge of the bed, feeling absolutely out of place because she was undressed. She pulled clothes on as fast as she could and packed whatever seemed important. After she had pushed her suitcase out the door, she remembered the wooden bowls and the poster. These she took along the path and threw in the Reeves' foul incinerator, as if to get rid of all traces of witchery, goodness, and love. She realized she was leaving, a decision as final and as stunning as her having crossed the promenade in Nice with Roy's hand on her arm.

She said through the white netting over the door, "I'm sorry, Roy." It was not enough; she added, "I'm sorry I don't understand you more." The stillness worried her. She limped near and bent over him. He was holding his breath, like a child in temper. She said softly, "I could stay a bit longer." No answer.

She said, "Of course, my foot will get better, but then you might find something else the matter with me." Still no answer, except that he began breathing. Nothing was wrong except that he was cruel, lunatic, Fascist – No, not even that. Nothing was wrong except that he did not love her. That was all.

She lugged her suitcase as far as the road and sat down beside it. Overnight a pocket of liquid the size of a lemon had formed near the anklebone. Her father would say it was all her own fault again. Why? Was it Sarah's fault that she had all this loving capital to invest? What was she supposed to do with it? Even if she always ended up sitting outside a gate somewhere, was she any the worse for it? The only thing wrong now was the pain she felt, not of her ankle but in her stomach. Her stomach felt as if it was filled up with old oyster shells. Yes, a load of old, ugly, used-up shells was what she had for stuffing. She had to take care not to breathe too deeply, because the shells scratched. In her research for Professor Downcast she had learned that one could be alcoholic, crippled, afraid of dying and of being poor, and she knew these things waited for everyone, even Sarah; but nothing had warned her that one day she would not be loved. That was the meaning of "less privileged." There was no other.

Now that she had vanished, Roy would probably get up, and shave, and stroll across to the Reeves, and share a good old fry-up. Then, his assurance regained, he would start prowling the bars and beaches, wearing worn immaculate whites, looking for a new, unblemished story. He would repeat the first soft words, "Don't be frightened," the charm, the gestures, the rituals, and the warning "It won't always be lovely." She saw him out in the open, in her remembered primrose light, before he was trapped in the tunnel again and had to play at death. "Roy's new pickup," the Reeves would bawl at each other. "I said, Roy's new one … he hardly knows how to get rid of her."

At that, Sarah opened her mouth and gave a great sobbing cry; only one, but it must have carried, for next thing she heard was the Reeves' door, and, turning, she saw Tim in a dressing gown, followed by Meg in her parachute of a robe. Sarah stood up to face them. The sun was on her back. She clutched the iron bars of the gate because she had to stand like a stork again. From their side of it, Tim looked down at her suitcase. He said, "Do you want – are you waiting to be driven somewhere?"

"To the airport, if you feel like taking me. Otherwise I'll hitch."

"Oh, please don't do that!" He seemed afraid of another outburst from her – something low-pitched and insulting this time.

"Come in this minute," said Meg. "I don't know what you are up to, but we do have neighbors, you know."

"Why should I care?" said Sarah. "They aren't my neighbors."

"You *are* a little coward," said Meg. "Running away only because ..." There were so many reasons that of course she hesitated.

Without unkind intention Sarah said the worst thing: "It's just that I'm too young for all of you."

Meg's hand crept between the bars and around her wrist. "Somebody had to be born before you, Sarah," she said, and unlocked her hand and turned back to the house. "Yes, boys, dear boys, here I am," she called.

Tim said, "Would you like – let me see – would you like something to eat or drink?" It seemed natural for him to talk through bars.

"I can't stay in the same bed with someone who doesn't care," said Sarah, beginning to cry. "It isn't right."

"It is what most people do," said Tim. "Meg has the dogs, and her television. She has everything. We haven't often lived together. We gradually stopped. When did we last live together? When we went home once for the motor show." She finally grasped what he meant by "live together." Tim said kindly, "Look, I don't mean to pry, but you didn't take old Roy too much to heart, did you? He wasn't what you might call the love of your life?"

"I don't know yet."

"Dear, dear," said Tim, as if someone had been spreading bad news. He seemed so much more feminine than his wife; his hands were powdery – they seemed dipped in talcum. His eyes were embedded in a little volcano of wrinkles that gave him in full sunlight the look of a lizard. A white lizard, Sarah decided. "This has affected Meg," he said. "The violence of it. We shall talk it over for a long time. Well. You have so much more time. You will bury all of us." His last words were loud and sudden, almost a squawk, because Meg, light of tread and silent on her feet, had come up behind him. She wore her straw hat and carried her morning glass of gin and orange juice.

"Sarah? She'll bury *you*," said Meg. "Fetch the car, Tim, and take Sarah somewhere. Come along. Get to Friday. *Tim*." He turned. "Dress first," she said.

The sun which had turned Tim into a white lizard now revealed a glassy stain on Meg's cheek, half under her hair. Sarah's attention jumped like a child's. She said, "Something's bitten you. Look. Something poisonous."

Meg moved her head and the poisoned bite vanished under the shade of her hat. "Observant. Tim has never noticed. Neither has Roy. It is only a small malignant thing," she said indifferently. "I've been going to the hospital in Nice twice a week for treatment. They burned it – that's the reason for the scar."

"Oh, Meg," said Sarah, drawn round the gate. "Nobody knew. That was why you went to Nice. I saw you on the bus."

"I saw you," said Meg, "but why talk when you needn't? I get plenty of talk at home. May I ask where you are going?"

"I'm going to the airport, and I'll sit there till they get me on a plane."

"Well, Sarah, you may be sitting for some time, but I know you know what you are doing," said Meg. "I am minding the summer heat this year. I feel that soon I won't be able to stand it anymore. When Tim's gone I won't ever marry again. I'll look for some woman to share expenses. If you ever want to come back for a holiday, Sarah, you have only to let me know."

And so Tim, the battery of his car leaking its lifeblood all over French roads, drove Sarah down to Nice and along to the airport. Loyal to the Reeve standards, he did not once glance at the sea. As for Sarah, she sat beside him crying quietly, first over Meg, then over herself, because she thought she had spent all her capital on Roy and would never love anyone again. She looked for the restaurant with the blue tablecloths, and for the beach where they had sat talking for a night, but she could not find them; there were dozens of tables and awnings and beaches, all more or less alike.

"You'll be all right?" said Tim. He wanted her to say yes, of course.

She said, "Tim, Roy needs help."

He did not know her euphemisms any more than she understood his. He said, "Help to do what?"

"Roy is unhappy and he doesn't know what he wants. If you're over forty and you don't know what you want, well, I guess someone should tell you."

"My dear Sarah," said the old man, "that is an unkind thing to say about a friend we have confidence in."

She said quickly, "Don't you see, before he had a life that suited him, inspecting people in jails. They didn't seem like people *or* jails. It kept him happy, it balanced ..." Suddenly she gave a great shiver in the heat of the morning and heard

Lisbet laugh and say, "Someone's walking on your grave." She went on, "For example, he won't eat."

"Don't you worry about that," cried Tim, understanding something at last. "Meg will see that he eats." Right to the end, everyone was at cross-purposes. "Think of it this way," said Tim. "You had to go home sometime."

"Not till September."

"Well, look on the happy side. Old Roy ... matrimony. You might not enjoy it, you know, unless you met someone like Meg." He obviously had no idea what he was saying anymore, and so she gave up talking until he set her down at the departures gate. Then he said, "Good luck to you, child," and drove away looking indescribably happy.

Sarah kept for a long time the picture of Judas with his guts spilling and with his soul (a shrimp of a man, a lesser Judas) reaching out for the Devil. It should have signified Roy, or even Lisbet, but oddly enough it was she, the victim, who felt guilty and maimed. Still, she was out of the tunnel. Unlike Judas she was alive, and that was something. She was so much younger than all those other people: as Tim had said, she would bury them all. She tacked the Judas card over a map of the world on a wall of her room. Plucked from its origins it began to flower from Sarah's; here was an image that might have followed her from the nursery. It was someone's photo, a family likeness, that could bear no taint of pain or disaster. One day she took the card down, turned it over, and addressed it to a man she was after. He was too poot to invite her anywhere and seemed too shy to make a move. He was also in terrible trouble – back taxes, ex-wife seizing his salary. He had been hounded from California to Canada for his political beliefs. She was in love with his mystery, his hardships, and the death of Trotsky. She wrote, "This person must have eaten my cooking. Others have risked it so please come to dinner on

Friday, Sarah." She looked at the words for seconds before hearing another voice. Then she remembered where the card was from, and she understood what the entire message was about. She could have changed it, but it was too late to change anything much. She was more of an *amoureuse* than a psycho-anything, she would never use up her capital, and some summer or other would always be walking on her grave.

THE ICE WAGON GOING DOWN THE STREET

Now that they are out of world affairs and back where they started, Peter Frazier's wife says, "Everybody else did well in the international thing except us."

"You have to be crooked," he tells her.

"Or smart. Pity we weren't."

It is Sunday morning. They sit in the kitchen, drinking their coffee, slowly, remembering the past. They say the names of people as if they were magic. Peter thinks, *Agnes Brusen*, but there are hundreds of other names. As a private married joke, Peter and Sheilah wear the silk dressing gowns they bought in Hong Kong. Each thinks the other a peacock, rather splendid, but they pretend the dressing gowns are silly and worn in fun.

Peter and Sheilah and their two daughters, Sandra and Jennifer, are visiting Peter's unmarried sister, Lucille. They have been Lucille's guests seventeen weeks, ever since they returned to Toronto from the Far East. Their big old steamer trunk blocks a corner of the kitchen, making a problem of the refrigerator door; but even Lucille says the trunk may as well stay where it is, for the present. The Fraziers' future is so unsettled; everything is still in the air.

Lucille has given her bedroom to her two nieces, and sleeps on a camp cot in the hall. The parents have the living-room divan. They have no privileges here; they sleep after Lucille has seen the last television show that interests her. In the hall closet their clothes are crushed by winter overcoats. They know they are being judged for the first time. Sandra and Jennifer are waiting for Sheilah and Peter to decide. They are waiting to learn where these exotic parents will fly to next. What sort of climate will Sheilah consider? What job will Peter consent to accept? When the parents are ready, the children will make a decision of their own. It is just possible that Sandra and Jennifer will choose to stay with their aunt.

The peacock parents are watched by wrens. Lucille and her nieces are much the same – sandy-colored, proudly plain. Neither of the girls has the father's insouciance or the mother's appearance – her height, her carriage, her thick hair, and sky-blue eyes. The children are more cautious than their parents; more Canadian. When they saw their aunt's apartment they had been away from Canada nine years, ever since they were two and four; and Jennifer, the elder, said, "Well, now we're home." Her voice is nasal and flat. Where did she learn that voice? And why should this be home? Peter's answer to anything about his mystifying children is, "It must be in the blood."

On Sunday morning Lucille takes her nieces to church. It seems to be the only condition she imposes on her relations: the children must be decent. The girls go willingly, with their new hats and purses and gloves and coral bracelets and strings of pearls. The parents, ramshackle, sleepy, dim in the brain because it is Sunday, sit down to their coffee and privacy and talk of the past.

"We weren't crooked," says Peter. "We weren't even smart."

Sheilah's head bobs up; she is no drowner. It is wrong to say they have nothing to show for time. Sheilah has the Balenciaga. It is a black afternoon dress, stiff and boned at the waist;

long for the fashions of now, but neither Sheilah nor Peter would change a thread. The Balenciaga is their talisman, their treasure; and after they remember it they touch hands and think that the years are not behind them but hazy and marvelous and still to be lived.

The first place they went to was Paris. In the early fifties the pick of the international jobs was there. Peter had inherited the last scrap of money he knew he was ever likely to see, and it was enough to get them over: Sheilah and Peter and the babies and the steamer trunk. To their joy and astonishment they had money in the bank. They said to each other, "It should last a year." Peter was fastidious about the new job; he hadn't come all this distance to accept just anything. In Paris he met Hugh Taylor, who was earning enough smuggling gasoline to keep his wife in Paris and a girl in Rome. That impressed Peter, because he remembered Taylor as a sour scholarship student without the slightest talent for life. Taylor had a job, of course. He hadn't said to himself, I'll go over to Europe and smuggle gasoline. It gave Peter an idea; he saw the shape of things. First you catch your fish. Later, at an international party, he met Johnny Hertzberg, who told him Germany was the place. Hertzberg said that anyone who came out of Germany broke now was too stupid to be here, and deserved to be back home at a desk. Peter nodded, as if he had already thought of that. He began to think about Germany. Paris was fine for a holiday, but it had been picked clean. Yes, Germany. His money was running low. He thought about Germany quite a lot.

That winter was moist and delicate; so fragile that they daren't speak of it now. There seemed to be plenty of everything and plenty of time. They were living the dream of a marriage, the fabric uncut, nothing slashed or spoiled. All winter they spent their money, and went to parties, and talked about Peter's future job. It lasted four months. They spent their money, lived in the future, and were never as happy again.

After four months they were suddenly moved away from Paris, but not to Germany – to Geneva. Peter thinks it was because of the incident at the Trudeau wedding at the Ritz. Paul Trudeau was a French Canadian Peter had known at school and in the Navy. Trudeau had turned into a snob, proud of his career and his Paris connections. He tried to make the difference felt, but Peter thought the difference was only for strangers. At the wedding reception Peter lay down on the floor and said he was dead. He held a white azalea in a brass pot on his chest, and sang, "Oh, hear us when we cry to Thee for those in peril on the sea." Sheilah bent over him and said, "Pete, darling, get up. Pete, listen, every single person who can do something for you is in this room. If you love me, you'll get up."

"I do love you," he said, ready to engage in a serious conversation. "She's so beautiful," he told a second face. "She's nearly as tall as I am. She was a model in London. I met her over in London in the war. I met her there in the war." He lay on his back with the azalea on his chest, explaining their history. A waiter took the brass pot away, and after Peter had been hauled to his feet he knocked the waiter down. Trudeau's bride, who was freshly out of an Ursuline convent, became hysterical; and even though Paul Trudeau and Peter were old acquaintances, Trudeau never spoke to him again. Peter says now that French Canadians always have that bit of spite. He says Trudeau asked the Embassy to interfere. Luckily, back home there were still a few people to whom the name "Frazier" meant something, and it was to these people that Peter appealed. He wrote letters saying that a French-Canadian combine was preventing his getting a decent job, and could anything be done? No one answered directly, but it was clear that what they settled for was exile to Geneva: a season of meditation and remorse, as he explained to Sheilah, and it was managed tactfully, through Lucille. Lucille wrote that a friend of hers, May Fergus, now a secretary in Geneva, had heard about a job. The job was filing pictures in the information service of an international agency in the Palais des Nations. The pay was so-so, but Lucille thought Peter must be getting fed up doing nothing.

Peter often asks his sister now who put her up to it – what important person told her to write that letter suggesting Peter go to Geneva?

"Nobody," says Lucille. "I mean, nobody in the way *you* mean. I really did have this girl friend working there, and I knew you must be running through your money pretty fast in Paris."

"It must have been somebody pretty high up," Peter says. He looks at his sister admiringly, as he has often looked at his wife.

Peter's wife had loved him in Paris. Whatever she wanted in marriage she found that winter, there. In Geneva, where Peter was a file clerk and they lived in a furnished flat, she pretended they were in Paris and life was still the same. Often, when the children were at supper, she changed as though she and Peter were dining out. She wore the Balenciaga, and put candles on the card table where she and Peter ate their meal. The neckline of the dress was soiled with make-up. Peter remembers her dabbing on the make-up with a wet sponge. He remembers her in the kitchen, in the soiled Balenciaga, patting on the make-up with a filthy sponge. Behind her, at the kitchen table, Sandra and Jennifer, in buttonless pajamas and bunny slippers, ate their supper of marmalade sandwiches and milk. When the children were asleep, the parents dined solemnly, ritually, Sheilah sitting straight as a queen.

It was a mysterious period of exile, and he had to wait for signs, or signals, to know when he was free to leave. He never saw the job any other way. He forgot he had applied for it. He thought he had been sent to Geneva because of a misdemeanor and had to wait to be released. Nobody pressed him at work. His immediate boss had resigned, and he was alone for months in a room with two desks. He read the *Herald-Tribune*, and tried to discover how things were here – how the others ran their lives on the pay they were officially getting. But it was a closed conspiracy. He was not dealing with adventures now but civil servants waiting for pension day. No one ever answered his questions. They pretended to think his questions were a form of wit. His only solace in exile was the few happy weekends he had in the late spring and early summer. He had met another old acquaintance, Mike Burleigh. Mike was a serious liberal who had married a serious heiress. The Burleighs had two guest lists. The first was composed of stuffy people they felt obliged to entertain, while the second was made up of their real friends, the friends they wanted. The real friends strove hard to become stuffy and dull and thus achieve the first guest list, but few succeeded. Peter went on the first list straight away. Possibly Mike didn't understand, at the beginning, why Peter was pretending to be a file clerk. Peter had such an air – he might have been sent by a universal inspector to see how things in Geneva were being run.

Every Friday in May and June and part of July, the Fraziers rented a sky-blue Fiat and drove forty miles east of Geneva to the Burleighs' summer house. They brought the children, a suitcase, the children's tattered picture books, and a token bottle of gin. This, in memory, is a period of water and water birds, swans, roses, and singing birds. The children were small and still belonged to them. If they remember too much, their mouths water, their stomachs hurt. Peter says, "It was fine while it lasted." Enough. While it lasted Sheilah and Madge Burleigh were close. They abandoned their husbands and spent long summer afternoons comparing their mothers and praising each other's skin and hair. To Madge, and not to Peter, Sheilah opened her Liverpool childhood with the words "rat poor." Peter heard about it later, from Mike. The women's friendship seemed to Peter a bad beginning. He trusted women but not with each other. It lasted ten weeks. One Sunday, Madge said she needed the two bedrooms the Fraziers usually occupied for a party of sociologists from Pakistan; and that was the end. In November, the Fraziers heard that the summer house had been closed, and that the Burleighs were in Geneva, in their winter flat; they gave no sign. There was no help for it, and no appeal.

Now Peter began firing letters to anyone who had ever known his late father. He was living in a mild yellow autumn. Why does he remember the streets of the city dark, and the windows everywhere black with rain? He remembers being with Sheilah and the children as if they clung together while just outside their small shelter it rained and rained. The children slept in the bedroom of the flat because the window gave on the street and they could breathe air. Peter and Sheilah had the living-room couch. Their window was not a real window but a square on a well of cement. The flat seemed damp as a cave. Peter remembers steam in the kitchen, pools under the sink, sweat on the pipes. Water streamed on him from the children's clothes, washed and dripping overhead. The trunk, upended in the children's room, was not quite unpacked. Sheilah had not signed her name to this life; she had not given in. Once Peter heard her drop her aitches. "You kids are lucky," she said to the girls. "I never 'ad so much as a sit-down meal. I ate chips out of a paper or I 'ad a butty out on the stairs." He never asked her what a butty was. He thinks it means bread and cheese.

The day he heard "You kids are lucky" he understood they were becoming in fact something they had only *appeared* to be until now – the shabby civil servant and his brood. If he had been European he would have ridden to work on a bicycle, in the uniform of his class and condition. He would have worn a tight coat, a turned collar, and a dirty tie. He wondered then if coming here had been a mistake, and if he should not, after all, still be in a place where his name meant something. Surely Peter Frazier should live where "Frazier" counts? In Ontario even now when he says "Frazier" an absent look comes over his hearer's face, as if its owner were consulting an interior guide. What is Frazier? What does it mean? Oil? Power? Politics? Wheat? Real estate? The creditors had the house sealed when Peter's father died. His aunt collapsed with a heart attack in somebody's bachelor apartment, leaving three sons and a widower to surmise they had never known her. Her will was a disappointment. None of that generation left enough. One made it: the granite Presbyterian immigrants from Scotland. Their children, a generation of daunted women and maiden men, held still. Peter's father's crowd spent: they were not afraid of their fathers, and their grandfathers were old. Peter and his sister and his cousins lived on the remains. They were left the rinds of income, of notions, and the memories of ideas rather than ideas intact. If Peter can choose his reincarnation, let him be the oppressed son of a Scottish parson. Let Peter grow up on cuffs and iron principles. Let him make the fortune! Let him flee the manse! When he was small his patrimony was squandered under his nose. He remembers people dancing in his father's house. He remembers seeing and nearly understanding adultery in a guest room, among a pile of wraps. He thought he had seen a murder; he never told. He remembers licking glasses wherever he found them – on window sills, on stairs, in the pantry. In his room he listened while Lucille read Beatrix Potter. The bad rabbit stole the carrot from the good rabbit without saying please, and downstairs was the noise of the party – the roar of the crouched lion. When his father died he saw the chairs upside down and the bailiff's chalk marks. Then the doors were sealed.

He has often tried to tell Sheilah why he cannot be defeated. He remembers his father saying, "Nothing can touch us," and Peter believed it and still does. It has prevented his taking his troubles too seriously. "Nothing can be as bad as this," he will tell himself. "It is happening to me." Even in Geneva, where his status was file clerk, where he sank and stopped on the level of the men who never emigrated, the men on the bicycles – even there he had a manner of strolling to work as if his office were a pastime, and his real life a secret so splendid he could share it with no one except himself.

In Geneva Peter worked for a woman – a girl. She was a Norwegian from a small town in Saskatchewan. He supposed they had been put together because they were Canadians; but they were as strange to each other as if "Canadian" meant any number of things, or had no real meaning. Soon after Agnes Brusen came to the office she hung her framed university degree on the wall. It was one of the gritty, prideful gestures that stand for push, toil, and family sacrifice. He thought, then, that she must be one of a family of immigrants for whom education is everything. Hugh Taylor had told him that in some families the older children never marry until the youngest have finished school. Sometimes every second child is sacrificed and made to work for the education of the next born. Those who finish college spend years paying back. They are white-hot Protestants, and they live with a load of work and debt and obligation. Peter placed his new colleague on scraps of information. He had never been in the West.

She came to the office on a Monday morning in October. The office was overheated and painted cream. It contained two desks, the filing cabinets, a map of the world as it had been in 1945, and the Charter of the United Nations left behind by Agnes Brusen's predecessor. (She took down the Charter without asking Peter if he minded, with the impudence of gesture you find in women who wouldn't say boo to a goose; and then she hung her college degree on the nail where the

Charter had been.) Three people brought her in – a whole committee. One of them said, "Agnes, this is Pete Frazier. Pete, Agnes Brusen. Pete's Canadian, too, Agnes. He knows all about the office, so ask him anything."

Of course he knew all about the office: he knew the exact spot where the cord of the venetian blind was frayed, obliging one to give an extra tug to the right.

The girl might have been twenty-three: no more. She wore a brown tweed suit with bone buttons, and a new silk scarf and new shoes. She clutched an unscratched brown purse. She seemed dressed in going-away presents. She said, "Oh, I never smoke," with a convulsive movement of her hand, when Peter offered his case. He was courteous, hiding his disappointment. The people he worked with had told him a Scandinavian girl was arriving, and he had expected a stunner. Agnes was a mole: she was small and brown, and round-shouldered as if she had always carried parcels or younger children in her arms. A mole's profile was turned when she said goodbye to her committee. If she had been foreign, ill-favored though she was, he might have flirted a little, just to show that he was friendly; but their being Canadian, and suddenly left together, was a sexual damper. He sat down and lit his own cigarette. She smiled at him, questioningly, he thought, and sat as if she had never seen a chair before. He wondered if his smoking was annoying her. He wondered if she was fidgety about drafts, or allergic to anything, and whether she would want the blind up or down. His social compass was out of order because the others couldn't tell Peter and Agnes apart. There was a world of difference between them, yet it was she who had been brought in to sit at the larger of the two desks.

While he was thinking this she got up and walked around the office, almost on tiptoe, opening the doors of closets and pulling out the filing trays. She looked inside everything except the drawers of Peter's desk. (In any case, Peter's desk was locked. His desk is locked wherever he works. In Geneva he went into Personnel one morning, early, and pinched his application form. He had stated on the form that he had seven years' experience in public relations and could speak French, German, Spanish, and Italian. He has always collected anything important about himself – anything useful. But he can never get on with the final act, which is getting rid of the information. He has kept papers about for years, a constant source of worry.)

"I know this looks funny, Mr. Ferris," said the girl. "I'm not really snooping or anything. I just can't feel easy in a new place unless I know where everything is. In a new place everything seems so hidden."

If she had called him "Ferris" and pretended not to know he was Frazier, it could only be because they had sent her here to spy on him and see if he had repented and was fit for a better place in life. "You'll be all right here," he said. "Nothing's hidden. Most of us haven't got brains enough to have secrets. This is Rainbow Valley." Depressed by the thought that they were having him watched now, he passed his hand over his hair and looked outside to the lawn and the parking lot and the peacocks someone gave the Palais des Nations years ago. The peacocks love no one. They wander about the parked cars looking elderly, bad-tempered, mournful, and lost.

Agnes had settled down again. She folded her silk scarf and placed it just so, with her gloves beside it. She opened her new purse and took out a notebook and a shiny gold pencil. She may have written

Duster for desk
Kleenex
Glass jar for flowers
Air-Wick because he smokes
Paper for lining drawers

because the next day she brought each of these articles to work. She also brought a large black Bible, which she unwrapped lovingly and placed on the left-hand corner of her desk. The flower vase – empty – stood in the middle, and the Kleenex made a counterpoise for the Bible on the right.

When he saw the Bible he knew she had not been sent to spy on his work. The conspiracy was deeper. She might have been dispatched by ghosts. He knew everything about her, all in a moment: he saw the ambition, the terror, the dry pride. She was the true heir of the men from Scotland; she was at the start. She had been sent to tell him, "You can begin, but not begin again." She never opened the Bible, but she dusted it as she dusted her desk, her chair, and any surface the cleaning staff had overlooked. And Peter, the first days, watching her timid movements, her insignificant little face, felt, as you feel the approach of a storm, the charge of moral certainty round her, the belief in work, the faith in undertakings, the bread of the Black Sunday. He recognized and tasted all of it: ashes in the mouth.

After five days their working relations were settled. Of course, there was the Bible and all that went with it, but his tongue had never held the taste of ashes long. She was an inferior girl of poor quality. She had nothing in her favor except the degree on the wall. In the real world, he would not have invited her to his house except to mind the children. That was what he said to Sheilah. He said that Agnes was a mole, and a virgin, and that her tics and mannerisms were sending him round the bend. She had an infuriating habit of covering her mouth when she talked. Even at the telephone she put up her hand as if afraid of losing anything, even a word. Her voice was nasal and flat. She had two working costumes, both dull as the wall. One was the brown suit, the other a navy-blue dress with changeable collars. She dressed for no one; she dressed for her desk, her jar of flowers, her Bible, and her box of Kleenex. One day she crossed the space between the two desks and stood over Peter, who was reading a newspaper. She could have spoken to him from her desk, but she may have felt that being on her feet gave her authority. She had plenty of courage, but authority was something else.

"I thought – I mean, they told me you were the person ..." She got on with it bravely: "If you don't want to do the filing or any work, all right, Mr. Frazier. I'm not saying anything about that. You might have poor health or your personal reasons. But it's got to be done, so if you'll kindly show me about the filing I'll do it. I've worked in Information before, but it was a different office, and every office is different."

"My dear girl," said Peter. He pushed back his chair and looked at her, astonished. "You've been sitting there fretting, worrying. How insensitive of me. How trying for you. Usually I file on the last Wednesday of the month, so you see, you just haven't been around long enough to see a last Wednesday. Not another word, please. And let us not waste another minute." He emptied the heaped baskets of photographs so swiftly, pushing "Iran – Smallpox Control" into "Irish Red Cross" (close enough), that the girl looked frightened, as if she had raised a whirlwind. She said slowly, "If you'll only show me, Mr. Frazier, instead of doing it so fast, I'll gladly look after it, because you might want to be doing other things, and I feel the filing should be done every day." But Peter was too busy to answer, and so she sat down, holding the edge of her desk.

"There," he said, beaming. "All done." His smile, his sunburst, was wasted, for the girl was staring round the room as if she feared she had not inspected everything the first day after all; some drawer, some cupboard, hid a monster. That evening Peter unlocked one of the drawers of his desk and took away the application form he had stolen from Personnel. The girl had not finished her search.

"How could you *not* know?" wailed Sheilah. "You sit looking at her every day. You must talk about *something*. She must have told you."

"She did tell me," said Peter, "and I've just told you."

It was this: Agnes Brusen was on the Burleighs' guest list. How had the Burleighs met her? What did they see in her? Peter could not reply. He knew that Agnes lived in a bed-sitting room with a Swiss family and had her meals with them. She had been in Geneva three months, but no one had ever seen her outside the office. "You *should* know," said Sheilah. "She must have something, more than you can see. Is she pretty? Is she brilliant? What is it?"

"We don't really talk," Peter said. They talked in a way: Peter teased her and she took no notice. Agnes was not a sulker. She had taken her defeat like a sport. She did her work and a good deal of his. She sat behind her Bible, her flowers, and her Kleenex, and answered when Peter spoke. That was how he learned about the Burleighs – just by teasing and being bored. It was a January afternoon. He said, "*Miss* Brusen. Talk to me. Tell me everything. Pretend we have perfect rapport. Do you like Geneva?"

"It's a nice clean town," she said. He can see to this day the red and blue anemones in the glass jar, and her bent head, and her small untended hands.

"Are you learning beautiful French with your Swiss family?"

"They speak English."

"Why don't you take an apartment of your own?" he said. Peter was not usually impertinent. He was bored. "You'd be independent then."

"I am independent," she said. "I earn my living. I don't think it proves anything if you live by yourself. Mrs. Burleigh wants me to live alone, too. She's looking for something for me. It mustn't be dear. I send money home."

Here was the extraordinary thing about Agnes Brusen: she refused the use of Christian names and never spoke to Peter unless he spoke first, but she would tell anything, as if to say, "Don't waste time fishing. Here it is."

He learned all in one minute that she sent her salary home,

and that she was a friend of the Burleighs. The first he had expected; the second knocked him flat.

"She's got to come to dinner," Sheilah said. "We should have had her right from the beginning. If only I'd known! But *you* were the one. You said she looked like – oh, I don't even remember. A Norwegian mole."

She came to dinner one Saturday night in January, in her navy-blue dress, to which she had pinned an organdy gardenia. She sat upright on the edge of the sofa. Sheilah had ordered the meal from a restaurant. There was lobster, good wine, and a *pièce-montée* full of kirsch and cream. Agnes refused the lobster; she had never eaten anything from the sea unless it had been sterilized and tinned, and said so. She was afraid of skin poisoning. Someone in her family had skin poisoning after having eaten oysters. She touched her cheeks and neck to show where the poisoning had erupted. She sniffed her wine and put the glass down without tasting it. She could not eat the cake because of the alcohol it contained. She ate an egg, bread and butter, a sliced tomato, and drank a glass of ginger ale. She seemed unaware she was creating disaster and pain. She did not help clear away the dinner plates. She sat, adequately nourished, decently dressed, and waited to learn why she had been invited here – that was the feeling Peter had. He folded the card table on which they had dined, and opened the window to air the room.

"It's not the same cold as Canada, but you feel it more," he said, for something to say.

"Your blood has gotten thin," said Agnes.

Sheilah returned from the kitchen and let herself fall into an armchair. With her eyes closed she held out her hand for a cigarette. She was performing the haughty-lady act that was a family joke. She flung her head back and looked at Agnes through half-closed lids; then she suddenly brought her head forward, widening her eyes.

"Are you skiing madly?" she said.

"Well, in the first place there hasn't been any snow," said Agnes. "So nobody's doing any skiing so far as I know. All I hear is people complaining because there's no snow. Personally, I don't ski. There isn't much skiing in the part of Canada I come from. Besides, my family never had that kind of leisure."

"Heavens," said Sheilah, as if her family had every kind.

I'll bet they had, thought Peter. On the dole.

Sheilah was wasting her act. He had a suspicion that Agnes knew it was an act but did not know it was also a joke. If so, it made Sheilah seem a fool, and he loved Sheilah too much to enjoy it.

"The Burleighs have been wonderful to me," said Agnes. She seemed to have divined why she was here, and decided to give them all the information they wanted, so that she could put on her coat and go home to bed. "They had me out to their place on the lake every weekend until the weather got cold and they moved back to town. They've rented a chalet for the winter, and they want me to come there, too. But I don't know if I will or not. I don't ski, and, oh, I don't know – I don't drink, either, and I don't always see the point. Their friends are too rich and I'm too Canadian."

She had delivered everything Sheilah wanted and more: Agnes was on the first guest list and didn't care. No, Peter corrected; doesn't know. Doesn't care and doesn't know.

"I thought with you Norwegians it was in the blood, skiing. And drinking," Sheilah murmured.

"Drinking, maybe," said Agnes. She covered her mouth and said behind her spread fingers, "In our family we were religious. We didn't drink or smoke. My brother was in Norway in the war. He saw some cousins. Oh," she said, unexpectedly loud, "Harry said it was just terrible. They were so poor. They had flies in their kitchen. They gave him something to eat a fly had been on. They didn't have a real toilet, and they'd been in the same house about two hundred years.

We've only recently built our own home, and we have a bathroom and two toilets. I'm from Saskatchewan," she said. "I'm not from any other place."

Surely one winter here had been punishment enough? In the spring they would remember him and free him. He wrote Lucille, who said he was lucky to have a job at all. The Burleighs had sent the Fraziers a second-guest-list Christmas card. It showed a Moslem refugee child weeping outside a tent. They treasured the card and left it standing long after the others had been given the children to cut up. Peter had discovered by now what had gone wrong in the friendship – Sheilah had charged a skirt at a dressmaker to Madge's account. Madge had told her she might, and then changed her mind. Poor Sheilah! She was new to this part of it – to the changing humors of independent friends. Paris was already a year in the past. At Mardi Gras, the Burleighs gave their annual party. They invited everyone, the damned and the dropped, with the prodigality of a child at prayers. The invitation said "in costume," but the Fraziers were too happy to wear a disguise. They might not be recognized. Like many of the guests they expected to meet at the party, they had been disgraced, forgotten, and rehabilitated. They would be anxious to see one another as they were.

On the night of the party, the Fraziers rented a car they had never seen before and drove through the first snowstorm of the year. Peter had not driven since last summer's blissful trips in the Fiat. He could not find the switch for the windshield wiper in this car. He leaned over the wheel. "Can you see on your side?" he asked. "Can I make a left turn here? Does it look like a one-way?"

"I can't imagine why you took a car with a right-hand drive," said Sheilah.

He had trouble finding a place to park; they crawled up and

down unknown streets whose curbs were packed with snow-covered cars. When they stood at last on the pavement, safe and sound, Peter said, "This is the first snow."

"I can see that," said Sheilah. "Hurry, darling. My hair."

"It's the first snow."

"You're repeating yourself," she said. "Please hurry, darling. Think of my poor shoes. My *hair*."

She was born in an ugly city, and so was Peter, but they have this difference: she does not know the importance of the first snow – the first clean thing in a dirty year. He would have told her then that this storm, which was wetting her feet and destroying her hair, was like the first day of the English spring, but she made a frightened gesture, trying to shield her head. The gesture told him he did not understand her beauty.

"Let me," she said. He was fumbling with the key, trying to lock the car. She took the key without impatience and locked the door on the driver's side; and then, to show Peter she treasured him and was not afraid of wasting her life or her beauty, she took his arm and they walked in the snow down a street and around a corner to the apartment house where the Burleighs lived. They were, and are, a united couple. They were afraid of the party, and each of them knew it. When they walk together, holding arms, they give each other whatever each can spare.

Only six people had arrived in costume. Madge Burleigh was disguised as Manet's "Lola de Valence," which everyone mistook for Carmen. Mike was an Impressionist painter, with a straw hat and a glued-on beard. "I am all of them," he said. He would rather have dressed as a dentist, he said, welcoming the Fraziers as if he had parted from them the day before, but Madge wanted him to look as if he had created her. "You know?" he said.

"Perfectly," said Sheilah. Her shoes were stained and the

snow had softened her lacquered hair. She was not wasted; she was the most beautiful woman here.

About an hour after their arrival, Peter found himself with no one to talk to. He had told about the Trudeau wedding in Paris and the pot of azaleas, and after he mislaid his audience he began to look round for Sheilah. She was on a window seat, partly concealed by a green velvet curtain. Facing her, so that their profiles were neat and perfect against the night, was a man. Their conversation was private and enclosed, as if they had in minutes covered leagues of time and arrived at the place where everything was implied, understood. Peter began working his way across the room, toward his wife, when he saw Agnes. He was granted the sight of her drowning face. She had dressed with comic intention, obviously with care, and now she was a ragged hobo, half tramp, half clown. Her hair was tucked up under a bowler hat. The six costumed guests who had made the same mistake – the ghost, the gypsy, the Athenian maiden, the geisha, the Martian, and the apache – were delighted to find a seventh; but Agnes was not amused; she was gasping for life. When a waiter passed with a crowded tray, she took a glass without seeing it; then a wave of the party took her away.

Sheilah's new friend was named Simpson. After Simpson said he thought perhaps he'd better circulate, Peter sat down where he had been. "Now look, Sheilah," he began. Their most intimate conversations have taken place at parties. Once at a party she told him she was leaving him; she didn't, of course. Smiling, blue-eyed, she gazed lovingly at Peter and said rapidly, "Pete, shut up and listen. That man. The man you scared away. He's a big wheel in a company out in India or someplace like that. It's gorgeous out there. Pete, the *servants*. And it's warm. It never never snows. He says there's heaps of jobs. You pick them off the trees like ... orchids. He says it's even easier now than when we owned all those places, because now the poor pets can't run anything and they'll pay *fortunes*.

Pete, he says it's warm, it's heaven, and Pete, they pay."

A few minutes later, Peter was alone again and Sheilah part of a closed, laughing group. Holding her elbow was the man from the place where jobs grew like orchids. Peter edged into the group and laughed at a story he hadn't heard. He heard only the last line, which was, "Here comes another tunnel." Looking out from the tight laughing ring, he saw Agnes again, and he thought, I'd be like Agnes if I didn't have Sheilah. Agnes put her glass down on a table and lurched toward the doorway, head forward. Madge Burleigh, who never stopped moving around the room and smiling, was still smiling when she paused and said in Peter's ear, "Go with Agnes, Pete. See that she gets home. People will notice if Mike leaves."

"She probably just wants to walk around the block," said Peter. "She'll be back."

"Oh, stop thinking about yourself, for once, and see that that poor girl gets home," said Madge. "You've still got your Fiat, haven't you?"

He turned away as if he had been pushed. Any command is a release, in a way. He may not want to go in that particular direction, but at least he is going somewhere. And now Sheilah, who had moved inches nearer to hear what Madge and Peter were murmuring, said, "Yes, go, darling," as if he were leaving the gates of Troy.

Peter was to find Agnes and see that she reached home: this he repeated to himself as he stood on the landing, outside the Burleighs' flat, ringing for the elevator. Bored with waiting for it, he ran down the stairs, four flights, and saw that Agnes had stalled the lift by leaving the door open. She was crouched on the floor, propped on her fingertips. Her eyes were closed.

"Agnes," said Peter. "*Miss* Brusen, I mean. That's no way to leave a party. Don't you know you're supposed to curtsey and say thanks? My God, Agnes, anybody going by here just now might have seen you! Come on, be a good girl. Time to go home."

She got up without his help and, moving between invisible crevasses, shut the elevator door. Then she left the building and Peter followed, remembering he was to see that she got home. They walked along the snowy pavement, Peter a few steps behind her. When she turned right for no reason, he turned, too. He had no clear idea where they were going. Perhaps she lived close by. He had forgotten where the hired car was parked, or what it looked like; he could not remember its make or its color. In any case, Sheilah had the key. Agnes walked on steadily, as if she knew their destination, and he thought, Agnes Brusen is drunk in the street in Geneva and dressed like a tramp. He wanted to say, "This is the best thing that ever happened to you, Agnes; it will help you understand how things are for some of the rest of us." But she stopped and turned and, leaning over a low hedge, retched on a frozen lawn. He held her clammy forehead and rested his hand on her arched back, on muscles as tight as a fist. She straightened up and drew a breath but the cold air made her cough. "Don't breathe too deeply," he said. "It's the worst thing you can do. Have you got a handkerchief?" He passed his own handkerchief over her wet weeping face, upturned like the face of one of his little girls. "I'm out without a coat," he said, noticing it. "We're a pair."

"I never drink," said Agnes. "I'm just not used to it." Her voice was sweet and quiet. He had never seen her so peaceful, so composed. He thought she must surely be all right, now, and perhaps he might leave her here. The trust in her tilted face had perplexed him. He wanted to get back to Sheilah and have her explain something. He had forgotten what it was, but Sheilah would know. "Do you live around here?" he said. As he spoke, she let herself fall. He had wiped her face and now she trusted him to pick her up, set her on her feet, take her wherever she ought to be. He pulled her up and she stood, wordless, humble, as he brushed the snow from her tramp's clothes. Snow horizontally crossed the lamplight. The street was silent. Agnes had lost her hat. Snow, which he tasted, melted on her hands. His gesture of licking snow from her hands was formal as a handshake. He tasted snow on her hands and then they walked on.

"I never drink," she said. They stood on the edge of a broad avenue. The wrong turning now could lead them anywhere; it was the changeable avenue at the edge of towns that loses its houses and becomes a highway. She held his arm and spoke in a gentle voice. She said, "In our house we didn't smoke or drink. My mother was ambitious for me, more than for Harry and the others." She said, "I've never been alone before. When I was a kid I would get up in the summer before the others, and I'd see the ice wagon going down the street. I'm alone now. Mrs. Burleigh's found me an apartment. It's only one room. She likes it because it's in the old part of town. I don't like old houses. Old houses are dirty. You don't know who was there before."

"I should have a car somewhere," Peter said. "I'm not sure where we are."

He remembers that on this avenue they climbed into a taxi, but nothing about the drive. Perhaps he fell asleep. He does remember that when he paid the driver Agnes clutched his arm, trying to stop him. She pressed extra coins into the driver's palm. The driver was paid twice.

"I'll tell you one thing about us," said Peter. "We pay everything twice." This was part of a much longer theory concerning North American behavior, and it was not Peter's own. Mike Burleigh had held forth about it on summer afternoons.

Agnes pushed open a door between a stationer's shop and a grocery, and led the way up a narrow inside stair. They climbed one flight, frightening beetles. She had to search every pocket for the latchkey. She was shaking with cold. Her apartment seemed little warmer than the street. Without speaking to Peter she turned on all the lights. She looked inside the kitchen and the bathroom and then got down on her hands and knees and looked under the sofa. The room was neat and belonged to no one. She left him standing in this unclaimed room – she had forgotten him – and closed a door behind her. He looked for something to do – some useful action he could repeat to Madge. He turned on the electric radiator in the fireplace. Perhaps Agnes wouldn't thank him for it; perhaps she would rather undress in the cold. "I'll be on my way," he called to the bathroom door.

She had taken off the tramp's clothes and put on a dressing gown of orphanage wool. She came out of the bathroom and straight toward him. She pressed her face and rubbed her cheek on his shoulder as if hoping the contact would leave a scar. He saw her back and her profile and his own face in the mirror over the fireplace. He thought, This is how disasters happen. He saw floods of sea water moving with perfect punitive justice over reclaimed land; he saw lava covering vineyards and overtaking dogs and stragglers. A bridge over an abyss snapped in two and the long express train, suddenly V-shaped, floated like snow. He thought amiably of every kind of disaster and thought, This is how they occur.

Her eyes were closed. She said, "I shouldn't be over here. In my family we didn't drink or smoke. My mother wanted a lot from me, more than from Harry and the others." But he knew all that; he had known from the day of the Bible, and because once, at the beginning, she had made him afraid. He was not afraid of her now.

She said, "It's no use staying here, is it?"

"If you mean what I think, no."

"It wouldn't be better anywhere."

She let him see full on her blotched face. He was not expected to do anything. He was not required to pick her up when she fell or wipe her tears. She was poor quality, really – he remembered having thought that once. She left him and went quietly into the bathroom and locked the door. He heard taps running and supposed it was a hot bath. He was pretty certain there would be no more tears. He looked at his watch: Sheilah must be home, now, wondering what had become of him. He descended the beetles' staircase and for forty minutes crossed the city under a windless fall of snow.

The neighbor's child who had stayed with Peter's children was asleep on the living-room sofa. Peter woke her and sent her, sleepwalking, to her own door. He sat down, wet to the bone, thinking, I'll call the Burleighs. In half an hour I'll call the police. He heard a car stop and the engine running and a confusion of two voices laughing and calling goodnight. Presently Sheilah let herself in, rosy-faced, smiling. She carried his trenchcoat over her arm. She said, "How's Agnes?"

"Where were you?" he said. "Whose car was that?"

Sheilah had gone into the children's room. He heard her shutting their window. She returned, undoing her dress, and said, "Was Agnes all right?"

"Agnes is all right. Sheilah, this is about the worst ..."

She stepped out of the Balenciaga and threw it over a chair. She stopped and looked at him and said, "Poor old Pete, are you in love with Agnes?" And then, as if the answer were of so little importance she hadn't time for it, she locked her arms around him and said, "My love, we're going to Ceylon."

Two days later, when Peter strolled into his office, Agnes was at her desk. She wore the blue dress, with a spotless collar. White and yellow freesias were symmetrically arranged in the glass jar. The room was hot, and the spring snow, glued for a second when it touched the window, blurred the view of parked cars.

"Quite a party," Peter said.

She did not look up. He sighed, sat down, and thought if the snow held he would be skiing at the Burleighs' very soon.

Impressed by his kindness to Agnes, Madge had invited the family for the first possible weekend.

Presently Agnes said, "I'll never drink again or go to a house where people are drinking. And I'll never bother anyone the way I bothered you."

"You didn't bother me," he said. "I took you home. You were alone and it was late. It's normal."

"Normal for you, maybe, but I'm used to getting home by myself. Please never tell what happened."

He stared at her. He can still remember the freesias and the Bible and the heat in the room. She looked as if the elements had no power. She felt neither heat nor cold. "Nothing happened," he said.

"I behaved in a silly way. I had no right to. I led you to think I might do something wrong."

"*I* might have tried something," he said gallantly. "But that would be my fault and not yours."

She put her knuckle to her mouth and he could scarcely hear. "It was because of you. I was afraid you might be blamed, or else you'd blame yourself."

"There's no question of any blame," he said. "Nothing happened. We'd both had a lot to drink. Forget about it. Nothing *happened*. You'd remember if it had."

She put down her hand. There was an expression on her face. Now she sees me, he thought. She had never looked at him after the first day. (He has since tried to put a name to the look on her face; but how can he, now, after so many voyages, after Ceylon, and Hong Kong, and Sheilah's nearly leaving him, and all their difficulties – the money owed, the rows with hotel managers, the lost and found steamer trunk, the children throwing up the foreign food?) She sees me now, he thought. What does she see?

She said, "I'm from a big family. I'm not used to being alone. I'm not a suicidal person, but I could have done something after that party, just not to see any more, or think or listen or expect anything. What can I think when I see these people? All my life I heard, Educated people don't do this, educated people don't do that. And now I'm here, and you're all educated people, and you're nothing but pigs. You're educated and you drink and do everything wrong and you know what you're doing, and that makes you worse than pigs. My family worked to make me an educated person, but they didn't know you. But what if I didn't see and hear and expect anything any more? It wouldn't change anything. You'd all be still the same. Only *you* might have thought it was your fault. You might have thought you were to blame. It could worry you all your life. It would have been wrong for me to worry you."

He remembered that the rented car was still along a snowy curb somewhere in Geneva. He wondered if Sheilah had the key in her purse and if she remembered where they'd parked.

"I told you about the ice wagon," Agnes said. "I don't remember everything, so you're wrong about remembering. But I remember telling you that. That was the best. It's the best you can hope to have. In a big family, if you want to be alone, you have to get up before the rest of them. You get up early in the morning in the summer and it's you, you, once in your life alone in the universe. You think you know everything that can happen ... Nothing is ever like that again."

He looked at the smeared window and wondered if this day could end without disaster. In his mind he saw her falling in the snow wearing a tramp's costume, and he saw her coming to him in the orphanage dressing gown. He saw her drowning face at the party. He was afraid for himself. The story was still unfinished. It had to come to a climax, something threatening to him. But there was no climax. They talked that day, and afterward nothing else was said. They went on in the same office for a short time, until Peter left for Ceylon; until somebody read the right letter, passed it on for the right initials, and the Fraziers began the Oriental tour that should have made their fortune. Agnes and Peter were too tired to speak after that morning. They were like a married couple in danger, taking care.

But what were they talking about that day, so quietly, such old friends? They talked about dying, about being ambitious, about being religious, about different kinds of love. What did she see when she looked at him – taking her knuckle slowly away from her mouth, bringing her hand down to the desk, letting it rest there? They were both Canadians, so they had this much together – the knowledge of the little you dare admit. Death, near-death, the best thing, the wrong thing – God knows what they were telling each other. Anyway, nothing happened.

When, on Sunday mornings, Sheilah and Peter talk about those times, they take on the glamor of something still to come. It is then he remembers Agnes Brusen. He never says her name. Sheilah wouldn't remember Agnes. Agnes is the only secret Peter has from his wife, the only puzzle he pieces together without her help. He thinks about families in the West as they were fifteen, twenty years ago – the iron-cold ambition, and every member pushing the next one on. He thinks of his father's parties. When he thinks of his father he imagines him with Sheilah, in a crowd. Actually, Sheilah and Peter's father never met, but they might have liked each other. His father admired good-looking women. Peter wonders what they were doing over there in Geneva – not Sheilah and Peter, *Agnes* and Peter. It is almost as if they had once run away together, silly as children, irresponsible as lovers. Peter and Sheilah are back where they started. While they were out in world affairs picking up microbes and debts, always on the fringe of disaster, the fringe of a fortune, Agnes went on and did – what? They lost each other. He thinks of the ice wagon going down the street. He sees something he has never seen in his life – a Western town that belongs to Agnes. Here is Agnes – small, mole-faced, round-shouldered because she has always carried a younger child. She watches the ice wagon and the trail of ice water in a morning invented for her: hers. He sees the weak prairie trees and the shadows on the sidewalk. Nothing moves except the shadows and the ice wagon and the changing amber of the child's eyes. The child is Peter. He has seen the grain of the cement sidewalk and the grass in the cracks, and the dust, and the dandelions at the edge of the road. He is there. He has taken the morning that belongs to Agnes, he is up before the others, and he knows everything. There is nothing he doesn't know. He could keep the morning, if he wanted to, but what can Peter do with the start of a summer day? Sheilah is here, it is a true Sunday morning, with its dimness and headache and remorse and regrets, and this is life. He says, "We have the Balenciaga." He touches Sheilah's hand. The children have their aunt now, and he and Sheilah have each other. Everything works out, somehow or other. Let Agnes have the start of the day. Let Agnes think it was invented for her. Who wants to be alone in the universe? No, begin at the beginning: Peter lost Agnes. Agnes says to herself somewhere, Peter is lost.

BONAVENTURE

He was besieged, he was invaded, by his mother's account of the day he was conceived; and his father confirmed her version of history, telling him *why*. He had never been able to fling in their faces "Why did you have me?" for they told him before he could reason, before he was ready to think. He was their marvel. Not only had he kept them together, he was a musical genius, the most gifted child any two people ever had, the most deserving of love. He began to doubt their legend when he discovered the casualness of sex, and understood that anyone who was not detached (which he believed his own talent would oblige him to be) could easily turn into parent and slave. He was not like his own father, who, as a parent, seemed a man who had been dying and all at once found himself in possession of a total life. His father never said this or anything like it, though he once committed himself dangerously in a letter. The father was more reticent than the mother; perhaps more Canadian. He could say what he thought, but not always what he felt. His memories, like the mother's, were silent, flickering areas of light, surrounded by buildings that no longer exist.

The son could not place himself in their epic story. They talked, but until the son became an eyewitness their lives were imaginary. Before he *was* – Douglas Ramsay – the world was covered with mist, palm fronds, and vegetarian reptiles. He said to his father, "The trouble is there are still too many people alive who remember all that." "All what?" "Oh, everything. The last war." He was trying to show the distance between them, yet he would have died for either one – perhaps the father first. That made him more violent toward them, and sometimes more indifferent. A year ago, when he was nineteen, he was awarded a fellowship that permitted him to study in Europe. He seldom wrote. Sometimes he forgot all about them. Their existence was pale, their adventure niggling, compared to his own. Family feeling had never dominated his actions; never would. Nevertheless, he discovered this: when he was confused, misunderstood, or insufficiently appreciated, a picture of his father stood upright in his mind. His father's face, stoic and watchful, transferred from a wartime photograph taken before true history began, appeared when Ramsay's emotions were dispersed, and his intellect, on which he depended, reduced to water.

He was in Switzerland, it was a June day, he was recently twenty, and he had to get rid of chocolate wrappers. He had spent the morning in Montreux, and in the short train journey between Montreux and the stop nearest the chalet where he was a guest for the summer, Ramsay had eaten three quarter-pound bars of the sweet, mild chocolate only women are said to like. He could not abandon the wrappers on the impeccable train; he was suddenly daunted by Swiss neatness and the eyes of strangers. Hobbling up the path from the station, he concealed the papers under ferns and stones.

The chalet, set up on its shelf of lawn, seemed to be watching. It was like an animal, a bison, or a bear, hairy with vines and dark because of its balconies. Once he had got rid of the evidence, he stared boldly back. Parts of his body were unhinged; he was clamped together by invisible hooks that tore the fabric. His knees, his shoulders, his neck were wrenched loose, like the punishment of Judas in an engraving Katharine Moser had put in his room. He had been in a car accident two years before, and would never mend entirely. "Neither will my father," he said to himself. Their suffering – his own and his father's – burned the day black. The shrieking of birds, which Katharine Moser thought he ought to like because he was a musician, sank and lodged in every bone. He shut his eyes and stood still, and waited for the seizure to pass, for the muscles to unlock; then he opened his eyes and looked at the lawn. It had not been wrecked by a war or by a woman in temper but by something ordinary – a country storm. The grass was bestrewn with branches, bark, leaves, peony petals, chairs knocked sideways, a child's watercolors, a strand of dripping vine. A branch shivered and the drops that fell were colder than any water he had ever touched. He imagined Katharine Moser standing here and saying to Heaven, "How dare you do this to my lawn?" As he thought this, the sun came on in a burst of fire, and his face and hands were riddled by stinging light. He saw the mountains, whose names he was daily told and at once forgot, and he saw the burning color of houses that were miles away. This was the landscape that had belonged to Adrien Moser, the great conductor; it had no other reason to command his gaze.

The prospects Ramsay had known until this summer were of cities – Montreal, and then Berlin. They were the same to him, whether their ruins were dark and soft, abandoned to pigeons and wavy pieces of sky, or created and destroyed by one process, like the machine that consumes itself. The air he had breathed was filled with particles of brick dust. He accepted faces, not one of which he would put a name to, and knew the smell and touch of wet raincoats worn by people he would never meet. In the streets of one place, Berlin, he walked on the dead, but both cities were built over annihilated walls scarcely anyone could remember. He knew that a lake is a lake – that is, a place to swim – and that parks and trees are good for children, but he had never known the name of a leaf or a tree until Moser's widow began telling him, comparing one wild grass with another, picking a flower, showing its picture in a book. In the morning, standing beside him in the ravine on the far side of the house, she pointed to fields of white anemones that seemed covered with frost, and she gathered forget-me-nots, wild geranium, mauve and violet and pink, and valerian like lace, and mare's-tails with fronds of green string. "The first plant life on earth," said Katharine, bending down. For a reason he could not immediately interpret, the words, and the sight of the plant in Katharine's hand, rushed him back to his mother screaming, and the wartime photograph of his father, which, of course, was mute.

Wishing for life without its past, for immeasurable distance from the first life on earth, he groped to Sabine and Berlin instead of Katharine and now. In the short daydream, Sabine frowned and turned her head sharply, then felt among the clothes on the floor for a cigarette. She told Ramsay she had had one abortion and would probably never marry. Later, she said she would travel and try a different husband in every country. She was not the doting German girl his father's crowd talked about in their anecdotes of the war. Her flat was shut up tight except when the janitor's wife came to clean and flung the windows wide. The janitor's wife was not concerned about Ramsay (who had not spent an entire night with a girl before) or Sabine dressed in two towels. "I saw a wild beast in the courtyard with black eyes, like an Italian," she said, scrubbing the sink. This was the only house on the street older than Ramsay, and the courtyard was full of rats and secrets. When it rained the courtyard smelled of ashes. Laughing about the janitor's wife and the Italian rat, Sabine stood naked before her mirror and said, "Look at how brown I am." One of her admirers had given her a sunlamp.

The first plant life on earth was spongy and weak; and the sun, in and out of clouds, sucked up every trace of color from Katharine Moser's hair and hand and eyes. He had seen color paler than Katharine's hand on angles of brick – was it paint splashed? Car lights washing by? There were no fissures in the brick, no space for fronds and stems, no room for leftovers. Why is brick ugly? Who says it is? Ramsay's father knows how much gravel per cubic centimeter is needed for several different sorts of concrete; he wrote his thesis on this twenty years ago, when he came back from the war.

"In Berlin," Ramsay started to say – something about bright weeds growing – but Katharine saw a magpie. "This is their season," she said. "They prey on fledglings." She told of the shrike, the jay, but he was thinking about the black, red-brown, smoke-marked courtyard in Berlin, and Sabine, shivering because she was suddenly cold, tender when it was too late, when there was no need for tenderness, asking what she considered serious questions in her version of English: "Was that all? Worth it? All that important?" She was not looking into space but at a clock she could not bother winding that was stopped forever at six minutes to three.

He and Katharine walked back to the lawn and the breakfast table, and she tipped her head like Sabine's, though not in remembrance of pleasure, only because the sun was strong again. She spoke to the cook's little boy, in straw hat and red shorts, pretending to garden; he was at their feet. Then behind and above them a branch rocked. It was Katharine's cat attacking a nest. The fury of the battle could be measured by the leaves rustling and thrashing in the windless day. A cat face the size of the moon must be over the nest; the eyes and the paws – there was no help for it – came through sunny leaves. The sky was behind the head. "Stop him, stop him!" Ramsay screamed like a girl or like a child.

"Pip! Naughty Pip!" She clapped her hands. "He's got one, I'm afraid." She was not disturbed. Neither was the cook's little boy, though he sucked his lip and stared up at the tree a moment more. "It is the cat's nature," she said. "Some things die – look at the spruce." (To encourage him.) "We think it is dying, but those fresh bits are new." The trees were devoured by something he did not understand – a web, a tent of gray, a hideous veil. The shadows netted on the breakfast table, on cups and milk and crumpled napkins, seemed a web to catch anything – lovers, stretched fingers, claws. He tried to see through Katharine's eyes: the cat had its nature, and every living thing carried a name.

"Do you notice that scent, Douglas? Does it bother you? It is the acacia flowering down the valley. Some people mind it. It gives them headaches. Poor Moser," she said, of her late husband, the conductor, who had died at Christmas and would have been seventy-four this summer. "When he began having headaches he thought all trees were poisonous. He breathed through a scarf. That was the form his fears took."

"It's only natural to be scared if you're dying," said Ramsay. He supposed this; until this moment he had not given it a thought.

"Old people are afraid," she said, as if she and Douglas were alike, without a time gap. (He had reckoned the difference in their ages to be twenty-five years.) "Although we'll know one day," she said, as if they would arrive at old age together. Lowering her voice, in case her adolescent daughter was spying and listening, she told how Moser had made her stop smoking. He did not want her to make a widower of him. He had chosen to marry Katharine because she was young, and he wished to be outlived. He was afraid of being alone. She, a mere child then, a little American girl nearly thirty but simple for her age, untalented, could not even play the piano, had been chosen by the great old man. But he forgot about being alone in eternity. "I told him," she said, putting the wild flowers in a glass of water on the breakfast table. "Unless two people die at exactly the same moment, they can never meet again." With such considerations had she entertained the ill old man. He had clasped her hands, weeping. His headache marched from the roots of his hair to his eyebrows, down the temples, around the eyes.

Ramsay was careful how he picked his way through this. For all his early dash and promise he was as Canadian as his father, which is to say cautious and single-minded. He had a mother younger than Katharine, who began all her conversations on a deep and intimate level, as if coming up for air was a waste of time. That made him more prudent still. He said, "Those the acacias?"

"The plum trees? They can't be what you mean, surely. That's the cuckoo you're hearing, by the way. If you count the calls, you can tell how many years before you get married. Peggy and Anne count the whole day." He considered the lunatic cuckoo, but having before him infinite time, he let the count trail off. The cook's small boy, squatting over one mauled, exhausted, eternally transplanted geranium, heard Ramsay and Katharine, but they might have been cuckoos too for all he cared. The only English words he knew were "What's that for?," "Shut up," and "Idiot." This child, who was a pet of Katharine's, lunched with the family. Until Ramsay had come, a few days ago, the boy had been the only man in the house. He sat on a cushion, an atlas, and a history of nineteenth-century painting, so as to reach the table, and he bullied and had his way; he had been obeyed and cherished by Katharine Moser and her daughter Anne; by fat Peggy Boon, who was Anne's friend; and by Nanette Stein, who was Katharine's. Now Ramsay was here, tall as a tree to the stooping child. When Ramsay said something to him, in French, he did not look, he went deaf, he muttered and sang to himself; and Ramsay, who had offered dominoes, and would have let the boy win the game, limped on up to the house, feeling wasted.

Peggy Boon, fourteen, too plump and too boring to be a friend for Anne – unless Anne, already, chose her friends for contrast – had been mooning about the lawn ever since the storm ended, watching for Ramsay to come up the path. She let him look at the Mosers' view a full minute, and then stepped round from behind a tree. She had been making up a poem, she said flutily. No one made up poetry; Ramsay had never seen anyone making up poems. He glared over her head. She stood there, straight of hair, small of eye, fat arms across new breasts she was flattening at night with a silk scarf – this information from Katharine, by way of Anne. She was an English rose, she feared silence, and pronounced her own name "Piggy."

"Everyone's out," she said, coloring deeply for no reason he cared to know. "Anne is playing tennis. I'm not keen ... so ... Nanette, well, I don't know *where* she is. She didn't say. Mrs. Moser went to visit the bees in case the thunder frightened them. She tells them everything. When Mr. Moser died she told the bees. She told them you were coming, and she's told them she is moving your things out of the house and into Mr. Moser's garden pavilion, and that you are his ... his ... " Unfolding her arms, stooping, she clutched at grass, as though weeding; she straightened up, she took courage, and announced, "*You* are Mr. Moser's spiritual heir." He was not listening to her. "If you don't tell the bees everything, Mrs. Moser says, they go away. But my mother," she added urgently, "says this is nonsense."

Like all English voices, hers sounded to him underdeveloped. He stared down at the cardigan, drooping and empty-armed, at the tight belt and bulging seat of what he supposed was a dainty frock. He had avoided one sort of Canadian girl all his life, and here was the pure, the original mold. He asked, "Did you know Adrien Moser?" It seemed impossible.

"Oh goodness, yes. This is the fourth time I've been here." She was gasping, as if he had splashed her with seawater. "I've been here a summer, and a Christmas, and an Easter, and *this* summer. Of course, he's not here now, is he?" If only Ramsay would say, "He must have been charming" – something like that. She pretended he had: "Oh he *was* charming! He used to do so many kind things. Once he offered to buy me a bicycle. I refused, of course. But imagine! He'd hardly known me five minutes then." Chewing on grass, airy and worldly now, she said, "I've been wondering.... No one's told me. Are you a composer?"

"I'm studying with Jekel in Berlin." And I am his best and strongest pupil, and if you knew anything you would know that, his mind continued. He had heard, for years, "Are you really only twelve? ... only sixteen?" The voices had stopped; no one is ever likely to say, "Are you really only twenty?"

"Don't you want a chair?" said Peggy, wiping the seat of one with her cardigan sleeve. "You're not supposed to stand too long. I've heard ... there's something wrong."

"Nothing's *wrong*. I was in a smash-up about two years ago, that's all. This girl was driving," he said. "It wasn't even her own car. There was all hell with the insurance. No one was killed."

"Oh, *good*." Having offered Moser's kindness, and had news of Ramsay's health, Peggy said, "Do you like Switzerland?" But she had lost him. Katharine Moser, with her cat in attendance, came toward them, smiling. The shadows that bent over her hair were cast by trees whose bark was like the skin of a snake. He had imagined another face for her; until a few days ago, he had known her only in letters. He had given her soft hair streaked with white, and humorous, intelligent eyes. His idea of a great man's wife was very near a good hospital nurse. Even now, when he thought, I am in Moser's house, he was grateful to the intelligent hospital nurse, who did not exist; at least she was not Katharine. Her eyes were green, uptilted. The straight parting in her hair was coquetry, to show how perfectly proportioned was her face. The only flaws he had seen were the shape of her nose, slightly bulbous at the tip, and the too straight body, which was a column for the fine head. The bees' scent, which clung to her hands and dress, was like incense. She was impressive, beautiful, fragrant, and until she lifted her arm to point to the pavilion where he would now sleep, and saw the skin of the arm, palely freckled, spotted, slack, he almost accepted her own idea of herself, which was that she was guileless, a child bride, touchingly young.

"I wanted to know you before I put you in the pavilion. You do understand why? It mustn't be a museum, but I want it kept alive just by people he liked, or might have loved. It's furnished with – What is it, Peggy?" The smitten girl was following them across the grass. Katharine watched Peggy Boon skip off (pretending joy) and become excluded. "That girl is having a rotten time. My daughter is so rude," she said, and sighed, and forgot all about it. "Now, Moser's bed and his tiled stove came from the curé's room in a château. I bought them at an auction."

He ducked his head to enter the pavilion. The first thing he saw was the piano, small and gaily colored, looking like the piano sometimes given a little girl for her first lessons. He could not see the name of the maker, which had been covered over with paint.

"Those engravings belonged to a fervent German monarchist who collected caricatures of the new rich, unaware that he was mocking himself. Moser liked objects that came from rich houses, providing they looked poor. He always thought he might die of hunger any day. He saved screws and tacks and elastic bands – you'll find boxes full of rubbish, all labelled. Moser told me that the walls of his family's house were covered with rugs they would not put on the floor, and that there were sheets over the rugs to protect them from light. I hope you will like your bed."

The bed was carved and bore a coat of arms and an angel's

head. The angel had a squint; Ramsay could not tell if it was looking reproachfully to Heaven or out of the window. The pavilion had been prepared in secret, while Ramsay was down in Montreux at a movie. He saw roses, a reading lamp, and then he saw the last photograph of the old man. The old man sat on a bench, in sunlight, holding a scarf. Katharine stood with one hand on his shoulder. Moser's eyes were wild and fixed.

"This is a great picture," he said, taking it up. "It was in the papers when he died. Someone in Berlin said it looked like a famous picture of Freud going into exile."

"I don't know what you mean by that. Moser was never in exile. He died in his native country." She shifted ornaments on the washstand. A shell porcelain soap dish was moved from the extreme left to the far right. The vase of roses took its place. "Now, there are things you can look at, if you want to. Testimonials. All the obituaries. Boxes of caramels – I found them after his last stroke. He loved them, but wasn't allowed to have any. When we found the empty boxes I knew he'd been eating on the quiet. I've kept them – I don't know why. This one wasn't opened." When she spoke of something she touched it. When she finished speaking she touched Ramsay's arm.

"Here's what they'll find after me," he said, and tumbled out of his pockets the marbles, the Yo-yo, and the sponge ball that were part of the reëducation of his injured hands. He was arrogant, he never doubted; it was a joke only in part. When Douglas Ramsay died, his Yo-yo and the plastic marbles would be placed on a shelf and labelled and dated, and dusted every day. He had never had parents; there was nothing behind him, nothing to come; the first plant life on earth had never existed; the cities would be reduced to mossy boulders; he would never have children; he would be mourned nevertheless. The curé's bed, Moser's bed, was Ramsay's bed. "How did he sleep in it?" they would say. "He was so big, and the bed is so small!"

The first night Ramsay spent in the pavilion a large moth brushed against his face. He knew it would not bite or sting, but its touch was pure horror, and his reaction uncontrolled. The moth was paper-white until it blundered against the pillow, and then he saw it was cream. Indigo eyes were painted upon its wings. He shot XEX out of the blue can Katharine had left for mosquito-killing. The battle the moth put up for its life now frightened him witless. It flapped its way under the bed. The frantic wings were louder than his heart. During the fight, scores of incidental casualties – gnats, midges, spiders, flies – dropped from the ceiling. He was afraid to open the window or the glass doors in case any more creatures came in, and he lay in the poisoned room blowing his nose all night long. He was on a mattress of straw that was just slightly too short. He was covered with tons of eiderdown. In his mind he had an image of his mended bones beginning to slip. If he got up now, he would not be able to stand. He could see, in moonlight, the paved terrace and the chair that had been the old man's. The pavilion was like another beehive, and the old man had been sent here, with a curé's bed and a doll's piano, and told something: "You will be alone in eternity." "Don't eat sweets." "If you think you are dying, ring that bell."

At a quarter to six the sunlight on the wall made a stately shadow of the roses. The sun was smaller than a marble. Hills and trees received its light at an angle that made them a single spongy substance. Birds were shrieking. Ramsay pulled the eiderdown up to his eyes, which left his feet bare. When he woke up two hours after this, he took inventory of the roses; there were four yellow, two pale pink, and two garnet, which were dying. These were probably sensitive – like him – to XEX. He had nothing better to do than count by color; he was in the grip of believing that he would fail, that he was ungifted, that his crushed body would betray him, and that the years of his life – fifteen out of twenty – involved with music were a waste. He had a premonition that he would be the victim of an inherited fault. His father should help him now. His father had willed his existence: he existed in his father's mind from the moment his father knew he had survived the Dieppe raid in the last war. This extra time, when Ramsay existed in desire, gave him a margin of safety. He felt as if he had been given a present of time; no one else had this. He would outlive everyone. Moser had wanted to be outlived. His father was better than Moser. His father would never have whimpered and breathed through a scarf. His father had a calm, closed, gentle disposition. Patience and endurance distinguished his face, which otherwise might have seemed boyish. If only his father had not depended on love, or on an ideal of what a woman must mean in his life; if only he had not been implicitly certain he could expect only good of women, that love was the constant survivor; if only he had let his wife leave him when she wanted to – but then, what about Ramsay? After his accident, his father had put something in a letter that he was too reserved to say when he came to see Ramsay in the hospital. (Where had he written the letter, and how had he slipped it out to the mail? From his office, probably. Ramsay's mother, having once tried to cast his father away, was now devoutly jealous – a wastebasket hunter, letter filcher, telephone spy. She thought his father's pocket diary was written in code.) His father wrote, "I suppose two things have bedevilled our life. First, that I am hideously shy and totally lacking inwardly in any confidence. Second (and this is fact, not fiction), that I've puzzled and puzzled over what happened in 1942, over the hundred-million-to-one shot that landed me back among living people when I had joined the dead. The greatest denial of death is to love as I always shall love you and your mother." Ramsay was too weak and too ill when he read it. He began to cry. They kept feeding him answers when he hadn't asked for anything. He would never say (though he thought it), "You both make me sick." There was still the early admiration for his father – not only for his unfaltering conduct but because of a childhood illusion that his father could, for example, look at the engine of a car and see what was wrong with it. And there was more – the conspiracy of two quiet men living in the same house with an intolerant woman.

As the sun above the dying spruce expanded, rose, became too brilliant to see, Ramsay surveyed his father's life and found it simple. "I love you" or "I don't love you" seemed puerile. His father had never had to cope – as Ramsay was doing – with doubts and terror and the possibility of lapsed genius. He had not even had to cope with a lot of women – only that one.

Owing to an exchange concluded with the enemy, Ramsay's father came back to Montreal about a year before the end of the war. He was part of a contingent of sick, wounded, and tubercular prisoners taken at Dieppe. Bonaventure Station received him. This was a dusty building with, on both the front and the back, a wooden porch that is called, in Montreal, a gallery. The paint on the gallery was scrofulous and diseased, and the station itself was the dark dry red that deflates the soul. It was at the foot of a steep hill; streetcars stopped before it after an awkward turn. For a long time the station had been used only for freight traffic, and then the Army took it over entirely. The Army put up cardboard squares with the letters of the alphabet so the next of kin would know where to wait, and assigned dozens of men to make sure the next of kin did not trample one another to death. Ramsay's mother was twenty-one. She sat under R for Ramsay the better part of a day, with her hands in the pockets of her camel-hair coat and her bare brown-painted legs stuck out straight before her. Ramsay knew, because she had told him, that there were no nylon stockings in those days, and that she wore her coat on a blazing hot day because of a guilty and confused desire to cover up. The men came through a door at the far end of the station, one by one.

His father appeared; swung his kit down from his shoulder; stared into the dark. It was like a monkey house by then, with the dirt of the place, and the stopped-up toilets, and the children frightened, and the women screaming. She pushed her way up to him and with her fists in her pockets said, "I don't want to live with you. I don't want to be married at all. I couldn't tell you while you were a prisoner. Anyway the censor might not have let it through." Some women took their husbands home and lay like corpses so the husbands could see for themselves the marriage was over, but Ramsay's mother wouldn't have that. She was fiercely honest and saw nothing the matter with manslaughter. In the slow-motion film of someone else's memory, Ramsay saw his father there, home, alive, yes, but in a sense never seen or heard of again. His father was Canadian-silent, Canadian-trained, and had to make an intellectual effort not to be proud. He struggled out of the station and walked up the hill beside his wife and sat down with her on a bench in Dominion Square. A Salvation Army band played "Lamb of God, Sheep of God," which was taken up by a drunk woman sharing their bench. His father was so stunned, so exhausted, he forgot his name. He forgot what he was doing here – forgot the name of his native city. His wife said he would be an invalid all his life. He heard her say she hated sick people, and had married too young. Yet at the end of the afternoon she led him home and turned out the girl whose apartment she shared. Why? Pity, she told Ramsay. No, said his father; it was justice, the power of love. Bonaventure Station was destroyed before Ramsay could see it. Most of the buildings his father and mother looked at when they were deciding his existence or nonexistence stand only on old post-cards and in their account of that day. The bed belonged to the girl turned temporarily out of the flat, and no one knows what became of her. She married some man, said Ramsay's mother, and they left Montreal.

Katharine Moser, companion of genius, generator of talent, dispenser of comfort, and mind reader as well, said, without leading up to it, "I suppose you were close to your mother?" They were in the car, and she was driving him he did not know quite where – to fetch drinking water from a spring, she said.

"I was closer to my father, actually" – this reluctantly. He pinched his lips together, for he had in his pocket one of his mother's long, self-justifying letters, jumpy with dates: "In January 1946," "Just after the Korean War," "When we met at Bonaventure" – that was the important date, when he was not conceived, was not present, was not even deaf, blind, and upside down. She defeated him by making him present on that occasion. He was still her witness, as if she had wanted nothing more than a witness. He saw her belted coat, her curly hair brushing the collar, her straight bare legs. He was afraid of contamination; his father's sweetness, his gentleness were in the blood. He knew – because many times told – how she had been persuaded. Victory for the man! Yet it was she who stood up abruptly, slung her handbag over her shoulder, and took him home to bed.

"You are so quiet – you live in music, I can see that," said Katharine, driving. "Do you have" – she sounded eighty-five and senile to him now – "time for girls?"

He had slept badly, and his legs were too long for the Mini-Minor. He edged slowly around so that he was facing her profile and, after the second's reflection in which he decided not to say, "Mind your own damn business," he suddenly told her about Sabine. He handed over Sabine, the slut, the innocent, the admirer of her own body, the good-natured, the stupid, the avaricious, the maker and seeker of love. The first woman he had spent a whole night with became an anecdote. He said, "Finally, she met an Arab prince. I mean a real one, in skirts. Jewelled dagger. He gave her some crappy bracelets that probably came from Hong Kong. She was excited. Every time you'd see her she'd be trying to write him a letter. But she made an awful mistake. When he left Berlin she said, 'Well, *shalom*.' She thought it was a kind of Middle Eastern '*Ciao*.' You know what the Arab said? He said, 'That's not exactly us.'" Ramsay's laughter was loud.

"And that wiped her out as a wife for you? Her *bêtise*?"

"I'm not looking for a *wife*." He wondered if she knew he was twenty and would have to live for a long time on grants and on the allowance his father gave him.

"Creative men should marry young. It stabilizes them."

What was she getting at? He looked at her calm profile, at her competent hands. She had the habit of opening and closing her hands as she drove, and slightly lifting her foot, so that the car, for a fraction of time, had to drive itself – though never long enough to take them off the road. He muttered about affinities and someone whose interests, whose mind and background …

"That's not marriage," said Katharine impatiently. "You didn't sleep with Sabine for her mind and background. Moser did his best work after he married me. I brought him back to the country, where he belonged. I made his life calm and easy, and kept him close to nature."

Owing to a mistake in time, he was having a conversation with a very young girl who was somehow old enough to be his mother.

"I would have thought that anything Moser did was separated from nature," he said. "He would have been what he was in a hotel room. In jail."

"Without the wind in the trees and the larks?"

Ramsay reflected that these had probably been a nuisance. Katharine's letters had been intelligent; she had used another vocabulary. If she had talked about the wind and larks, he would never have come. "I've explained it all wrong," he said, though he thought he had not. "I mean that everything he did was intellectual. He was divorced from nature by intention. Now do you see?"

"Nothing can be divorced from nature and survive." She looked angry, creased suddenly. He saw how she would be fifteen years from now. "Look at what has happened to music. To painting. It is the fault of people like you."

He should have let it go, but he was angry too. Who was she to attack him? She had invited him here; he had not arrived like a baby on the doorstep. When the old man died, Ramsay had written a polite and thoughtful letter to his widow, in care of the Swiss nation, and had been surprised to receive a warm embrace of an answer, in English. *She* had kept on writing; *she* had – the fine, and humorous, and courageous hospital nurse. (He forgot how it had pleased him, for once in his life, to play up to a situation, to pretend it was not over his head, to show off his opinions, pretending all the while to be diffident – to gather favor, to charm.)

If, at this moment, she was thinking, You are not what I expected, she was to blame. She was ignorant of music. She was the persistent artists' friend who inspires nothing but a profound lack of gratitude. He was feeling it now. He said, "Painters learn to paint by looking at pictures, not at hills and valleys, and musicians listen to music, not the wind in the trees. Everything Moser said and wrote was unnatural. It was unnatural because he was sophisticated." Her head shot round, and to her blazing eyes he said, bewildered, "It is a compliment."

They drove on in a silence that presently became unbearable. "Very soon it's too late," his mother had remarked, of quarrels. Her staccato letter jumped through his mind: "I said if you can't take a holiday when I need one I had better go without you. I shall go where there are plenty of men, I promise you that. He said, Go where you like my darling. I said, A woman like me shouldn't travel alone. I must have bitched up my life. He had the gall to say, All right I agree you've bitched it up but it wasn't all my fault. I was driving and I felt his crippled existence beside me and I thought mine might not be better. The weather is beautiful as it always is in Montreal when he is being impossible. There must be more accidents more murders more nervous breakdowns more hell in October and June. Where was I? Oh yes. When I got out of the car I saw he was crying. Pity for himself? Guilt over me?"

All at once Katharine parked sharply. Reaching behind her for a basket of empty bottles that had been rattling on the floor, she said (smiling to show they were friends again), "Is it true you have never seen a spring?" In an evil grotto a trickle of water squeezed out of the rock. A mossy stone pipe rested on the edge of a very old bathtub and dispensed a stream that overflowed the tub and ran deviously along a bed of stones, under a stone bridge, and out of sight. They stood, she worshipping, he blinking merely, each crowned with a whirling wreath of gnats. "I *own* this source," she said, and to his horror she immersed the bottles one by one in the tub. She filled each with typhoid fever, conjunctivitis, amoebic dysentery, blood poisoning, and boils. She capped them, smiling all the while, and put them back dripping in the basket; the basket was packed in the car, and they drove away.

Night after night he fought flies, midges, mosquitoes, and moths, most of which expired on his pillow or on the white bedsheet. They seemed determined to perish upon a white expansion – some mountaintop of their own insect literature and mythology – instead of going and dying in a corner where Ramsay need never see them again. One night a dying fly got in his wastebasket and thrashed and buzzed. Every time he thought it had stopped it began again. At luncheon next day he told how it had kept him awake.

"All you had to do was squash it," said Anne. She was tall, and still growing. She looked at him intently. The others seemed to concur – piggy Peggy (whom he had just interrupted) and Katharine and her friend Nanette Stein.

"Shut up," said the cook's little boy, but they turned to English now, putting a stop to Peggy's recital, in creeping French, of a visit she had made three days before to the market at Vevey. She rushed into English too: "There was nothing Swiss in Vivey, you know, nothing but vigitables." They were all sick of her. She was Anne's guest, but Anne had left her once again for the whole morning. "Time went so fast when you were away," Peggy went on calmly. "Goodness, it was half past ten before I knew *when* it was. I washed my green woolly and I wrote Mummy and Phyllis and I went for a lovely walk." A barely perceptible collective sigh went round the table, a collective breath of boredom. "I went farther and farther, straight on and up and on. The road was so steep! I thought, What if I should slip and fall? What a long way it would be! And so I turned and came back. I saw a herd of lovely Jersey cows, each wearing a bill, and I thought, How lovely! The biggest cow had the biggest bill, and the smallest one had the smallest bill. They made heavenly music."

"Bell?" said Nanette.

"Yes, bill," said the crimson child. "I thought, Goodness, why haven't I got a camera here?"

"I would have lent you a camera," Nanette said. "For such an original photograph."

Peggy's flush now seemed merely gratitude that the subject had been taken up. "If they don't move the cows, I could find them again easily."

"Aren't you afraid, going out alone among a herd?" said Nanette. She seemed subordinate, playing up to the others, and Ramsay wondered exactly what her role had been when the old man was alive.

"Not of cows, no, but actually as I went up and up I was thinking of that English lady who was waylaid and killed on a lonely road in Switzerland. It was near here."

"Never in Switzerland," said Nanette.

"And then there was that other one, a younger one. I

remember it. You know, knocked down and bashed about. I'm sure it was here. I thought, Well, there's no use hanging about here waiting for *that*."

"Men do attack girls," said Anne suddenly. The rest were uneasy, for now the ridiculous obsession had shifted from Peggy, who was a joke, to Anne, whom they were expected to take seriously. Peggy had touched an apprehension so deeply shared by the women that Ramsay felt himself in league with the cook's child, and suspected of something. For some reason, confirmation that she had been in danger made Peggy cheerful. She passed around a trunk key found on the road half an hour away from the house. No one claimed it, and so she dropped the key back in the pocket of her blazer and went skipping out of the house and across the lawn, fat and maddening, with Anne behind her. The others sat smoking, watching the pair through the dining-room window.

"I hope her holiday is a success this time," said Katharine gravely.

"It never will be," said Nanette. "This is as successful as life can ever be for that girl – going to stay with a friend and talking twaddle."

Katharine waited until she and Ramsay were alone. "I want to ask you something," she said. "A great favor. Would you be nice to Nanette? Pay attention to her? She's a lost, unhappy creature. She was a bright young pianist, though you wouldn't know it now. Moser encouraged her. Do you notice how Anne ignores her? About two years ago Nanette began writing to Anne, who wasn't quite thirteen. What could I do? Anne had often seen her here. But I didn't understand why Nanette should write every day to a child half her age." Moser was too old to be bothered. What Katharine had done, she said, was slip into her daughter's room and find Nanette's letters. Anne had gone out early. She found the letters easily; Anne had her father's Swiss neatness. She saved programs, menus, anything to do with herself. There was a narcissism about Anne....

"What happened?"

But Katharine would not be rushed. Her own upbringing, she said, had risen like a wave. She felt watched by her own mother, who would never have done such a thing. She almost put the letters back.

This, Ramsay thought, was a lie. Katharine had sat on her daughter's bed, like her mother before her, like his mother pursuing his father, and read methodically, smoothing the pages on her knee. What Katharine saw, she said (holding up thumb and finger joined, to show with what distaste she had invaded Anne's life, and how revolting the letters were), made her see that the correspondence must stop. She drove to Ascona to have a word with Nanette, who was discovered sharing a cottage with a gendarme Englishwoman. She described that too: the rage, the tears, the abject guilt. Katharine looked tolerant and sad.

"What's Nanette doing here now?"

"But she's a friend – an excellent person. Besides, Anne has outgrown her. I sent Anne to a school where her letters are surveyed. She needed English, and her manners wanted straightening out."

Reflecting on Anne's treatment of Peggy, he thought the school wanting. And he still did not see why Nanette should be here, in the house.

He started to write to someone back home, "Honest to God, the *radar* around here," but tossed it in his basket. When it disappeared from the basket, he remembered something his father had said about women's curiosity: "You can't leave a thing around. They *uncrumple* everything."

Nanette Stein was a slight woman of twenty-seven, with a small, squashed face and a fringe of curly hair that seemed to start up from the middle of her forehead. She watched Ramsay eating his breakfast, and asked fierce questions about the racial problem in America. She told him that when an African concert tour had been organized for her (and a lot of work it had been, Katharine put in, letting Ramsay know who had been the influence behind it), she had been asked to leave South Africa. She had been shunned by British women in Northern Rhodesia. She was proud of it. Music was a waste of time when you saw the condition of the world.

Katharine, shelling peas under a large hat, seemed grave and interested, and nodded without committing herself. Nanette had gone to Barcelona just to help a strike once. She had been arrested and conducted to the frontier. When she saw the mounted policemen, the horses, something in her, a revolt against injustice (she brought her fist down on the table, remembering), made her scream and curse and fling herself against them, pummelling the horses, swearing at the police.

"I know, they say you made a lot of noise," said Katharine mildly.

Ramsay's mind snapped off; he tuned them out. He could see how this would appeal to an extremely bright girl of twelve or thirteen. Katharine might have been wrong. Nanette had perhaps been proselyting impersonally, politically.

"I decided never to touch a piano again," said Nanette.

No one touched a piano here. He had expected it to be the house of music, but he heard only the very light quarrelling of women. The music room with its records and library of scores might have been surrounded with vines and brambles. Nothing had been added for years. When he asked Nanette to play for him one evening (his way of answering Katharine's request to be nice to her), she fetched a tape recorder and they sat in the garden listening to her repeating one movement of a Haydn concerto. When she stumbled she said "*Merde*," and that was the clearest part of the tape. He thanked her when she turned the machine off.

"It's about three years old," she said. "I was trying to make something decent for Katharine."

"Does she like music?"

Nanette looked completely scandalized, as if he had been angling for gossip. She scowled and said, "I don't know what either of them liked, finally. He was old when I met him. He came to a concert in Lausanne. It meant a lot to me. He never came out anymore. It was known he hated crowds and towns. If you wanted to play for him, you had to come up here, and then you might get a telegram at the last minute telling you not to come. He had something like asthma. Some days he lay gasping – there." She pointed to the chair where Ramsay sat. "He sat with a shawl over his knees, looking down at the lights of towns he never went to. I'd played the Prokofieff Second. I hardly dared ask what he thought. He said, 'Very pretty, my child, very pretty.' Pretty! It's so Swiss – everything is *joli*. But *she* fascinated me. She was in green, in a dress like a sari, with the black hair, and the eyes. I felt like a little provincial. She had so much more than anyone, and he was fine-looking, still. I never had seen a couple like them and never will again. And then she called me and said, 'We would like to see you again.' Oh, they were such a couple. People fell in love with them. And Moser – of course, he stopped doing anything here. All that wild grass was bad for his asthma. But *before*! He was a conductor and a teacher and . . ."

"I know."

"Look at them now. Look at your hero, Jekel, in Berlin. What does he write? A ten-minute opus every other year."

"Not my hero – my teacher." Ramsay was secretly reassured. He admired his teacher but did not mind hearing him attacked.

"My mother thinks activity is genius," he said, and smiled.

He was a bit dotty at the end," said Nanette, trusting Ramsay. She walked beside him with the docility of a little dog. As they passed the kitchen – Nanette staring straight before her and talking in a low voice – Ramsay turned and saw the face of the cook, which was frightened and haggard, and so exhausted that, although her eyes met Ramsay's, she did not see he was there. The kitchen was on the north side of the house, under a long balcony; a single light above the stove had already been turned on, and the cook moved toward it and became saffron-colored. "They dote on her little boy and spoil him," Ramsay said to himself, "but I have never even been told the cook's name."

"He was a bit touched, at the end," Nanette said. "He was fond of Peggy in a senile way, but she was so stupid she didn't seem to notice she was being pawed. He would offer to buy her presents, and she would simper and say no. Katharine was deathly afraid the child would tell her mother. That's why she's asked her back now; she wants to show it is a normal household."

"Did Moser like living here?"

"It was his house."

"You don't feel he lived here. That piano ..."

"He didn't need a piano. He used to go for walks and be lost or tired, and then he would get some farmer to ring her. She was always rushing off in the car to bring him home. She would find him sitting in a hot kitchen, and he would get in the car smelling of cabbages and cooked fat. His clothes reeked of farm kitchens, but that isn't to say he felt at home there either. He was never comfortable with country people. He would sit with his hands on his walking stick, waiting for Katharine. Katharine was foreign-looking, but she got to them. She would sit down, and she would just begin telling about herself and her bees, never asking questions. Why, I've seen farmers come to help her get a swarm back, and you know they don't bother about each other, let alone strangers. As for him, oh, presently he began to hate walking. And the doctor said he had to walk, he had so much wrong with him. She had to coax him out, bribe him with caramels – because he wasn't supposed to have them and they were a treat. 'Just one ten-minute walk,' I've heard her say, 'ten out, ten back, twenty minutes in all,' but he was too muddled to count. It was along here." She meant the path where stones were now hurting Ramsay's feet. He also was supposed to exercise, but he hated it. He trudged on with Nanette, counting ten out, ten back, twenty minutes in all. She plunged her hands in the pockets of her leather coat. Her Aberdeen Angus hair seemed to him touching. Old maid at twenty-seven, older than Katharine, she let her hands pull at the shape of her coat.

The old man was dragged for a walk along this road, Ramsay reflected, looking at the silken grasses he did not care to identify, though he knew they were not alike. Like Moser, he craved anything sweet. He would have gone to the village, but if he asked for the car, Katharine would know. She would have driven him, without reproach, but he did not want her to know. Ramsay saw the old man on a bench on this stony road with smuggled chocolate in his mouth. He broke off only one square and let it melt slowly. If the old man had chocolate, then he would look at anything she wanted – at fields and chalets catching the strong evening sunlight, and clouds going pink, and one cloud pressing like a headache on a peak. If he walked to the village – but that was impossible, he never would again, for it was thirty-five minutes down, even on the shortcut by the tracks, and nearly fifty back, because it was so steep. Perhaps she thought he was meditating here on the bench. He was huddled into his cape because the evening was suddenly cold. His intellect dissolved, his mind was like water, his powers centered only on the things to eat he was forbidden to have.

"This is where the picture was taken," Ramsay said, stopping before the bench. "The old man, with Katharine beside him. Now I know why he looked in exile. He had to go for walks, and he couldn't eat what he wanted. Like a kid."

Nanette looked at the bench too. "Everyone in music is

childish," she said. "Our mothers stand beside us when we practice, from the age of four."

"Somebody has to."

"Musicians live between their mothers and their confessors, forever and ever. If they lose them, they find substitutes. They invent them. *Marry* them. They marry one or the other. Always two in their lives, you'll notice. The mother and the confessor."

"No, it is not childish," Ramsay was saying to himself. "I know that *I* am not childish, I am older than my parents, but sometimes, even when I am not hungry ..." He stopped; it was too secret. Then, crossing his mind, unsummoned, came "cruelty." It was only a word, a tag on a tree; it was like Katharine's voice saying "larch," "spruce," "acacia."

"He should have been in a city," said Ramsay. "It's as simple as that. That mania he had for collecting, even. It's a clue. They are all things you use in cities – pieces of metal, paper clips."

"A simple case of thrift," said Nanette. "Very Swiss."

He looked down at her face. "Where's your home?" he said. "Where are you from?"

"I've told you. Ascona." Her face seemed smaller all at once. "All right. From Vienna. Before that, Poland. Now you know everything. If you want the whole truth, the real truth, he didn't like foreigners. He made horrible jokes about Jews in front of me, to see if I would laugh." All Nanette had done was apply a new name, just as Katharine had said grass was millet. Ramsay would see her now wearing a tag. They heard cowbells from the valley. "Katharine thinks they sound like Oriental music," she said, smiling miserably.

"Shows how much she knows about that."

But she would not follow up what she had been saying. Without meaning to, he had made her unhappy. She talked as if they had only just met, and began all over again about the racial question in the United States.

Ramsay had accepted the old man's bed, but the bath repelled him. He was glad when, one day, the taps ran nothing but rust and he was obliged to share one of the bathrooms in the house. He came into an early-morning house, with the cook stirring and the little boy eating bread on the stairs, and Nanette, encountered in the hall, wearing a striped bathrobe. Nanette had left the room full of steam and lavender. Wet washcloths festooned the tub. He removed a wire hanger holding six stockings, and, just before he turned the shower on, he listened to church bells and to thunder. Ten minutes later the lawn was obliterated by gray smoke. The tree where Pip had hunted was still. Over the thunderclap came more bells, as if to silence the sky. The wind rose all in a moment, and the first drops of rain were flung against the house. By the time he had finished shaving, soft silent rain fell from a bright sky. The air was cold. Birds sang, but the strongest sound was a brook. Now a voice covered it – Katharine's voice, complaining about last night's supper. "The soup was out of a can, the hamburger was cooked black, and I don't call half a slice of tinned pineapple on a bit of rusk a pudding. It really is unfair – I take the boy over entirely. I keep him out of the kitchen. You've got nothing to do but the meals. As for the salad, there was too much vinegar *and* too much oil. I don't know how you manage to have too much of both."

In the room where the young girls slept, light came through flimsy curtains. Ramsay, coming into the room, saw Peggy hunched, sheet up to her forehead, tufts of coarse fair hair showing like bristles. Her pillows were on the floor. Anne lay with a leg and an arm and a small breast outside the blanket. On the pillow a wreath of dead wild flowers was half crushed by her head. Her brown smooth face was lightly oiled. Watching the sleeping girl, he knew what he could be capable of, provided she loathed him, or was frightened of him. Better fear than hate. When he touched Anne her breathing changed; he thought he saw a gleam between her lashes. Watching, she made no move. She was waiting to see what could happen. Outside, Katharine called, "Pip, Pip!," beating her hands. Peggy awoke and, with a rapidity he would never have thought possible in the dull girl, sat up and looked. There they were, Anne cold and excited, her heart like a machine under his hand, and Ramsay the vivisectionist, and poor Peggy, who had been in love.

To amuse Ramsay, Katharine now organized excursions. She took them to restaurants where they lunched sitting on balconies brilliant with roses, where she ordered the food with frowning care, putting on her glasses to read the menu, suggesting and planning for them all. She had noticed that he was greedy. She watched him, sagely and fondly. She had wakened something – perhaps only a craving for strawberries and cream – she later intended to curb. Nanette looked at her, and at Ramsay, and began having headaches, and finally dropped out of their party altogether. She looked dark and wretched when she was left behind. "The truth is, she gets carsick," said Katharine, as if some other excuse had been offered and was a lie. The young girls looked through Ramsay and round him and not much at each other. They played an acquisitive game called Take It Home and fought over museums, ancient jewelry, ski lifts, whole restaurants, a view, a horse, other people's cars, but stopped short of people. Peggy was pink with joy at being included, but Ramsay knew that she, and not Anne, had been scared to death that morning in their bedroom.

After these excursions he was stiff and sore, and could hardly move his arms and legs at night or turn in bed. His memory of each day was of eating and drinking beer on blowy terraces and of parasols knocked down by wind. Katharine took him to see a famous church treasure, and to Zurchers for tea, where they sat next to Noël Coward, and to Lausanne for an exhibition of French sculpture and painting. She brought the cook's child this time, and the two girls went to a movie. Katharine wore her glasses, and looked at the catalogue in her hand before examining any of the paintings. The two men of the household walked one on each side of her. Ramsay, shut up in a series of large rooms full of paintings, rid of three out of four of the women, began to breathe.

"These Impressionists," he began. "They seem kind of tied to their wives, you know what I mean. They were limited to their wives' gardens. You feel they all had something wrong with them and that the wife was waiting with a cup of tea and some medicine." Katharine glanced at him. That had been her role, and she knew that he knew it.

"Sit down, Douglas," she said, suggesting the circular sofa in the middle of the room. "You must be tired, after all this walking around. There is nothing more tiring than looking at things that don't interest one."

Ramsay found himself sitting and looking at the headless statue of an adolescent girl. He looked at the small breasts, slightly down-pointed. The hips were wider than the chest, the legs columns. A piece of bronze, he told himself. No one had ever been like that. He put Anne's head on the bronze neck, and presently was conscious of being watched. It was the boy, who was running round and round the sofa. The little boy circled closer. He sat down, and Ramsay smiled into what seemed an open face. The child breathed something difficult to hear. He pointed at Ramsay (and he had to bring his hand all the way from a far place to do so; he liked great gestures). He breathed again – something that sounded like "Idiot."

"What?"

"Idiot," the child said. The index finger still pointed; the arm was a soft arc.

"Who?"

"*Vous*."

Ramsay stared down at him in fury and outrage. "Idiot, am

I? What do you think you are? You supposed to be clever?"

The child did not understand English, but he understood the tone. A mistake had been made; he had been bolder than he intended. "You, for instance," said Ramsay. "What are you supposed to be? *Tu n'es pas un peu idiot?*"

"*Moi, je suis gentil,*" said the child, sliding off the sofa and beginning to back away. His face trembled. He said "*zentil,*" but this evidence of his age – his inability to pronounce some letters – did not endear him to Ramsay, who rushed on, "You're a rude little bastard. *Gentil!* You're a little bastard, that's what you are."

From the safety of Katharine, the child looked boldly back. What a fool I've been, Ramsay thought. Of course the child had not remarked he was looking at the statue of an adolescent girl and thinking spellbound thoughts about Anne.

Peggy wants to go back to England," said Katharine, and sighed.

"But she hates her family," Nanette protested.

"She may not know she does."

"She's fourteen and old enough to admit that her father isn't a god and her mother an angel," said Nanette.

"That is true." Katharine bowed her head with simulated meekness.

Anne appeared, with wet hair plastered on her cheeks. She washed it daily. She was struggling with a pullover. "Are you talking about me?" she said as her head emerged. "I thought I heard my name. Peggy is packing, by the way." She plunged down on the grass at their feet and said, "We've decided she's leaving because I've been so awful to her."

"I shall speak to her," Katharine said, looking oddly like the woman Ramsay had imagined before he ever saw her.

"I have been awful to her," said Anne. "You won't make her change her mind."

"It is the same story every time she comes here," said Katharine. "That wretched girl always threatens to leave because of some nonsense she has imagined. It used to be – " Nanette stopped her. "Now it is Anne she complains of," Katharine said.

"I want to see you alone," said Anne to her mother casually, "when you've finished with Peggy."

Katharine was already walking across the lawn, in her striped dress, in an old, large straw hat, with all her bracelets rattling. Throughout this exchange Ramsay might as well have been invisible. The group was disintegrating. The cook's child no longer came to lunch. Ramsay could observe all he liked now, for there was no one to catch him at it. Even the old man's phantom had vanished. Ramsay no longer saw or felt him, demanding chocolate, querulous and lost, too cosseted, smothered, destroyed. "Yesterday," said Nanette's small radio, "was the hottest twenty-second of June since 1873." Ramsay isolated three birds by sound: one asking a question, one cackling derisively, one talking to itself in a conversational tone.

Picked out in the headlights, a badger crossed the road, steadily, like an enormous dachshund. It turned and looked into the lights, and Ramsay, sitting next to Katharine, experienced the revulsion he felt in the presence of animals and wild creatures in particular. They had taken Peggy to the airport at Geneva and there – as at the exhibition of French paintings – he had felt completely himself and at home.

Back at the chalet was the incomprehensible language of birds, and the cat with its savage nature, and the cannibal magpies, the cannibal jays.

"If we park here, the car will be in shade tomorrow," he said.

"No, the trees are on the wrong side," Katharine said.

"There must be some shade, no matter which side they're on."

"You would have thought that after years of this, they would either have enlarged the garage," Ramsay remarked to himself, "or built another, or figured out which side of the trees received the morning sun." The car lights were put out, and flashlights distributed. Larch branches pressed on the car windows, white in the night. Katharine sat as the others – Anne and Nanette – got out. Ramsay, holding the door for her, shone his flashlight on her face.

"Do you think much about that girl in Berlin?" she said.

No. He thought of his mother in a camel-hair coat, her legs thrust out, staring straight before her. He said, "Most of the time I never think about her."

"Anne had a conversation with me today," she said. His stomach contracted; his hands were without strength. He released the switch of the pocket light. "Never mind about it," said Katharine. "There's a moon. Anne wants to go to Ascona with Nanette this week. She wants to stay all July. She and Peggy have funny holidays – school in August."

"Are you letting her?"

"Why not?" she said, without looking at him. "She wants to get away from home, which is normal. I told her she could go wherever she liked. She is old enough. I can't …"

You can't read her mail forever, he thought.

"What are your plans, Douglas? You can stay as long as you like. I feel there have been too many people around. We've never had a real conversation, have we? I'm afraid you'll have to put up with my cooking in July. I've fired the cook."

The cuckoo, at daybreak, was an interruption to his sleep. He saw the notes – not as notes of music but as a new kind of shorthand. He did not know enough of the shorthand to read the notes, or enough of the new language to reply. He dreamed that everyone was skeletal, while he had got enormously fat. He got up and dressed – by flashlight, to avoid doing battle with insects – and packed, not caring much what he left behind, and stepped out into the garden. Across the front of the house was a carved inscription, naming the builder, and giving a date – 1780 – and reminding Ramsay, or anyone who stopped to read it, that death waits for life. The motto did not belong to this chalet but came from another region. Katharine had bought it and put it there about a year before Moser's last stroke. The chalet – like a bison, like a bear – watched him slip and slide down the path with his two suitcases. He sat down in the station shelter in a state of such lunatic joy at his deliverance that presently he was close to tears.

At the pension he went to in Montreux, a tall, dignified woman wearing a white apron greeted Ramsay. His cases were put in an ice-cold room with a linoleum floor. He looked through the north window at another pension, then at the varnished bed, the eiderdown, the table, and the clean, unironed checked cloth. A small Buddha, the only ornament in the room, sat on the chest of drawers. Ramsay picked him up, but no matter how he tried he could not catch Buddha's eye.

"That was left behind," the woman said, "by a Professor Doctor. The meal hours are eight, twelve, and seven. Breakfast in your room will be fifty centimes more. With the prices we charge we cannot afford extras." From the kitchen came a crash of plates and loud cursing. When that died away he heard the soft silent crunching, like silkworms feeding, that came from the dining room, where the others were all at breakfast.

The first thing he unpacked was the unopened box of caramels: Caramels à la crème de Gruyères. He tangled with the Scotch Tape and pulled the box open. It's only fudge, he thought. He did not know what he had been expecting. He ate half the box – Moser's legacy – and felt sick, and drank tap water. "Good thing I left," he told himself, realizing indignantly what he had been driven to. By now they would know he had gone. He had left them up there with the cat and the cannibals. He was down where there were signs of life and work. He found one of the signs in a drawer, left by the Professor Doctor – a drawing of a naked and faceless woman wearing a pearl necklace. At ten he went to a film and watched a pretty German girl mixed up with some man who looked like a toad. But they were all so comfortable and so well dressed, and their problems were real problems, such as money lost and found. He could not sit in the cinema forever, but first things first: his room in the students' residence in Berlin was taken by someone else until July. He said, "Look here, Katharine, I'm not interested in weather and the color of the sky. I hate knowing what the weather is. I don't know what you mean by having inner resources. Are you supposed to recite poems from memory while the whole world dissolves into fog, goes away, and stays gone?" He blinked at the sleepy noon streets, the petunias in tubs, the brown balconies with washing under the eaves. He bought a newspaper and saw a prime minister wearing a miner's helmet. In the middle of the front page, boxed to show its importance, was this:

LES PREMIÈRES FRAMBOISES

Les premières framboises mûrissent
sur la rive droite de la vallée.

He translated everything except "*mûrissent*," which he could have sworn he had never seen before. He substituted for it "have exploded," which gave the item some stature. He did not know what he was doing here, unless he was waiting for

Katharine to come and find him. In the pension dining room he was the victim of provincial staring, because of his youth and his limp. There came the memory of the months he had spent after his accident completely at the mercy of other people, depending on nurses and resenting it. He had always been active, had lived on decisions; he remembered how his parents had respected him, let him make his own choices about what he would study and the life he would lead. He ate steadily grated carrots, meat, potatoes, wet salad, gray bread. A bowl of custard was placed beside him. He spooned some of it onto his plate, where it ran everywhere. Since the orgy of caramels sweets disgusted him. He dreaded the mattress in his room, but it was only for a night. In the morning he would take the train to Zurich and from there fly to Berlin. His room there was taken, and his girl had vanished – she was too old for him anyway. "Listen, Sabine," he had said, "is the guy really a prince?" "No, only his bodyguard. But I ruined it anyway with '*shalom*.'" Ramsay laughed. "Is not funny," Sabine said. She showed him what remained of the railway station where both her parents were killed. "Who cares?" she said, meaning "Do you?"

Two days later he was still there. He looked at the sky, the blue on the horizon, the gray, then the pink. When he entered his room, mist arose outside the window as if it had been lying waiting for him to approach. One night in the dining room he started up from the table, thinking she had come. Katharine in her silk dress could save him from everything mediocre, commonplace, vile, and poor. The room was filled with solemn English couples; the women wore heavy white shoes and yards of stoles. Katharine might enter this room, warm and inquisitive, as if it were a new experience. It was not new: "He used to go for walks and be lost or tired, and then he would get some farmer to ring her." In the pension dining room, television accompanied their supper. Chairs were arranged so that everyone faced in the same direction. A girl who looked like Sabine lay on a piano and sang. Every few seconds, though the song continued without interruption, the girl wore different clothes. Now she stood with her hand on the pianist's shoulder; he looked up into her eyes, and the pair posed that way. The screen went blank, but the sound continued. They listened to a chorus from *West Side Story*, in a foreign language. Everyone looked at the empty, glowing screen, across which sticks and marbles moved, ran together, parted. Faces were lifted, for the set was high on a corner shelf. Again he thought Katharine had arrived. Nothing had happened. The screen had not changed, and the sound was nearly gone.

Early in July, in his old room in Berlin, Ramsay opened the letters that had been kept for his return. There was a letter from Katharine, written at the end of May, that must have arrived the day he departed for Switzerland. The great conductor's widow wrote that now the rain had stopped. She had seen young Italians in spotless shirts hanging about waiting for the cinemas to open – their Sundays were sad. On the promenades, by the lake, in the towns, couples are strolling. The sky changes color; the girls' white skirts are flattened against their legs. The lake is harsh-looking. The wind shakes the trees. Flower petals are strewn on the grass, and it is like the end of a season instead of the beginning. This was a letter written before she had ever met him. He felt buoyant and lightheaded tearing it to shreds. He was amazed at how simple it became. He was not sure if he had left Sabine, for example, or if she had rejected him. She had said, "Oh, I like you, but now is enough," spitting grape seed into her palm; but Ramsay had his ticket to Switzerland, bought that very day. What his father would like would be to start again, to arrive at Bonaventure, but how can he? The station is no longer there. "Lamb of God, Sheep of God," sings a woman, and the Sally Ann band is nearby. Very attractive, very nostalgic, he said to the remains of Katharine's letter, but what about the pension and the smell of mediocrity? What about your cook in the kitchen, with frightened eyes? We drove slowly, crawling, because Katharine had seen a white orchis somewhere. Did anyone dare say this was a waste of time? The orchis was a straggly poor thing with sparse anemic flowers.... Surely he had passed a test safely and shown he was immune to the inherited blight?

Only afterward did he think that he might be mistaken, but that day, the day he arrived in Berlin, he was triumphant because he sat with his back to the window and did not know or care what the weather was like outside.

VIRUS X

A bunch of holly hanging upside down at the entrance to her hotel was the first thing Lottie Benz saw in all of Paris that seemed right to her. Even a word like "hotel" was subject to suspicion, since it was attached to a black façade in no way distinguished from the rest of the street. The people walking on the street did not look as if they had sisters or brothers or childhood friends, and their clothes and haircuts in no manner indicated to her a station in life. The New Look had spread from this place, but none of the women appeared to have given it a thought. As for the men, alike in their gray raincoats, only their self-absorbed but inquisitive faces kept them from seeming unemployed. Lottie, whose mother had made the dress she was wearing from a Vogue pattern, could have filled the back seat of her taxi with polka dots, the skirt was so wide. Stepping down, she shook order into the polka dots and her mother's ankle-length Persian-lamb coat, lent for the voyage. That was when she saw the holly. Even as the taxi-driver plucked every bit of change from her outstretched hand, she turned to this one familiar thing. A city that knew about holly would know about Christmas, true winter, everything.

That day, which was Tuesday, December 9, 1952, was laid on with a light brush. The street had been cut out of charcoal-colored paper with extremely fine scissors. Lottie had come here out of a tempest of snow. She drew a breath of air that seemed mild – her first breath of Paris. It swept into her lungs and was immediately converted into iron. She withdrew her hand, relieved of its francs, and pressed it against her chest.

Two boys passed her, walking in step, without a glance at Lottie stranded, the taxi grinding out and away, or the bags the driver had dumped upon the curb. One boy said to the other, in an American accent, "If people depress you, why do you bother seeing them?" The iron weight shifted as she bent to pick up her suitcases. An old man in porter's uniform watched Lottie through the frosted glass door. His eye appeared as part of the pattern of lilies etched on the glass, and then his nose. He consented to hold open the door. Lottie offered him a tip, which he pocketed. She had been advised to tip for consideration, however slight, no matter how discourteously shown. In a place where Americans were said to be hated because of the Korean War, she intended to put up a show for her own country, which was Canada. She smiled. The hotel, or France, personified by the woman at the desk with frizzy red hair, did not care. Lottie conveyed with a second smile that it was of no importance.

For the first time in her life she was compelled to put her name to a police questionnaire. Bending over the form, she wrote "Charlotte Maria," and wanted to put "Lottie" in brackets, but there was no room. Her home address – the Princess Pat Apartments, in Winnipeg – also seemed to want explaining. She could have written reams of explanation about everything, had there been space. She imagined a policeman reading her answers attentively. Next to "Profession" she wrote "none yet." The woman with frizzy hair made her cross this out and write "student" in its place. Lottie gave up the questionnaire, and with it her new blue passport.

Three messages awaited her. First, a letter from her mother, written four days before Lottie left home. Though sent with loving intention, so that Lottie would have news the instant she arrived, it contained no news. As for Kevin, he had cabled, "MISS YOU ALREADY LOVE," a few hours after her plane took off. Supposing he discovered twenty hours later that he did not miss her at all? She examined the cable gravely. The last message was from a girl named Vera Rodna. It welcomed Lottie to Paris, and gave a telephone number. Upstairs, in her ice-cold, beige-colored hotel room, Lottie tore all three messages across, then found there was no wastebasket.

A sunbeam revealed dust on the window and dust on the floor but, curiously, none in the air. (Perhaps in this place they deliberately allowed dust to settle. Was this better? Better for Lottie – for her asthma, her chronic bronchitis, her fragile lungs?) The bed, the cupboard containing a washbasin, the wardrobe that contained one bent wire hanger were all clean. There were no pillows, window shades, towels, or drinking glass. There were any number of mirrors, however, evenly shaded with dust, and velvet curtains that she accepted as luxurious.

Wondering why she was noticing so much, checking herself lest she become introspective or moody, she remembered that this was the first time she had ever been anywhere alone. The notes she was taking mentally were for future letters – the first to Dr. Keller, her thesis director, the second most likely for Kevin. She unpacked her new cake of Palmolive, her toothbrush, her unworn dressing gown with rose-pink petal neckline. A hot bath, she learned, from a notice posted on the back of the door, would cost three hundred and sixty francs, which was more than a dollar. Lottie was to live on a Royal Society scholarship, supplied out of Canadian funds frozen abroad. Any baths from now on would be considered pampering. She intended to profit from this winter of opportunities, and was grateful to her country for having provided it, but in no sense did she desire to change or begin a new life.

By Sunday the weather in the street was the weather of

spring. The iron of the first breath had disintegrated, vaporized. At the bottom of her lungs was a pool of mist. She reminded herself that back home the day had not begun. The city she had left was under snow, ransacked by wind, and on the dark side of the globe. She was not homesick.

Vera Rodna, whose message had so quickly been turned into paper scrap, came to the hotel one day when Lottie was visiting the "Mona Lisa." She left a new letter, this time asking Lottie to come to lunch, and she indicated the restaurant with a great X on a map. "*Une jeune fille très élégante*," the frizzy redhead down at the desk remarked. Lottie had to smile at that. No one here could know that Vera was only a girl from Winnipeg who had flunked out of high school and, on a suspicion of pregnancy, been shipped abroad to an exile without glamour. Some of the men in her family called themselves Rodney, and at least one was in politics. End syllables had been dropped from the name in any case, to make it less specifically Ukrainian. Vera had big hands and feet, a slouching walk, a head of blond steel wool. The nose was large, the eyes green and small. She played rough basketball, but also used to be seen downtown, Sunday-dressed, wearing ankle-strap shoes. Vera had made falsies out of a bra and gym socks – there were boys could vouch for it. In cooking class it turned out that she thought creamed carrots were made with real cream. She didn't know what white sauce was because they had never eaten it at home. That spoke volumes for the sort of home it must be.

Lottie accepted Vera's invitation, though there was no real reason for them to meet. Having been raised in the same city did not give them a common past. Attempting to impose a past, beginning with a meal in a restaurant, Vera would not establish herself as a friend from home, if that was what she was trying to do. But Vera, being Ukrainian, and probably no moron in spite of her scholastic and morals records, would have enough sense to know this.

The restaurant was an Italian place on the Rue Bonaparte. Wavy, sooty dust masked the wall paintings except for a corner where someone had been at work with a sponge. There Vera waited, backed up by frothing geraniums and blue-as-laundry-bluing seas. Ashes, Sunday papers, spilled cigarettes, and bread crumbs gave her table the look of an unswept floor. Vera's eyes tore over Lottie, head to foot, gardenia hat to plastic overshoes. She said, in a full voice that all at once became familiar and a second later had never been forgotten, "Well, this is great. Sit down."

"This is very nice," said Lottie neutrally.

"It's not bad. I've tried most of them."

Lottie had not meant the restaurant but the occasion of their meeting. Vera began to wave at a waiter and also to talk. She sloshed wine from a bottle that was nearly empty into a glass that seemed none too clean, and pushed this at Lottie. "Some rich bastard's Chambertin," she said. "Might as well lap up the dregs."

Lottie lifted the glass and sipped, and put it down forever, having shown she was game. She said, "How did you know I was in Paris, Vera?"

"My mother, from my sister Frannie. Fran's in your father's math-and-Latin. She's smart – makes up for me."

The name Frannie Rodna conveyed nothing, and Lottie accepted with some pride and some melancholy that she was now part of an older crowd.

"By the way, what are you doing here, exactly?" Vera asked. She was dressed in a black-and-brown checked cape, and a wool hat pulled straight down to her eyebrows. She may have been quite smart by local standards, which undoubtedly she knew about by now, but Lottie could not help thinking how hunkie she looked. Vera's crocheted gloves fell off the table. Her hands looked as if they could easily deal with the oilier parts of a motorbike. "Whadja say?" said Vera, after fishing round for her gloves.

"I *said*, Vera, that my *professor*, Dr. *Keller*, is *from* Alsace, and that's the reason I'm going there. My thesis is about the integration of minority groups without a loss of ethnic characteristics."

"Come again?" Vera's elbows were planted in ashes and crumbs. She turned from Lottie to deal with the waiter, and ordered an unknown something on Lottie's behalf.

"Like at home," Lottie said, when the waiter had left. "Vera, you do know. That's the strength of Canada, that it hasn't been a melting pot. Everybody knows that. The point is, I'm taking it as a good thing. Alsace is an example in an older civilization. With Dr. Keller's contacts in Strasbourg ... Vera, don't stare just on purpose; I do find it unpleasant. I'll give you a simple example. Take the Poles." Delicacy with regard to Vera's possible feelings prevented her saying Ukrainians. "The Poles paint traditional Easter eggs. Right? They stop doing it in the States after one generation, two at most. In Canada they never stop. Now do you see?"

Vera was listening to this open-mouthed. Lottie felt she had sounded stupid, yet the idea, a favorite of Dr. Keller's, was not stupid at all. She knew it was a theory, but she was taking it for granted that it could be applied. If it could not, let Vera prove it. Vera closed her mouth, drew her lips in between her teeth, let go her breath, and when all that was accomplished said, "You crazy or something?"

"Think whatever you like."

"Do you even know what a minority is?"

"I ought to," said Lottie, and she took the bread and began peeling off the crust, after cracking its surface with her nails.

"You don't. It was always right to be what *you* are."

"Oh, was it, now?"

An explanation for Lottie's foolishness suddenly brightened Vera's face. She clasped her hands, her big mechanic's hands, and cried, "Keller's in love with you! He's meeting you in Alsace."

"He's got a wife and everything. Children, I mean. Honestly, Vera!"

"I think everybody's in love," said Vera, and indeed looked as if she thought so. "Who is it, then? Still Kevin?"

"Yes, still."

"You're going to be away, in Alsace or someplace? That's taking a chance." She seemed to be fumbling over something in her mind, perhaps a memory of Kevin. "I guess you needn't worry," she said. "You've kept him on the string since you were sixteen. You'll bring it off."

"What do you mean, Vera, 'bring it off'?"

Vera looked as if Lottie should know what she meant. A platter of something strange was placed between them. Vera dug into a bone full of marrow, extricated the marrow, and spread it over a mound of rice. It might have been dog food.

"Delicious," said Vera with her mouth full. "Know one thing I remember, Lottie? You used to choose the meals at home, and your brothers had to eat whatever you happened to like. That's what they told around, anyway."

Lottie, surprised at Vera's knowing about this, said, "Everybody favors girls."

"Boy, my father didn't," said Vera. "He kind of respects me now, though. Your father used to scare me even more than my own. His voice was just a squeak when he got mad. You could hear every word, but the voice was up around the ceiling. When he told my father I wasn't college material, and not even high-school material, his voice sounded artificial. You take after him a little, but your voice just gets slower and slower. Your father was a fine man, all the same. Old Captain Hook."

Mr. Benz had been called Captain Hook by his pupils, but there was a further matter, which Vera did not mention – Captain von Hook. That was an old wartime joke. You would have thought the mean backwash of war could never have reached them there, in the middle of another country.

Lottie said with slow care, "How is your brother, Vera, the one who went into politics? Wasn't there some kind of row about him? Honest Stan Rodney?"

"Honest slob. Listen, what are you doing over Christmas? I'm going to Rome. I've got this friend there. He's from home, but you don't know him. He's a Pole. Far as I know, he doesn't paint any Easter eggs. I used to think he was a spy, but he turned out to be a teacher. Slav lit. *When* he's working. Boy, the trouble *he* gets into." Vera's admiration for the trouble made her go limp. "Do you want to do something in Paris before I go? See a play or something? You've been up the Eiffel Tower, I suppose. I like going up and looking down. You see this shadow like a kind of basket, when there's any sun. There's Versailles and that. Euh, Fontainebleau ... boring. Katherine Mansfield's grave, how about that? Remember Miss Pink? She fed us old Mansfield till it ran out of our ears. She's buried around Fontainebleau. Mansfield is, not Miss Pink." Vera laughed with her mouth wide.

"She was my favorite author until I specialized," said Lottie primly. "Then, I'm sorry to say, I had to restrict my reading."

Vera dug into her rice as if looking for treasure. "Right," she said. "We'll go out to the grave." Lottie consented to nothing of the kind.

Vera must have mistaken Lottie's silent refusal, for the next Saturday, at half past ten, she turned up while Lottie was still in bed.

Lottie had been out with a cousin of Kevin's, who worked at the Embassy. He had made her pay for her own drinks, as if they were still students having cafeteria coffee. Lottie was puzzled by the bar he took her to, full of youngish American men, and even more by the hateful, bitter singer at the piano. Kevin's cousin seemed to feel that she had no right to criticize anything, having only just arrived, though he himself never stopped complaining. His landlord was swindling him; he was sick of dark rooms and gas heaters. He blamed Paris for its size. Until now he had lived in a house, never in a flat. His accent shot from one extreme of broad vowels to the opposite. He did not want to sound American but looked it. In the bar full of crew cuts, he matched any one of them except in assurance. Toward the end of the night, he began bemoaning his own Canadian problems of national identity, which Lottie thought a sign of weakness in a man. Moreover, she learned nothing new. What he was telling her was part of Dr. Keller's course in Winnipeg Culture Patterns. She had wasted the government's money and her own time.

Vera said she was leaving for Rome, which she called Roma, any minute. Slumped over an ashtray on the foot of Lottie's bed, she urged an excursion to Fontainebleau. It was a lovely sunny day – just the weather for visiting graveyards. Sleepy and pale, caught with curlers in her hair, Lottie rose and dressed, turning her back. Vera scarcely allowed her time to brush her teeth. They were doomed to catch, and they caught, the Lyon noon express. The train was filled with *hommes d'affaires*, who had all the seats. Lottie stood crushed against a window, looking at the backs of towns. She was cold, and speechless with hunger. After Melun she began to feel calmer, and less hungry and unwashed. Trees such as she had never seen before, and dense with ivy, met and glided apart in the winter light. Touching the window, she felt a thin cool film of sunlight. The ivy shone and suddenly darkened, as if a shutter had been swung to. Lottie forgot she had asthma, chronic colds, low blood pressure, and that Vera would regret this.

"I always thought I was going to die at the same age as Mansfield," she remarked to Vera. "I may still."

"Not the same way."

"At my age, you already know what you're going to die of." Lottie was thirteen months older than Vera, who would be twenty-one in February. Unspecified illnesses of a bronchial nature had kept Lottie out of school for months on end. A summer grippe only last August had prevented her coming over here in September.

"You used to wear those hand-smocked dresses," Vera suddenly chose to recall.

"A friend of Mother's made them," said Lottie, and closed a door on that with her tone of voice. Though ignominiously clothed then, she had been small for her age, and almost unnoticeable in the classes of children younger than herself. She skipped grades, catching up, passing, but no one praised her. They said Captain Hook had helped.

Vera explained her commitment to Mansfield, which was an old crush on Miss Pink. It had led Vera to read this one writer when she never read anything else, or wanted to. Now that she was away from the Miss Pinks of this world, she read all the time.

Lottie's transparent reflection was ivy green. "Do you think I look weak?" she asked, meaning that she wanted her health kept in mind.

Vera, who was tall, caught Lottie's face at an angle Lottie had never seen. "Weak, in a way," she said, "but not frail." Lottie's reflection went smug. Vera, squinting down and sideways, looked as if she thought weakness could not account for everything.

When they alighted at the station, Vera consulted a taxi-driver, whose head was a turtle's between muffler and cap. Showing off in French, she seemed to think the driver would think she was French and take them to a gem of a restaurant. Lottie felt cold and proud. She would not mention her low blood pressure. Actually, she was supposed to drink tea or coffee almost the minute she wakened; her mother usually brought it to her in bed. She had never fainted, but that was not to say she never would. Their driver rushed them up a dirt road and abandoned them before a billboard upon which was painted in orange "RESTAURANT – BAR – DOLLARS ACCEPTED – PARKING."

"We aren't going to like it," said Vera. "He took you for an American." Nevertheless, she rushed Lottie onward, through a room where an American soldier slept in a leather armchair, past a bar where more soldiers sat as if Saturday drinking were a cheerless command, and into a totally empty dining room that smelled of eggs frying. Not empty: out of the dim corner where he was counting empty bottles came the proprietor of the place, unshaven, clad in an American gabardine. His thick eyelids drooped; he had already seen enough of Vera and Lottie. Vera was tossing her scarf and her cape and saying chummily, "Just an omelette, really – we aren't at all hungry," and then they were in a small room, and the door to the room shut behind them. Here ashes and orange peel spilled out of a cold grate. Three tables pushed against the wall were barricaded behind armchairs, an upright piano, dining chairs, and a cheval glass. The two girls pulled a table and chairs clear and sat down. Lottie had a view of a red clay tennis court strung with Christmas lights. She turned to see what Vera was staring at. Another table was taken, but the noise and confusion coming from it at first seemed part of the chaos in the room. Lottie now saw two American soldiers and two adolescent girls who might be their wives. One of the girls, the prettier of the two, cried out, "But tell me now, am I talking loud? Because I sound to myself like I am talking loud." The laughter from the others was a kettledrum, and Lottie and Vera displayed their first pathetic complicity: "*We* aren't Yanks," said the look they exchanged.

Dissociating herself and perhaps Lottie from the noisy four, Vera gave their waitress a great smile and a skyrocket of French. "*On n'a que ça, les Américains*," said the waitress, shrugging. Vera's flashy French, her flashy good will did not endear her. Lottie watched the waitress's face and understood: she didn't like them, either. When Vera praised the small neat lighter she kept in her apron pocket, the waitress said, "*C'est un briquet, tout simplement*." She served a tepid omelette on cold plates and disappeared into a more interesting region, whence came the sound of men's voices. Lottie and Vera sat on, forgotten.

Vera said, "There should be a thing on the table you could hit that would go cling, cling."

"A bell," said Lottie, taken in. "The thing is a bell."

"*I* know. I was showing you how Al talks." Smoking, Vera told about walks in Roma and meals when she and her Polish friend from home had nothing to eat but hard-as-a-rock cheese. Once, he gave his share to a dog.

"Are you hard up for money, Vera?" Lottie did not mean by this she had any to lend.

"No, not really. But I sort of am when I'm with him. I pretend not to have any at all and live the way he does." Vera was bored; she was always quickly bored. Blowing smoke all over Lottie, she began defending the four Americans. "You've never seen how abominable Canadians can be."

Americans could be trained to set an example, Lottie insisted. They should be loved. Who was to blame if they were not?

Vera mashed her cigarette out on her plate. "D'you know how Canadian soldiers used to cut the Germans' throats?" she said. "Al showed me. You push the helmet like this," and she reached across quick as a snake and pressed the long helmet Lottie Benz would have been wearing had she been a soldier into the nape of her neck and drew her forefinger under Lottie's chin.

Lottie understood that an attempt had been made against her life and that she was safe. She said, "I love my country, Vera, and even if I didn't I wouldn't run it down."

"I'm not running it down. I'm telling you stories."

The bill was nineteen hundred francs. Vera said it was grossly excessive. "They took you for an American," she said. "It's those damned overshoes."

The air outside smelled of earth and eternally wet leaves, as though this place were unmindful of seasons. At the end of a walled lane the walled graveyard was a box. The sky (the sun was covered up now) was the lid. Lottie was still disturbed by Vera's attack. She knew if you show nothing, eventually you feel nothing; presently, feeling nothing, she was just herself, a visitor here – not a guest, because she was paying her way. She walked a pace or two behind Vera, who had taken on a serious and rather reproachful air, sniffing at rusty iron crosses, shaking her head beside a fresh grave covered over with planks. At the only plot of grass in the cemetery, she stopped and announced that this was it. A brownish shrub had been clipped so that it neatly surrounded a stone bench. Someone – now, in December – had planted a border of yellow pansies. Vera, stalking dramatically in her cape, left Lottie to think her thoughts. A restless pilgrim, she slashed at weeds with her handbag and all at once called, "It's not where you are, Lottie. It's over here." Lottie rose slowly from the bench, where she had not been thinking about Katherine Mansfield but simply nursing her several reasons for not feeling well. Where Vera stood, a block of polished granite weighed upon a block still larger. The base was cemented to the ground.

"'Katherine Mansfield,'" Vera droned. "'Wife of John Middleton Murry. 1888-1923. But I tell you, my lord fool, out of this nettle, danger, we pluck this flower, safety.' Well, I don't know what *that* means. Another thing I wish you'd tell me – what is that awful china rose doing there instead of real flowers? It's so puritan. You can't just abandon people that way, under all that granite. It's less than love. It's just considering your own taste."

"She is not abandoned, Vera; she is buried."

The orator heard only herself. "The stone is even moss-resistant," she said. But no, for the first wash of green crept up the granite step and touched a capital "M."

Lottie, whose ears might have been deaf to everything but

Vera until now, heard other sounds – a rooster crowing, a sudden rush of motors somewhere, a metallic clanging that certainly had to do with troops. Vera planted one foot upon the step and with more effort than seemed needed removed the rose. She tossed it aside; it landed in the tall grass of another grave. Then she picked a handful of yellow pansies and strewed them where the rose had been. Like all gestures, it seemed to Lottie suspect.

Lottie need never have seen Vera again after this. Vera departed for Rome, having first turned out her bureau drawers and left at Lottie's hotel a number of things she did not require. Lottie still had not looked up all the people to whom she had been given introductions. She woke up early each day wondering whom she would be seeing that night. Despite Vear's remark about overshoes, she went on wearing hers, and she wore her hats – the gardenia bandeau, the feather toque with veil, the suède beret – even though people turned and smiled and stared. Lottie told her new acquaintances that she had only just arrived and was eager to get to Strasbourg, where the university library contained everything she wanted; but she made no move to go. One mild rainy night, like a night in April displaced, a couple she had talked to on the plane from Canada invited her to the Comédie-Caumartin to see Danièle Delorme in an Ibsen revival. The theatre reminded Lottie of Vera, although she could not think why. It was stuffy and hot, and had been redecorated, and it smelled of paint. "We may get a headache from this," Lottie warned. The new friends, whose name was Morrow, thought she had said something remarkable about the play. The Morrows were dressed as if they had not planned to spend the evening together – he in tweeds and flannel, she in a sleeveless black dress with layers of silk fringe overlapping down the skirt. The bracelets on her arm jangled. Her hair was short (it had been long on the plane) and pushed behind the ears. They had both changed since the journey, but nothing about them seemed definite. Lottie thought they were not wearing their clothes from home but new outfits they were trying for effect.

Soon after the lights went down, a quarrel began in the audience. Groans and hisses and shouts of "*Mal élevé!*" covered the actors' voices, and the curtains had to be drawn. The actors tried again, and got on safely until one of them said how hot it was, upon which the audience began to laugh, a spectator shouted "*Oui, en effet!*" and threats were exchanged, though no one was struck. Baited by the public, the actors seemed to Lottie too intimate, too involved. She lost the thread of the story and became self-conscious, as though *she* were on the stage.

Languidly, the Morrows glanced about as if they knew people, or expected to know them soon. "I can't imagine why she revived it," Mrs. Morrow said during the interval.

"The sets are dull," said the husband. "The rest of the cast is weak."

Lottie said, "We had better stuff than this in Winnipeg; we had these really good actors from England, and the audience knows how to behave." Why should that make the Morrows so distant, all at once?

The husband was the first to unbend. Forgiving Lottie for her provincialism, he described the play he was over here to write – a murder, and several people who are really all one person. The several persons are either the victim, or the murderer, or a single witness. It was all the same thing.

"What will you be doing apart from that?" said Lottie.

"Nothing. That is what I *am* doing."

There was something fishy about him. He was too old to be a student, yet clearly wasn't working. Did he have money, or what?

"What do you think Ibsen did apart from that?" said the wife, turning her big black-rimmed eyes on Lottie. She held her elbow in one hand and a cigarette holder in the other.

"Nobody knows," said Lottie. "Anyway, goodness, we're none of us Ibsen."

When Lottie called the Morrows at their hotel a day later, Mrs. Morrow said that Lottie was not to take this personally but she and her husband were working hard – she was typing for him – and her husband did not want to spend too much time with Canadians over here. Lottie was not offended. It confirmed her suspicion of fishiness. Nevertheless, she did want to be with someone familiar at Christmas, and so was not displeased when she found a telegram from Vera. The telegram said, "MEET YOU ALSACE SEE LETTER." The letter came two days later. Pages long, it told where and how they were to meet, although not why.

II

Vera was dressed this time in a purple skirt and sweater she said had come from a five-and-ten in Rome. She stood idly, hand on one hip, in the lobby of their hotel while Lottie filled out a questionnaire for the police of Colmar. If her answers varied by so much as a spelling mistake from the answers she had given in Paris, she was sure she would be summoned for an explanation. Vera's hair was thick and straight and blonder than it had been. "Didn't I have a good idea about Christmas?" she said.

"It seemed like a good idea," said Lottie, in the tone of one only prudently ready for anything.

"You couldn't of done any work over Christmas anyway."

"But why Colmar, Vera?"

"You'll see enough of Strasbourg. You might as well look at something else." Lottie let Vera link an arm through hers and guide her out of the hotel into a light-blue evening. The shape of what seemed to be a street of very old houses was outlined in colored lights. Near a church someone had propped a ladder and climbed into a spruce tree to hang tinsel balls. The spire of the church had been lighted as well, but halfheartedly, as if the electrician in charge had run out of light bulbs. Lottie thought, I have not sent Kevin a cable for Christmas.

In the restaurant Vera chose for their dinner that night, she was loud and too confident, and Lottie felt undervalued. She had submitted to a wearing journey from Paris, with a change of trains at Strasbourg. From Strasbourg to Colmar she stood, her luggage in everyone's way, until she saw a city in a plain as flat as home, and understood this to be her destination. This much she let Vera know. What she did not say was how she had without a trace of fatigue left her luggage in the station at Strasbourg and gone out to find the cathedral. It was an important element of her thesis, for both Catholic and Protestant services were held inside; also, Dr. Keller had said something about an astronomical clock he admired. Flocks of bicycles swooped at Lottie, more unnerving than the screaming cabs of Paris. She heard German. Once, she was unable to get directions in French. When the first words of German crossed her lips, she thought they would remain, engraven, to condemn her. Speaking the secret language, she spoke in the name of unknown Grandmother Benz, whom she was said to resemble. The cathedral seemed to right itself before her – frosty, chalky, pink and trembling in the snowy air. A brown swift river divided that part of the city from the station. True Christmas was praised in shopwindows, with wine and nuts and candied peel. A gingerbread angel with painted paper face and paper wings cried of home – not of Winnipeg but of a vestigial ceremony, never mentioned as German, never confirmed as Canadian. The Paris promise of Christmas had been nonsense – all but the holly outside the hotel, and one night someone stole even that. The cold air and certain warm memories tinged her cheeks pink. She saw herself without disapproval in a glass. Sometimes strangers smiled. They were not smiling meanly at her overshoes or her hat. None of this was Vera's business.

Vera chewed on a drumstick, and told what had happened in Rome. She had found her friend Al Wiczinski living with a French family in a crummy unheated palazzo. He was adored by the daughter of the family, aged seventeen, and also by her father. Al was just too nice to people. But he was coming to Alsace. ("Coincidence, eh, Lottie?") A college had been opened for refugees in Strasbourg, and Al had been offered a teaching job. Politics, in a way, said Vera, but mostly the culture racket. After all, teaching Slav lit to a bunch of Slavs was what, culture or politics? Radio Free Europe was running the place. Lottie had never heard of it. Vera glanced at her oddly. Al had been told that he could obtain the visa he needed in Colmar more easily than in Strasbourg, and had sent Vera on to see what she could do. In theory, Al was not allowed to live along any frontier, especially this one.

"Why not?"

"Don't ask me. Ask the police."

"I don't see why a Canadian should have any trouble," said Lottie.

"He's only sort of Canadian," said Vera. "If you ask me, I don't think he should have a passport. I mean, he sort of picks on the place."

"You can't be sort of Canadian. If he is, he doesn't have to be in trouble anywhere."

"Oh, come off it, Lottie," said Vera, smiling at her. "Suppose you had to explain what you were doing here this very minute, what would you say?"

Lottie gave up. Sulking and pale, she let Vera glance at her several times but would not say what the matter was. She thought she had been taken in.

After dinner they walked beside a black gelatinous canal in which stood, upside down, a row of crooked houses. Lottie said, "Sometimes I think I've got no brains."

"You've got brains, all right," said Vera.

"No." Out of the protective dark she spoke to upside-down houses. "I've got a good memory. I can remember anything. But I've never worked on my own."

Lottchen. When she stuffed her mouth full of candy, her mother knew it had been taken without permission, but the boys were scolded instead of the little girl. Why? Oh, yes – they had put her up to it. Captain von Hook told them what he thought of it, in a high and frightening voice. He was meant to be principal of his school, but after 1939 his career was blocked.

The promenade along the canal ended Lottie's first evening in Alsace. She and Vera parted in the hotel lobby – Vera was going to stay and converse with total strangers in the bar – and without waiting to see if this was all right with Lottie she kissed her good night.

On the morning of Christmas Eve, Vera rose at seven and, after shaking Lottie awake, dragged her – cold, stunned, already weary – into streets where pale lamps flickered and aboard a bus filled with pale people asleep. They rolled into dark hills, which, as the day lightened, became blotter green. Lottie was not yet accustomed to steep hills and valleys; she wanted them to be more beautiful than they were. Desolate, she shut her eyes, believing herself close to a dead faint. She heard a girl cry "*C'est épouvantable*," but it was only because an elderly Alsatian peasant could not speak French. In the town of Munster, they descended before a shuttered hotel. The dining room was closed, glacial – Lottie had a glimpse of stacked chairs. In the kitchen a maid was ironing sheets, while another fed two little boys bread in the shape of men with pointed heads and feet. Vera ordered red wine and cheese for breakfast, and asked the price of rooms. Lottie wondered why. The wine stung and burned, the cheese made her lips swell. One day she would tell Vera about her low blood pressure, and how her temperature was often lower than normal, too, and she would let Vera understand how selfish and thoughtless she had been. On their way out through the courtyard, Vera banged on a door marked "*Pissoir.*" Lottie walked on. "You'll have to get over being fussy," Vera remarked. Lottie affected not to hear. She concentrated on the view of Munster, smoke and blue in a hollow. Above the town a blue gap broke open the metal sky. They set off downhill over wet earth and melting snow. Lottie walked easily in her comic overshoes, but Vera was pitched forward by the heels on her Italian shoes. They saw no one except a troop of little boys in sabots and square blue caps who engulfed them, fell silent, giggled after they had gone by. A snowball struck the back of Vera's cape. The boy who had thrown it wore rimless glasses and was absolutely cross-eyed. "Brat," said Lottie, who did not care for children. But Vera laughed back at him and put out her tongue.

They missed the bus they ought to have taken back to Colmar and had a three-hour wait. Vera pretended it had been planned that way. Tugging at Lottie, she made for a café. Here a Christmas tree gave off fragrance in waves, like a hyacinth. Radio Stuttgart offered them carols. Vera ate a mountain of sauerkraut and ham and sausage and drank a bottle of white wine. "Poor old Al, he's got no one but me, and here it is Christmas Eve!" she said gaily.

Elbows on table, head in her hands, Lottie read a newspaper. "Pinay has resigned," she said.

"No skin off my nose," said Vera.

"It'll skin theirs. He was keeping the franc up." Hearing the carols on the radio, Lottie wished she were religious. It might take her mind off such things as high finance, her own health, and scholarship.

"You know about exchange and all that," said Vera. "I just know when I can't afford to do what I want."

"May I ask, Vera, what you live on?"

"My family, for the moment. But Frannie and my brother Joe will both be in college in about a year and then I'll have to be on my own. The family can't keep all three of us."

"It's good of them to keep you now," said Lottie. "You don't work or anything."

"They get me instead of a holiday in California. I'm their luxury."

"Don't they think you should work?"

"They haven't said," said Vera, grinning. "I'm waiting for the right suggestion. You know where I was this time last year? In Rome. I'd just met Al."

"You've been away a long time," Lottie said. "I could never stay away that long."

"Who wants you to?"

The trouble with Vera was that she was indifferent. She had made Lottie come all the way to Colmar, with a complicated change of trains, and had tramped her up and down the rainy slopes on Christmas Eve, just so that she, Vera, would not feel lonely. Vera whistled with the radio, stopped, and said, "I had a little girl."

"I don't understand you. Oh, I'm sorry. I do."

"She's been adopted."

Lottie said stiffly, "I'm sure she's in a good home."

"I dream she's following me. In the dream I'm not like me. I look like Michèle Morgan. I dream I'm leading her through woods and holding branches so they won't snap back in her face. She could be dead. When it's raining like it was this afternoon, she could be outside, with nobody looking after her."

The only protection Lottie had received until now in her native country was an implicit promise that no one would ever talk this way.

"The family were over here a couple of times. Nothing's changed. They still say, 'Why don't you do something about your hair?' They don't seem to think I'll ever come back, or want to. The doctor who looked after the adoption kept writing to them, '*Il faut lui trouver un bon mari*.' Instead of doing that, they put me in a sort of convent school, and I nearly died. You don't know how it was over here four, five years ago. Now they let me do what I like. I'll find a *mari* if I feel like it. If I don't, too bad for them." Vera at this moment looked despairingly plain.

"It's a sad sort of life for you, Vera. You've been on your own since you were what – seventeen?"

"You feeling sorry for me?"

Feeling sorry had not occurred to Lottie; she was astonished that Vera would think it possible. Feeling sorry would have meant she was not minding her own business. Vera had certainly been away a long time. Otherwise she would never have supposed such a thing.

The next morning at breakfast, in a coffee shop Vera liked because the *croissants* were stuffed with almond paste, Lottie gave Vera her Christmas present – a leather case that would hold a pack of Gauloises. Vera had nothing for Lottie. She turned the case over in her hand, as if wondering what the occasion was. Lottie, slightly embarrassed, picked up from the leather seat beside her a folded, harsh-looking tract. She spread it on the glass-topped table. It was cheaply printed. In German, it informed its finder that "in the mountains" a Separatist movement that seemed to have died had only been sleeping. Recent injustices had warmed it to life.

"I know all about this," said Vera importantly, snatching it away. Her political eye looked for the printer, and she was triumphant pointing out that the name was absent, which proved that the tract was from a clandestine press.

"Of course," said Lottie, puzzled. "Who else would print it? That's what it's about, a clandestine movement. What I don't understand is, what do they want to separate from?"

"France, you dope," said Vera.

"I know all that," said Lottie, in her slowest voice. "I'm only trying to say that if there are people here who don't want to belong to France, then my proposition doesn't hold water. The idea is, these people are supposed to be loyal but still keep their national characteristics."

"There aren't many. Just a couple of nuts."

"There mustn't even be one."

"It's your own fault for inventing something and then trying to stick people in it." Vera talked, or, rather, rambled on, until the arrival of hot chocolate and *croissants*, when she began to stuff her mouth. Lottie folded the tract with care. A few minutes later she was once more rattling around inside a bus, headed now for Kaysersberg. "Good place for Christmas," Vera decreed, consulting but not sharing a green guidebook she kept in the pocket of her cape.

"You said Colmar was a good place for Christmas!" Lottie said. Vera took no notice of this.

Kaysersberg might have been chewed by rats. The passage of armies seven years ago still littered the streets. They walked away from here and over fields toward another town Vera said would be better. The sun was warm on Lottie's back, and her mother's Persian-lamb coat was a suit of armor. Beside the narrow road, vines tied to sticks seemed to be sliding uphill. It was a trick of the eye. Another illusion was the way the mountains moved: they rose and collapsed, soft-looking, green, purple, charcoal, deserting Lottie when she turned her head. All at once a vineyard fell away, and there for one minute, spread before her, was the plain of the Rhine, strung with glistening villages, and a church steeple here and there poking through the mist. Across the river were dark clouds or dark hills. She could not see where they joined the horizon or where they rose from the plain. So this was the place she loathed and craved, and never mentioned. It was the place where her mother and father had been born, and which they seemed unable to imagine, forgive, or describe.

"Well, that's Germany," said Vera. "I'll have to go over one of these days and get my passport stamped. They didn't stamp it when I came in from Italy, and it has to be done every three months."

Lottie wished she were looking at a picture and not a real place. She wished she were a child and could *pretend* it was a picture. "I'll never go there!" she said.

They walked on and entered Riquewihr in a soft wash of mud that came over the tops of Vera's shoes. "Three stars in the book," said Vera, not even trying to be jaunty anymore. "God, what a tomb! You expect people here to come crawling out of their huts covered with moss and weeds."

"But you've been here, Vera? You said you had been all over."

"I haven't been exactly here. I thought it would be nice for you for Christmas."

Lottie considered briefly the preposterous thought that Vera had not been trying to wear her out but to entertain her. Suddenly, as if it were Lottie's fault, Vera began to complain about the way streets had been in Winnipeg when Vera's mother was a girl. Where Vera's mother had lived, there hadn't been any sidewalks; there were wooden planks. If Vera's mother stepped off a plank, she was likely to lose her overshoe in the gumbo mud. In the good part of town, on Wellington Crescent, there were no pavements either, but for a different reason. When Ukrainian children were taken across the city on digestive airings, after Sunday lunch, to look at Wellington Crescent houses – when their parents had at last lost the Old Country habit of congregating in public parks and learned the New World custom of admiring the houses of people more fortunate than they were – the children, wondering at the absence of sidewalks, were told that people here had always had carriages and then motorcars and had never needed to walk.

Vera was passionate over a past she knew nothing about. It was just her mother's folklore. Vera's mother, Lottie now learned, had washed in snow water. Vera herself could remember snow carried into the house and melted on the kitchen stove.

"Well, then, your father moved the whole family, I suppose," said Lottie, remembering Winnipeg Culture Patterns with Dr. Keller.

"That's right," said Vera, without inflection. "To your part of town."

Lottie had still not sent the Christmas cable to Kevin. Could she send it from here? It was early morning in Winnipeg – scarcely dawn.

Lottie intended to set off for Strasbourg the instant Christmas was over, but Vera gained another day. In the morning they went to see a movie called *Das Herz Einer Frau*, subtitled *Ich Suche Eine Mutti* – an incredibly sad story about a laundress and her little boy. Lottie, exasperated, turned to say something but saw that Vera was wiping tears. Later, she and Vera boldly entered a police station, where Vera asked questions on Al's behalf. Lottie sat staring at a sign: *C'est* CHIC *de parler Français!*" "*Chic*" was in red.

It was plain that Vera's plans had gone wrong; Al's arrival should have coincided with Lottie's going. Vera did not want to go off to Strasbourg in case he came here, and she did not want Lottie to desert her. She coaxed from Lottie one more excursion, this time not far away. After a mercifully short bus trip, they walked under pines. In these woods, so tame, so gardened, that Lottie did not know what to call them, they stumbled on a ruin covered with moss and ivy. "It is part of the Maginot Line, I think," said Vera.

Lottie, frantic with being where she did not want to be, turned from her and cried, "Is that what it is? The Maginot Line? No wonder they lost the war."

"Is that what Dr. Keller taught you? Why do you think one piece is all of everything?"

"What else can you do?" said Lottie. The mist carried in her lungs since Paris darkened and filled her chest. "You don't understand, Vera. I'm not strong physically. That's what I meant that day on the train, when you said 'weak, not frail.' I *am* frail, and I have to do this thesis on my own. I have to choose my own books and work with people I've never met before. I've never used a strange library. You've made me walk a lot. I've got this very low blood pressure. One day my heart might just stop."

"Yes, well, it was a mistake," said Vera. She folded her arms under her cape and kicked at the Maginot Line instead of kicking herself, or Al, or Lottie.

III

The advantage of Strasbourg over any other place was that Lottie here had a warm room. In a hotel on the Quai des Bateliers, discovered by Vera, she unpacked the notes and files. She could see the spire of the cathedral, encased in scaffolding, rosy and buoyed up on plain air. Chimes and bells evenly punctuated her days and nights. Every night, at a dark foggy hour, she heard strange tunes – tunes that seemed to be trying to escape from between two close parallel lines. The sound came from a shack full of Arabs, across from the hotel, on the bank of a canal. In the next room but one, Lottie had a neighbor, a man who typed. The empty room between them was a sounding box. She heard him talking to himself sometimes and walking about. His step was quick. Vera was also on this floor, at the end of a corridor papered with lettuce-sized roses. Her room gave onto nothing of interest, and her window sill was already a repository for bread, butter, dime-store knives, and old newspapers.

On January 9th, a month to the day after her arrival in France, Lottie wrote her first long letter to Kevin. The postcards she had sent from Paris and Colmar said, "I am working hard," which was not so, and "It is terribly cold," and "I'm saving it up to tell you when I get back." Her real letters to him were those she composed in her head and was too shy to write. She could imagine him listening to anything she had to tell him but not reading what she wrote. "I went to the opening of the European Assembly in a new prefab building that already looks like a shack, looks left over from the war," she wrote, hoping that this would be a letter of such historical importance he would keep it in a folder. "A sign said that anyone showing approval *or* disapproval would be thrown out. There were hardly any visitors, and I did not have the feeling that history was being made. It was all dry and dull. I listened to the translators through the headphones, but it was more of a strain than just hearing an unknown language. Sort of English-English and bored French. M. Spaak was not there, because he had rheumatism (at least that's what I understood) and just when this was announced I felt the start of a chill and had to rush out and home in a cab. I was shaking so much in my fur coat that Vera was frightened. It's not serious" – she felt her beginning going off the rails – "but I've got a chill and a fever and a bad cough and a pain in my chest and a sore throat. Vera has bought me some pills full of codeine. Vera believes in sweat. A dog that belongs to this hotel, name of Bonzo, came in to see me. I gave him a piece of stale bread and he took it under the bed, with his legs and tail sticking out flat. It suddenly occurred to me today that there is no such thing as sociology. When you are a sociologist, all you can do is teach more of the same, and every professor has his own idea about what it is. Vera says that if I were studying the integration of Indians, which never happened anyway, it would not be called sociology. Vera will take this out to mail."

Lottie could eat nothing until the next day, when, mostly to pacify Vera, she picked at a helping of macaroni and gravy. Vera sat at Lottie's clean table and proceeded to make a mess of it. She drank beer out of a bottle and, when she had drunk all she wanted, poured the rest in the washbasin. "Do you mind the smell?" she asked, too late, peering down. Vera was already on a first-name basis with the whole hotel, and particularly friendly with the man who typed. He was an elderly madman, who had only a week before been released from the mental ward of a military hospital.

"What do you type?" Vera had asked him.

"Poems," he replied, looking at her with one eye. (The other was glass.)

Vera read aloud from *France-Soir* to Lottie, who disliked being read to. "*Le trentième anniversaire de la mort de Katherine Mansfield est célébré aujourd'hui à Avon.*"

"They'll see I got rid of that china rose," said Vera, very pleased.

In the night, Lottie spat blood. It looked bright and pure, like a chip of jewel. She had coughed enough to rupture a small blood vessel. Out of childhood came recollections of monumental nosebleeds, and of the whole family worried. As if to confirm the memory, Vera came bustling in, for all the world like Lottie's mother. She found Lottie lying across the bed with her head hanging back. She closed the window, then covered Lottie with the eiderdown. Lottie was irritated. "I need lots and lots of air," she said. Being irritated brought on an attack of coughing and pain. Vera began opening and closing windows again.

Lottie wanted to write to Kevin, "My coldness to Vera frightens me. She came in again now and was sweet and kind, and I thought I would scream. She smelled of the bar downstairs in the hotel where she likes to hang out eating stale chips and talking to men. She sat on the bed and stroked my pillow saying, 'Isn't there anything I can do for you?' She seems lost and lonely because Al hasn't turned up. She offers all the kindness she can in exchange for something I don't want to give because I can't spare it. A grain of love? Maybe the Pole, Al, is hell. It is not my fault. I shrank into myself, cold, cold.

We are all like that. So are you, Kevin. Finally I said, 'Vera, would you mind awfully opening the window?' and she aired the room (she likes doing that) and held her cape so as to protect me from the draft. She looked around for something else to do. 'I'll go and complain about that washbasin,' she said. 'Yes, do go,' I said. I wanted to be left alone. She felt it, and went away looking as if she would never understand why."

This composed, but not written, Lottie dragged herself from her bed and down the rose-papered hall to Vera's room, on an impulse, to say something like "You were kind," but Vera's door was locked. She thought she heard Vera whispering to someone – or else she heard the curtains moving, or the rustle of the papers Vera kept on her window sill.

"Even when I am nice to Vera," she finished the letter, "it doesn't mean anything, because I don't honestly like her."

Vera had complained about the washbasin and then proceeded to the post office to collect her mail. She and Lottie were both using poste restante, because they thought the Quai des Bateliers was temporary. Lottie wanted to get into a students' residence where she would meet interesting people, and Vera was waiting for Al. Vera came back from the post office with a picture of Al. He was in Paris now – he seemed to be approaching in stages and halts, like a traveller in an earlier century – and had sent, along with his photograph, a letter full of requests and instructions. Lottie looked at a round face and enormous dark eyes with fixed, staring pupils. He seemed drugged or startled. "His eyes are blue," said Vera. "They look dark with that fancy lighting. I've been out to the refugee college, asking around. He's got it all wrong. It's only a dorm. They go to the university for classes. It sounded funny in the first place, teaching Slav lit to Slavs. Maybe he's found something else to do. Or not to do, more like it. He's got in with some Poles who live outside Paris and do weaving. They may also have prayer and patriotic evenings. Right Wing Bohemia," said Vera, looking down her large nose, "lives in the country and weaves its own skirts. *You* know." Over Lottie's cringing mind crept the fear that Vera might be some sort of radical. Ukrainians were extreme one way or another. You would have to know which of the Uke papers Vera's parents subscribed to, and even that wouldn't help unless you could read the language. "Get this," said Vera, and, adopting a manner Lottie assumed must be Al's, she read aloud, "'You cannot imagine what a change it is for me – yesterday *le grand luxe* in Roma, today here. But I must say, even though I have the palate of a gourmet, I find nothing wrong with the cooking.'"

"He just doesn't sound Canadian," Lottie said.

"In the evening the old man came to my room," composed Lottie, introducing the old man to Kevin without warning. "He stood in the doorway, with his battered face and his one eye, and said, 'I am going to write a poem about Canada in honor of you and your friend Mademoiselle Vera. In which city is there a street called Saint-Jean-Louis?'"

"In the first place," Lottie had said earnestly, "is there any such saint?"

"Could it be in Winnipeg?" the old man said.

"No, Quebec." She recalled crooked streets, and one street where the houses were frozen and old; over the top of a stone wall had bloomed a cold spring tree.... But I was never in Quebec, she remembered next.

There was no transition from day to night. She heard him typing, like someone dropping china beads one by one. She coughed, and put the pillow over her face. If he comes in and talks about the poem again, she thought, it might make me homesick. If something made me homesick I might cry, and that could break the fever. If something could make me homesick, I would go home and not wait for someone to come and fetch me. But when she wanted to think of home, she thought of a church in Quebec, and a dark recess where the skull of General Montcalm, preserved by Ursuline nuns, and exposed by them, rested in a gold-and-glass cage. But I have never seen it – someone described it to me. It has nothing to do with home. Her eyes filled with tears, but not of homesickness.

A mounting litter of paper handkerchiefs and empty yoghurt jars spilled out of the paper carton Vera had put beside Lottie's bed. "*À quoi bon?*" said the hotel maid when Lottie asked her to empty the box. The maid was not obliged to clean a room unless the tenant went out. It was a rule. Bribed, she said she would see about the washbasin but nothing more.

Lottie wanted to give the old man something better than an imaginary street for his poem, but now the idea of a city she had not seen obscured her memory. "What, do you mean you were never there?" he might ask if she told him she had never been to Quebec. "It was a tremendous excursion," she would have to say. "Nobody over here knows how far it was, or how much it would have cost," and tears of self-pity followed the others.

Bonzo, the hotel dog, stole under the bed and tore to pieces a box of matches. Lottie had lost her voice. She whispered, "Bad dog!" and "You'll make yourself very sick!" and on her hands and knees retrieved a slimy piece of wood. She had a high fever now. She knew it by the trouble she had getting back into bed – she could not judge its height – and she saw it reflected on the face of the nurse who had been summoned by Vera. The nurse, a peasant girl in a soiled head scarf, twin sister to the maid in appearance, told Lottie what her temperature was, in a disapproving voice. It was in centigrade and meant nothing.

"*Ma voisine!*" cried the old man, standing in the hall. "It is very warm outside, so warm that one can go out without a coat."

"Good," whispered Lottie. She heard him go out into the bitter day, perhaps without a coat.

She felt well enough to go on with her letter to Kevin: "My neighbor does exercises in the doorway to show me how spry he is. At the end of each one he hops up and stands at attention, giving just one small disciplined bound in place. He is like someone who has done these things for years in a row with other men – in a jail, or a military hospital, or a prison camp, or the Army, or a mental home. In any one, or two, or three …"

Lottie and the old man shared a view. At night they heard the iron chimes of the cathedral. At dawn they could see the pink spire briefly red. Inside the cathedral, Death struck the hours in Dr. Keller's clock, and at noon Our Lord blessed in turn each of the Apostles. Every noon – or, rather, at half past twelve, for the clock was half an hour off – the betrayal was announced by a mechanical cock flapping stiff wings. One night the neighbor typed all night, and, talking loudly to himself, went to bed before six, the hour at which the whole clumsy performance of the clock – chariots, pagan deities, signs of the zodiac, days of the week, Christ and the Apostles, the betrayal – finished its round. Lottie understood that night and day were done for before time from home could overtake them. She was dislocated, perhaps forever, like the clock.

The nurse returned next day with a doctor, who said, "It is a little fever."

"What kind?" Lottie asked. Her teeth were chattering. "What about my nosebleeds?"

"A little simple cough. You take yourself too seriously." He wrote out a prescription for three kinds of remedy, which were all patent medicines. Two of the three Vera had already bought. Lottie composed for Kevin: "I imagined – because with a fever you don't know where imagination begins and a dream leaves off – that my mad neighbor had to repaint the outside of the high school. I said, 'Can't the parishioners afford to hire someone?' Isn't it funny, my thinking it was a church?"

Her health improved; she got dressed and walked along the river, with Vera beside her. At the post office was a letter from Kevin, and for Vera a receipt from American Express in Rome for five hundred lire she had left as a deposit for forwarding her mail. This Vera misread as five hundred dollars she had received from home, and even when Lottie pointed out the error she continued to prattle on about what she was going to do with the money. She would take Lottie south! They would visit Al Wiczinski in Paris! Laughing, she picked up a glove someone had dropped on the pavement and put it in her pocket. Lottie was suddenly wildly angry about the glove, as if all the causes Vera had ever given for anger were pale compared with this particular offense. She walked back to the hotel, trembling with weakness and fury, and plotting some sort of obscure revenge.

The letter she had from Kevin began, "I'm fine. Sorry you aren't feeling well." She put it away with the Separatist tract found in the coffee shop. They were documents to be analyzed.

Vera said, "Listen, Lottie, I'm hard up for the moment. No, don't look scared. I'll just pawn something. If you've got anything you could lend me to pawn, that would be great."

"Kevin," Lottie thought she would write, "this morning I bundled all my trinkets into a scarf of Vera's – Granny's pearl and sapphire earrings I can't wear because my ears aren't pierced, and my cameo, which turned out to be worth nothing – and I went with Vera, who was whistling and singing and not worried at all. I had to leave my passport, because they said they were giving me a lot of money – fifteen thousand francs, which I handed to Vera, who took it as if it were a gift. She paid her hotel bill. In the afternoon, she forgot where the money came from and what it was for, and she invited me with a grand air to the Kléber, a big café like a railway station. We drank three thousand and fifty francs' worth of kümmel. Vera also invited the mad party from down the hall. He said he could read English and had been reading the love letters of Mark Twain. The band wore red coats and played 'L'Amour Est un Bouquet de Violettes.' Everywhere you go, you hear that played. The waiters were reading newspapers; there were high ceilings and trays of beer and enormous pretzels. Vera sang with the band. I wonder if I shall ever get my passport back."

Whatever Lottie's fever had been, it had worn itself down to bouts of coughing. Her head was stuffed with felt. When she looked at her old notes or tried to read anything, her eyes shut of their own accord. Without her passport she could not collect her mail. Why had Vera not given up her own? Because, said Vera, astonished at the question, then she would not have been able to get *her* mail, and, as she was expecting money from home, she needed it.

Lottie began to be worried about money. She had spent more than ever planned for on medicines, on the doctor and nurse, on the Christmas holiday in Colmar, which now seemed wild, wine-drenched.

On a cold, foggy winter Saturday, when she could hope for nothing in the post, and could not shake off her cough or rid herself of her pallor, the newspapers finally mentioned an epidemic of grippe that was sweeping through Europe. The symptoms resembled those of pneumonia. The popular name for it was Virus X. There had been two new deaths in Clermont-Ferrand. "Why do they always tell about what happens in Clermont-Ferrand?" said Vera.

She had received three hundred dollars from home. Without making a particular point of it, or showing any gratitude, she returned the fifteen thousand francs. "What I never did understand," she said, as if discussing ancient history, "was why you didn't just take your own money and unpawn your stuff and get your passport back."

Lottie could not make sense of that. The passport had been tied up by Vera, and only Vera could undo the knot.

Vera had also received a birthday box from her sister-in-law, the wife of Honest Stan. It contained aspirin, Life Savers, two cards of snap fasteners, colored ribbon, needles, thread, a bottle of vitamin pills, Band-Aids, and Ivory soap. One aspirin was missing in each tin. "She sends me old clothes sometimes," said Vera, groping at the bottom of the box. "She's from a good old United Empire Loyalist family, true-blue Tory, one-hundred-per-cent Anglo-Saxon taste in clothes." Lottie felt obscurely offended, as if her own taste had been impugned. Kevin was probably Irish, but, being Protestant, he counted as English. Remembering that Vera was a nut who collected lost gloves, Lottie ranged herself and Kevin on the side of Honest Stan's wife. "There," said Vera, with satisfaction, and pulled out a summer frock of blue voile sprigged with roses. It had puffed sleeves and reached midway between Vera's hip and knee. Vera opened the window, shook out the dress, and sent it off. The dress, picked up by the wind, rose and then floated down. The Arab music had begun – it accompanied a certain dark hour of the day – and Vera said the dress was dancing to it.

On Sunday, when the sky was full of bells, and the snow along the canals a blue that was nearly white, Lottie walked with Vera, believing that this was spring. Upon the water was the swift circle of a flight of birds. When the girls looked up from the reflection, the birds were white dots in the sky. Bridges, bare trees, and cobbles passed them, and Lottie, walking on a treadmill, was all at once drenched in sweat, and trembling, and had to lean on Vera's arm. Put to bed, she lay limp, mute, her mouth dry, her hands burning. There was a new electric pain in her lungs. In her mind she wrote to Kevin, "My thesis is a mess. I haven't done any work, and here it is past the middle of January. Most of the things Keller let me think weren't true...."

The firemen's band marching beneath the window played a fat, German-sounding military air. She was like a wooden toy apart at the joints, scattered to the four corners of the room. Each of the pieces was marred. Yet by evening she was suddenly better. She got up again and walked with Vera in the cold, snowy night, dragging Bonzo on the end of a rope. She thought, but did not say, that it was the most beautiful night she had ever seen. She admired, in silence, the lamps in the brown canals and in the icy branches above. Suddenly Vera snatched Bonzo's rope and, cape flying, ran like a streak. Vera could be perfectly happy with or without Al, probably with or without Lottie. The important thing was feeling free, and never being alone.

Only one letter was waiting at the post office when Lottie turned up, passport in hand. Kevin wrote, "A funny-looking girl called Rose Perry has been around this winter. Some friend of yours introduces us saying we have a lot in common because she is a sociologist, like you, and also High Anglican, though I don't know why that gives us something in common. She's around thirty, red hair, funny-looking – I already said that. She's from England, either taking some other degree or just picking up material on the white-collar class in the prairie provinces for her own fun. Now, why couldn't you have done just that and never left home? Rose says the integration idea isn't new. She's been having a hungry winter. Her scholarship isn't a hell of a lot, and it's in pounds, not dollars. We've had her over to the house."

He likes her, and I know why, Lottie thought. Because she is English. His family will look after her, feed her, find her a place to stay. If I were having a hungry winter, I would be the immigrants' child who hadn't made it. I wouldn't dare have a hungry winter.

The sun shone – a pale sunlight, the first of 1953. Vera climbed up the spire of the cathedral while Lottie waited below – two hundred-odd steps of winding stone to a snowy platform where pigeons hopped on the ledge, and where eighteenth-century tourists had carved the record of their climb. Up there, Vera heard the piercing screams of a schoolyard full of children. She went up a smaller and older-seeming spiral to the very top, above the cathedral bells, which she could see through windows carved in stone. Ice formed on the soles of her shoes.

She was mystically moved, she declared, by the appearance of the bells, which seemed to hang over infinite space.

Walking in Vera's shadow, Lottie thought, I should never have seen her after that trip to Fontainebleau.

The days were lighter and longer. The rivers and canals became bottle green, and the delicate trees beside them were detached from fog. Vera and Lottie went often to the Grande Taverne de Kléber. When Lottie had enough kümmel to drink, Vera made sense. On one brilliantly sunny day, two girls came into the Kléber laughing the indomitable laughter of girls proving they can be friends, and Lottie said, "Look, Vera, that is like you and me." Presently they got up and changed cafés, moving by this means four streets nearer the hotel. The table here was covered with someone's cigarette ash – someone who had been here for a long time. There was in the air, with the smell of beer and fresh coffee, a substance made up of old conversations. The windows were black and streaked with melted snow. Each rivulet reflected the neon inside.

"Let's go over to Germany," Vera said for the second time. "It's nothing – just another bus ride. Maybe a train this time. All I have to do is get my passport stamped and come right back. It's just like crossing a road."

"Not for me it isn't."

Falling asleep that night, Lottie heard, pounding outside her window, a steam-driven machine the Arab workers had somehow got their hands on but could not operate. They sounded as if they were cursing each other. The sounds of Strasbourg were hard and ugly sometimes: trams and traffic, and in the night drunken people shouting the thick dialect.

Lottie, wake up," Vera said.

Lottie thought she was in a café and that the waitress had said, "If you fall asleep here, I shall call the police." The room was full of white snow light, and Lottie was still clothed, under the eiderdown. Someone had taken off her shoes. She saw a bunch of anemones, red and blue, in a glass on the edge of the hopelessly plugged washbasin. "The nut next door brought us each a bunch of them," said Vera. She was bright and dressed, wearing tangerine lipstick that made her mouth twice as big as it should have been. "You know what time it is? One o'clock. Boy, do you look terrible! Al's just called from Paris. I wonder who paid for *that*? I thought he was calling because it's my twenty-first birthday, but he's just lonely. He wants me to come. I said, 'Why are we always doing something for *your* good? You've already left me stranded in Alsace.' I don't think he ever intended to come. He said, 'You know I need you, but I leave it up to you.' It's this moral-pressure business. Would it work with you?"

"Yes," said Lottie. She lay with her eyes open, imagining Strasbourg empty. How would she go alone to the post office?

"I hate letting him down. He's been through a lot."

"Then go."

"I don't think I should leave you. You look worse than when you had Virus X."

"We'll go out and drink to your birthday," Lottie said. "I'll look better then."

Walking again, crossing rivers and canals, they saw a man in a canoe. The water was green and thick and still. Along the banks the trees seemed bedded out, like the pansies in the graveyard. How rough and shaggy woods at home seemed now! Nothing there was ever dry underfoot until high summer, and then in a short time the ground was boggy again.

"I always felt I had less right to be Canadian than you, even though we've been there longer," Vera said. "I've never understood that coldness. I know you aren't English, but it's all the same. You can be a piece of ice when you want to. When you walked into the restaurant that day in Paris, I felt cold to the bone."

The canoe moved without a sound.

In a *brasserie* opposite the cathedral, where they celebrated Vera's coming of age, smoke lay midway between floor and ceiling, a motionless layer of blue. "I only want one thing for my birthday and there it is," said Vera, pointing to a player piano. Rolls were fed to the piano ("Poet and Peasant," the overture to "William Tell," "Vienna Blood") and not only did the piano keys rise and fall but the circle of violins, upside down, as if reflected, revolved and ground out spirited melodies. Two little lamps with spangled shades decorated the instrument, which the waitress said was German and very old. That reminded Lottie, and she said, "I'll go with you tomorrow, if you want to, to get your passport stamped."

"It's not Moscow, for God's sake," said Vera. "It's only over there."

They stayed after everyone else had gone, and the smoke and the smell of pork and cabbage grew cold. They drank kümmel and made perfect sense.

"But Vera" – Lottie tried to be serious – "what are you going to *do* now that you are twenty-one?"

"I don't know. Find out why one aspirin was missing from each tin."

When they reached the hotel, drunk on friendship and with nothing to worry about but what to do with the rest of the day, Kevin was there. He sat with his habitual patience, in the hotel lobby, wearing his overcoat, reading a stained, plastic-covered, and over-confident bar list – the hotel served only coffee and chips and beer. He was examining the German and French columns of the menu with equal forbearance; he understood neither, and probably had no desires.

One day, she would become accustomed to Kevin, Lottie said to herself; stop seeing him, as she had nearly grown used to mountains. She thought, crazily, that if it had been Dr. Keller or any other man here to take her away, she would have clung to his hands and wept all over them. He looked so reassuring. She thought, A conservative Canadian type, and the words made her want to marry him. The confidence he assumed for them both let her know that if she had not worked on her thesis it was Dr. Keller's fault; he had prepared her badly. If she had been taken ill, it was because of a virus no one had ever heard of at home. When she saw the shapeless overcoat and the rubbers over his shoes that would make people laugh in Paris, she did not care, and she was happy because he could not read anything but English. That was the way he had to be.

"We can't talk here," she said. "Come upstairs."

"Is it all right?"

"Oh, *they* don't care."

He followed her up the stairs. He was ill at ease. He was worried about the hotel detectives.

"It's a lovely room, Kevin. Wait till you see the view, like a Flemish painting. And so warm. They leave the heat on all night. In Paris ..."

From the doorway, looking around, he took in the half-drained basin with its greasy rim, the carton she used as a wastebasket, her underthings drying on a wire hanger, the table covered with a wine-stained cloth, the unmade bed. Lottie thought he was admiring her anemones. "My crazy neighbor gave them to me," she said. "The old boy from the military hospital. The one who's been writing the poem for Vera and me."

"No," said Kevin. "You never mentioned him. You mentioned this Vera just once. Then you stopped writing."

"I wrote all the time."

"I never got the letters. One of mine was returned. I guess the mail system here isn't exactly up to date."

"It must have been returned when I was too sick to go to the post office. You have to show your passport."

"I know, but I got just this one letter. If Vera hadn't been writing and telling your mother not to worry, I'd have been over before. It was a long time of nothing – not even a card for Christmas. Vera said how hard you were working, how busy." He left the door ajar but consented to sit on the unmade bed. "So, when I got the chance of a free hop to Zurich, a press flight ..." He looked as if he would never grow old. The lines in his face might deepen, that was all. "I knew you'd had this flu. That can take a lot out of you."

"Yes. It was good of you to come and see how I was. How long can you stay?"

"One, two days. I don't want to interfere with your work."

Vera had said, "You've kept him on the string since you were sixteen. You'll bring it off." Ah, but it was one thing to be sixteen, pretty but modest, brilliant but unassuming. Her frail health had been slightly in her favor then. She had made the mistake of going away, and she had let Kevin discover he could get on without her. She held his hands and pretended to be as conscious as he was of the half-open door. They had never been as alone as at this moment and might never be again. They were almost dangerously on the side of friendship. If she began explaining everything that had taken place, from the moment she saw the holly in Paris and filled out her first police questionnaire, then they might become very good friends indeed, but would probably never marry.

"What I would like, Kevin – I don't know if you'll think it's a good idea – would be to go back with you. If I stay here, I'll get pneumonia. It's a good thing you came. Vera was killing me."

"Her letters didn't sound like it. Who is she, anyway?"

"A girl from home. A Ukrainian. She got in trouble, and they sent her away. Forget Vera."

"They could have just sent her to Minneapolis," said Kevin.

"Too close," said Lottie. "She might have slipped back."

"I guess you'll be glad to get out of here," said Kevin, as the bells struck the hour. He left her and returned to the hotel near the station, where he had taken a room. He could not rid himself of the fear that there might be detectives.

As she had promised, Lottie accompanied Vera to Germany. Kevin was with them. Once her passport was stamped, Vera thought she would go to Paris and help Al out of whatever predicament he was in, perhaps for the last time. "I liked it in Rome, where it was sort of crazy, but Paris is cold and dirty, and now he's twenty-six," said Vera.

"You mean, he should settle down," said Kevin, not making of it a question, and without asking what Vera imagined her help to Al could consist of.

Vera was hypocritically meek with Kevin, though she smiled when he said "Ukarainian," in five syllables. Lottie saw that if Vera had for one moment wavered, if she had considered going home because Lottie was leaving, the voice from home saying "Ukarainian" had reminded her of what the return would be. That was Vera's labyrinth. Lottie was on her way out. Kevin held Lottie's hand when Vera wasn't looking. He was friendly toward Vera, but protective of Lottie, which was the right imbalance. Lottie guessed he had made up his mind.

They walked on a coating of slush and ice – they had left the sun and the rivers on the other side.

In a totally gray village nothing stirred. Beyond it, on the dirty, icy highway by some railway tracks, they came upon a knot of orphans and a clergyman. The two groups passed each other without a glance. In a moment the children were out of sight. Answering a remark of Kevin's, Vera said they were ten or eleven years old, and unlikely to remember the air raids eight years ago. The sky was low and looked unwashed. On the horizon the dark blue mountains were so near now that Lottie saw where they rose from the plain. "Appenweier" – that was the name of the place. It was like those mysterious childhood railway journeys that begin and end in darkness.

"Are you girls by any chance going anyplace in particular?" said Kevin.

They turned and looked at him. No, they were just walking. Vera was not even leading the way.

"Well, I'm sorry then," said Kevin, "but as the saying goes, I've had it," and he marched them to the bombed station, and onto a train, and so back to France.

If that was Germany, there was nothing to wait for, expect, or return to. She had not crossed a frontier but come up to another limit.

Vera packed some things and left some, and departed for Paris. She and Lottie did not kiss, and Vera left the hotel without looking back. Her room – because it was cheaper – was instantly taken over by the mad neighbor. Kevin spent the evening, supperless, and part of the night with Lottie. Vera also must have been an inhibiting factor for him, Lottie decided – not just the phantom detectives. He might have taken Lottie to his hotel, which was more comfortable, but he thought it would look funny. They had given Vera a day's start. Kevin and Lottie were leaving for Zurich in the morning, and from Zurich flying home. Lottie did not think this night would give her a claim on Kevin, but when she woke, at an hour she could not place – woke because the Arabs were quarrelling outside the window, got up to shut the window and, in the dark, comb her hair – she thought that a memory of it could. Vera had left a parcel of food. If she had not been afraid of disturbing Kevin, she would have spread it on the table and eaten a meal – salami, pickles, butter, and bread, half a bottle of Sylvaner.

Kevin now rose, obsessed by what the people who owned the hotel might be supposing. He smoked a cigarette, refused the wine, and put on his clothes. He and Lottie were to meet next morning at the station; there was some confusion about the time. Kevin remarked, with a certain pride, that as far as he was concerned it was now around seven at night. He had brought a travelling clock to lend to Lottie so that she could wake up in plenty of time to pack. He set it for six, and placed the clock where she could reach it.

Lottie made a list not of what she was taking but of what

she was leaving behind: food, wilted anemones, medicine, all Vera's residue as well as her own. The hotel maid would have a full day of it, and could not get away with saying "À *quoi bon?*" Lottie could not make herself believe that someone else would be sleeping in this room and that there would be no trace of Lottie and Vera anywhere. She rose before the alarm rang, and stood at the window with the curtain in her hand. She composed, "Last night, just at the end of the night, the sky and the air were white as milk. Snow had fallen and a thick low fog lay in the streets and on the water, filling every crack between the houses. The cathedral bells were iron and muffled in snow. I heard drunks up and down the sidewalk most of the night."

This could not be a letter to Kevin; he was there, across the city, and had never received any of the others. It was not a letter to anyone. There was no sense to what she was doing. She would never do it again. That was the first of many changes.

LINNET MUIR

IN YOUTH IS PLEASURE

My father died, then my grandmother; my mother was left, but we did not get on. I was probably disagreeable with anyone who felt entitled to give me instructions and advice. We seldom lived under the same roof, which was just as well. She had found me civil and amusing until I was ten, at which time I was said to have become pert and obstinate. She was impulsive, generous, in some ways better than most other people, but without any feeling for cause and effect; this made her at the least unpredictable and at the most a serious element of danger. I was fascinated by her, though she worried me; then all at once I lost interest. I was fifteen when this happened. I would forget to answer her letters and even to open them. It was not rejection or anything so violent as dislike but a simple indifference I cannot account for. It was much the way I would be later with men I fell out of love with, but I was too young to know that then. As for my mother, whatever I thought, felt, said, wrote, and wore had always been a positive source of exasperation. From time to time she attempted to alter the form, the outward shape at least, of the creature she thought she was modelling, but at last she came to the conclusion there must be something wrong with the clay. Her final unexpected upsurge of attention coincided with my abrupt unconcern: one may well have been the reason for the other.

It took the form of digging into my diaries and notebooks and it yielded, among other documents, a two-year-old poem, Kiplingesque in its rhythms, entitled "Why I Am a Socialist." The first words of the first line were "You ask …," then came a long answer. But it was not an answer to anything she'd wondered. Like all mothers – at least, all I have known – she was obsessed with the entirely private and possibly trivial matter of a daughter's virginity. Why I was a Socialist she rightly conceded to be none of her business. Still, she must have felt she had to say something, and the something was "You had better be clever, because you will never be pretty." My response was to take – take, not grab – the poem from her and tear it up. No voices were raised. I never mentioned the incident to anyone. That is how it was. We became, presently, mutually unconcerned. My detachment was put down to the coldness of my nature, hers to the exhaustion of trying to bring me up. It must have been a relief to her when, in the first half of Hitler's war, I slipped quietly and finally out of her life. I was now eighteen, and completely on my own. By "on my own" I don't mean a show of independence with Papa-Mama footing the bills: I mean that I was solely responsible for my economic survival and that no living person felt any duty toward me.

On a bright morning in June I arrived in Montreal, where I'd been born, from New York, where I had been living and going to school. My luggage was a small suitcase and an Edwardian picnic hamper – a preposterous piece of baggage my father had brought from England some twenty years before; it had been with me since childhood, when his death turned my life into a helpless migration. In my purse was a birth certificate and five American dollars, my total fortune, the parting gift of a Canadian actress in New York, who had taken me to see *Mayerling* before I got on the train. She was kind and good and terribly hard up, and she had no idea that apart from some loose change I had nothing more. The birth certificate, which testified I was Linnet Muir, daughter of Angus and of Charlotte, was my right of passage. I did not own a passport and possibly never had seen one. In those days there was almost no such thing as a "Canadian." You were Canadian-born, and a British subject, too, and you had a third label with no consular reality, like the racial tag that on Soviet passports will make a German of someone who has never been to Germany. In Canada you were also whatever your father happened to be, which in my case was English. He was half Scot, but English by birth, by mother, by instinct. I did not feel a scrap British or English, but I was not an American either. In American schools I had refused to salute the flag. My denial of that curiously Fascist-looking celebration, with the right arm stuck straight out, and my silence when the others intoned the trusting "... and justice for all" had never been thought offensive, only stubborn. Americans then were accustomed to gratitude from foreigners but did not demand it; they quite innocently could not imagine any country fit to live in except their own. If I could not recognize it, too bad for me. Besides, I was not a refugee – just someone from the backwoods. "You got schools in Canada?" I had been asked. "You got radios?" And once, from a teacher, "What do they major in up there? Basket-weaving?"

My travel costume was a white piqué jacket and skirt that must have been crumpled and soot-flecked, for I had sat up all night. I was reading, I think, a novel by Sylvia Townsend Warner. My hair was thick and long. I wore my grandmother's wedding ring, which was too large, and which I would lose before long. I desperately wanted to look more than my age, which I had already started to give out as twenty-one. I was travelling light; my picnic hamper contained the poems and journals I had judged fit to accompany me into my new, unfettered existence, and some books I feared I might not find again in clerical Quebec – Zinoviev and Lenin's *Against the Stream*, and a few beige pamphlets from the Little Lenin Library, purchased second hand in New York. I had a picture of Mayakovsky torn out of *Cloud in Trousers* and one of Paddy Finucane, the Irish R.A.F. fighter pilot, who was killed the following summer. I had not met either of these men, but I approved of them both very much. I had abandoned my beloved but cumbersome anthologies of American and English verse, confident that I had whatever I needed by heart. I knew every word of Stephen Vincent Benét's "Litany for Dictatorships" and "Notes to be Left in a Cornerstone," and the other one that begins:

> They shot the Socialists at half-past five
> In the name of victorious Austria....

I could begin anywhere and rush on in my mind to the end. "Notes ..." was the New York I knew I would never have again, for there could be no journeying backward; the words "but I walked it young" were already a gate shut on a part of my life. The suitcase held only the fewest possible summer clothes. Everything else had been deposited at the various war-relief agencies of New York. In those days I made symbols out of everything, and I must have thought that by leaving a tartan skirt somewhere I was shedding past time. I remember one of those wartime agencies well because it was full of Canadian matrons. They wore pearl earrings like the Duchess of Kent's and seemed to be practicing her tiny smile. Brooches pinned to their cashmere cardigans carried some daft message about the Empire. I heard one of them exclaiming, "You don't expect me, a Britisher, to drink tea made with tea bags!" Good plain girls from the little German towns of Ontario, christened probably Wilma, Jean, and Irma, they had flowing eighteenth-century names like Georgiana and Arabella now. And the

Americans, who came in with their arms full of every stitch they could spare, would urge them, the Canadian matrons, to stand fast on the cliffs, to fight the fight, to slug the enemy on the landing fields, to belt him one on the beaches, to keep going with whatever iron rations they could scrape up in Bronxville and Scarsdale; and the Canadians half-shut their eyes and tipped their heads back like Gertrude Lawrence and said in thrilling Benita Hume accents that they would do that – indeed they would. I recorded "They're all trained nurses, actually. The Canadian ones have a good reputation. They managed to marry these American doctors."

Canada had been in Hitler's war from the very beginning, but America was still uneasily at peace. Recruiting had already begun; I had seen a departure from New York for Camp Stewart in Georgia, and some of the recruits' mothers crying and even screaming and trying to run alongside the train. The recruits were going off to drill with broomsticks because there weren't enough guns; they still wore old-fashioned headgear and were paid twenty-one dollars a month. There was a song about it: "For twenty-one dollars a day, once a month." As my own train crossed the border to Canada I expected to sense at once an air of calm and grit and dedication, but the only changes were from prosperous to shabby, from painted to unpainted, from smiling to dour. I was entering a poorer and a curiously empty country, where the faces of the people gave nothing away. The crossing was my sea change. I silently recited the vow I had been preparing for weeks: that I would never be helpless again and that I would not let anyone make a decision on my behalf.

When I got down from the train at Windsor Station, a man sidled over to me. He had a cap on his head and a bitter Celtic face, with deep indentations along his cheeks, as if his back teeth were pulled. I thought he was asking a direction. He repeated his question, which was obscene. My arms were pinned by the weight of my hamper and suitcase. He brushed the back of his hand over my breasts, called me a name, and edged away. The murderous rage I felt and the revulsion that followed were old friends. They had for years been my reaction to what my diaries called "their hypocrisy." "They" was a world of sly and mumbling people, all of them older than myself. I must have substituted "hypocrisy" for every sort of aggression, because fright was a luxury I could not afford. What distressed me was my helplessness – I who had sworn only a few hours earlier that I'd not be vulnerable again. The man's gaunt face, his drunken breath, the flat voice which I assigned to the graduate of some Christian Brothers teaching establishment haunted me for a long time after that. "The man at Windsor Station" would lurk in the windowless corridors of my nightmares; he would be the passenger, the only passenger, on a dark tram. The first sight of a city must be the measure for all second looks.

But it was not my first sight. I'd had ten years of it here – the first ten. After that, and before New York (in one sense, my deliverance), there had been a long spell of grief and shadow in an Ontario city, a place full of mean judgments and grudging minds, of paranoid Protestants and slovenly Catholics. To this day I cannot bear the sight of brick houses, or of a certain kind of empty treeless street on a Sunday afternoon. My memory of Montreal took shape while I was there. It was not a random jumble of rooms and summers and my mother singing "We've Come to See Miss Jenny Jones," but the faithful record of the true survivor. I retained, I rebuilt a superior civilization. In that drowned world, Sherbrooke Street seemed to be glittering and white; the vision of a house upon that street was so painful that I was obliged to banish it from the memorial. The small hot rooms of a summer cottage became enormous and cool. If I say that Cleopatra floated down the Chateauguay River, that the Winter Palace was stormed on Sherbrooke Street, that Trafalgar was fought on Lake St. Louis, I mean it naturally; they were the natural backgrounds of my exile and fidelity. I saw now at the far end of Windsor Station – more foreign, echoing, and mysterious than any American station could be – a statue of Lord Mount Stephen, the founder of the Canadian Pacific, which everyone took to be a memorial to Edward VII. Angus, Charlotte, and the smaller Linnet had truly been: this was my proof; once upon a time my instructions had been to make my way to Windsor Station should I ever be lost and to stand at the foot of Edward VII and wait for someone to find me.

I have forgotten to say that no one in Canada knew I was there. I looked up the number of the woman who had once been my nurse, but she had no telephone. I found her in a city directory, and with complete faith that "O. Carette" was indeed Olivia and that she would recall and welcome me I took a taxi to the east end of the city – the French end, the poor end. I was so sure of her that I did not ask the driver to wait (to take me where?) but dismissed him and climbed two flights of dark-brown stairs inside a house that must have been built soon after Waterloo. That it was Olivia who came to the door, that the small gray-haired creature I recalled as dark and towering had to look up at me, that she unhesitatingly offered me shelter all seem as simple now as when I broke my fiver to settle the taxi. Believing that I was dead, having paid for years of Masses for the repose of my heretic soul, almost the first thing she said to me was "*Tu vis?*" I understood "*Tu es ici?*" We straightened it out later. She held both my hands and cried and called me *belle et grande. Grande* was good, for among American girls I'd seemed a shrimp. I did not see what there was to cry for; I was here. I was as naturally selfish with Olivia as if her sole reason for being was me. I stayed with her for a while and left when her affection for me made her possessive, and I think I neglected her. On her deathbed she told one of her daughters, the reliable one, to keep an eye on me forever. Olivia was the only person in the world who did not believe

I could look after myself. Where she and I were concerned I remained under six. . .

Now, at no moment of this remarkable day did I feel anxious or worried or forlorn. The man at Windsor Station could not really affect my view of the future. I had seen some of the worst of life, but I had no way of judging it or of knowing what the worst could be. I had a sensation of loud, ruthless power, like an enormous waterfall. The past, the part I would rather not have lived, became small and remote, a dark pinpoint. My only weapons until now had been secrecy and insolence. I had stopped running away from schools and situations when I finally understood that by becoming a name in a file, by attracting attention, I would merely prolong my stay in prison – I mean, the prison of childhood itself. My rebellions then consisted only in causing people who were physically larger and legally sovereign to lose their self-control, to become bleached with anger, to shake with such temper that they broke cups and glasses and bumped into chairs. From the malleable, sunny child Olivia said she remembered, I had become, according to later chroniclers, cold, snobbish, and presumptuous. "You need an iron hand, Linnet." I can still hear that melancholy voice, which belonged to a friend of my mother's. "If anybody ever marries you he'd better have an iron hand." After today I would never need to hear this, or anything approaching it, for the rest of my life.

And so that June morning and the drive through empty, sunlit, wartime streets are even now like a roll of drums in the mind. My life was my own revolution – the tyrants deposed, the constitution wrenched from unwilling hands; I was, all by myself, the liberated crowd setting the palace on fire; I was the flags, the trees, the bannered windows, the flower-decked trains. The singing and the skyrockets of the 1848 I so trustingly believed would emerge out of the war were me, no one but me; and, as in the lyrical first days of any revolution, as in the first days of any love affair, there wasn't the whisper of a voice to tell me, "You might compromise."

If making virtue of necessity has ever had a meaning it must be here: for I was independent *inevitably*. There were good-hearted Americans who knew a bit of my story – as much as I wanted anyone to know – and who hoped I would swim and not drown, but from the moment I embarked on my journey I went on the dark side of the moon. "You seemed so sure of yourself," they would tell me, still troubled, long after this. In the cool journals I kept I noted that my survival meant nothing in the capitalist system; I was one of those not considered to be worth helping, saving, or even investigating. Thinking with care, I see this was true. What could I have turned into in another place? Why, a librarian at Omsk or a file clerk at Tomsk. Well, it hadn't happened that way; I had my private revolution and I settled in with Olivia in Montreal. Sink or swim? Of course I swam. Jobs were for the having; you could pick them up off the ground. Working for a living meant just what it says – a brisk necessity. It would be the least important fragment of my life until I had what I wanted. The cheek of it, I think now: penniless, sleeping in a shed room behind the kitchen of Olivia's cold-water flat, still I pointed across the wooden balustrade in a long open office where I was being considered for employment and said, "But I won't sit there." Girls were *there*, penned in like sheep. I did not think men better than women – only that they did more interesing work and got more money for it. In my journals I called other girls "coolies." I did not know if life made them bearers or if they had been born with a natural gift for giving in. "Coolie" must have been the secret expression of one of my deepest fears. I see now that I had an immense conceit: I thought I occupied a world other people could scarcely envision, let alone attain. It involved giddy risks and changes, stepping off the edge blindfolded, one's hand on nothing more than a birth certificate and a five-dollar bill. At this time of sitting in judgment I was earning nine dollars a week (until I was told by someone that the local minimum wage was twelve, on which I left for greener fields) and washing my white piqué skirt at night and ironing at dawn, and coming home at all hours so I could pretend to Olivia I had dined. Part of this impermeable sureness that I needn't waver or doubt came out of my having lived in New York. The first time I ever heard people laughing in a cinema was there. I can still remember the wonder and excitement and amazement I felt. I was just under fourteen and I had never heard people expressing their feelings in a public place in my life. The easy reactions, the way a poignant moment caught them, held them still – all that was new. I had come there straight from Ontario, where the reaction to a love scene was a kind of unhappy giggling, while the image of a kitten or a baby induced a long flat "Aaaah," followed by shamed silence. You could imagine them blushing in the dark for having said that – just that "Aaaah." When I heard that open American laughter I thought I could be like these people too, but had been told not to be by everyone, beginning with Olivia: "*Pas si fort*" was something she repeated to me so often when I was small that my father had made a tease out of it, called "passy four." From a tease it became oppressive too: "For the love of God, Linnet, passy four." What were these new people? Were they soft, too easily got at? I wondered that even then. Would a dictator have a field day here? Were they, as Canadian opinion had it, vulgar? Perhaps the notion of vulgarity came out of some incapacity on the part of the refined. Whatever they were, they couldn't all be daft; if they weren't I probably wasn't either. I supposed I stood as good a chance of being miserable here as anywhere, but at least I would not have to pretend to be someone else.

Now, of course there is much to be said on the other side: people who do not display what they feel have practical advantages. They can go away to be killed as if they didn't mind; they can see their sons off to war without a blink. Their upbringing is intended for a crisis. When it comes, they behave themselves. But it is murder in everyday life – truly murder. The dead of heart and spirit litter the landscape. Still, keeping a straight face makes life tolerable under stress. It makes *public* life tolerable – that is all I am saying; because in private people still got drunk, went after each other with bottles and knives, rang the police to complain that neighbors were sending poison gas over the transom, abandoned infant children and aged parents, wrote letters to newspapers in favor of corporal punishment, with inventive suggestions. When I came back to Canada that June, at least one thing had been settled: I knew that it was all right for people to laugh and cry and even to make asses of themselves. I had actually known people like that, had lived with them, and they were fine, mostly – not crazy at all. That was where a lot of my confidence came from when I began my journey into a new life and a dream past.

My father's death had been kept from me. I did not know its exact circumstances or even the date. He died when I was ten. At thirteen I was still expected to believe a fable about his being in England. I kept waiting for him to send for me, for my life was deeply wretched and I took it for granted he knew. Finally I began to suspect that death and silence can be one. How to be sure? Head-on questions got me nowhere. I had to create a situation in which some adult (not my mother, who was far too sharp) would lose all restraint and hurl the truth at me. It was easy: I was an artist at this. What I had not foreseen was the verbal violence of the scene or the effect it might have. The storm that seemed to break in my head, my need to maintain the pose of indifference ("What are you telling me that for? What makes you think I care?") were such a strain that I had physical reactions, like stigmata, which doctors would hopelessly treat on and off for years and which vanished when I became independent. The other change was that if anyone asked about my father I said, "Oh, he died." Now, in Montreal, I could confront the free adult world of falsehood and evasion on an equal footing; they would be forced to talk to me as they did to each other. Making appointments to meet my father's friends – Mr. Archie McEwen, Mr. Stephen Ross-Colby, Mr. Quentin Keller – I left my adult name, "Miss Muir." These were the men who eight, nine, ten years ago had asked, "Do you like your school?" – not knowing what else to say to children. I had curtsied to them and said, "Good night." I think what I wanted was special information about despair, but I should have known that would be taboo in a place where "like" and "don't like" were heavy emotional statements.

Archie McEwen, my father's best friend, or the man I mistook for that, kept me standing in his office on St. James Street West, he standing too, with his hands behind his back, and he said the following – not reconstructed or approximate but recalled, like "The religions of ancient Greece and Rome are extinct" or "O come, let us sing unto the Lord":

"Of course, Angus was a very sick man. I saw him walking along Sherbrooke Street. He must have just come out of hospital. He couldn't walk upright. He was using a stick. Inching along. His hair had turned gray. Nobody knew where Charlotte had got to, and we'd heard you were dead. He obviously wasn't long for this world either. He had too many troubles for any one man. I crossed the street because I didn't have the heart to shake hands with him. I felt terrible."

Savage? Reasonable? You can't tell, with those minds. Some recent threat had scared them. The Depression was too close, just at their heels. Archie McEwen did not ask where I was staying or where I had been for the last eight years; in fact, he asked only two questions. In response to the first I said, "She is married."

There came a gleam of interest – distant, amused: "So she decided to marry him, did she?"

My mother was highly visible; she had no secrets except

unexpected ones. My father had nothing but. When he asked, "Would you like to spend a year in England with your Aunt Dorothy?" I had no idea what he meant and I still don't. His only brother, Thomas, who was killed in 1918, had not been married; he'd had no sisters, that anyone knew. Those English mysteries used to be common. People came out to Canada because they did not want to think about the Thomases and Dorothys anymore. Angus was a solemn man, not much of a smiler. My mother, on the other hand – I won't begin to describe her, it would never end – smiled, talked, charmed anyone she didn't happen to be related to, swam in scandal like a partisan among the people. She made herself the central figure in loud, spectacular dramas which she played with the houselights on; you could see the audience too. That was her mistake; they kept their reactions, like their lovemaking, in the dark. You can imagine what she must have been in this world where everything was hushed, muffled, disguised: she must have seemed all they had by way of excitement, give or take a few elections and wars. It sounds like a story about the old and stale, but she and my father had been quite young eight and ten years before. The dying man creeping along Sherbrooke Street was thirty-two. First it was light chatter, then darker gossip, and then it went too far (*he* was ill and he couldn't hide it; *she* had a lover and didn't try); then suddenly it became tragic, and open tragedy was disallowed. And so Mr. Archie McEwen could stand in his office and without a trace of feeling on his narrow Lowland face – not unlike my father's in shape – he could say, "I crossed the street."

Stephen Ross-Colby, a bachelor, my father's painter chum: the smell of his studio on St. Mark Street was the smell of a personal myth. I said timidly, "Do you happen to have anything of his – a drawing or anything?" I was humble because I was on a private, personal terrain of vocation that made me shy even of the dead.

He said, "No, nothing. You could ask around. She junked

a lot of his stuff and he junked the rest when he thought he wouldn't survive. You might try ..." He gave me a name or two. "It was all small stuff," said Ross-Colby. "He didn't do anything big." He hurried me out of the studio for a cup of coffee in a crowded place – the Honey Dew on St. Catherine Street, it must have been. Perhaps in the privacy of his studio I might have heard him thinking. Years after that he would try to call me "Lynn," which I never was, and himself "Steve." He'd come into his own as an artist by then, selling wash drawings of Canadian war graves, sun-splashed, wisteria-mauve, lime-green, with drifts of blossom across the name of the regiment; gained a reputation among the heartbroken women who bought these impersonations, had them framed – the only picture in the house. He painted the war memorial at Caen. ("Their name liveth forever.") His stones weren't stones but mauve bubbles – that is all I have against them. They floated off the page. My objection wasn't to "He didn't do anything big" but to Ross-Colby's way of turning the dead into thistledown. He said, much later, of that meeting, "I felt like a bastard, but I was broke, and I was afraid you'd put the bite on me."

Let me distribute demerits equally and tell about my father's literary Jewish friend, Mr. Quentin Keller. He was older than the others, perhaps by some twelve years. He had a whispery voice and a long pale face and a daughter older than I. "Bossy Wendy" I used to call her when, forced by her parents as I was by mine, Bossy Wendy had to take a whole afternoon of me. She had a room full of extraordinary toys, a miniature kitchen in which everything worked, of which all I recall her saying is "Don't touch." Wendy Keller had left Smith after her freshman year to marry the elder son of a Danish baron. Her father said to me, "There is only one thing you need to know and that is that your father was a gentleman."

Jackass was what I thought. Yes, Mr. Quentin Keller was a jackass. But he was a literary one, for he had once written a play called *Forbearance*, in which I'd had a role. I had bounded across the stage like a tennis ball, into the arms of a young woman dressed up like an old one, and cried my one line: "Here I am, Granny!" Of course, he did not make his living fiddling about with amateur theatricals; thanks to our meeting I had a good look at the inside of a conservative architect's private office – that was about all it brought me.

What were they so afraid of, I wondered. I had not yet seen that I was in a false position where they were concerned; being "Miss Muir" had not made equals of us but lent distance. I thought they had read my true passport, the invisible one we all carry, but I had neither the wealth nor the influence a provincial society requires to make a passport valid. My credentials were lopsided: the important half of the scales was still in the air. I needed enormous collateral security – fame, an alliance with a powerful family, the power of money itself. I remember how Archie McEwen, trying to place me in some sensible context, to give me a voucher so he could take me home and show me to his wife, perhaps, asked his second question: "Who inherited the – ?"

"The what, Mr. McEwen?"

He had not, of course, read "Why I Am a Socialist." I did not believe in inherited property. "Who inherited the – ?" would not cross my mind again for another ten years, and then it would be a drawer quickly opened and shut before demons could escape. To all three men the last eight years were like minutes; to me they had been several lives. Some of my confidence left me then. It came down to "Next time I'll know better," but would that be enough? I had been buffeted until now by other people's moods, principles, whims, tantrums; I had survived, but perhaps I had failed to grow some outer skin it was now too late to acquire. Olivia thought that; she was the only one. Olivia knew more about the limits of nerve than I did. Her knowledge came out of the clean, swept, orderly poverty that used to be tucked away in the corners of cities. It didn't spill out then, or give anyone a bad conscience. Nobody took its picture. Anyway, Olivia would not have sat for such a portrait. The fringed green rug she put over her treadle sewing machine was part of a personal fortune. On her mantelpiece stood a copper statuette of Voltaire in an armchair. It must have come down to her from some robustly anticlerical ancestor. "Who is he?" she said to me. "You've been to school in a foreign country." "A governor of New France," I replied. She knew Voltaire was the name of a bad man and she'd have thrown the figurine out, and it would have made one treasure less in the house. Olivia's maiden name was Ouvrardville, which was good in Quebec, but only really good if you were one of the rich ones. Because of her maiden name she did not want anyone ever to know she had worked for a family; she impressed this on me delicately – it was like trying to understand what a dragonfly wanted to tell. In the old days she had gone home every weekend, taking me with her if my parents felt my company was going to make Sunday a very long day. Now I understood what the weekends were about: her daughters, Berthe and Marguerite, for whose sake she worked, were home from their convent schools Saturday and Sunday and had to be chaperoned. Her relatives pretended not to notice that Olivia was poor or even that she was widowed, for which she seemed grateful. The result of all this elegant sham was that Olivia did not say, "I was afraid you'd put the bite on me," or keep me standing. She dried her tears and asked if there was a trunk to follow. No? She made a pot of tea and spread a starched cloth on the kitchen table and we sat down to a breakfast of toast and honey. The honey tin was a ten-pounder decorated with bees the size of hornets. Lifting it for her, I remarked, "*C'est collant*," a word out of a frozen language that started to thaw when Olivia said, "*Tu vis?*"

On the advice of her confessor, who was to be my rival from now on, Olivia refused to tell me whatever she guessed or knew, and she was far too dignified to hint. Putting together the three men's woolly stories, I arrived at something about tuberculosis of the spine and a butchery of an operation. He started back to England to die there but either changed his mind or was too ill to begin the journey; at Quebec City, where he was to have taken ship, he shot himself in a public park at five o'clock in the morning. That was one version; another was that he died at sea and the gun was found in his luggage. The revolver figured in all three accounts. It was an officer's weapon from the Kaiser's war, that had belonged to his brother. Angus kept it at the back of a small drawer in the tall chest used for men's clothes and known in Canada as a highboy. In front of the revolver was a pigskin stud box and a pile of ironed handkerchiefs. Just describing that drawer dates it. How I happen to know the revolver was loaded and how I learned never to point a gun even in play is another story. I can tell you that I never again in my life looked inside a drawer that did not belong to me.

I know a woman whose father died, she thinks, in a concentration camp. Or was he shot in a schoolyard? Or hanged and thrown in a ditch? Were the ashes that arrived from some eastern plain his or another prisoner's? She invents different deaths. Her inventions have become her conversation at dinner parties. She takes on a child's voice and says, "My father died at Buchenwald." She chooses and rejects elements of the last act; one avoids mentioning death, shooting, capital punishment, cremation, deportation, even fathers. Her inventions are not thought neurotic or exhibitionist but something sanctioned by history. Peacetime casualties are not like that. They are lightning bolts out of a sunny sky that strike only one house. All around the ashy ruin lilacs blossom, leaves gleam. Speculation in public about the disaster would be indecent. Nothing remains but a silent, recurring puzzlement to the survivors: Why here and not there? Why this and not that?

Before July was out I had settled his fate in my mind and I never varied: I thought he had died of homesickness; sickness for England was the consumption, the gun, the everything. "Everything" had to take it all in, for people in Canada then did not speak of irrational endings to life, and newspapers did not print that kind of news: this was because of the spiritual tragedy for Catholic families, and because the act had long been considered a criminal one in British law. If Catholic feelings were spared it gave the impression no one but Protestants ever went over the edge, which was unfair; and so the possibility was eliminated, and people came to a natural end in a running car in a closed garage, hanging from a rafter in the barn, in an icy lake with a canoe left to drift empty. Once I had made up my mind, the whole story somehow became none of my business: I had looked in a drawer that did not belong to me. More, if I was to live my own life I had to let go. I wrote in my journal that "they" had got him but would not get me, and after that there was scarcely ever a mention.

My dream past evaporated. Montreal, in memory, was a leafy citadel where I knew every tree. In reality I recognized nearly nothing and had to start from scratch. Sherbrooke Street had been the dream street, pure white. It was the avenue poor Angus descended leaning on a walking stick. It was a moat I was not allowed to cross alone; it was lined with gigantic spreading trees through which light fell like a rain of coins. One day, standing at a corner, waiting for the light to change, I understood that the Sherbrooke Street of my exile – my Mecca, my Jerusalem – was this. It had to be: there could not be two. It was *only* this. The limitless green where in a perpetual spring I had been taken to play was the campus of McGill University. A house, whose beauty had brought tears to my sleep, to which in sleep I'd returned to find it inhabited by ugly strangers, gypsies, was a narrow stone thing with a shop on the ground floor and offices above – if that was it, for there were several like it. Through the bare panes of what might have been the sitting room, with its deep private window seats, I saw neon striplighting along a ceiling. Reality, as always, was narrow and dull. And yet what dramatic things had taken place on this very corner: Once Satan had approached me – furry dark skin, claws, red eyes, the lot. He urged me to cross the street and I did, in front of a car that braked in time. I explained, "The Devil told me to." I had no idea until then that my parents did not believe what I was taught in my convent school. (Satan is not bilingual, by the way; he speaks Quebec French.) My parents had no God and therefore no Fallen Angel. I was scolded for lying, which was a thing my father detested, and which my mother regularly did but never forgave in others.

Why these two nonbelievers wanted a strong religious education for me is one of the mysteries. (Even in loss of faith they were unalike, for he was ex-Anglican and she was ex-Lutheran and that is not your same atheist – no, not at all.) "To make you tolerant" was a lame excuse, as was "French," for I spoke fluent French with Olivia, and I could read in two languages before I was four. Discipline might have been one reason – God knows, the nuns provided plenty of that – but according to Olivia I did not need any. It cannot have been for the quality of the teaching, which was lamentable. I suspect that it was something like sending a dog to a trainer (they were passionate in their concern for animals, especially dogs), but I am not certain it ever brought me to heel. The first of my schools, the worst, the darkest, was on Sherbrooke Street too. When I heard, years later, it had been demolished, it was like the burial of a witch. I had remembered it penitentiary size, but what I found myself looking at one day was simply a very large stone house. A crocodile of little girls emerged from the front gate and proceeded along the street – white-faced, black-clad, eyes cast down. I knew they were bored, fidgety, anxious, and probably hungry. I should have felt pity, but at eighteen all that came to me was thankfulness that I had been correct about one thing throughout my youth, which I now considered ended: time had been on my side, faithfully, and unless you died you were always bound to escape.

BETWEEN ZERO AND ONE

When I was young I thought that men had small lives of their own creation. I could not see why, born enfranchised, without the obstacles and constraints attendant on women, they set such close limits for themselves and why, once the limits had been reached, they seemed so taken aback. I could not tell much difference between a man aged thirty-six, about, and one forty or fifty; it was impossible to fix the borderline of this apparent disappointment. There was a space of life I used to call "between Zero and One" and then came a long mystery. I supposed that men came up to their wall, their terminal point, quite a long way after One. At that time I was nineteen and we were losing the war. The news broadcast in Canada was flatly optimistic, read out in the detached nasal voices de rigueur for the CBC. They were voices that seemed to be saying, "Good or bad, it can't affect *us*." I worked in a building belonging to the federal government – it was a heavy Victorian structure of the sort that exists on every continent, wherever the British thought they'd come to stay. This one had been made out of the reddish-brown Montreal stone that colors, in memory, the streets of my childhood and that architects have no use for now. The office was full of old soldiers from one war before: Ypres (pronounced "Wipers") and Vimy Ridge were real, as real as this minute, while Singapore, Pearl Harbor, Voronezh were the stuff of fiction. It seemed as if anything that befell the young, even dying, was bound to be trivial.

"Half of 'em'll never see any fighting," I often heard. "Anyway not like in the trenches." We did have one veteran from the current war – Mac Kirkconnell, who'd had a knock on the head during his training and was now good for nothing except civilian life. He and two others were the only men under thirty left in the place. The other two were physical crocks, which was why they were not in uniform (a question demented women sometimes asked them in the street). Mr. Tracy had been snow-blinded after looking out of a train window for most of a sunny February day; he had recovered part of his sight but had to wear mauve glasses even by electric light. He was nice but strange, infirm. Mr. Curran, reputed to have one kidney, one lung, and one testicle, and who was the subject of endless rhymes and ditties on that account, was not so nice: he had not wanted a girl in the office and had argued against my being employed. Now that I was there he simply pretended that he had won. There were about a dozen other men – older, old. I can see every face, hear every syllable, which evoked, for me, a street, a suburb, a kind of schooling. I could hear just out of someone's saying to me, "Say, Linnet, couja just gimme a hand here, please?" born here, born in Glasgow; immigrated early, late; raised in Montreal, no, farther west. I can see the rolled shirtsleeves, the braces, the eyeshades, the hunched shoulders, the elastic armbands, the paper cuffs they wore sometimes, the chopped-egg sandwiches in waxed paper, the apples, the oatmeal cookies ("Want any, Linnet? If you don't eat lunch nobody'll marry you"), the thermos flasks. Most of them lived thinly, paying for a bungalow, a duplex flat, a son's education: a good Protestant education was not to be had for nothing then. I remember a day of dark spring snowstorms, ourselves reflected on the black windows, the pools of warm light here and there, the green-shaded lamps, the dramatic hiss and gurgle of the radiators that always sounded like the background to some emotional outburst, the sudden slackening at the end of the afternoon when every molecule of oxygen in the room had turned into poison. Assistant Chief Engineer Macaulay came plodding softly along the wintry room and laid something down on my desk. It was a collection of snapshots of a naked woman prancing and skipping in what I took to be the back yard of his house out in Cartierville. In one she was in a baby carriage with her legs spread over the sides, pretending to drink out of an infant's bottle. The unknown that this represented was infinite. I also wondered what Mr. Macaulay wanted – he didn't say. He remarked, shifting from foot to foot, "Now, Linnet, they tell me you like modern art." I thought then, I think now, that the tunnel winters, the sudden darkness that April day, the years he'd had of this long green room, the knowledge that he would die and be buried "Assistant Chief Engineer Grade II" without having overtaken Chief Engineer McCreery had simply snapped the twig, the frail matchstick in the head that is all we have to keep us sensible.

Bertie Knox had a desk facing mine. He told the other men I'd gone red in the face when I saw Macaulay's fat-arsed wife. (He hadn't seen *that* one; I had turned it over, like a bad card.) The men teased me for blushing, and they said, "Wait till you get married, Linnet, you haven't done with shocks." Bertie Knox had been in this very office since the age of twelve. The walls had been a good solid gray then – not this drawing-room green. The men hadn't been pampered and coddled, either. There wasn't even a water cooler. You were fined for smoking, fined for lateness, fined for sick leave. He had worked the old ten-hour day and given every cent to his mother. Once he pinched a dime of it and his mother went for him. He locked himself in a cupboard. His mother took the door off its hinges and beat him blue with a wooden hanger. During the Depression, married, down to half pay, four kids in the house, he had shovelled snow for twenty cents an hour. "And none the worse for it," he would always wind up. Most of the men seemed to have been raised in hardship by stern, desperate parents. What struck me was the good they thought it had done them (I had yet to meet an adult man with a poor opinion of himself) and their desire to impose the same broken fortunes on other people, particularly on the young – though not their own young, of course. There was a touch of sadness, a touch of envy to it, too. Bertie Knox had seen Mr. Macaulay and Mr. McCreery come in as Engineers Grade II, wet behind the ears, puffed up with their new degrees, "just a couple more college punks." He said that engineering was the world's most despised profession, occupied mainly by human apes. Instead of a degree he had a photograph of himself in full kilt, Highland Light Infantry, 1917: he had gone "home," to a completely unknown Old Country, and joined up there. "Will you just look at that lad?" he would plead. "Do they come like him today? By God, they do not!" Bertie Knox could imitate any tone and accent, including mine. He could do a CBC announcer droning, "The British have ah taken ah Tobruk," when we knew perfectly well the Germans had. (One good thing about the men was that when anything seemed hopeless they talked nonsense. The native traits of pessimism and constant grumbling returned only when there was nothing to grumble about.) Bertie Knox had a wooden leg, which he showed me; it was dressed in a maroon sock with clocks up the sides and a buckled garter. He had a collection of robust bawdy songs – as everyone (all the men, I mean) had in Canada, unless they were pretending – which I copied in a notebook, verse upon verse, with the necessary indications: Tune – "On, Wisconsin!," Tune – "Men of Harlech," Tune – "We Gather Together to Ask the Lord's Blessing." Sometimes he took the notebook and corrected a word here and there. It doesn't follow that he was a cheerful person. He laughed a lot but he never smiled. I don't think he liked anyone, really.

The men were statisticians, draftsmen, civil engineers. Painted on the frosted glass of the office door was

REVIEW AND DEVELOPMENT
RESEARCH AND EXPANSION
OF
WARTIME INDUSTRY
"REGIONAL AND URBAN"

The office had been called something else up until September, 1939; according to Bertie Knox they were still doing the same work as before, and not much of it. "It looks good," he said. "It sounds good. What is its meaning? Sweet buggerall." A few girls equipped with rackety typewriters and adding machines sat grouped at the far end of the room, separated from the men by a balustrade. I was the first woman ever permitted to work on the men's side of this fence. A pigeon among the cats was how it sometimes felt. My title was "aide." Today it would be something like "trainee." I was totally unqualified for this or any other kind of work and had been taken on almost at my own insistence that they could not do without me.

"Yes, I know all about that," I had replied, to everything.

"Well, I *suppose* it's all right," said Chief Engineer. The hiring of girls usually fell to a stout grim woman called "Supervisor," but I was not coming in as a typist. He had never interviewed a girl before and he was plainly uncomfortable, asking me questions with all the men straining to hear. There were no young men left on account of the war, and the office did need someone. But what if they trained me, he said, at great cost and expense to the government, and what if I then did the dreadful thing girls were reputed to do, which was to go off and get married? It would mean a great waste of time and money just when there was a war on.

I was engaged, but not nearly ready for the next step. In any case, I told him, even if I did marry I would need to go on working, for my husband would more than likely be sent overseas. What Chief Engineer did not know was that I was a minor with almost no possibility of obtaining parental consent. Barring some bright idea, I could not do much of anything until I was twenty-one. For this interview I had pinned back my long hair; I wore a hat, gloves, earrings, and I folded my hands on my purse in a conscious imitation of older women. I did not mind the interview, or the furtively staring men. I was shy, but not self-conscious. Efforts made not to turn a young girl's head – part of an education I had encountered at every stage and in every sort of school – had succeeded in making me invisible to myself. My only commercial asset was that I knew French, but French was of no professional use to anyone in Canada then – not even to French Canadians; one might as well have been fluent in Pushtu. Nevertheless I listed it on my application form, along with a very dodgy "German" (private lessons between the ages of eight and ten) and an entirely impudent "Russian": I was attending Russian evening classes at McGill, for reasons having mainly to do with what I believed to be the world's political future. I recorded my age as twenty-two, hoping to be given a grade and a salary that would correspond. There were no psychological or aptitudes tests; you were taken at your word and lasted according to performance. There was no social security and only the loosest sort of pensions plan; hiring and firing involved no more paperwork than a typed letter – sometimes not even that. I had an unmistakably Montreal accent of a kind now almost extinct, but my having attended school in the United States gave me a useful vagueness of background.

And so, in an ambience of doubt, apprehension, foreboding, incipient danger, and plain hostility, for the first time in the history of the office a girl was allowed to sit with the men. And it was here, at the desk facing Bertie Knox's, on the only uncomfortable chair in the room, that I felt for the first time that almost palpable atmosphere of sexual curiosity, sexual resentment, and sexual fear that the presence of a woman can create where she is not wanted. If part of the resentment vanished when it became clear that I did not know what I was doing, the feeling that women were "trouble" never disappeared. However, some of the men were fathers of daughters, and they quickly saw that I was nothing like twenty-two. Some of them helped me then, and one man, Hughie Pryor, an engineer, actually stayed late to do some of my work when I fell behind.

Had I known exactly what I was about, I might not have remained for more than a day. Older, more experienced, I'd have called it a dull place. The men were rotting quietly until pension time. They kept to a slow English-rooted civil-service pace; no one wasted office time openly, but no one produced much, either. Although they could squabble like hens over mislaid pencils, windows open or shut, borrowed triangles, special and sacred pen nibs used for tracing maps, there was a truce about zeal. The fact is that I did not know the office was dull. It was so new to me, so strange, such another climate, that even to flow with the sluggish tide draining men and women into the heart of the city each day was a repeated experiment I sensed, noted, recorded, as if I were being allowed to be part of something that was not really mine. The smell of the building was of school – of chalk, dust, plaster, varnish, beeswax. Victorian, Edwardian, and early Georgian oil portraits of Canadian captains of industry, fleshed-out pirate faces, adorned the staircase and halls – a daily reminder that there are two races, those who tread on people's lives, and the others. The latest date on any of the portraits was about 1925: I suppose photography had taken over. Also by then the great fortunes had been established and the surviving pirates were retired, replete and titled, usually to England. Having had both French and English schooling in Quebec, I knew that these pink-cheeked marauders were what English-speaking children were led to admire (without much hope of emulation, for the feast was over). They were men of patriotism and of action; we owed them everything. They were in a positive, constructive way a part of the Empire and of the Crown; this was a good thing. In a French education veneration was withheld from anyone except the dead and defeated, ranging from General Montcalm expiring at his last battle to a large galaxy of maimed and crippled saints. Deprivation of the senses, mortification of mind and body were imposed, encouraged, for phantom reasons – something to do with a tragic past and a deep fear of life itself. Montreal was a city where the greater part of the population were wrapped in myths and sustained by belief in magic. I had been to school with little girls who walked in their sleep and had visions; the nuns who had taught me seemed at ease with the dead. I think of them even now as strange, dead, punishing creatures who neither ate nor breathed nor slept. The one who broke one of my fingers with a ruler was surely a spirit without a mind, tormented, acting in the vengeful driven way of homeless ghosts. In an English school visions would have been smartly dealt with – cold showers, the parents summoned, at the least a good stiff talking to. These two populations, these two tribes, knew nothing whatever about each other. In the very poorest part of the east end of the city, apparitions were commonplace; one lived among a mixture of men and women and their imaginings. I would never have believed then that anything could ever stir them from their dark dreams. The men in the portraits were ghosts of a kind, too; they also seemed to be saying, "Too late, too late for you," and of course in a sense so it was: it was too late for anyone else to import Chinese and Irish coolie labor and wring a railway out of them. That had already been done. Once I said to half-blind Mr. Tracy, "Things can't just stay this way."

"Change is always for the worse" was his reply. His own

father had lost all his money in the Depression, ten years before; perhaps he meant that.

I climbed to the office in a slow reassuring elevator with iron grille doors, sharing it with inexpressive women and men – clearly, the trodden on. No matter how familiar our faces became, we never spoke. The only sound, apart from the creaking cable, was the gasping and choking of a poor man who had been gassed at the Somme and whose lungs were said to be in shreds. He had an old man's pale eyes and wore a high stiff collar and stared straight before him, like everyone else. Some of the men in my office had been wounded, too, but they made it sound pleasant. Bertie Knox said he had hobbled on one leg and crutches in the 1918 Allied victory parade in Paris. According to him, when his decimated regiment followed their Highland music up the Champs-Élysées, every pretty girl in Paris had been along the curb, fighting the police and screaming and trying to get at Bertie Knox and take him home.

"It was the kilts set 'em off," said Bertie Knox. "That and the wounds. And the Jocks played it up for all they was worth, bashing the very buggery out of the drums." "Jocks" were Scots in those days – nothing more.

Any mention of that older war could bring the men to life, but it had been done with for more than twenty years now. Why didn't they move, walk, stretch, run? Each of them seemed to inhabit an invisible square; the square was shared with *my* desk, *my* graph paper, *my* elastic bands. The contents of the square were tested each morning: The drawers of my own desk – do they still open and shut? My desk lamp – does it still turn on and off? Have my special coat hanger, my favorite nibs, my drinking glass, my calendar, my children's pictures, my ash-tray, the one I brought from home, been tampered with during the night? Sometimes one glimpsed another world, like an extra room ("It was my young daughter made my lunch today" – said with a dismissive shrug, lest it be taken for boasting) or a wish outdistanced, reduced, shrunken, trailing somewhere in the mind: "I often thought I wanted …" "Something I wouldn't have minded having …" Easily angry, easily offended, underpaid, at the mercy of accidents – an illness in the family could wipe out a life's savings – still they'd have resisted change for the better. Change was double-edged; it might mean improving people with funny names, letting them get uppity. What they had instead were marks of privilege – a blind sureness that they were superior in every way to French Canadians, whom in some strange fashion they neither heard nor saw (a lack of interest that was doubly and triply returned); they had the certainty they'd never be called on to share a washroom or a drawing board or to exchange the time of day with anyone "funny" (applications from such people, in those days, would have been quietly set aside); most important of all, perhaps, they had the distinction of the individual hand towel. These towels, as stiff as boards, reeking of chloride bleach, were distributed once a week by a boy pushing a trolley. They were distributed to men, but not even to *all* men. The sanctioned carried them to the washroom, aired and dried them on the backs of chairs, kept them folded in a special drawer. Assimilated into a male world, I had one too. The stenographers and typists had to make do with paper towels that scratched when new and dissolved when damp. Any mistake or oversight on towel day was a source of outrage: "Why the bejesus do I get a torn one three times running? You'd think I didn't count for anything round here." It seemed a true distress; someday some simple carelessness might turn out to be the final curse: they were like that prisoner of Mussolini, shut up for life, who burst into tears because the soup was cold. When I received presents of candy I used to bring them in for the staff; these wartime chocolates tasted of candlewax but were much appreciated nonetheless. I had to be careful to whom I handed the box first: I could not begin with girls, which I'd have thought natural, because Supervisor did not brook interruptions. I would transfer the top layer to the lid of the box for the girls, for later on, and then consider the men. A trinity of them occupied glass cubicles. One was diabetic; another was Mr. Tracy, who, a gentle alcoholic, did not care for sweets; and the third was Mr. Curran. Skipping all three I would start with Chief Engineer McCreery and descend by way of Assistant Chief Engineers Grade I and then II – I approached them by educational standards, those with degrees from McGill and Queen's – Queen's first – to, finally, the technicians. By that time the caramels and nougats had all been eaten and nothing left but squashy orange and vanilla creams nobody liked. Then, then, oh God, who was to receive the affront of the last chocolate, the one reposing among crumbs and fluted paper casings? Sometimes I was cowardly and left the box adrift on a drawing board with a murmured "Pass it along, would you?"

I was deeply happy. It was one of the periods of inexplicable grace when every day is a new parcel one unwraps, layer on layer of tissue paper covering bits of crystal, scraps of words in a foreign language, pure white stones. I spent my lunch hours writing in notebooks, which I kept locked in my desk. The men never bothered me, apart from trying to feed me little pieces of cake. They were all sad when I began to smoke – I remember that. I could write without hearing anyone, but poetry was leaving me. It was not an abrupt removal but like a recurring tide whose high-water mark recedes inch by inch. Presently I was deep inland and the sea was gone. I would mourn it much later: it was such a gentle separation at the time that I scarcely noticed. I had notebooks stuffed with streets and people: my journals were full of "but what he *really* must have meant was ..." There were endless political puzzles I tried to solve by comparing one thing with another, but of course nothing matched; I had not lost my adolescent habit of private, passionate manifestos. If politics were nothing but chess – Mr. Tracy's ways of sliding out of conviction – K was surely Social

Justice and Q Extreme Morality. I was certain of this, and that after the war – unless we were completely swallowed up, like those Canadian battalions at Hong Kong – K and Q would envelop the world. Having no one to listen to, I could not have a thought without writing it down. There were pages and pages of dead butterflies, wings without motion or lift. I began to ration my writing, for fear I would dream through life as my father had done. I was afraid I had inherited a poisoned gene from him, a vocation without a gift. He had spent his own short time like a priest in charge of a relic, forever expecting the blessed blood to liquefy. I had no assurance I was not the same. I was so like him in some ways that a man once stopped me in front of the Bell Telephone building on Beaver Hall Hill and said, "Could you possibly be Angus Muir's sister?" That is how years telescope in men's minds. That particular place must be the windiest in Montreal, for I remember dust and ragged papers blowing in whirlpools and that I had to hold my hair. I said, "No, I'm not," without explaining that I was not his sister but his daughter. I had heard people say, referring to me but not knowing who I was, "He had a daughter, but apparently she died." We couldn't *both* be dead. Having come down on the side of life, I kept my distance. Writing now had to occupy an enormous space. I had lived in New York until a year before and there were things I was sick with missing. There was no theatre, no music; there was one museum of art with not much in it. There was not even a free public lending library in the sense of the meaning that would have been given the words "free public lending library" in Toronto or New York. The municipal library was considered a sinister joke. There was a persistent, apocryphal story among English Canadians that an American philanthropic foundation (the Carnegie was usually mentioned) had offered to establish a free public lending library on condition that its contents were not to be censored by the provincial government of Quebec or by the Catholic Church, and that the offer had been turned down. The story may not have been true but its persistence shows the political and cultural climate of Montreal then. Educated French Canadians summed it up in shorter form: their story was that when you looked up "Darwin" in the card index of the Bibliothèque de Montréal you found "See anti-Darwin." A Canadian actress I knew in New York sent me the first published text of *The Skin of Our Teeth.* I wrote imploring her to tell me everything about the production – the costumes, the staging, the voices. I've never seen it performed – not read it since the end of the war. I've been told that it doesn't hold, that it is not rooted in anything specific. It was then; its Ice Age was Fascism. I read it the year of Dieppe, in a year when "Russia" meant "Leningrad," when Malta could be neither fed nor defended. The Japanese were anywhere they wanted to be. Vast areas of the world were covered with silence and ice. One morning I read a little notice in the *Gazette* that Miss Margaret Urn would be taking auditions for the Canadian Broadcasting Corporation. I presented myself during my lunch hour with *The Skin of Our Teeth* and a manuscript one-act play of my own, in case. I had expected to find queues of applicants but I was the only one. Miss Urn received me in a small room of a dingy office suite on St. Catherine Street. We sat down on opposite sides of a table. I was rendered shy by her bearing, which had a headmistress quality, and perplexed by her accent – it was the voice any North American actor will pick up after six months of looking for work in the West End, but I did not know that. I opened *The Skin of Our Teeth* and began to read. It was floating rather than reading, for I had much of it by heart. When I read "Have you milked the mammoth?" Miss Urn stopped me. She reached over the table and placed her hand on the page.

"My dear child, what is this rubbish?" she said.

I stammered, "It is a … a play in New York."

Oh, fool. The worst thing to say. If only I had said, "Tallulah Bankhead," adding swiftly, "London, before the war." Or, better, "An Edwardian farce. Queen Alexandra, deaf though she was, much appreciated the joke about the separation of 'm' and 'n.' " "A play in New York" evoked a look Canada was making me familiar with: amusement, fastidious withdrawal, gentle disdain. What a strange city to have a play in, she might have been thinking.

"Try reading this," she said.

I shall forget everything about the war except that at the worst point of it I was asked to read *Dear Octopus.* If Miss Urn had never heard of Thornton Wilder I had never heard of Dodie Smith. I read what I took to be parody. Presently it dawned on me these were meant to be real people. I broke up laughing because of Sabina, Fascism, the Ice Age that was perhaps upon us, because of the one-act play still in my purse. She took the book away from me and closed it and said I would, or would not, be hearing from her.

Now there was excitement in the office: a second woman had been brought in. Mrs. Ireland was her name. She had an advanced degree in accountancy and she was preparing a doctorate in some branch of mathematics none of the men were familiar with. She was about thirty-two. Her hair was glossy and dark; she wore it in braids that became a rich mahogany color when they caught the light. I admired her hair, but the rest of her was angry-looking – flushed cheeks, red hands and arms. The scarf around her throat looked as though it had been wound and tied in a fury. She tossed a paper on my desk and said, "Check this. I'm in a hurry." Chief Engineer looked up, looked at her, looked down. A play within the play, a subplot, came to life; I felt it exactly as children can sense a situation they have no name for. In the afternoon she said, "Haven't you done that yet?" She had a positive, hammering sort of voice. It must have carried as far as the portraits in the hall. Chief Engineer unrolled a large map showing the mineral resources of eastern Canada and got behind it. Mrs. Ireland called, to the room in general, "Well, is she supposed to be working for me or isn't she?" Oh? I opened the bottom drawer of my desk, unlocked the middle drawer, began to pack up my personal affairs. I saw that I'd need a taxi: I had about three pounds of manuscripts and notes, and what seemed to amount to a wardrobe. In those days girls wore white gloves to work; I had two extra pairs of these, and a makeup kit, and extra shoes. I began filling my wastebasket with superfluous cargo. The room had gone silent: I can still see Bertie Knox's ratty little eyes judging, summing up, taking the measure of this new force. Mr. Tracy, in his mauve glasses, hands in his pockets, came strolling out of his office; it was a sort of booth, with frosted-glass panels that did not go up to the ceiling. He must have heard the shouting and then the quiet. He and Mr. Curran and Mr. Elwitt, the diabetic one, were higher in rank than Chief Engineer, higher than Office Manager; they could have eaten Supervisor for tea and no one would dare complain. He came along easily – I never knew him to rush. I remember now that Chief Engineer called him "Young Tracy," because of his father; "Old Tracy" – the real Tracy, so to speak – was the one who'd gone bust in the Depression. That was why Young Tracy had this job. He wasn't all that qualified, really; not so different from me. He sat down on Bertie Knox's desk with his back to him.

"Well, Bolshie," he said to me. This was a long joke: it had to do with my political views, as he saw them, and it was also a reference to a character in an English comic called "Pip and Squeak" that he and I had both read as children – we'd discussed it once. Pip and Squeak were a dog and a penguin. They had a son called Wilfred, who was a rabbit. Bolshie seemed to be a sort of acquaintance. He went around carrying one of those round black bombs with a sputtering fuse. He had a dog, I think – a dog with whiskers. I had told Mr. Tracy how modern educators were opposed to "Pip and Squeak." They thought that more than one generation of us had been badly misled by the unusual family unit of dog, penguin, and rabbit. It was argued that millions of children had grown up believing that if a dog made advances to a female penguin she would produce a rabbit. "Not a *rabbit*," said Mr. Tracy reasonably. "*Wilfred*."

I truly liked him. He must have thought I was going to say something now, if only to rise to the tease about "Bolshie," but I was in the grip of that dazzling anger that is a form of snow blindness, too. I could not speak, and anyway didn't want to. I could only go on examining a pencil to see if it was company property or mine – as if that mattered. "Are you taking the day off or trying to leave me?" he said. I can feel that tense listening of men pretending to work. "I was looking over your application form," he said. "D'you know that your father knew my father? Yep. A long time ago. My father took it into his head to commission a mural for a plant in Sorel. Brave thing to do. Nobody did anything like that. Your father said it wasn't up his street. Suggested some other guy. My old man took the *two* of them down to Sorel. Did a lot of clowning around, but the Depression was just starting, so the idea fell through. My old man enjoyed it, though."

"Clowning around" could not possibly have been my father, but then the whole thing was so astonishing. "I should have mentioned it to you when you first came in," he said, "but I didn't realize it myself. There must be a million people called Muir; I happened to be looking at your form because apparently you're due for a raise." He whistled something for a second or two, then laughed and said, "Nobody ever quits around here. It can't be done. It upsets the delicate balance between labor and government. You don't want to do that. What do you want to do that for?"

"Mr. Curran doesn't like me."

"Mr. Curran is a brilliant man," he said. "Why, if you knew Curran's whole story you'd" – he paused – "you'd stretch out the hand of friendship."

"I've been asking and asking for a chair that doesn't wobble."

"Take the day off," he said. "Go to a movie or something. Tomorrow we'll start over." His life must have been like that. "You know, there's a war on. We're all needed. Mrs. Ireland has been brought here from ..."

"From Trahnah," said Mrs. Ireland.

"Yes, from Toronto, to do important work. I'll see something gets done about that chair."

He stood up, hands in his pockets, slouching, really; gave an affable nod all round. The men didn't see; their noses were almost touching their work. He strolled back to his glass cubicle, whistling softly. The feeling in the room was like the sight of a curtain raised by the wind now sinking softly.

"Oh, Holy Hannah!" Mrs. Ireland burst out. "I thought this was supposed to be a wartime agency!"

No one replied. *My father knew your father. I'll see something gets done about that chair.* So that is how it works among men. To be noted, examined, compared.

Meanwhile I picked up the paper she'd tossed on my desk hours before and saw that it was an actuarial equation. I waited until the men had stopped being aware of us and took it over and told her I could not read it, let alone check it. It had obviously been some kind of test.

She said, "Well, it was too much to hope for. I have to single-handedly work out some wartime overtime pensions plan taking into account the cost of living and the earnest hope that the Canadian dollar won't sink." And I was to have been her assistant. I began to admire the genius someone – Assistant Chief Engineer Macaulay, perhaps – had obviously seen in me. Mrs. Ireland went on, "I gather after this little comic opera we've just witnessed that you're the blue-eyed girl around here." (Need I say that I'd hear this often? That the rumor I was Mr. Tracy's mistress now had firm hold on the feminine element in the room – though it never gained all the men – particularly on the biddies, the two or three old girls loafing along to retirement, in comfortable corsets that gave them a sort of picket fence around the middle? That the obscene anonymous notes I sometimes found on my desk – and at once unfairly blamed on Bertie Knox – were the first proof I had that prolonged virginity can be the mother of invention?) "You can have your desk put next to mine," said Mrs. Ireland. "I'll try to dig some good out of you."

But I had no intention of being mined by Mrs. Ireland. Remembering what Mr. Tracy had said about the hand of friendship I told her, truthfully, that it would be a waste for her and for me. My name was down to do documentary-film work, for which I thought I'd be better suited; I was to be told as soon as a vacancy occurred.

"Then you'll have a new girl," I said. "You can teach her whatever you like."

"*Girl?*" She could not keep her voice down, ever. "There'll not be a girl in this office again, if I have a say. Girls make me sick, sore, and weary."

I thought about that for a long time. I had believed it was only because of the men that girls were parked like third-class immigrants at the far end of the room – the darkest part, away from the windows – with the indignity of being watched by Supervisor, whose whole function was just that. But there, up on the life raft, stepping on girls' fingers, was Mrs. Ireland, too. If that was so, why didn't Mrs. Ireland get along with the men, and why did they positively and openly hate her – openly especially after Mr. Tracy's extraordinary and instructive sorting out of power?

"What blinking idiot would ever marry *her*?" said Bertie Knox. "Ten to one she's not married at all. Ireland must be her maiden name. She thinks the 'Mrs.' sounds good." I began to wonder if she was not a little daft sometimes: she used to talk to herself; quite a lot of it was about me.

"You can't run a wartime agency with *that* going on," she'd say loudly. "That" meant poor Mr. Tracy and me. Or else she would declare that it was unpatriotic of me to be drawing a man's salary. Here I think the men agreed. The salary was seventy-five dollars a month, which was less than a man's if he was doing the same work. The men had often hinted it was a lot for a girl. Girls had no expenses; they lived at home. Money paid them was a sort of handout. When I protested that I had the same expenses as any bachelor and did not live at home, it was countered by a reasonable "Where you live is up to you." They looked on girls as parasites of a kind, always being taken to restaurants and fed by men. They calculated the cost of probable outings, even to the Laura Secord chocolates I might be given, and rang the total as a casual profit to me. Bertie Knox used to sing, "I think that I shall never see a dame refuse a meal that's free." Mrs. Ireland said that all this money would be better spent on soldiers who were dying, on buying war bonds and plasma, on the purchase of tanks and Spitfires. "When I think of parents scrimping to send their sons to college!" she would conclude. All this was floods of clear water; I could not give it a shape. I kept wondering what she expected me to *do*, for that at least would throw a shadow on the water, but then she dropped me for a time in favor of another crusade, this one against Bertie Knox's singing. He had always sung. His voice conveyed rakish parodies of hymns and marches to every corner of the room. Most of the songs were well-known; they came back to us from the troops, were either simple and rowdy or expressed a deep skepticism about the war, its aims and purposes, the way it was being conducted, and about the girls they had left at home. It was hard to shut Bertie Knox up: he had been around for a long time. Mrs. Ireland said she had not had the education she'd had to come here and listen to foul language. Now absolutely and flatly forbidden by Chief Engineer to sing any ribald song *plainly*, Bertie Knox managed with umptee-um syllables as best he could. He became Mrs. Ireland's counterpoint.

"I know there's a shortage of men," Mrs. Ireland would suddenly burst out.

"Oh umptee tum titty," sang Bertie Knox.

"And that after this war it will be still worse ..."

"Ti umpty dum diddy."

"There'll hardly be a man left in the world worth his salt ..."

"Tee umpty tum tumpty."

"But what I do not see ..."

"Tee diddle dee dum."

"Is why a totally unqualified girl ..."

"Tum tittle umpty tumpty."

"Should be subsidized by the taxpayers of this country ..."

"Pum pum tee umpty pumpee."

"Just because her father failed to paint ..."

"Oh umpty tumpty tumpty."

"A mural down in ..."

"Tee umpty dum dum."

"Sorel."

"Tum tum, oh, dum dum, oh, pum pum, oh, oh, uuuum."

"Subsidized" stung, for I worked hard. Having no training I had no shortcuts. There were few mechanical shortcuts of any kind. The engineers used slide rules, and the machines might baffle today because of their simplicity. As for a computer, I would not have guessed what it might do or even look like. Facts were recorded on paper and stored in files and summarized by doing sums and displayed in some orderly fashion on graphs. I sat with one elbow on my desk, my left hand concealed in my hair. No one could see that I was counting on my fingers, in units of five and ten. The system by twelves would have finished me; luckily no one mentioned it. Numbers were a sunken world; they were a seascape from which perfect continents might emerge at any minute. I never saw more than their outline. I was caught on Zero. If zero meant Zero, how could you begin a graph on nothing? How could anything under zero be anything but Zero too? I spoke to Mr. Tracy: What occupied the space between Zero and One? It must be something arbitrary, not in the natural order of numbers. If One was solid ground, why not begin with One? Before One there was what? Thin air? Thin air must be Something. He said kindly, "Don't worry your head," and if I had continued would certainly have added, "Take the day off." Chief Engineer McCreery often had to remind me, "But we're not *paying* you to think!" If that was so, were we all being paid not to think? At the next place I worked things were even worse. It was another government agency, called Dominion Film Centre – my first brush with the creative life. Here one was handed a folded thought like a shapeless school uniform and told, "There, wear that." Everyone had it on, regardless of fit. It was one step on: "We're not paying you to think about whatever you are thinking." I often considered approaching Mrs. Ireland, but she would not accept even a candy from me, let alone a question. "There's a war on" had been her discouraging refusal of a Life Saver once.

The men by now had found out about her husband. He had left school at Junior Fourth (Grade Seven) and "done nothing to improve himself." He was a Pole. She was ashamed of having a name that ended in "ski" and used her maiden name; Bertie Knox hadn't been far off. Thinking of it now, I realize she might not have been ashamed but only aware that the "ski" name on her application could have relegated it to a bottom drawer. Where did the men get their information, I wonder. Old "ski" was a lush who drank her paycheck and sometimes beat her up; the scarves she wound around her neck were meant to cover bruises.

That she was unhappily married I think did not surprise me. What impressed me was that so many of the men were too. I had become engaged to be married, for the third time. There was a slight overlapping of two, by which I mean that the one in Halifax did not know I was also going to marry the one from the West. To the men, who could not follow my life as closely as they'd have wanted – I gave out next to nothing – it seemed like a long betrothal to some puppy in uniform, whom they had never seen, and whose Christian name kept changing. One of my reasons for discretion was that I was still under age. Until now I had been using my minority as an escape hatch, the way a married man will use his wife – for "Ursula will never divorce" I substituted "My mother will never consent." Once I had made up my mind I simply began looking for roads around the obstacle; it was this search, in fact, that made me realize I must be serious. No one, no one at all, knew what I was up to, or what my entirely apocryphal emancipation would consist of; all that the men knew was that this time it did look as if I was going through with it. They took me aside, one after the other, and said, "Don't do it, Linnet. Don't do it." Bertie Knox said, "Once you're in it, you're in it, kiddo." I can't remember any man ever criticizing his own wife – it is something men don't often do, anywhere – but the warning I had was this: marriage was a watershed that transformed sweet, cheerful, affectionate girls into, well, their own mothers. Once a girl had caught (their word) a husband she became a whiner, a snooper, a killjoy, a wet blanket, a grouch, and a bully. What I gleaned out of this was that it seemed hard on the men. But then even Mrs. Ireland, who never said a word to me, declared, "I think it's terrible." She said it was insane for me to marry someone on his way overseas, to tie up my youth, to live like a widow without a widow's moral status. Why were she and I standing together, side by side, looking out the window at a gray sky, at pigeons, at a streetcar grinding up the steep street? We could never possibly have stood close, talking in low voices. And yet there she is; there I am with Mrs. Ireland. For once she kept her voice down. She looked out – not at me. She said the worst thing of all. Remembering it, I see the unwashed windowpane. She said, "Don't you girls ever know when you're well off? Now you've got no one to lie to you, to belittle you, to make a fool of you, to stab you in the back." But we were different – different ages, different women, two lines of a graph that could never cross.

Mostly when people say "I know exactly how I felt" it can't be true, but here I am sure – sure of Mrs. Ireland and the window and of what she said. The recollection has something to do with the blackest kind of terror, as stunning as the bolts of happiness that strike for no reason. This blackness, this darkening, was not wholly Mrs. Ireland, no; I think it had to do with the men, with squares and walls and limits and numbers. How do you stand if you stand upon Zero? What will the passage be like between Zero and One? And what will happen at One? Yes, what will happen?

VARIETIES OF EXILE

In the third summer of the war I began to meet refugees. There were large numbers of them in Montreal – to me a source of infinite wonder. I could not get enough of them. They came straight out of the twilit Socialist-literary landscape of my reading and my desires. I saw them as prophets of a promised social order that was to consist of justice, equality, art, personal relations, courage, generosity. Each of them – Belgian, French, Catholic German, Socialist German, Jewish German, Czech – was a book I tried to read from start to finish. My dictionaries were films, poems, novels, Lenin, Freud. That the refugees tended to hate one another seemed no more than a deplorable accident. Nationalist pigheadedness, that chronic, wasting, and apparently incurable disease, was known to me only on Canadian terms and I did not always recognize its symptoms. Anything I could not decipher I turned into fiction, which was my way of untangling knots. At the office where I worked I now spent my lunch hour writing stories about people in exile. I tried to see Montreal as an Austrian might see it and to feel whatever he felt. I was entirely at home with foreigners, which is not surprising – the home was all in my head. They were the only people I had met until now who believed, as I did, that our victory would prove to be a tidal wave nothing could stop. What I did not know was how many of them hoped and expected their neighbors to be washed away too.

I was nineteen and for the third time in a year engaged to be married. What I craved at this point was not love, or romance, or a life added to mine, but conversation, which was harder to find. I knew by now that a man in love does not necessarily have anything interesting to say: If he has, he keeps it for other men. Men in Canada did not talk much to women and hardly at all to young ones. The impetus of love – of infatuation, rather – brought on a kind of conversation I saw no reason to pursue. A remark such as "I can't live without you" made the speaker sound not only half-witted to me but almost truly, literally, insane. There is a girl in a Stefan Zweig novel who says to her lover, "Is that all?" I had pondered this carefully many years before, for I supposed it had something unexpected to do with sex. Now I gave it another meaning, which was that where women were concerned men were satisfied with next to nothing. If every woman was a situation, she was somehow always the same situation, and what was expected from the woman – the situation – was so limited it was insulting. I had a large opinion of what I could do and provide, yet it came down to "Is that all? Is that all you expect?" Being promised to one person after another was turning into a perpetual state of hesitation and refusal: I was not used to hesitating over anything and so I supposed I must be wrong. The men in my office had warned me of the dangers of turning into a married woman; if this caution affected me it was only because it coincided with a misgiving of my own. My private name for married women was Red Queens. They looked to me like the Red Queen in *Through the Looking-Glass*, chasing after other people and minding their business for them. To get out of the heat that summer I had taken a room outside

Montreal in an area called simply "the Lakeshore." In those days the Lakeshore was a string of verdant towns with next to no traffic. Dandelions grew in the pavement cracks. The streets were thickly shaded. A fragrance I have never forgotten of mown grass and leaf smoke drifted from yard to yard. As I walked to my commuters' train early in the morning I saw kids still in their pajamas digging holes in the lawns and Red Queen wives wearing housecoats. They stuck their heads out of screen doors and yelled instructions – to husbands, to children, to dogs, to postmen, to a neighbor's child. How could I be sure I wouldn't sound that way – so shrill, so discontented? As for a family, the promise of children all stamped with the same face, cast in the same genetic mold, seemed a cruel waste of possibilities. I would never have voiced this to anyone, for it would have been thought unnatural, even monstrous. When I was very young, under seven, my plan for the future had been to live in every country of the world and have a child in each. I had confided it: with adult adroitness my listener led me on. How many children? Oh, one to a country. And what would you do with them? Travel in trains. How would they go to school? I hate schools. How will they learn to read and write, then? They'll know already. What would you live on? It will all be free. That's not very sensible, is it? Why not? As a result of this idyll, of my divulgence of it, I was kept under watch for a time and my pocket money taken away lest I save it up and sail to a tropical island (where because of the Swiss Family Robinson I proposed to begin) long before the onset of puberty. I think no one realized I had not even a nebulous idea of how children sprang to life. I merely knew two persons were required for a ritual I believed had to continue for nine months, and which I imagined in the nature of a long card game with mysterious rules. When I was finally "told" – accurately, as it turned out – I was offended at being asked to believe something so unreasonable, which could not be true because I had never come across it in books. This trust in the printed word seems all the more remarkable when I remember that I thought children's books were written by other children. Probably at nineteen I was still dim about relevant dates, plain facts, brass tacks, consistent reasoning. Perhaps I was still hoping for magic card games tc short-circuit every sort of common sense – common sense is only an admission we don't know much. I know that I wanted to marry this third man but that I didn't want to be anybody's Red Queen.

The commuters on the Montreal train never spoke much to each other. The mystifying and meaningless "Hot enough for you?" was about the extent of it. If I noticed one man more than the anonymous others it was only because he looked so hopelessly English, so unable or unwilling to concede to anything, even the climate. Once, walking a few steps behind him, I saw him turn into the drive of a stone house, one of the few old French-Canadian houses in that particular town. The choice of houses seemed to me peculiarly English too – though not, of course, what French Canadians call "English," for that includes plain Canadians, Irish, Swedes, anything you like not natively French. I looked again at the house and at the straight back going along the drive. His wife was on her knees holding a pair of edging shears. He stopped to greet her. She glanced up and said something in a carrying British voice so wild and miserable, so resentful, so intensely disagreeable that it could not have been the tag end of a morning quarrel; no, it was the thunderclap of some new engagement. After a second he went on up the walk, and in another I was out of earshot. I was persuaded that he had seen me; I don't know why. I also thought it must have been humiliating for him to have had a witness.

Which of us spoke first? It could not have been him and it most certainly could not have been me. There must have been a collision, for there we are, speaking, on a station platform. It is early morning, already hot. I see once again, without surprise, that he is not dressed for the climate.

He said he had often wondered what I was reading. I said I was reading "all the Russians." He said I really ought to read Arthur Waley. I had never heard of Arthur Waley. Similar signalling takes place between galaxies rushing apart in the outer heavens. He said he would bring me a book by Arthur Waley the next day.

"Please don't. I'm careless with books. Look at the shape this one's in." It was the truth. "All the Russians" were being published in a uniform edition with flag-red covers, on grayish paper, with microscopic print. The words were jammed together; you could not have put a pin between the lines. It was one of those cheap editions I think we were supposed to be sending the troops in order to cheer them up. Left in the grass beside a tennis court *The Possessed* now curved like a shell. A white streak ran down the middle of the shell. The rest of the cover had turned pink. That was nothing, he said. All I needed to do was dampen the cover with a sponge and put a weight on the book. *The Wallet of Kai Lung* had been to Ceylon with him and had survived. Whatever bait "Ceylon" may have been caught nothing. Army? Civil Service? I did not take it up. Anyway I thought I could guess.

"You'd better not bring a book for nothing. I don't always take this train."

He had probably noticed me every morning. The mixture of reserve and obstinacy that next crossed his face I see still. He smiled, oh, not too much: I'd have turned my back on a grin. He said, "I forgot to … Frank Cairns."

"Muir. Linnet Muir." Reluctantly.

The thing is, I knew all about him. He was, one, married and, two, too old. But there was also three: Frank Cairns was stamped, labelled, ticketed by his tie (club? regiment? school?); by his voice, manner, haircut, suit; by the impression he gave of being stranded in a jungle, waiting for a rescue party – from England, of course. He belonged to a species of British immigrant known as remittance men. Their obsolescence began on

3 September 1939 and by 8 May 1945 they were extinct. I knew about them from having had one in the family. Frank Cairns worked in a brokerage house – he told me later – but he probably did not need a job, at least not for a living. It must have been a way of ordering time, a flight from idleness, perhaps a means of getting out of the house.

The institution of the remittance man was British, its genesis a chemical structure of family pride, class insanity, and imperial holdings that seemed impervious to fission but in the end turned out to be more fragile than anyone thought. Like all superfluous and marginal persons, remittance men were characters in a plot. The plot began with a fixed scene, an immutable first chapter, which described a powerful father's taking umbrage at his son's misconduct and ordering him out of the country. The pound was then one to five dollars, and there were vast British territories everywhere you looked. Hordes of young men who had somehow offended their parents were shipped out, golden deportees, to Canada, South Africa, New Zealand, Singapore. They were reluctant pioneers, totally lacking any sense of adventure or desire to see that particular world. An income – the remittance – was provided on a standing banker's order, with one string attached: "Keep out of England." For the second chapter the plot allowed a choice of six crimes as reasons for banishment: Conflict over the choice of a profession – the son wants to be a tap-dancer. Gambling and debts – he has been barred from Monte Carlo. Dud checks – "I won't press a charge, sir, but see that the young rascal is kept out of harm's way." Marriage with a girl from the wrong walk of life – "Young man, you have made your bed!" Fathering an illegitimate child: " … and broken your mother's heart." Homosexuality, if discovered: too grave for even a lecture – it was a criminal offense.

This is the plot of the romance: this is what everyone

repeated and what the remittance man believed of himself. Obviously, it is a load of codswallop. A man legally of age could marry the tattooed woman in a circus, be arrested for check-bouncing or for soliciting boys in Green Park, be obliged to recognize his by-blow and even to wed its mother, become a ponce or a professional wrestler, and still remain where he was born. All he needed to do was eschew the remittance and tell his papa to go to hell. Even at nineteen the plot was a story I wouldn't buy. The truth came down to something just as dramatic but boring to tell: a classic struggle for dominance with two protagonists – strong father, pliant son. It was also a male battle. No son was ever sent into exile by his mother, and no one has ever heard of a remittance *woman*. Yet daughters got into scrapes nearly as often as their brothers. Having no idea what money was, they ran up debts easily. Sometimes, out of ignorance of another sort, they dared to dispose of their own virginity, thus wrecking their value on the marriage market and becoming family charges for life. Accoucheurs had to be bribed to perform abortions; or else the daughters were dispatched to Austria and Switzerland to have babies they would never hear of again. A daughter's disgrace was long, expensive, and hard to conceal, yet no one dreamed of sending her thousands of miles away and forever: on the contrary, she became her father's unpaid servant, social secretary, dog walker, companion, sick nurse. Holding on to a daughter, dismissing a son were relatively easy: it depended on having tamely delinquent children, or a thunderous personality no child would dare to challenge, and on the weapon of money – bait or weapon, as you like.

Banished young, as a rule, the remittance man (the RM, in my private vocabulary) drifted for the rest of his life, never quite sounding or looking like anyone around him, seldom raising a family or pursuing an occupation (so much for the "choice of profession" legend) – remote, dreamy, bored. Those who never married often became low-key drunks. The remittance was usually ample without being handsome, but enough to keep one from doing a hand's turn; in any case few remittance men were fit to do much of anything, being well schooled but half educated, in that specifically English way, as well as markedly unaggressive and totally uncompetitive, which would have meant early death in the New World for anyone without an income. They were like children waiting for the school vacation so that they could go home, except that at home nobody wanted them: the nursery had been turned into a billiards room and Nanny dismissed. They were parted from mothers they rarely mentioned, whom in some way they blended with a Rupert Brooke memory of England, of the mother country, of the Old Country as everyone at home grew old. Often as not the payoff, the keep-away blackmail funds, came out of the mother's marriage settlement – out of the capital her own father had agreed to settle upon her unborn children during the wear and tear of Edwardian engagement negotiations. The son disgraced would never see more than a fixed income from this; he was cut off from a share of inheritance by his contract of exile. There were cases where the remittance ended abruptly with the mother's death, but that was considered a bad arrangement. Usually the allowance continued for the exile's lifetime and stopped when he died. No provision was made for his dependents, if he had them, and because of his own subject attitude to money he was unlikely to have made any himself. The income reverted to his sisters and brothers, to an estate, to a cat-and-dog hospital – whatever his father had decreed on some black angry day long before.

Whatever these sons had done their punishment was surely a cruel and singular one, invented for naughty children by a cosmic headmaster taking over for God: they were obliged to live over and over until they died the first separation from home, and the incomparable trauma of rejection. Yes, they were like children, perpetually on their way to a harsh school;

they were eight years of age and sent "home" from India to childhoods of secret grieving among strangers. And this wound, this amputation, they would mercilessly inflict on their own children when the time came – on sons always, on daughters sometimes – persuaded that early heartbreak was right because it was British, hampered only by the financial limit set for banishment: it costs money to get rid of your young.

And how they admired their fathers, those helpless sons! They spoke of them with so much admiration, with such a depth of awe: only in memory can such voices still exist, the calm English voice on a summer night – a Canadian night so alien to the speaker – insisting, with sudden firmness, with a pause between words, "My ... father ... once ... said ... to ... me ..." and here would follow something utterly trivial, some advice about choosing a motorcar or training a dog. To the Canadian grandchildren the unknown grandfather was seven foot tall with a beard like George V, while the grandmother came through weepy and prissy and not very interesting. It was the father's Father, never met, never heard, who made Heaven and earth and Eve and Adam. The father in Canada seemed no more than an apostle transmitting a paternal message from the Father in England – the Father of us all. It was, however, rare for a remittance man to marry, rarer still to have any children; how could he become a father when he had never stopped being a son?

If the scattered freemasonry of offspring the remittance man left behind, all adult to elderly now, had anything in common it must have been their degree of incompetence. They were raised to behave well in situations that might never occur, trained to become genteel poor on continents where even the concept of genteel poverty has never existed. They were brought up with plenty of books and music and private lessons, a nurse sometimes, in a household where certain small luxuries were deemed essential – a way of life that, in North America at least, was supposed to be built on a sunken concrete base of money;

otherwise you were British con men, a breed of gypsy, and a bad example.

Now, your remittance man was apt to find this assumption quite funny. The one place he would never take seriously was the place he was in. The identification of prominent local families with the name of a product, a commodity, would be his running joke: "The Allseeds are sugar, the Bilges are coal, the Cumquats are cough medicine, the Doldrums are coffins, the Earwigs are saucepans, the Fustians are timber, the Grindstones are beer." But his young, once they came up against it, were bound to observe that their concrete base was the dandelion fluff of a banker's order, their commodity nothing but "life in England before 1914," which was not negotiable. Also, the constant, nagging "What does your father really *do*?" could amount to persecution.

"Mr. Bainwood wants to know what you do."

"Damned inquisitive of him."

Silence. Signs of annoyance. Laughter sometimes. Or something silly: "What do *you* do when you aren't asking questions?"

No remittance man's child that I know of ever attended a university, though care was taken over the choice of schools. There they would be, at eighteen and nineteen, the boys wearing raincoats in the coldest weather, the girls with their hair ribbons and hand-knits and their innocently irritating English voices, well read, musical, versed in history, probably because they had been taught that the past is better than now, and somewhere else better than here. They must have been the only English-Canadian children to speak French casually, as a matter of course. Untidy, unpunctual, imperially tactless, they drifted into work that had to be "interesting," "creative," never demeaning, and where – unless they'd had the advantage of a rough time and enough nous to draw a line against the past – they seldom lasted. There was one in every public-relations firm, one to a radio station, two to a publisher – forgetting appointments, losing contracts, jamming typewriters, sabotaging telephones, apologizing in accents it would have taken elocution lessons to change, so strong had been paternal pressure against the hard Canadian "r," not to mention other vocables:

"A-t-e is *et* darling, not ate."

"I can't say *et*. Only farmers say it."

"Perhaps here, but you won't always be here."

Of course the children were guilt-drenched, wondering which of the six traditional crimes they ought to pin on their father, what his secret was, what his past included, why he had been made an outcast. The answer was quite often "Nothing, no reason," but it meant too much to be unravelled and knit up. The saddest were those unwise enough to look into the families who had caused so much inherited woe. For the family was often as not smaller potatoes than the children had thought, and their father's romantic crime had been just the inability to sit for an examination, to stay at a university, to handle an allowance, to gain a toehold in any profession, or even to decide what he wanted to do – an ineptitude so maddening to live with that the Father preferred to shell out forever rather than watch his heir fall apart before his eyes. The male line, then, was a ghost story. A mother's vitality would be needed to create ectoplasm, to make the ghost offspring visible. Unfortunately the exiles were apt to marry absentminded women whose skirts are covered with dog hairs – the drooping, bewildered British-Canadian mouse, who counts on tea leaves to tell her "what will happen when Edward goes." None of us is ever saved entirely, but even an erratic and alarming maternal vitality could turn out to be better than none.

Frank Cairns was childless, which I thought wise of him. He had been to Ceylon, gone back to England with a stiff case of homesickness disguised as malaria, married, and been shipped smartly out again, this time to Montreal. He was a neat, I think rather a small, man, with a straight part in his hair and a quick, brisk walk. He noticed I was engaged. I did not reply. I told him I had been in New York, had come back about a year ago, and missed "different things." He seemed to approve. "You can't make a move here," he said more than once. I was not sure what he meant. If he had been only the person I have described I'd have started taking an earlier train to be rid of him. But Frank Cairns was something new, unique of his kind, and almost as good as a refugee, for he was a Socialist. At least he said he was. He said he had never voted anywhere but that if he ever in the future happened to be in England when there was an election he would certainly vote Labour. His Socialism did not fit anything else about him, and seemed to depend for its life on the memory of talks he'd once had with a friend whom he described as brilliant, philosophical, farseeing, and just. I thought, Like Christ, but did not know Frank Cairns well enough to say so. The nonbeliever I had become was sometimes dogged by the child whose nightly request had been "Gentle Jesus, meek and mild, look upon a little child," and I sometimes got into ferocious arguments with her, as well as with other people. I was too curious about Frank Cairns to wish to quarrel over religion – at any rate not at the beginning. He talked about his friend without seeming able to share him. He never mentioned his name. I had to fill in the blank part of this conversation without help; I made the friend a high-ranking civil servant in Ceylon, older than anyone – which might have meant forty-two – an intellectual revolutionary who could work the future out on paper, like arithmetic.

Wherever his opinions came from, Frank Cairns was the first person ever to talk to me about the English poor. They seemed to be a race, different in kind from other English. He showed me old copies of *Picture Post* he must have saved up from the Depression. In our hot summer train, where everyone was starched and ironed and washed and fed, we considered slum doorways and the faces of women at the breaking point. They looked like Lenin's "remnants of nations" except that there were too many of them for a remnant. I thought of my mother and her long preoccupation with the fate of the Scottsboro Boys. My mother had read and mooned and fretted about the Scottsboro case, while I tried to turn her attention to something urgent, such as that my school uniform was now torn in three places. It is quite possible that my mother had seldom seen a black except on railway trains. (If I say "black" it is only because it is expected. It was a rude and offensive term in my childhood and I would not have been allowed to use it. "Black" was the sort of thing South Africans said.) Had Frank Cairns actually seen those *Picture Post* faces, I wondered. His home, his England, was every other remittance man's – the one I called "Christopher-Robin-land" and had sworn to keep away from. He hated Churchill, I remember, but I was used to hearing that. No man who remembered the Dardanelles really trusted him. Younger men (I am speaking of the handful I knew who had any opinion at all) were not usually irritated by his rhetoric until they got into uniform.

Once in a book I lent him he found a scrap of paper on which I had written the title of a story I was writing, "The Socialist RM," and some scrawls in, luckily, a private shorthand of mine. A perilous moment: "remittance man" was a term of abuse all over the Commonwealth and Empire.

"What is it?" he asked. "Resident Magistrate?"

"It might be Royal Marine. Royal Mail. I honestly don't remember. I can't read my own writing sometimes." The last sentence was true.

His Socialism was unlike a Czech's or a German's; though he believed that one should fight hard for social change, there was a hopelessness about it, an almost moral belief that improving their material circumstances would get the downtrodden nowhere. At the same time, he thought the poor *were* happy, that they had some strange secret of happiness – the way people often think all Italians are happy because they have large families. I wondered if he really believed that a man with no prospects and no teeth in his head was spiritually better off than Frank Cairns and why, in that case, Frank Cairns did not let him alone with his underfed children and his native good nature. This was a British left-wing paradox I was often to encounter later on. What it seemed to amount to was leaving people more or less as they were, though he did speak about basic principles and the spread of education. It sounded dull. I was Russian-minded; I read Russian books, listened to Russian music. After Russia came Germany and Central Europe – that was where the real mystery and political excitement lay. His Webbs and his Fabians were plodding and gray. I saw the men with thick mustaches, wearing heavy boots, sharing lumpy meals with moral women. In the books he brought me I continued to find his absent friend. He produced Housman and Hardy (I could not read either), Siegfried Sassoon and Edmund Blunden, H.G. Wells and Bernard Shaw. The friend was probably a Scot – Frank Cairns admired them. The Scots of Canada, to me, stood for all that was narrow, grasping, at a standstill. How I distrusted those granite bankers who thought it was sinful to smoke! I was wrong, he told me. The true Scots were full of poetry and political passion. I said, "Are you sure?" and turned his friend into a native of Aberdeen and a graduate from Edinburgh. I also began a new notebook: "Scottish Labour Party. Keir Hardie. Others." This was better than the Webbs but still not as good as Rosa Luxemburg.

It was Frank Cairns who said to me "Life has no point," without emphasis, in response to some ignorant assumption of mine. This was his true voice. I recall the sidelong glance, the lizard's eye that some men develop as they grow old or when they have too much to hide. I was no good with ages. I cannot place him even today. Early thirties, probably. What else did he tell me? That "Scotch" was the proper term and "Scots" an example of a genteelism overtaking the original. That unless the English surmounted their class obsessions with speech and accent Britain would not survive in the world after the war. His remedy (or his friend's) was having everyone go to the same schools. He surprised me even more by saying, "I would never live in England, not as it is now."

"Where, then?"

"Nowhere. I don't know."

"What about Russia? They all go to the same schools."

"Good Lord," said Frank Cairns.

He was inhabited by a familiar who spoke through him, provided him with jolting outbursts but not a whole thought. Perhaps that silent coming and going was the way people stayed in each other's lives when they were apart. What Frank Cairns was to me was a curio cabinet. I took everything out of the cabinet, piece by piece, examined the objects, set them down. Such situations, riddled with ambiguity, I would blunder about with for a long time until I learned to be careful.

The husband of the woman from whom I rented my summer room played golf every weekend. On one of those August nights when no one can sleep and the sky is nearly bright enough to read by, I took to the back yard and found him trying to cool off with a glass of beer. He remembered he had offered to give me golf lessons. I did not wish to learn, but did not say so. His wife spoke up from a deck chair: "You've never offered to teach me, I notice." She then compounded the error by telling me everyone was talking about me and the married man on the train. The next day I took the Käthe Kollwitz prints down from the walls of my room and moved back to Montreal without an explanation. Frank Cairns and I met once more that summer to return some books. That was all. When he called me at my office late in November, I said, "*Who?*"

He came into the coffee shop at Windsor Station, where I

was waiting. He was in uniform. I had not noticed he was good-looking before. It was not something I noticed in men. He was a first lieutenant. I disapproved: "Couldn't they make you a private?"

"Too old," he said. "As it is I am too old for my rank." I thought he just meant he might be promoted faster because of that.

"You don't look old." I at once regretted this personal remark, the first he had heard from me. Indeed, he had shed most of his adult life. He must have seemed as young as this when he started out to Ceylon. The uniform was his visa to England; no one could shut him away now. His face was radiant, open: he was halfway there. This glimpse of a purpose astonished me; why should a uniform make the change he'd been unable to make alone? He was not the first soldier I saw transfigured but he was the first to affect me.

He kept smiling and staring at me. I hoped he was not going to make a personal remark in exchange for mine. He said, "That tam makes you look, I don't know, Canadian. I've always thought of you as English. I still think England is where you might be happy."

"I'm happy here. You said you'd never live there."

"It would be a good place for you," he said. "Well, well, we shall see."

He would see nothing. My evolution was like freaky weather then: a few months, a few weeks even, were the equivalent of long second thoughts later on. I was in a completely other climate. I no longer missed New York and "different things." I had become patriotic. Canadian patriotism is always anti-American in part, and feeds upon anecdotes. American tourists were beginning to arrive in Montreal looking for anything expensive or hard to find in the United States; when they could not buy rationed food such as meat and butter, or unrationed things such as nylon stockings (because they did not exist), they complained of ingratitude. This was because Canada was thought to be a recipient of American charity and on the other end of Lend-Lease. Canadians were, and are, enormously touchy. Great umbrage had been taken over a story that was going around in the States about Americans who had been soaked for black-market butter in Montreal; when they got back across the border they opened the package and found the butter stamped "Gift of the American People." This fable persisted throughout the war and turned up in print. An American friend saw it in, I think, Westbrook Pegler's column and wrote asking me if it was true. I composed a letter I meant to send to the *New York Times*, demolishing the butter story. I kept rewriting and reshaping it, trying to achieve a balance between crippling irony and a calm review of events. I never posted it, finally, because my grandmother appeared to me in a dream and said that only fools wrote to newspapers.

Our coffee was tepid, the saucers slopped. He complained, and the waitress asked if we knew there was a war on. "Christ, what a bloody awful country this is," he said.

I wanted to say, Then why are you with a Canadian regiment? I provided my own answer: They pay more than the Brits. We were actually quarrelling in my head, and on such a mean level. I began to tear up a paper napkin and to cry.

"I have missed you," he remarked, but quite happily; you could tell the need for missing was over. I had scarcely thought of him at all. I kept taking more and more napkins out of the container on the table and blotting my face and tearing the paper up. He must be the only man I ever cried about in a public place. I hardly knew him. He was not embarrassed, as a Canadian would have been, but looked all the happier. The glances we got from other tables were full of understanding. Everything gave the wrong impression – his uniform, my engagement ring, my tears. I told him I was going to be married.

"Nonsense," he said.

"I'm serious."

"You seem awfully young."

"I'll soon be twenty." A slip. I had told him I was older. It amazed me to remember how young I had been only the summer before. "But I won't actually be a married woman," I said, "because I hate everything about them. Another thing I won't be and that's the sensitive housewife – the one who listens to Brahms while she does the ironing and reads all the new books still in their jackets."

"No, don't be a sensitive housewife," he said.

He gave me *The Wallet of Kai Lung* and *Kai Lung's Golden Hours*, which had been in Ceylon with him and had survived.

Did we write to each other? That's what I can't remember. I was careless then; I kept moving on. Also I really did, that time, get married. My husband was posted three days afterward to an American base in the Aleutian Islands – I have forgotten why. Eight months later he returned for a brief embarkation leave and then went overseas. I had dreaded coming in to my office after my wedding for fear the men I worked with would tease me. But the mixture of war and separation recalled old stories of their own experiences, in the First World War. Also I had been transformed into someone with a French surname, which gave them pause.

"Does he – uh – speak any French?"

"Not a word. He's from the West." Ah. "But he ought to. His father is French." Oh.

I had disappeared for no more than four days, but I was Mrs. Something now, not young Linnet. They spoke about me as "she," and not "Linnet" or "the kid." I wondered what they saw when they looked at me. In every head bent over a desk or a drawing board there was an opinion about women; expressed, it sounded either prurient or coarse, but I still cannot believe that is all there was to it. I know I shocked them profoundly once by saying that a wartime ditty popular with the troops, "Rock me to sleep, Sergeant-Major, tuck me in my little bed," was innocently homosexual. That I could have such a turn of thought, that I could use such an expression, that I even knew it existed seemed scandalous to them. "You read too damned much," I was told. Oddly enough, they had never minded my hearing any of the several versions of the song, some of which were unspeakable; all they objected to was my unfeminine remark. When I married they gave me a suitcase, and when I left for good they bought me a Victory Bond. I had scrupulously noted every detail of the office, and the building it was in, yet only a few months later I would walk by it without remembering I had ever been inside, and it occurs to me only now that I never saw any of them again.

I was still a minor, but emancipated by marriage. I did not need to ask parental consent for anything or worry about being brought down on the wing. I realized how anxious I had been once the need for that particular anxiety was over. A friend in New York married to a psychiatrist had sent me a letter saying I had her permission to marry. She did not describe herself as a relative or state anything untrue – she just addressed herself to whom it may concern, said that as far as *she* was concerned I could get married, and signed. She did not tell her husband, in case he tried to put things right out of principle, and I mentioned to no one that the letter was legal taradiddle and carried about as much weight as a library card. I mention this to show what essential paperwork sometimes amounts to. My husband, aged twenty-four, had become my legal guardian under Quebec's preposterous Napoleonic law, but he never knew that. When he went overseas he asked me not to join any political party, which I hadn't thought of doing, and not to enlist in the Army or the Air Force. The second he vanished I tried to join the Wrens, which had not been on the list only because it slipped his mind. Joining one of the services had never been among my plans and projects – it was he who accidentally put the idea in my head. I now decided I would turn up overseas, having made it there on my own, but I got no further than the enlistment requirements, which included "... of the white race only." This barrier turned out to be true of nearly all the navies of the Commonwealth countries. I supposed everyone must have wanted it that way, for I never heard it questioned. I was only beginning to hear the first rumblings of hypocrisy on our side – the right side; the wrong side seemed to be guilty of every sin humanly possible except simulation of virtue. I put the blame for the racial barrier on Churchill, who certainly *knew*, and had known since the First World War; I believed that Roosevelt, Stalin, Chiang Kai-shek, and de Gaulle did not know, and that should it ever come to their attention they would be as shocked as I was.

Instead of enlisting I passed the St. John Ambulance first-aid certificate, which made me a useful person in case of total war. The Killed-Wounded-Missing columns of the afternoon paper were now my daily reading. It became a habit so steadfast that I would automatically look for victims even after the war ended. The summer of the Scottish Labour Party, Keir Hardie, and Others fell behind, as well as a younger, discarded Linnet. I lighted ferocious autos-da-fé. Nothing could live except present time. In the ever-new present I read one day that Major Francis Cairns had died of wounds in Italy. Who remembers now the shock of the known name? It was like a flat white light. One felt apart from everyone, isolated. The field of vision drew in. Then, before one could lose consciousness, vision expanded, light and shadow moved, voices pierced through. One's heart, which had stopped, beat hard enough to make a room shudder. All this would occupy about a second. The next second was inhabited by disbelief. I saw him in uniform, so happy, halfway there, and myself making a spectacle of us, tearing a paper napkin. I was happy for him that he would never need to return to the commuting train and the loneliness and be forced to relive his own past. I wanted to write a casual letter saying so. One's impulse was always to write to the dead. Nobody knew I knew him, and in Canada it was not done to speak of the missing. I forgot him. He went under. I was doing a new sort of work and sharing a house with another girl whose husband was also overseas. Montreal had become a completely other city. I was no longer attracted to refugees. They were going through a process called "integrating." Some changed their names. Others applied for citizenship. A refugee eating cornflakes was of no further interest. The house I now lived in contained a fireplace, in which I burned all my stories about Czech and German anti-Fascists. In the picnic hamper I used for storing journals and notebooks I found a manila envelope marked "Lakeshore." It contained several versions of "The Socialist RM" and a few other things that sounded as if they were translated from the Russian by Constance Garnett. I also found a brief novel I had no memory of having written, about a Scot from Aberdeen, a left-wing civil servant in Ceylon – a man from somewhere, living elsewhere, confident that another world was entirely possible, since he had got it all down. It had shape, density, voice, but I destroyed it too. I never felt guilt about forgetting the dead or the living, but I minded about that one manuscript for a time. All this business of putting life through a sieve and then discarding it was another variety of exile; I knew that even then, but it seemed quite right and perfectly natural.

VOICES LOST IN SNOW

Halfway between our two great wars, parents whose own early years had been shaped with Edwardian firmness were apt to lend a tone of finality to quite simple remarks: "Because I say so" was the answer to "Why?," and a child's response to "What did I just tell you?" could seldom be anything but "Not to" – not to say, do, touch, remove, go out, argue, reject, eat, pick up, open, shout, appear to sulk, appear to be cross. Dark riddles filled the corners of life because no enlightenment was thought required. Asking questions was "being tiresome," while persistent curiosity got one nowhere, at least nowhere of interest. How much has changed? Observe the drift of words descending from adult to child – the fall of personal questions, observations, unnecessary instructions. Before long the listener seems blanketed. He must hear the voice as authority muffled, a hum through snow. The tone has changed – it may be coaxing, even plaintive – but the words have barely altered. They still claim the ancient right-of-way through a young life.

"Well, old cock," said my father's friend Archie McEwen, meeting him one Saturday in Montreal. "How's Charlotte taking life in the country?" Apparently no one had expected my mother to accept the country in winter.

"Well, old cock," I repeated to a country neighbor, Mr. Bainwood. "How's life?" What do you suppose it meant to me, other than a kind of weathervane? Mr. Bainwood thought it over, then came round to our house and complained to my mother.

"It isn't blasphemy," she said, not letting him have much satisfaction from the complaint. Still, I had to apologize. "I'm sorry" was a ritual habit with even less meaning than "old cock." "Never say that again," my mother said after he had gone.

"Why not?"

"Because I've just told you not to."

"What does it mean?"

"Nothing."

It must have been after yet another "nothing" that one summer's day I ran screaming around a garden, tore the heads off tulips, and – no, let another voice finish it; the only authentic voices I have belong to the dead: " ... then she *ate* them."

It was my father's custom if he took me with him to visit a friend on Saturdays not to say where we were going. He was more taciturn than any man I have known since, but that wasn't all of it; being young, I was the last person to whom anyone owed an explanation. These Saturdays have turned into one whitish afternoon, a windless snowfall, a steep street. Two persons descend the street, stepping carefully. The child, reminded every day to keep her hands still, gesticulates wildly – there is the flash of a red mitten. I will never overtake this pair. Their voices are lost in snow.

We were living in what used to be called the country and is now a suburb of Montreal. On Saturdays my father and I came in together by train. I went to the doctor, the dentist, to my German lesson. After that I had to get back to Windsor Station by myself and on time. My father gave me a boy's watch so that the dial would be good and large. I remember the No. 83 streetcar trundling downhill and myself, wondering if the watch was slow, asking strangers to tell me the hour. Inevitably – how could it have been otherwise? – after his death, which would not be long in coming, I would dream that someone important had taken a train without me. My route to the meeting place – deviated, betrayed by stopped clocks – was always downhill. As soon as I was old enough to understand from my reading of myths and legends that this journey was a pursuit of darkness, its terminal point a sunless underworld, the dream vanished.

Sometimes I would be taken along to lunch with one or another of my father's friends. He would meet the friend at Pauzé's for oysters or at Drury's or the Windsor Grill. The friend would more often than not be Scottish- or English-sounding, and they would talk as if I were invisible, as Archie McEwen had done, and eat what I thought of as English food – grilled kidneys, sweetbreads – which I was too finicky to touch. Both my parents had been made wretched as children by having food forced on them and so that particular torture was never inflicted on me. However, the manner in which I ate was subject to precise attention. My father disapproved of the North American custom that he called "spearing" (knife laid on the plate, fork in the right hand). My mother's eye was out for a straight back, invisible chewing, small mouthfuls, immobile silence during the interminable adult loafing over dessert. My mother did not care for food. If we were alone together, she would sit smoking and reading, sipping black coffee, her elbows used as props – a posture that would have called for instant banishment had I so much as tried it. Being constantly observed and corrected was like having a fly buzzing around one's plate. At Pauzé's, the only child, perhaps the only female, I sat up to an oak counter and ate oysters quite neatly, not knowing exactly what they were and certainly not that they were alive. They were served as in "The Walrus and the Carpenter," with bread and butter, pepper and vinegar. Dessert was a chocolate biscuit – plates of them stood at intervals along the counter. When my father and I ate alone, I was not required to say much, nor could I expect a great deal in the way of response. After I had been addressing him for minutes, sometimes he would suddenly come to life and I would know he had been elsewhere. "Of course I've been listening," he would protest, and he would repeat by way of proof the last few words of whatever it was I'd been saying. He was seldom present. I don't know where my father spent his waking life: just elsewhere.

What was he doing alone with a child? Where was his wife? In the country, reading. She read one book after another without looking up, without scraping away the frost on the windows. "The Russians, you know, the Russians," she said to her mother and me, glancing around in the drugged way adolescent readers have. "They put salt on the window sills in winter." Yes, so they did, in the nineteenth century, in the boyhood of Turgenev, of Tolstoy. The salt absorbed the moisture between two sets of windows sealed shut for half the year. She must have been in a Russian country house at that moment, surrounded by a large Russian family, living out vast Russian complications. The flat white fields beyond her imaginary windows were like the flat white fields she would have observed if only she had looked out. She was myopic; the pupil when she had been reading seemed to be the whole of the eye. What age was she then? Twenty-seven, twenty-eight. Her husband had removed her to the country; now that they were there he seldom spoke. How young she seems to me now – half twenty-eight in perception and feeling, but with a husband, a child, a house, a life, an illiterate maid from the village whose life she confidently interfered with and mismanaged, a small zoo of animals she alternately cherished and forgot; and she was the daughter of such a sensible, truthful, pessimistic woman – pessimistic in the way women become when they settle for what actually exists.

Our rooms were not Russian – they were aired every day and the salt became a great nuisance, blowing in on the floor.

"There, Charlotte, what did I tell you?" my grandmother said. This grandmother did not care for dreams or for children. If I sensed the first, I had no hint of the latter. Out of decency she kept it quiet, at least in a child's presence. She had the reputation, shared with a long-vanished nurse named Olivia, of being able to "do anything" with me, which merely meant an ability to provoke from a child behavior convenient for adults. It was she who taught me to eat in the Continental way, with both hands in sight at all times upon the table, and who made me sit at meals with books under my arms so I would learn not to stick out my elbows. I remember having accepted this nonsense from her without a trace of resentment. Like Olivia, she could make the most pointless sort of training seem a natural way of life. (I think that as discipline goes this must be the most dangerous form of all.) She was one of three godparents I had – the important one. It is impossible for me to enter the mind of this agnostic who taught me prayers, who had already shed every remnant of belief when she committed me at the font. I know that she married late and reluctantly; she would have preferred a life of solitude and independence, next to impossible for a woman in her time. She had the positive voice of the born teacher, sharp manners, quick blue eyes, and the square, massive figure common to both lines of her ancestry – the West of France, the North of Germany. When she said "There, Charlotte, what did I tell you?" without obtaining an answer, it summed up mother and daughter both.

My father's friend Malcolm Whitmore was the second godparent. He quarrelled with my mother when she said something flippant about Mussolini, disappeared, died in Europe some years later, though perhaps not fighting for Franco, as my mother had it. She often rewrote other people's lives, providing them with suitable and harmonious endings. In her version of events you were supposed to die as you'd lived. He would write sometimes, asking me, "Have you been confirmed yet?" He had never really held a place and could not by dying leave a gap. The third godparent was a young woman named Georgie Henderson. She was my mother's choice, for a long time her confidante, partisan, and close sympathizer. Something happened, and they stopped seeing each other. Georgie was not her real name – it was Edna May. One of the reasons she had fallen out with my mother was that I had not been called Edna May too. Apparently, this had been promised.

Without saying where we were going, my father took me along to visit Georgie one Saturday afternoon.

"You didn't say you were bringing Linnet" was how she greeted him. We stood in the passage of a long, hot, high-ceilinged apartment, treading snow water into the rug.

He said, "Well, she is your godchild, and she has been ill."

My godmother shut the front door and leaned her back against it. It is in this surprisingly dramatic pose that I recall her. It would be unfair to repeat what I think I saw then, for she and I were to meet again once, only once, many years after this, and I might substitute a lined face for a smooth one and tough, large-knuckled hands for fingers that may have been delicate. One has to allow elbowroom in the account of a rival: "She must have had something" is how it generally goes, long after the initial "What can he see in her? He must be deaf and blind." Georgie, explained by my mother as being the natural daughter of Sarah Bernhardt and a stork, is only a shadow, a tracing, with long arms and legs and one of those sightly puggy faces with pulled-up eyes.

Her voice remains – the husky Virginia-tobacco whisper I associate with so many women of that generation, my parents' friends; it must have come of age in English Montreal around 1920, when girls began to cut their hair and to smoke. In middle life the voice would slide from low to harsh, and develop a chronic cough. For the moment it was fascinating to me – opposite in pitch and speed from my mother's, which was slightly too high and apt to break off, like that of a singer unable to sustain a long note.

It was true that I had been ill, but I don't think my godmother made much of it that afternoon, other than saying, "It's all very well to talk about that now, but I was certainly never told much, and as for that doctor, you ought to just hear what Ward thinks." Out of this whispered jumble my mother stood accused – of many transgressions, certainly, but chiefly of having discarded Dr. Ward Mackey, everyone's doctor and a family friend. At the time of my birth my mother had all at once decided she liked Ward Mackey better than anyone else and had asked him to choose a name for me. He could not think of one, or, rather, thought of too many, and finally consulted his own mother. She had always longed for a daughter, so that she could call her after the heroine of a novel by, I believe, Marie Corelli. The legend so often repeated to me goes on to tell that when I was seven weeks old my father suddenly asked, "What did you say her name was?"

"*Votre fille a frôlé la phtisie*," the new doctor had said, the one who had now replaced Dr. Mackey. The new doctor was known to me as Uncle Raoul, though we were not related. This manner of declaring my brush with consumption was worlds away from Ward Mackey's "subject to bilious attacks." Mackey's objections to Uncle Raoul were neither envious nor personal, for Mackey was the sort of bachelor who could console himself with golf. The Protestant in him truly believed those other doctors to be poorly trained and superstitious, capable of recommending the pulling of teeth to cure tonsillitis, and of letting their patients cough to death or perish from septicemia just through Catholic fatalism.

What parent could fail to gasp and marvel at Uncle Raoul's announcement? Any but either of mine. My mother could invent and produce better dramas any day; as for my father, his French wasn't all that good and he had to have it explained. Once he understood that I had grazed the edge of tuberculosis, he made his decision to remove us all to the country, which he had been wanting a reason to do for some time. He was, I think, attempting to isolate his wife, but by taking her out of the city he exposed her to a danger that, being English, he had never dreamed of: this was the heart-stopping cry of the steam train at night, sweeping across a frozen river, clattering on the ties of a wooden bridge. From our separate rooms my mother and I heard the unrivalled summons, the long, urgent, uniquely North American beckoning. She would follow and so would I, but separately, years and desires and destinations apart. I think that women once pledged in such a manner are more steadfast than men.

"*Frôler*" was the charmed word in that winter's story; it was a hand brushing the edge of folded silk, a leaf escaping a spider-web. Being caught in the web would have meant staying in bed day and night in a place even worse than a convent school. Charlotte and Angus, whose lives had once seemed so enchanted, so fortunate and free that I could not imagine lesser persons so much as eating the same kind of toast for breakfast, had to share their lives with me, whether they wanted to or not – thanks to Uncle Raoul, who always supposed me to be their principal delight. I had been standing on one foot for months now, midway between *frôler* and *falling into*, propped up by a psychosomatic guardian angel. Of course I could not stand that way forever; inevitably my health improved and before long I was declared out of danger and then restored – to the relief and pleasure of all except the patient.

"I'd like to see more of you than eyes and nose," said my

godmother. "Take off your things." I offer this as an example of unnecessary instruction. Would anyone over the age of three prepare to spend the afternoon in a stifling room wrapped like a mummy in outdoor clothes? "She's smaller than she looks," Georgie remarked, as I began to emerge. This authentic godmother observation drives me to my only refuge, the insistence that she must have had something – he could not have been completely deaf and blind. Divested of hat, scarf, coat, overshoes, and leggings, grasping the handkerchief pressed in my hand so I would not interrupt later by asking for one, responding to my father's muttered "Fix your hair," struck by the command because it was he who had told me not to use "fix" in that sense, I was finally able to sit down next to him on a white sofa. My godmother occupied its twin. A low table stood between, bearing a decanter and glasses and a pile of magazines and, of course, Georgie's ashtrays; I think she smoked even more than my mother did.

On one of these sofas, during an earlier visit with my mother and father, the backs of my dangling feet had left a smudge of shoe polish. It may have been the last occasion when my mother and Georgie were ever together. Directed to stop humming and kicking, and perhaps bored with the conversation in which I was not expected to join, I had soon started up again.

"It doesn't matter," my godmother said, though you could tell she minded.

"Sit up," my father said to me.

"I am sitting up. What do you think I'm doing?" This was not answering but answering back; it is not an expression I ever heard from my father, but I am certain it stood like a stalled truck in Georgie's mind. She wore the look people put on when they are thinking, Now what are you spineless parents going to do about that?

"Oh, for God's sake, she's only a child," said my mother, as though that had ever been an excuse for anything.

Soon after the sofa-kicking incident she and Georgie moved into the hibernation known as "not speaking." This, the lingering condition of half my mother's friendships, usually followed her having said the very thing no one wanted to hear, such as "Who wants to be called Edna May, anyway?"

Once more in the hot pale room where there was nothing to do and nothing for children, I offended my godmother again, by pretending I had never seen her before. The spot I had kicked was pointed out to me, though, owing to new slipcovers, real evidence was missing. My father was proud of my quite surprising memory, of its long backward reach and the minutiae of detail I could describe. My failure now to shine in a domain where I was naturally gifted, that did not require lessons or create litter and noise, must have annoyed him. I also see that my guileless-seeming needling of my godmother was a close adaptation of how my mother could be, and I attribute it to a child's instinctive loyalty to the absent one. Giving me up, my godmother placed a silver dish of mint wafers where I could reach them – white, pink, and green, overlapping – and suggested I look at a magazine. Whatever the magazine was, I had probably seen it, for my mother subscribed to everything then. I may have turned the pages anyway, in case at home something had been censored for children. I felt and am certain I have not invented Georgie's disappointment at not seeing Angus alone. She disliked Charlotte now, and so I supposed he came to call by himself, having no quarrel of his own; he was still close to the slighted Ward Mackey.

My father and Georgie talked for a while – she using people's initials instead of their names, which my mother would not have done – and they drank what must have been sherry, if I think of the shape of the decanter. Then we left and went down to the street in a wood-panelled elevator that had sconce lights, as in a room. The end of the afternoon had a particular shade of color then, which is not tinted by distance or enhancement but has to do with how streets were lighted. Lamps were still gas, and their soft gradual blooming at dusk made the sky turn a peacock blue that slowly deepened to marine, then indigo. This uneven light falling in blurred pools gave the snow it touched a quality of phosphorescence, beyond which were night shadows in which no one lurked. There were few cars, little sound. A fresh snowfall would lie in the streets in a way that seemed natural. Sidewalks were dangerous, casually sanded; even on busy streets you found traces of the icy slides children's feet had made. The reddish brown of the stone houses, the curve and slope of the streets, the constantly changing sky were satisfactory in a way that I now realize must have been aesthetically comfortable. This is what I saw when I read "city" in a book; I had no means of knowing that "city" one day would also mean drab, filthy, flat, or that city blocks could turn into dull squares without mystery.

We crossed Sherbrooke Street, starting down to catch our train. My father walked everywhere in all weathers. Already mined, colonized by an enemy prepared to destroy what it fed on, fighting it with every wrong weapon, squandering strength he should have been storing, stifling pain in silence rather than speaking up while there might have been time, he gave an impression of sternness that was a shield against suffering. One day we heard a mob roaring four syllables over and over, and we turned and went down a different street. That sound was starkly terrifying, something a child might liken to the baying of wolves.

"What is it?"

"Howie Morenz."

"Who is it? Are they chasing him?"

"No, they like him," he said of the hockey player admired to the point of dementia. He seemed to stretch, as if trying to keep every bone in his body from touching a nerve; a look of helplessness such as I had never seen on a grown person gripped his face and he said this strange thing: "Crowds eat me. Noise eats me." The kind of physical pain that makes one seem rat's prey is summed up in my memory of this.

When we came abreast of the Ritz-Carlton after leaving Georgie's apartment, my father paused. The lights within at that time of day were golden and warm. If I barely knew what "hotel" meant, never having stayed in one, I connected the lights with other snowy afternoons, with stupefying adult conversation (Oh, those shut-in velvet-draped unaired low-voice problems!) compensated for by creamy bitter hot chocolate poured out of a pink-and-white china pot.

"You missed your gootay," he suddenly remembered. Established by my grandmother, "*goûter*" was the family word for tea. He often transformed French words, like putty, into shapes he could grasp. No, Georgie had not provided a *goûter*, other than the mint wafers, but it was not her fault – I had not been announced. Perhaps if I had not been so disagreeable with her, he might have proposed hot chocolate now, though I knew better than to ask. He merely pulled my scarf up over my nose and mouth, as if recalling something Uncle Raoul had advised. Breathing inside knitted wool was delicious – warm, moist, pungent when one had been sucking on mint candies, as now. He said, "You didn't enjoy your visit much."

"Not very," through red wool.

"No matter," he said. "You needn't see Georgie again unless you want to," and we walked on. He must have been smarting, for he liked me to be admired. When I was not being admired I was supposed to keep quiet. "You needn't see Georgie again" was also a private decision about himself. He was barely thirty-one and had a full winter to live after this one – little more. Why? "Because I say so." The answer seems to speak out of the lights, the stones, the snow; out of the crucial second when inner and outer forces join, and the environment becomes part of the enemy too.

Ward Mackey used to mention me as "Angus's precocious pain in the neck," which is better than nothing. Long after that afternoon, when I was about twenty, Mackey said to me, "Georgie didn't play her cards well where he was concerned. There was a point where if she had just made one smart move she could have had him. Not for long, of course, but none of us knew that."

What cards, I wonder. The cards have another meaning for me – they mean a trip, a death, a letter, tomorrow, next year. I saw only one move that Saturday: my father placed a card face up on the table and watched to see what Georgie made of it. She shrugged, let it rest. There she sits, looking puggy but capable, Angus waiting, the precocious pain in the neck turning pages, hoping to find something in the *National Geographic* harmful for children. I brush in memory against the spiderweb: what if she had picked it up, remarking in her smoky voice, "Yes, I can use that" ? It was a low card, the kind that only a born gambler would risk as part of a long-term strategy. She would never have weakened a hand that way; she was not gambling but building. He took the card back and dropped his hand, and their long intermittent game came to an end. The card must have been the eight of clubs – "a female child."

THE DOCTOR

Who can remember now a picture called "The Doctor"? From 1891, when the original was painted, to the middle of the Depression, when it finally went out of style, reproductions of this work flowed into every crevice and corner of North America and the British Empire, swamping continents. Not even "The Angelus" supplied as rich a mixture of art and lesson. The two people in "The Angelus" are there to tell us clearly that the meek inherit nothing but seem not to mind; in "The Doctor" a cast of four enacts a more complex statement of Christian submission or Christian pessimism, depending on the beholder: God's Will is manifested in a dying child, Helpless Materialism in a baffled physician, and Afflicted Humanity in the stricken parents. The parable is set in a spotless cottage; the child's bed, composed of three chairs, is out of a doll's house. In much of the world – the world as it was, so much smaller than now – two full generations were raised with the monochrome promise that existence is insoluble, tragedy static, poverty endearing, and heavenly justice a total mystery.

It must have come as a shock to overseas visitors when they

discovered "The Doctor" incarnated as an oil painting in the Tate Gallery in London, in the company of other Victorian miseries entitled "Hopeless Dawn" and "The Last Day in the Old Home." "The Doctor" had not been divinely inspired and distributed to chasten us after all, but was the work of someone called Sir Luke Fildes – nineteenth-century rationalist and atheist, for all anyone knew. Perhaps it was simply a scene from a three-decker novel, even a joke. In museum surroundings – classified, ticketed – "The Doctor" conveyed a new instruction: Death is sentimental, art is pretense.

Some people had always hated "The Doctor." My father, for one. He said, "You surely don't want *that* thing in your room."

The argument (it became one) took place in Montreal, in a house that died long ago without leaving even a ghost. He was in his twenties, to match the century. I had been around about the length of your average major war. I had my way but do not remember how; neither tears nor temper ever worked. What probably won out was his wish to be agreeable to Dr. Chauchard, the pediatrician who had given me the engraving. My father seemed to like Chauchard, as he did most people – just well enough – while my mother, who carried an uncritical allegiance from person to person, belief to belief, had recently declared Chauchard to be mentally, morally, and spiritually without fault.

Dr. Chauchard must have been in his thirties then, but he seemed to me timeless, like God the Father. When he took the engraving down from the wall of his office, I understood him to be offering me a portrait of himself. My mother at first refused it, thinking I had asked; he assured her I had not, that he had merely been struck by my expression when I looked at the ailing child. "*C'est une sensible*," he said – an appraisal my mother dismissed by saying I was as tough as a boot, which I truly believe to have been her opinion.

What I was sensitive to is nearly too plain to be signalled: the dying child, a girl, is the heart of the composition. The parents are in the shadow, where they belong. Their function is to be sorry. The doctor has only one patient; light from a tipped lampshade falls on her and her alone.

The street where Dr. Chauchard lived began to decline around the same time as the popularity of "The Doctor" and is now a slum. No citizens' committee can restore the natural elegance of those gray stone houses, the swept steps, the glittering windows, because, short of a miracle, it cannot resurrect the kind of upper-bourgeois French Canadians who used to live there. They have not migrated or moved westward in the city – they have ceased to exist. The handful of dust they sprang from, with its powerful components of religion and history, is part of another clay. They were families who did not resent what were inaccurately called "the English" in Montreal; they had never acknowledged them. The men read a newspaper sometimes, the women never. The women had a dark version of faith for private drama, a family tree to memorize for intellectual exercise, intense family affection for the needs of the heart. Their houses, like Dr. Chauchard's, smelled of cleanness as if cleanness were a commodity, a brand of floor wax. Convents used to have that smell; the girls raised in them brought to married life an ideal of housekeeping that was a memory of the polished convent corridor, with strict squares of sunlight falling where and as they should. Two sons and five daughters was the average for children; Simone, Pauline, Jeanne, Yvonne, and Louise the feminine names of the decade. The girls when young wore religious medals like golden flower petals on thin chains, had positive torrents of curls down to their shoulder blades, and came to children's parties dressed in rose velvet and white stockings, too shy to speak. Chauchard, a bachelor, came out of this world, which I can describe best only through its girls and women.

His front door, painted the gloomy shade my father called Montreal green, is seen from below, at an angle – a bell too high for me during the first visits, a letter box through which I called, "Open the door; *c'est moi*," believing still that *moi* would take me anywhere. But no one could hear in any language, because two vestibules, one behind the other, stood in the way. In the first one overshoes dripped on a mat, then came a warmer place for coats. Each vestibule had its door, varnished to imitate the rings of a tree trunk, enhanced by a nature scene made of frosted glass; you unbuckled galoshes under herons and palm trees and shed layers of damp wool under swans floating in a landscape closer to home.

Just over the letter box of the green door a large, beautifully polished brass plate carried, in sloped writing:

Docteur Raoul Chauchard
Spécialiste en Médecine Infantile
Ancien Externe et Interne
des Hôpitaux de Paris
Sur Rendez-vous

On the bottom half of the plate this information was repeated in English, though the only English I recall in the waiting room was my mother's addressed to me.

He was not Parisian but native to the city, perhaps to the street, even to the house, if I think of how the glass-shaded lamps and branched chandeliers must have followed an evolution from oil to kerosene to gas to electricity without changing shape or place. Rooms and passages were papered deep blue fading to green (the brighter oblong left by the removal of "The Doctor" was about the color of a teal), so that the time of day indoors was winter dusk, with pools of light like uncurtained windows. An assemblage of gilt-framed pictures began between the heron and swan doors with brisk scenes of Biblical injustice – the casting-out of Hagar, the swindling of Esau – and moved along the hall with European history: Vercingetorix surrendering to the Romans, the earthquake at Lisbon,

Queen Victoria looking exactly like a potato pancake receiving some dark and humble envoy; then, with a light over him to mark his importance, Napoleon III reviewing a regiment from a white horse. (The popularity of "Napoléon" as a Christian name did not connect with the first Bonaparte, as English Canadians supposed – when any thought was given to any matter concerning French Canadians at all – but with his nephew, the lesser Bonaparte, who had never divorced or insulted the Pope, and who had established clerical influence in the saddle as firmly as it now sat upon Quebec.) The sitting-room-converted-to-waiting-room had on display landmarks of Paris, identified in two languages:

Le Petit Palais – The Petit Palais
Place Vendôme – Place Vendôme
Rue de la Paix – Rue de la Paix

as if the engraver had known they would find their way to a wall in Montreal.

Although he had trained in Paris, where, as our English doctor told my mother, leeches were still sold in pharmacies and babies died like flies, Chauchard was thought modern and forward-looking. He used the most advanced methods imported from the United States, or, as one would have said then, "from Boston," which meant both stylish and impeccably right. Ultraviolet irradiation was one, recommended for building up delicate children. I recall the black mask tied on, and the danger of blindness should one pull it off before being told. I owe him irradiation to the marrow and other sources of confusion: it was he who gave my mother the name of a convent where Jansenist discipline still had a foot on the neck of the twentieth century and where, as an added enchantment, I was certain not to hear a word of English. He never dreamed, I am sure, that I would be packed off there as a boarder from the age of four. Out of goodness and affection he gave me books to read – children's stories from nineteenth-century France which I hated and still detest. In these oppressive stories children were punished and punished hard for behavior that seemed in another century, above all on another continent, natural and right. I could never see the right-and-wrong over which they kept stumbling and only much later recognized it in European social fiddle-faddle – the trivial yardsticks that measure a man's character by the way he eats a boiled egg. The prose was stiff, a bit shrill, probably pitched too high for a North American ear. Even the bindings, a particularly ugly red, were repellent to me, while their gilt titles lent them the ceremonial quality of school prizes. I had plenty of English Victorian books, but the scolding could be got over, because there was no unfairness. Where there was, it was done away with as part of the plot. The authors were on the side of morality but also of the child. For a long time I imagined that most of my English books had been written by other children, but I never made that mistake with French; I saw these authors as large, scowling creatures with faces as flushed with crossness as the books' covers. Still, the books were presents, therefore important, offered without a word or a look Dr. Chauchard would not have bestowed on an adult. They had been his mother's; she lived in rooms at the top of the house, receiving her own friends, not often mingling with his. She must have let him have these treasures for a favored patient who did not understand the courtesy, even the sacrifice, until it was too late to say "Thank you." Another child's name – his mother's – was on the flyleaf; I seldom looked at it, concentrated as I was on my own. It is not simply rhetoric to say that I see him still – Fildes profile, white cuff, dark sleeve, writing the new dedication with a pen dipped in a blue inkwell, hand and book within the circle cast by the lamp on his desk. At home I would paste inside the front cover the plate my father had designed for me, which had "Linnet: Her Book" as ex libris, and the drawing of a stream flowing between grassy banks – his memory of the unhurried movement of England, no reflection of anything known to me in Quebec – bearing a single autumn leaf. Under the stream came the lines

Time, Time which none can bind
While flowing fast leaves love
behind.

The only child will usually give and lend its possessions easily, having missed the sturdy training in rivalry and forced sharing afforded by sisters and brothers, yet nothing would have made me part willingly with any of the grim red books. Grouped on a special shelf, seldom opened after the first reading, they were not reminders but a true fragment of his twilit house, his swan and heron doors, Napoleon III so cunningly lighted, "Le Petit Palais – The Petit Palais," and, finally, Dr. Chauchard himself at the desk of his shadowy room writing *"Pour ma chère petite Linnet"* in a book that had once belonged to another girl.

Now, how to account for the changed, stern, disapproving Chauchard who in that same office gave me not a book but a lecture beginning "Think of your unfortunate parents" and ending "You owe them everything; it is your duty to love them." He had just telephoned for my father to come and fetch me. "How miserable they would be if anything ever happened to you," he said. He spoke of my *petit Papa* and my *petite Maman* with that fake diminution of authority characteristic of the Latin tongues which never works in English. I sat on a chair still wearing outdoor clothes – navy reefer over my convent uniform, HMS *Nelson* sailor hat held on by a black elastic – neither his patient nor his guest at this dreadful crisis, wondering, What does he mean? For a long time now my surprise visits to friends had been called, incorrectly, "running away." Running away was one of the reasons my parents gave when anyone asked why I had been walled up in such a severe school at an early age. Dr. Chauchard, honored by one of my visits, at once asked his office nurse, "Do her parents know she's here?" Women are supposed to make dangerous patients for bachelor doctors; besotted little girls must seem even worse. But I was not besotted; I believed we were equals. It was he who had set up the equality, and for that reason I still think he should have invited me to remove my coat.

The only thing worth remarking about his dull little sermon is that it was in French. French was his language for medicine; I never heard him give an opinion in English. It was evidently the language to which he retreated if one became a nuisance, his back to a wall of white marble syntax. And when it came to filial devotion he was one with the red-covered books. Calling on my parents, not as my doctor but as their friend, he spoke another language. It was not merely English instead of French but the private dialect of a younger person who was playful, charming, who smoked cigarettes in a black-and-silver holder, looking round to see the effect of his puns and jokes. You could notice then, only then, that his black-currant eyes were never still.

The house he came to remained for a long time enormous in memory, though the few like it still standing – "still living," I nearly say – are narrow, with thin, steep staircases and close, high-ceilinged rooms. They were the work of Edinburgh architects and dated from when Montreal was a Scottish city; it had never been really English. A Saturday-evening gathering of several adults, one child, and a couple of dogs created a sort of tangle in the middle of the room – an entwining that was surely not of people's feet: in those days everyone sat straight. The women had to, because their girdles had hooks and stays. Men sat up out of habit, probably the habit of prosperity; the Depression created the physical slump, a change in posture to match the times. Perhaps desires and secrets and second thoughts threading from person to person, from bachelor to married woman, from mother of none to somebody's father, formed a cat's cradle – matted, invisible, and quite dangerous. Why else would Ruby, the latest homesick underpaid Newfoundland import, have kept tripping up as she lurched across the room with cups and glasses on a tray?

Transformed into jolly Uncle Raoul (his request), Dr. Chauchard would arrive with a good friend of his, divorced Mrs. Erskine, and a younger friend of both, named Paul-Armand. Paul-Armand was temporary, one of a sequence of young men who attended Mrs. Erskine as her bard, her personal laureate. His role did not outlive a certain stage of artless admiration; at the first sign of falling away, the first mouse squeak of disenchantment from him, a replacement was found. All of these young men were good-looking, well brought up, longing to be unconventional, and entirely innocent. Flanked by her pair of males, Mrs. Erskine would sway into the room, as graceful as a woman can be when she is boned from waist to thigh. She would keep on her long moleskin coat, even though like all Canadian rooms this one was vastly overheated, explaining that she was chilly. This may have been an attempt to reduce the impression she gave of general largeness by suggesting an inner fragility. Presently the coat would come off, revealing a handwoven tea-cozy sort of garment – this at a time when every other woman was showing her knees. My mother sat with her legs crossed and one sandal dangling. Her hair had recently been shingled; she seemed to be groping for its lost comfortable warmth. Other persons, my father apart, are a dim choir muttering, "Isn't it past your bedtime?" My father sat back in a deep, chintz-covered chair and said hardly anything except for an occasional "Down" to his dogs.

In another season, in the country, my parents had other friends, summer friends, who drank Old-Fashioneds and danced to gramophone records out on the lawn. Winter friends were mostly coffee drinkers, who did what people do between wars and revolutions – sat in a circle and talked about revolutions and wars. The language was usually English, though not everyone was native to English. Mrs. Erskine commanded what she called "*good* French" and rather liked displaying it, but after a few sentences, which made those who could not understand French very fidgety and which annoyed the French Canadians present exactly in the way an affected accent will grate on Irish nerves, she would pick her way back to English. In mixed society, such little of it as existed, English seemed to be the social rule. It did not enter the mind of any English speaker that the French were at a constant disadvantage, like a team obliged to play all their matches away from home. Dr. Chauchard never addressed me in French here, not even when he would ask me to recite a French poem learned at my convent school. It began, "If I were a fly, Maman, I would steal a kiss from your lips." The nun in charge of memory work was fiddly about liaison, which produced an accidentally appropriate "*Si j'étaiszzzzzzzzune mouche, Maman*." Dr. Chauchard never seemed to tire of this and may have thought it a reasonable declaration to make to one's mother.

It was a tactless rhyme, if you think of all the buzzing and stealing that went on in at least part of the winter circle, but I could not have known that. At least not consciously. Unconsciously, everyone under the age of ten knows everything. Under-ten can come into a room and sense at once everything felt, kept silent, held back in the way of love, hate, and desire, though he may not have the right words for such sentiments. It is part of the clairvoyant immunity to hypocrisy we are born with and that vanishes just before puberty. I knew, though no one had told me, that my mother was a bit foolish about Dr. Chauchard; that Mrs. Erskine would have turned cartwheels to get my father's attention but that even cartwheels would have failed; that Dr. Chauchard and Mrs. Erskine were somehow together but never went out alone. Paul-Armand was harder to place; too young to be a parent, he was a pest, a tease to someone smaller. His goading was never noticed, though my reaction to it, creeping behind his chair until I was in a position to punch him, brought an immediate response from the police: "Linnet, if you don't sit down I'm afraid you will have to go to your room." "If" and "I'm afraid" meant there was plenty of margin. Later: "Wouldn't you be happier if you just went to bed? No? Then get a book and sit down and read it." Presently, "Down, I said, sit down; did you hear what I've just said to you? I said, sit down, *down*." There came a point like convergent lines finally meeting where orders to dogs and instructions to children were given in the same voice. The only difference was that a dog got "Down, damn it," and, of course, no one ever swore at me.

This overlapping in one room of French and English, of Catholic and Protestant – my parents' way of being, and so to me life itself – was as unlikely, as unnatural to the Montreal climate as a school of tropical fish. Only later would I discover that most other people simply floated in mossy little ponds labelled "French and Catholic" or "English and Protestant," never wondering what it might be like to step ashore; or wondering, perhaps, but weighing up the danger. To be out of a pond is to be in unmapped territory. The earth might be flat; you could fall over the edge quite easily. My parents and their friends were, in their way, explorers. They had in common a fear of being bored, which is a fear one can afford to nourish in times of prosperity and peace. It makes for the most ruthless kind of exclusiveness, based as it is on the belief that anyone can be the richest of this or cleverest of that and still be the dullest dog that ever barked. I wince even now remembering those wretched once-only guests who were put on trial for a Saturday night and unanimously condemned. This heartlessness apart, the winter circle shared an outlook, a kind of humor, a certain vocabulary of the mind. No one made any of the standard Montreal statements, such as "What a lot of books you've got! Don't tell me you've read them," or "I hear you're some kind of artist. What do you really *do*?" Explorers like Dr. Chauchard and Mrs. Erskine and my mother and the rest recognized each other on sight; the recognition cut through disguisements of class, profession, religion, language, and even what polltakers call "other interests."

Once you have jumped out of a social enclosure, your eye is bound to be on a real, a geographical elsewhere; theirs seemed to consist of a few cities of Europe with agreeable-sounding names like Vienna and Venice. The United States consisted only of Boston and Florida then. Adults went to Florida for therapeutic reasons – for chronic bronchitis, to recover from operations, for the sake of mysterious maladies that had no names and were called in obituaries "a long illness bravely borne." Boston seemed to be an elegant little republic with its own parliament and flag. To English Montreal, cocooned in that other language nobody bothered to learn, the rest of the continent, Canada included, barely existed; travellers would disembark after long, sooty train trips expressing relief to be in the only city where there were decent restaurants and well-dressed women and where proper English could be heard. Elsewhere, then, became other people, and little groups would form where friends, to the tune of vast mutual admiration, could find a pleasing remoteness in each other. They resembled, in their yearnings, in their clinging together as a substitute for motion, in their craving for "someone to talk to," the kind of marginal social clans you find today in the capitals of Eastern Europe.

I was in the dining room cutting up magazines. My mother brought her coffee cup in, sat down, and said, "Promise me you will never be caught in a situation where you have to compete with a younger woman."

She must have been twenty-six at the very most; Mrs. Erskine was well over thirty. I suppose she was appraising the amount of pickle Mrs. Erskine was in. They had become rivals. With her pale braids, her stately figure, her eyes the color of a stoneware teapot, Mrs. Erskine seemed to me like a white statue with features painted on. I had heard my mother praising her beauty, but for a child she was too large, too still. "Age has its points," my mother went on. "The longer your life goes on, the more chance it has to be interesting. Promise me that when you're thirty you'll have a lot to look back on."

My mother had on her side her comparative youth, her quickness, her somewhat giddy intelligence. She had been married, as she said, "for ever and ever" and was afraid nothing would ever happen to her again. Mrs. Erskine's chief advantage over my mother – being unmarried and available – was matched by an enviable biography. "Ah, don't ask me for my life's story now," she would cry, settling back to tell it. When the others broke into that sighing, singing recital of cities they went in for, repeating strings of names that sounded like sleigh bells (Venice, London, Paris, Rome), Mrs. Erskine would narrow her stoneware eyes and annihilate my mother with "But Charlotte, I've *been* to all those places, I've *seen* all those people." What, indeed, hadn't she seen – crown princes dragged out of Rolls-Royces by cursing mobs, duchesses clutching their tiaras while being raped by anarchists, strikers in England kicking innocent little Border terriers.

"... And as for the Hun*gar*ians and that Béla *Kun*, let me tell *you* ... tore the uniforms right off the Red Cross *nurses* ... made them dance the Charleston naked on top of *street*cars ..."

"Linnet, wouldn't you be better off in your room?"

The fear of the horde was in all of them; it haunted even their jokes. "Bolshevik" was now "Bolshie," to make it harmless. Petrograd had been their early youth; the Red years just after the war were still within earshot. They dreaded yet seemed drawn to tales of conspiracy and enormous might. The English among them were the first generation to have been raised on *The Wind in the Willows*. Their own Wild Wood was a dark political mystery; its rude inhabitants were still to be tamed. What was needed was a leader, a Badger. But when a Badger occurred they mistrusted him, too; my mother had impressed on me early that Mussolini was a "bad, wicked man." Fortunate Mrs. Erskine had seen "those people" from legation windows; she had, in another defeat for my mother, been married twice, each time to a diplomat. The word "diplomat" had greater cachet then than it has now. Earlier in the century a diplomat was believed to have attended universities in more than one country, to have two or three languages at his disposal and some slender notion of geography and history. He could read and write quite easily, had probably been born in wedlock, possessed tact and discretion, and led an exemplary private life. Obviously there were no more of these paragons then than there might be now, but fewer were needed, because there were only half as many capitals. Those who did exist spun round and round the world, used for all they were worth, until they became like those coats that outlast their buttons, linings, and pockets: your diplomat, recalled from Bulgaria, by now a mere warp and woof, would be given a new silk lining, bone buttons, have his collar turned, and, after a quick reading of Norse myths, would be shipped to Scandinavia. Mrs. Erskine, twice wedded to examples of these freshened garments, had been everywhere – everywhere my mother longed to be.

"My *life*," said Mrs. Erskine. "Ah, Charlotte, don't ask me to tell you everything – you'd never believe it!" My mother asked, and believed, and died in her heart along with Mrs. Erskine's first husband, a Mr. Sparrow, shot to death in Berlin by a lunatic Russian refugee. (Out of the decency of his nature Mr. Sparrow had helped the refugee's husband emigrate accompanied by a woman Mr. Sparrow had taken to be the Russian man's wife.) In the hours that preceded his "going," as Mrs. Erskine termed his death, Mr. Sparrow had turned into a totally other person, quite common and gross. She had seen exactly how he would rise from the dead for his next incarnation. She had said, "Now then, Alfred, I think it has been a blissful marriage but perhaps not blissful enough. As I am the best part of your karma, we are going to start all over again in another existence." Mr. Sparrow, in his new coarse, uneducated voice, replied, "Believe you me, Bimbo, if I see you in another world, this time I'm making a detour." His last words – not what every woman hopes to hear, probably, but nothing in my mother's experience could come ankle-high to having a husband assassinated in Berlin by a crazy Russian. Mr. Erskine, the second husband, was not quite so interesting, for he merely "drank and drank and *drank*," and finally, unwittingly, provided grounds for divorce. Since in those days adultery was the only acceptable grounds, the divorce ended his ambitions and transformed Mrs. Erskine into someone déclassée; it was not done for a woman to spoil a man's career, and it was taken for granted that no man ever ruined his own. I am certain my mother did not see Mr. Sparrow as an ass and Mr. Erskine as a soak. They were men out of novels – half diplomat, half secret agent. The natural progress of such men was needed to drag women out of the dullness that seemed to be woman's fate.

There was also the matter of Mrs. Erskine's French: my mother could read and speak it but had nothing of her friend's intolerable fluency. Nor could my mother compete with her special status as the only English and Protestant girl of her generation to have attended French and Catholic schools. She had spend ten years with the Ursulines in Quebec City (languages took longer to learn in those days, when you were obliged to start by memorizing all the verbs) and had emerged with the chic little Ursuline lisp.

"Tell me again," my entranced mother would ask. "How do you say 'squab stuffed with sage dressing'?"

"Charlotte, I've told you and told you. *'Pouthin farthi au thauge.'*"

"Thankth," said my mother. Such was the humor of that period.

For a long time I would turn over like samples of dress

material the reasons why I was sent off to a school where by all the rules of the world we lived in I did not belong. A sample that nearly matches is my mother's desire to tease Mrs. Erskine, perhaps to overtake her through me: if she had been unique in her generation, then I would be in mine. Unlikely as it sounds today, I believe that I was. At least I have never met another, just as no French-Canadian woman of my period can recall having sat in a classroom with any other English-speaking Protestant disguised in convent uniform. Mrs. Erskine, rising to the tease, warned that convents had gone downhill since the war and that the appalling French I spoke would be a handicap in Venice, London, Paris, Rome; if the Ursuline French of Quebec City was the best in the world after Tours, Montreal French was just barely a language.

How could my mother, so quick and sharp usually, have been drawn in by this? For a day or two my parents actually weighed the advantages of sending their very young daughter miles away, for no good reason. Why not even to France? "You know perfectly well why not. Because we can't afford it. Not that or anything like it."

Leaning forward in her chair as if words alone could not convince her listener, more like my mother than herself at this moment, Mrs. Erskine with her fingertips to her cheek, the other hand held palm outward, cried, "Ah, Angus, don't ask me for my life's story now!" This to my father, who barely knew other people had lives.

My father made this mysterious answer: "Yes, Frances, I do see what you mean, but I have a family, and once you've got children you're never quite so free."

There was only one child, of course, and not often there, but in my parents' minds and by some miracle of fertility they had produced a whole tribe. At any second this tribe might rampage through the house, scribbling on the wallpaper, tearing up books, scratching gramophone records with a stolen diamond brooch. They dreaded mischief so much that I can only suppose them to have been quite disgraceful children.

"What's Linnet up to? She's awfully quiet."

"Sounds suspicious. Better go and look."

I would be found reading or painting or "building," which meant the elaboration of a foreign city called Marigold that spread and spread until it took up a third of my room and had to be cleared away when my back was turned upon which, as relentless as a colony of beavers, I would start building again. To a visitor Marigold was a slum of empty boxes, serving trays, bottles, silver paper, overturned chairs, but these were streets and houses, churches and convents, restaurants and railway stations. The citizens of Marigold were cut out of magazines: Gloria Swanson was the Mother Superior, Herbert Hoover a convent gardener. Entirely villainous, they did their plotting and planning in an empty cigar box.

Whatever I was doing, I would be told to do something else immediately: I think they had both been brought up that way. "Go out and play in the snow" was a frequent interruption. Parents in bitter climates have a fixed idea about driving children out to be frozen. There was one sunken hour on January afternoons, just before the street lamps were lighted, that was the gray of true wretchedness, as if one's heart and stomach had turned into the same dull, cottony stuff as the sky; it was attached to a feeling of loss, of helpless sadness, unknown to children in other latitudes.

I was home weekends but by no means every weekend. Friday night was given to spoiling and rejoicing, but on Saturday I would hear "When does she go back?"

"Not till tomorrow night."

Ruby, the homesick offshore import, sometimes sat in my room, just for company. She turned the radiator on so that you saw a wisp of steam from the overflow tap. A wicker basket of mending was on her lap; she wiped her eyes on my father's socks. I was not allowed to say to anyone "Go away," or anything like it. I heard her sniffles, her low, muttered grievances. Then she emerged from her impenetrable cloud of Newfoundland gloom to take an interest in the life of Marigold. She did not get down on the floor or in the way, but from her chair suggested some pretty good plots. Ruby was the inspirer of "The Insane Stepmother," "The Rich, Selfish Cousins," "The Death from Croup of Baby Sister" ("Is her face blue yet?" "No; in a minute"), and "The Broken Engagement," with its cast of three – rejected maiden, fickle lover, and chaperon. Paper dolls did the acting, the voices were ours. Ruby played the cast-off fiancée from the heart: "Don't chew men ever know what chew want?" Chaperon was a fine bossy part: "That's enough, now. Sit down; I said, *down*."

My parents said, "What does she see in Ruby?" They were cross and jealous. The jealousness was real. They did not drop their voices to say "When does she go back?" but were alert to signs of disaffection, and offended because I did not crave their company every minute. Once, when Mrs. Erskine, a bit of a fool probably, asked, "Who do you love best, your father or your mother?" and I apparently (I have no memory of it) answered, "Oh, I'm not really dying about anybody," it was recalled to me for a long time, as if I had set fire to the curtains or spat on the Union Jack.

"Think of your unfortunate parents," Dr. Chauchard had said in the sort of language that had no meaning to me, though I am sure it was authentic to him.

When he died and I read his obituary, I saw there had been still another voice. I was twenty and had not seen him since the age of nine. "The Doctor" and the red-covered books had been lost even before that, when during a major move from Montreal to a house in the country a number of things that belonged to me and that my parents were tired of seeing disappeared.

There were three separate death notices, as if to affirm that

Chauchard had been three men. All three were in a French newspaper; he neither lived nor died in English. The first was a jumble of family names and syntax: "After a serene and happy life it has pleased our Lord to send for the soul of his faithful servant Raoul Étienne Chauchard, piously deceased in his native city in his fifty-first year after a short illness comforted by the sacraments of the Church." There followed a few particulars – the date and place of the funeral, and the names and addresses of the relatives making the announcement. The exact kinship of each was mentioned: sister, brother-in-law, uncle, nephew, cousin, second cousin.

The second obituary, somewhat longer, had been published by the medical association he belonged to; it described all the steps and stages of his career. There were strings of initials denoting awards and honors, ending with: "Dr. Chauchard had also been granted the Medal of Epidemics (Belgium)." Beneath this came the third notice: "The Arts and Letters Society of Quebec announces the irreparable loss of one of its founder members, the poet R.É. Chauchard." R.É. had published six volumes of verse, a book of critical essays, and a work referred to as "the immortal 'Progress,' " which did not seem to fall into a category or, perhaps, was too well known to readers to need identification.

That third notice was an earthquake, the collapse of the cities we build over the past to cover seams and cracks we cannot account for. He must have been writing when my parents knew him. Why they neglected to speak of it is something too shameful to dwell on; he probably never mentioned it, knowing they would believe it impossible. French books were from France; English books from England or the United States. It would not have entered their minds that the languages they heard spoken around them could be written, too.

I met by accident years after Dr. Chauchard's death one of Mrs. Erskine's ex-minnesingers, now an elderly bachelor. His name was Louis. He had never heard of Paul-Armand, not even by rumor. He had not known my parents and was certain he had never accompanied Dr. Chauchard and Mrs. Erskine to our house. He said that when he met these two he had been fresh from a seminary, aged about nineteen, determined to live a life of ease and pleasure but not sure how to begin. Mrs. Erskine had by then bought and converted a farmhouse south of Montreal, where she wove carpets, hooked rugs, scraped and waxed old tables, kept bees, and bottled tons of pickled beets, preparing for some dark proletarian future should the mob – the horde, "those people" – take over after all. Louis knew the doctor only as the poet R.É. of the third notice. He had no knowledge of the Medal of Epidemics (Belgium) and could not explain it to me. I had found "Progress" by then, which turned out to be R.É.'s diary. I could not put faces to the X, Y, and Z that covered real names, nor could I discover any trace of my parents, let alone of *ma chère petite Linnet*. There were long thoughts about Mozart – people like that.

Louis told me of walking with Mrs. Erskine along a snowy road close to her farmhouse, she in a fur cape that came down to her boot tops and a fur bonnet that hid her braided hair. She talked about her unusual life and her two husbands and about what she now called "the predicament." She told him how she had never been asked to meet Madame Chauchard *mère* and how she had slowly come to realize that R.É. would never marry. She spoke of people who had drifted through the predicament, my mother among them, not singling her out as someone important, just as a wisp of cloud on the edge of the sky. "Poor Charlotte" was how Mrs. Erskine described the thin little target on which she had once trained her biggest guns. Yet "poor Charlotte" – not even an X in the diary, finally – had once been the heart of the play. The plot must have taken a full turning after she left the stage. Louis became a new young satellite, content to circle the powerful stars, to keep an eye on the predicament, which seemed to him flaming, sulphurous.

Nobody ever told him what had taken place in the first and second acts.

Walking, he and Mrs. Erskine came to a railway track quite far from houses, and she turned to Louis and opened the fur cloak and said, smiling, "*Viens voir Mrs. Erskine*." (Owing to the Ursuline lisp this must have been "Mitheth Erthkine.") Without coyness or any more conversation she lay down – he said "on the track," but he must have meant near it, if you think of the ties. Folded into the cloak, Louis at last became part of a predicament. He decided that only further experience could only fall short of it, and so he never married.

In this story about the cloak Mrs. Erskine is transmuted from the pale, affected statue I remember and takes on a polychrome life. She seems cheerful and careless, and I like her for that. Carelessness might explain her unreliable memory about Charlotte. And yet not all that careless: "She even knew the train times," said Louis. "She must have done it before." Still, on a sharp blue day, when some people were still in a dark classroom writing "*abyssus abyssum invocat*" all over their immortal souls, she, who had been through this and escaped with nothing worse than a lisp, had the sun, the snow, the wrap of fur, the bright sky, the risk. There is a raffish kind of nerve to her, the only nerve that matters.

For that one conversation Louis and I wondered what our appearance on stage several scenes apart might make us to each other: if A was the daughter of B, and B rattled the foundations of C, and C, though cautious and lazy where women were concerned, was committed in a way to D, and D was forever trying to tell her life's story to E, the husband of B, and E had enough on his hands with B without taking on D, too, and if D decided to lie down on or near a railway track with F, then what are A and F? Nothing. Minor satellites floating out of orbit and out of order after the stars burned out. Mrs. Erskine reclaimed Dr. Chauchard but he never married anyone. Angus reclaimed Charlotte but he died soon after. Louis, another old bachelor, had that one good anecdote about the fur cloak. I lost even the engraving of "The Doctor," spirited away quite shabbily, and I never saw Dr. Chauchard again or even tried to. What if I had turned up one day, aged eighteen or so, only to have him say to his nurse, "Does anyone know she's here?"

When I read the three obituaries it was the brass plate on the door I saw and "Sur Rendez-vous." That means "no dropping in." After the warning came the shut heron door and the shut swan door and, at another remove, the desk with the circle of lamplight and R.É. himself, writing about X, Y, Z, and Mozart. A bit humdrum perhaps, a bit prosy, not nearly as good as his old winter Saturday self, but I am sure that it was his real voice, the voice that transcends this or that language. His French-speaking friends did not hear it for a long time (his first book of verse was not sold to anyone outside his immediate family), while his English-speaking friends never heard it at all. But I should have heard it then, at the start, standing on tiptoe to reach the doorbell, calling through the letter box every way I could think of, "I, me." I ought to have heard it when I was still under ten and had all my wits about me.

WITH A CAPITAL T

For Madeleine and Jean-Paul Lemieux

In wartime, in Montreal, I applied to work on a newspaper. Its name was *The Lantern*, and its motto, "My light shall shine," carried a Wesleyan ring of veracity and plain dealing. I chose it because I thought it was a place where I would be given a lot of different things to do. I said to the man who consented to see me, "But not the women's pages. Nothing like that." I was eighteen. He heard me out and suggested I come back at twenty-one, which was a soft way of getting rid of me. In the meantime I was to acquire experience; he did not say of what kind. On the stroke of twenty-one I returned and told my story to a different person. I was immediately accepted; I had expected to be. I still believed, then, that most people meant what they said. I supposed that the man I had seen that first time had left a memorandum in the files: "To whom it may concern – Three years from this date, Miss Linnet Muir will join the editorial staff." But after I'd been working for a short time I heard one of the editors say, "If it hadn't been for the god-damned war we would never have hired even one of the god-damned women," and so I knew.

In the meantime I had acquired experience by getting married. I was no longer a Miss Muir, but a Mrs. Blanchard. My husband was overseas. I had longed for emancipation and independence, but I was learning that women's autonomy is like a small inheritance paid out a penny at a time. In a journal I kept I scrupulously noted everything that came into my head about this, and about God, and about politics. I took it for granted that our victory over Fascism would be followed by a sunburst of revolution – I thought that was what the war was about. I wondered if going to work for the capitalist press was entirely moral. "Whatever happens," I wrote, "it will be the Truth, nothing half-hearted, the Truth with a Capital T."

The first thing I had to do was write what goes under the pictures. There is no trick to it. You just repeat what the picture has told you like this:

"Boy eats bun as bear looks on."

The reason why anything has to go under the picture at all is that a reader might wonder, "Is that a bear looking on?" It looks like a bear, but that is not enough reason for saying so. Pasted across the back of the photo you have been given is a strip of paper on which you can read: "Saskatoon, Sask. 23 Nov. Boy eats bun as bear looks on." Whoever composed this knows two things more than you do – a place and a time.

You have a space to fill in which the words must come out even. The space may be tight; in that case, you can remove "as" and substitute a comma, though that makes the kind of terse statement to which your reader is apt to reply, "So what?" Most of the time, the Truth with a Capital T is a matter of elongation: "Blond boy eats small bun as large bear looks on."

"Blond boy eats buttered bun ... " is livelier, but unscrupulous. You have been given no information about the butter. "Boy eats bun as hungry bear looks on," has the beginnings of a plot, but it may inspire your reader to protest: "That boy must be a mean sort of kid if he won't share his food with a starving creature." Child-lovers, though less prone to fits of anguish than animal-lovers, may be distressed by the word "hungry" for a different reason, believing "boy" subject to attack from "bear." You must not lose your head and type, "Blond bear eats large boy as hungry bun looks on," because your reader may notice, and write a letter saying, "Some of you guys around there think you're pretty smart, don't you?" while another will try to enrich your caption with, "Re your bun write-up, my wife has taken better pictures than that in the very area you mention."

At the back of your mind, because your mentors have placed it there, is an obstruction called "the policy factor." Your paper supports a political party. You try to discover what this party has had to say about buns and bears, how it intends to approach them in the future. Your editor, at golf with a member of parliament, will not want to have his game upset by: "It's not that I want to interfere but some of that bun stuff seems pretty negative to me." The young and vulnerable reporter would just as soon not pick up the phone to be told, "I'm ashamed of your defeatist attitude. Why, I knew your father! He must be spinning in his grave!" or, more effectively, "I'm telling you this for your own good – I think you're subversive without knowing it."

Negative, defeatist and subversive are three of the things you have been cautioned not to be. The others are seditious, obscene, obscure, ironic, intellectual and impulsive.

You gather up the photo and three pages of failed captions, and knock at the frosted glass of a senior door. You sit down and are given a view of boot soles. You say that the whole matter comes down to an ethical question concerning information and redundancy; unless "reader" is blotto, can't he see for himself that this is about a boy, a bun, and a bear?

Your senior person is in shirtsleeves, hands clasped behind his neck. He thinks this over, staring at the ceiling; swings his feet to the floor; reads your variations on the bear-and-bun theme; turns the photo upside-down. He tells you patiently, that it is not the business of "reader" to draw conclusions. Our subscribers are not dreamers or smart alecks; when they see a situation in a picture, they want that situation confirmed. He reminds you about negativism and obscuration; advises you to go sit in the library and acquire a sense of values by reading the back issues of *Life*.

The back numbers of *Life* are tatty and incomplete, owing to staff habits of tearing out whatever they wish to examine at leisure. A few captions, still intact, allow you to admire a contribution to pictorial journalism, the word "note":

"American flag flies over new post office. Note stars on flag."

"GI waves happily from captured Italian tank. Note helmet on head."

So, "Boy eats bun as bear looks on. Note fur on bear." All that can happen now will be a letter asking, "Are you sure it was a bun?"

From behind frosted-glass doors, as from a leaking intellectual bath, flow instructions about style, spelling, caution, libel, brevity, and something called "the ground rules." A few of these rules have been established for the convenience of the wives of senior persons and reflect their tastes and interests, their inhibitions and fears, their desire to see close friends' pictures when they open to the social page, their fragile attention span. Other rules demand that we pretend to be independent of British foreign policy and American commerce – otherwise our readers, discouraged, will give up caring who wins the war. (Soon after victory British foreign policy will cease to exist; as for American commerce, the first grumbling will be heard when a factory in Buffalo is suspected of having flooded the country with defective twelve-inch pie tins.) Ground rules maintain that you must not be flippant about the Crown – an umbrella term covering a number of high-class subjects, from the Royal Family to the nation's judicial system – or about our war effort or, indeed, our reasons for making any effort about anything. Religions, in particular those observed by decent Christians, are not up for debate. We may however, describe and denounce marginal sects whose puritanical learnings are even more dizzily slanted than our own. The Jehovah's Witnesses, banned as seditious, continue to issue inflammatory pamphlets about Jesus; patriotic outrage abounds over this. The children of Witnesses are beaten up in public schools for refusing to draw Easter bunnies. An education officer, interviewed, declares that the children's obstinate observance of the Second Commandment is helping Hitler. Everyone knows that the Easter bunny, along with God and Santa Claus, is on our side.

To argue a case for the children is defeatist; to advance reasons against their persecution is obscure. Besides, your version of the bunny conflict may be unreliable. Behind frosted-glass doors lurk male fears of female mischief. Women, having no inborn sense of history, are known to invent absurd stories. Celebrated newspaper hoaxes (perpetrated by men, as it happens) are described to you, examples of irresponsible writing that have brought down trusting editors. A few of these stories have been swimming, like old sea turtles, for years now, crawling ashore wherever British possessions are still tinted red on the map. "As the niece of the Governor-General rose from a deep curtsey, the Prince, with the boyish smile that has made him the darling of five continents, picked up a bronze bust of his grandmother and battered Lady Adeline to death" is one version of a perennial favorite.

Privately, you think you could do better. You will never get the chance. The umpires of ground rules are nervous and watchful behind those doors. Wartime security hangs heavy. So does the fear that the end of hostilities will see them turfed out to make way for war correspondents wearing nonchalant mustaches, battered caps, carelessly-knotted white scarves, raincoats with shoulder tabs, punctuating their accounts of Hunnish atrocities perceived at Claridges and the Savoy with "Roger!" and "Jolly-oh!" and "Over to you!"

Awaiting this dreadful invasion the umpires sit, in shirt-sleeves and braces, scribbling initials with thick blue pencils. "NDG" stands for "No Damned Good." (Clairvoyant, you will begin to write "NBF" in your journal meaning "No Bloody Future.") As a creeping, climbing wash of conflicting and contradictory instructions threatens to smother you, you discover the possibilities of the quiet, or lesser, hoax. Obeying every warning and precept, you will write, turn in, and get away with, "Dressed in shoes, stockings and hat appropriate to the season, Mrs. Horatio Bantam, the former Felicity Duckpond, grasped the bottle of champagne in her white-gloved hand and sent it swinging against the end of HMCS *Makeweight* that was nearest the official party, after which, swaying slightly, she slid down the ways and headed for open waters."

As soon as I realized that I was paid about half the salary men were earning, I decided to do half the work. I had spent much of my adolescence as a resourceful truant, evolving the good escape dodges that would serve one way and another all my life. At *The Lantern* I used reliable school methods. I would knock on a glass door – a door that had nothing to do with me.

"Well, Blanchard, what do you want?"

"Oh, Mr. Watchmaster – it's just to tell you I'm going out to look something up."

"What for?"

"An assignment."

"Don't tell *me*. Tell Amstutz."

"He's organizing fire-drill in case of air-raids."

"Tell Cranach. He can tell Amstutz."

"Mr. Cranach has gone to stop the art department from striking."

"*Striking*? Don't those buggers know there's a war on? I'd like to see Accounting try that. What do they want now?"

"Conditions. They're asking for conditions. Is it all right if I go now, Mr. Watchmaster?"

"You know what we need around here, don't you? One German regiment. Regiment? What am I saying? *Platoon*. That'd take the mickey out of 'em. Teach them something about hard work. Loving your country. Your duty. Give me one trained German sergeant. I'd lead him in. 'O.K. – you've been asking for this!' Ratatatat. You wouldn't hear any more guff about conditions. What's your assignment?"

"The Old Presbyterians. They've decided they're against killing people because of something God said to Moses."

"Seditious bastards. Put 'em in work camps, the whole damned lot. All right, Blanchard, carry on."

I would go home, wash my hair, listen to Billie Holiday records.

"Say, Blanchard, where the hell were you yesterday? Seventy-nine people were poisoned by ham sandwiches at a wedding party on Durocher Street. The sidewalk was like a morgue."

"Actually, I just happened to be in Mr. Watchmaster's office. But only for a minute."

"Watchmaster's got no right to ask you to do anything. One of these days I'm going to close in on him. I can't right now – there's a war on. The only good men we ever had in this country were killed in the last one. Look, next time Watchmaster gets you to run his errands, refer it to Cranach. Got that? All right, Blanchard, on your way."

No good dodge works forever.

"Oh, Mr. Watchmaster, I just wanted to tell you I'm going out for an hour or two. I have to look something up. Mr. Cranach's got his door locked, and Mr. Amstutz had to go home to see why his wife was crying."

"Christ, what an outfit. What do you have to look up?"

"What Mussolini did to the Red Cross dogs. It's for the 'Whither Italy?' supplement."

"You don't need to leave the building for that. You can get all you want by phone. You highbrows don't even know what a phone is. Drop around Advertising some time and I'll show you down-to-earth people using phones as working instruments. All you have to do is call the Red Cross, a veterinarian, an Italian priest, maybe an Italian restaurant, and a kennel. They'll tell you all you need to know. Remember what Churchill said about Mussolini, eh? That he was a fine Christian gentleman. If you want my opinion, whatever those dogs got they deserved."

Interviews were useful: you could get out and ride around in taxis and waste hours in hotel lobbies reading the new American magazines, which were increasingly difficult to find.

"I'm just checking something for *The Lantern* – do you mind?"

"Just so long as you don't mar the merchandise. I've only got five *Time*, three *Look*, four *Photoplay* and two *Ladies' Home*. Don't wander away with the *Esquire*. There's a war on."

Once I was sent to interview my own godmother. Nobody knew I knew her, and I didn't say. She was president of a committee that sent bundles to prisoners-of-war. The committee was launching an appeal for funds; that was the reason for the interview. I took down her name as if I had never heard it before: Miss Edna May Henderson. My parents had called her "Georgie," though I don't know why.

I had not seen my godmother since I was eight. My father had died, and I had been dragged away to be brought up in different cities. At eighteen, I had summoned her to a telephone: "It's Linnet," I said. "I'm here, in Montreal. I've come back to stay."

"Linnet," she said. "Good gracious me." Her chain-smoker's

voice made me homesick, though it could not have been for a place – I was in it. Her voice, and her particular Montreal accent, were like the unexpected signatures that underwrite the past: If this much is true, you will tell yourself, then so is all the rest I have remembered.

She was too busy with her personal war drive to see me then, though she did ask for my phone number. She did not enquire where I had been since my father's death, or if I had anything here to come back to. It is true that she and my mother had quarrelled years before; still, it was Georgie who had once renounced in my name "the devil and all his works, the vain pomp and glory of the world, with all covetous desires of the same, and carnal desires of the flesh." She might have been curious to see the result of her bizarre undertaking, but a native canny Anglo-Montreal prudence held her still.

I was calling from a drugstore; I lived in one room of a cold-water flat in the east end. I said, "I'm completely on my own, and entirely self-supporting." That was so Georgie would understand I was not looking for help; at all events, for nothing material.

I realize now how irregular, how fishy even, this must have sounded. Everybody has a phone, she was probably thinking. What is the girl trying to hide?

"Nothing" would have been the answer. There seemed no way to connect. She asked me to call her again in about a month's time, but of course I never did.

My godmother spent most of her life in a block of granite designed to look like a fortress. Within the fortress were sprawling apartments, drawn to an Edwardian pattern of high ceilings, dark corridors, and enormous kitchens full of pipes. Churches and schools, banks and prisons, dwellings and railway stations were part of an imperial convallation that wound round the globe, designed to impress on the minds of indigenous populations that the builders had come to stay. In Georgie's redoubt, the doorman was shabby and lame; he limped beside me along a gloomy passage as far as the elevator, where only one of the sconce lights fixed to the panelling still worked. I had expected someone else to answer my ring, but it was Georgie who let me in, took my coat, and indicated with a brusque gesture, as if I did not know any English, the mat where I was to leave my wet snowboots. It had not occurred to me to bring shoes. Padding into her drawing room on stockinged feet, I saw the flash photograph her memory would file as further evidence of Muir incompetence; for I believe to this day that she recognized me at once. I was the final product, the last living specimen of a strain of people whose imprudence, lack of foresight, and refusal to take anything seriously had left one generation after another unprepared and stranded, obliged to build life from the ground up, fashioning new materials every time.

My godmother was tall, though not so tall as I remembered. Her face was wide and flat. Her eyes were small, deep-set, slightly tilted, as if two invisible thumbs were pulling at her temples. Her skin was as coarse and lined as a farm woman's; indifference to personal appearance of that kind used to be a matter of pride.

Her drawing room was white, and dingy and worn-looking. Curtains and armchairs needed attention, but that may have been on account of the war: it had been a good four years since anyone had bothered to paint or paper or have slipcovers made. The lamps were blue-and-white, and on this winter day already lighted. The room smelled of the metallic central heating of old apartment buildings, and of my godmother's Virginia cigarettes. We sat on worn white sofas, facing each other, with a table in between.

My godmother gave me Scotch in a heavy tumbler and pushed a dish of peanuts towards me, remarking in that harsh evocative voice, "Peanuts are harder to find than Scotch now."

Actually, Scotch was off the map for most people; it was a civilian casualty, expensive and rare.

We were alone except for a Yorkshire terrier, who lay on a chair in the senile sleep that is part of dying.

"I would like it if Minnie could hang on until the end of the war," Georgie said. "I'm sure she'd like the victory parades and the bands. But she's thirteen, so I don't know."

That was the way she and my parents and their friends had talked to each other. The duller, the more earnest, the more literal generation I stood for seemed to crowd the worn white room, and to darken it further.

I thought I had better tell her straightaway who I was, though I imagined she knew. I did not intend to be friendly beyond that, unless she smiled. And even there, the quality of the smile would matter. Some smiles are instruments of repression.

Telling my new name, explaining that I had married, that I was now working for a newspaper, gave an accounting only up to a point. A deserted continent stretched between us, cracked and fissured with bottomless pits over which Georgie stepped easily. How do you deal with life? her particular Canadian catechism asked. By ignoring its claims on feeling. Any curiosity she may have felt about such mysteries as coincidence and continuity (my father was said to have been the love of her life; I was said to resemble him) had been abandoned, like a game that was once the rage. She may have been unlucky with games, which would explain the committee work; it may be dull, but you can be fairly sure of the outcome. I often came across women like her, then, who had no sons or lovers or husbands to worry about, and who adopted the principle of the absent, endangered male. A difference between us was that, to me, the absence and danger had to be taken for granted; another was that what I thought of as men, Georgie referred to as "boys." The rest was beyond my reach. Being a poor judge of probabilities, she had expected my father to divorce. I was another woman's child, foolish and vulnerable because I had lost my dignity along with my boots; paid to take down her words in a notebook; working not for a lark but for a living, which was unforgivable even then within the shabby fortress. I might have said, "I am innocent," but she already knew that.

My godmother was dressed in a jaunty blue jacket with a double row of brass buttons, and a pleated skirt. I supposed this must be the costume she and her committee wore when they were packing soap and cigarettes and second-hand cheery novels for their boys over there in the coop. She told me the names of the committee women, and said, "Are you getting everything down all right?" People ask that who are not used to being interviewed. "They told me there'd be a picture," she complained. That explained the uniform.

"I'm sorry. He should be here now."

"Do you want me to spell those names for you?"

"No. I'm sure I have them."

"You're not writing much."

"I don't need to," I said. "Not as a rule."

"You must have quite a memory."

She seemed to be trying to recall where my knack of remembering came from, if it was inherited, wondering whether memory is of any use to anyone except to store up reasons for discord.

We gave up waiting for the photographer. I stood stork-like in the passage, pulling on a boot. Georgie leaned on the wall, and I saw that she was slightly tight.

"I have four godchildren," she said. "People chose me because I was an old maid, and they thought I had money to leave. Well, I haven't. There'll be nothing for the boys. All my godchildren were boys. I never liked girls."

She had probably been drinking for much of the day, on and off; and of course there was all the excitement of being interviewed, and the shock of seeing me: still, it was a poor thing to say. Supposing, just supposing, that Georgie had been all I had left? My parents had been perfectly indifferent to money – almost pathologically so, I sometimes thought. The careless debts they had left strewn behind and that I kept picking up and trying to settle were not owed in currency.

Why didn't I come straight out with that? Because you can't – not in that world. No one can have the last retort, not even when there is truth to it. Hints and reminders flutter to the ground in overheated winter rooms, lie stunned for a season, are reborn as everlasting grudges.

"Goodbye, Linnet," she said.

"Goodbye."

"Do you still *not* have a telephone?" No answer. "When will it come out?" She meant the interview.

"On Saturday."

"I'll be looking for it." On her face was a look I took to mean anxiety over the picture, and that I now see to have been mortal terror. I never met her again, not even by accident. The true account I wrote of her committee and its need for public generosity put us at a final remove from each other.

I did not forget her, but I forgot about her. Her life seemed silent and slow and choked with wrack, while mine moved all in a rush, dislodging every obstacle it encountered. Then mine slowed too; stopped flooding its banks. The noise of it abated and I could hear the past. She had died by then – thick-skinned, chain-smoking survivor of the regiment holding the fort.

I saw us in the decaying winter room, saw the lamps blazing coldly on the dark window panes; I heard our voices: "Peanuts are harder to find than Scotch now." "Do you send parcels to Asia, or just to Germany?"

What a dull girl she is, Georgie must have thought; for I see, now, that I was seamless, and as smooth as brass; that I gave her no opening.

When she died, the godsons mentioned in her will swarmed around for a while, but after a certain amount of scuffling with trustees they gave up all claim, which was more dignified for them than standing forlorn and hungry-looking before a cupboard containing nothing. Nobody spoke up for the one legacy the trustees would have relinquished: a dog named Minnie, who was by then the equivalent of one hundred and nineteen years old in human time, and who persisted so unreasonably in her right to outlive the rest of us that she had to be put down without mercy.